'A won

'This novel is chillingly good.'
The Book Trail

'Wonderfully atmospheric, this immersive tale grips
the reader to the final page.'
Woman & Home

'A fascinating read for any fans of historical fiction,
magical realism, intrigue and mystery, dealing with themes of
female power, patriarchal religion and the power of books.'
Somerset Life

'*The Book of Eve* draws you into its rich, unsettling world
from the first page and refuses to let go until the very end.
Vividly drawn characters and a totally transporting setting
with timely undertones, like *The Handmaid's Tale*
meets *The Devil and the Dark Water*.'
Bobby Palmer, author of *Isaac and the Egg*

'*The Book of Eve* completely captured me with its
intricately and delicately woven world, filled with strange
and entrancing magic. A powerful novel that grips with
its compelling mystery and unforgettable heroine.'
Eleanor Shearer, author of *River Sing Me Home*

'What a spellbinding tale! I can't remember the last time I was
so captivated by a novel that I had to put everything else on
hold to read it. Tense and claustrophobic, with a creeping sense
of dread that builds throughout the story, *The Book of Eve*
is a beautifully written, utterly enthralling read.'
Karen Coles, author of *The Asylum*

'Expertly crafted and beautifully told, this is an intriguing tale of ancient power and mystery with female strength and solidarity at its core. Haunting, magical and moving.'
Jennifer Saint, author of *Atalanta*

'Can a book be both fast-paced and a slow-burn? I read Meg Clothier's *The Book of Eve* in a quick burst, enchanted by the plot, the mysterious manuscript, and the unfolding relationships between characters. Weeks later I'm still thinking about the compelling and complex treatments of themes of knowledge, community, agency and kinship. At times brutal and haunting, this is a beautiful book and one whose ideas resound long after the final page is turned.'
Melissa Fu, author of *Peach Blossom Spring*

'What an extraordinary book – rich in historical detail and full of esoteric knowledge yet wearing its learning lightly while tapping into a rage that's universal at men's endless attempts to control the doings and thinkings of women. It's an education hidden in a tense, compelling, anger-driven narrative, Beatrice and Diana both knock-out characters. No mean feat!'
Harriet Tyce, author of *It Ends at Midnight*

'*The Book of Eve* is a dark, magical tale of women called upon to find their strength and sisterhood in order to protect an ancient power. Mysterious, bewitching and beautiful.'
Elizabeth Lee, author *Cunning Women*

'A ravishing, erudite feminist hijack of Renaissance Florence and the Bonfire of the Vanities.'
Alice Albinia, author of *Cwen*

'A truly beautiful book, brimming with unsettling magic and the love of literature. It's erudite and bewitching, with a heroine I will never forget. Like a feminist *Name of the Rose*.'
Costanza Casati, author of *Clytemnestra*

Meg Clothier studied Classics at Cambridge, sailed from England to Alaska, and worked as a journalist in London and Moscow. She now lives and writes in Somerset. *The Book of Eve* is her third novel.

The
BOOK
of
EVE

MEG CLOTHIER

WILDFIRE

First published in 2023 by
WILDFIRE
an imprint of HEADLINE PUBLISHING GROUP

First published in paperback in 2024 by
WILDFIRE
an imprint of HEADLINE PUBLISHING GROUP

1

Cataloguing in Publication Data is available from the British Library

ISBN 978 1 4722 7612 4

Map illustration by Tim Peters

Typeset by EM&EN
Printed and bound in Great Britain by Clays Ltd, Elcograf S.p.A.

Headline's policy is to use papers that are natural, renewable and recyclable
products and made from wood grown in well-managed forests and other
controlled sources. The logging and manufacturing processes are expected
to conform to the environmental regulations of the country of origin.

HEADLINE PUBLISHING GROUP
An Hachette UK Company
Carmelite House
50 Victoria Embankment
London EC4Y 0DZ

www.headline.co.uk
www.hachette.co.uk

FOR MUFFIN AND ENNEA

I think your mother would have liked this one

Don't you know that you are Eve?

TERTULLIAN

The Book of Eve

OH, BUT IT'S QUITE SOMETHING UP HERE.

The sky above, the crumbling stones of the pass. The sun setting to our right, trees darkening, snowbanks aflame. The lights of that city, burning beckoning burning—

But why have we stopped?

The nice boy – names, names, they don't stay with me these days – he's jumped down from his wagon – he's calling to my daughter. The pair of them, they've been fretting all day, ever since he came hammering at our door before dawn, saying men were looking, men were asking, saying we must hurry, hurry. Saying don't worry, Mistress, don't be scared – as if we'd never had men after us, as if we'd never run for our lives before.

My girl pats my knee, climbs down from our wretched cart, strides ahead to talk to him. What – what's he saying? Something about nightfall, something about gates, something about – ah, I understand, he's going to speed ahead, stir his friends. They'll see us safe inside this city of theirs.

And now he's gone. Hopped back up on his wagon, flick of the reins, gone. He's a nice boy. A good boy. I thought that, even before he showed me the blessed mark upon his face.

My daughter's wrestling with that brake block again. Maybe I've got time to get down. Get down and kneel and trace the mark. Watch my finger melt the snow – it'd be a good omen, no? – silver shimmer, droplets of moonlight—

'What you doing, Ma?' She's by my side. Red cheeks. Sweat

steaming off her. Trying to tuck that mangy bit of blanket back round me.

Say with a gasp, 'What's it look like?'

I'm trying to stand, but I can't. But I can't. Push down again, harder. No luck. Stuck.

'Easy now, Ma,' she says.

Before we set out, all those weeks ago, she'd tried telling me that I was too old, too weak, too this, too that. That there'd be trouble on the road. Trouble! What don't I know about trouble? The king's men, didn't they used to come poking round our marshes, and didn't I wisp them on the lost paths and watch them sink? Mud bleeding from their noses, their gullets full of weeds, their long swords sinking into the—

'Ma?'

For lifetimes I've been waiting, waiting, watching the birds swoop and the seas rise and fall and the rippling of the reeds, and always I knew, didn't I, I always said that

one day

one day—

'*Ma?*'

She's climbed back up. She's holding my hand. She's giving it a squeeze. I bend my head, kiss her knuckles, breathe.

'Hold on tight, Ma,' she says, and tells the donkey to get a move on.

And we're travelling fast now. Down and down. Jolting now. Wheels now. My ears are singing and the trees on either side, they're bending to listen. My head is light, my spirits too. We look at one another – and then we both look to her breast, to where it's strapped, there, there, against her heart.

The book. *Her* book. The book we're taking to—

But what's that? Glimpse of a girl like a thief between the trees. Sound of bells. Sound of bleating. The girl's waving, and now she's on the road behind us, watching us go. She can't take her eyes off us. She's drawn to us, drawn to the long dance, the long song, heartbeat and drumbeat and the beat of—

Hooves.

Hooves, hooves, like thunder, like lightning, on the road above us. My daughter's heard it too. She's leaning forwards, cursing the donkey, urging it faster and faster. Speed now, hooves now, wheels skidding and sheering. And when next I look to her breast, the book's no longer held by a shawl, but by twining and quickening shoots of—

Shouts now, closer and closer, telling us halt, halt, pull up.

'Faster,' my daughter cries. 'Faster!'

I want to tell her to have no fear, to tell her that though they'll try to stop us, to bend us, to break us, we shall not let them. Not this time.

Can't she hear it? The book. The forest. It's singing. Singing. Can't you hear—?

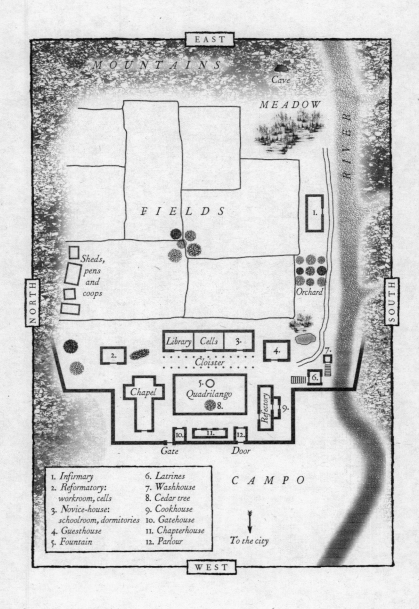

EAST

MOUNTAINS

Cave

MEADOW

RIVER

FIELDS

1.

Sheds,
pens
and
coops

Orchard

NORTH

SOUTH

Library | Cells | 3.

4.

7.

2.

Cloister

6.

Chapel

5.
Quadrilango
8.

Refectory

9.

10. | 11. | 12.

Gate   Door

CAMPO

1. Infirmary
2. Reformatory:
   workroom, cells
3. Novice-house:
   schoolroom, dormitories
4. Guesthouse
5. Fountain

6. Latrines
7. Washhouse
8. Cedar tree
9. Cookhouse
10. Gatehouse
11. Chapterhouse
12. Parlour

To the city

WEST

The Gate

Fat Tuesday

'Help!' A voice calls from beyond our walls. 'Help –
I found them – on the mountain – two women – strangers –
help! Holy sisters, I beg you, open, open the gate!'

The cry sounds shrill and ragged, desperate even, but no
pleading will tempt me from my station beneath the chapel
portico. How can we help? It is carnival and the sun has long
since set. The city will grow wild tonight, and we must be
on our guard. It is a prank, a ruse – of that I am certain. A
cartload of revellers, already buoyed by wine. A young man
falsettoing, affecting the cries of a girl distressed, while his
friends snort and nudge—

'They're dying, I tell you. Dying!'

I grimace – such absurd persistence – although sometimes
it pays off. Sometimes, every three years or four, a few boys
do get in. Stumbling shadows breach our walls, tilt across
the quadrilango, splash in the fountain, cooing and crooning,
begging the pretty girls to come out, come out, wherever they
are. Mother Chiara greets them – the novices watch on tiptoes
from their dormitory – and quickly the boys lose their brag-
gadocio. They want shrieks and screams, not Mother Chiara's
homely face, her stout contours, her amiable enquiries. 'Lost

are you, pets?' She chucks their chins, and they retreat. Still, they come. New year, new boys.

The plaints crescendo, finally rousing old Poggio, our decrepit chaperon. By what little light remains in the sky, I watch him shuffle from his gatehouse, scratching his scrofula, grumbling as his foot plashes in a puddle of slush lingering beneath the walls. His sight – like all his faculties – is poor, but nevertheless, I shrink deeper into the shadows. I should not, of course, be shivering out here. I should be in the chapel, beside my sisters, joining my voice to theirs as they sing the penultimate psalm of the sixth office.

'For shame—' Poggio is attempting to address whoever stands beyond the gate, but his words quaver and crack. He clears his throat – ever an undertaking – and begins again. 'For shame, for shame, to disturb the ladies at their prayers. Begone, jackanapes, or I'll call—'

The triumphant bang of the night's first fire-rocket cuts him off, followed by the affronted hinny of a frighted donkey. I strain my ears while the braying subsides, but hear nothing more, and for a moment I savour the vindication of my suspicions. They are giving up, I think, untangling my fingers, which had knotted together. They will go away and leave us alone. But I am wrong. I hear a bestial squeal – has somebody kicked the donkey? – followed by a frenzy of pounding and a pugnacious cry.

'I'll leave them, you hear me? You don't open up, I'll leave them. And if they die, let it be on you! On your heads – you hear me? Not mine!'

My perception lists. A girl's voice – assuredly, it is a girl's. Those cries are truth, not buffoonery. I banish the snickering youths from my thoughts – and replace them with somebody young, frantic. Poggio, it seems, is of the same mind. Already, he has advanced upon the gate and is fumbling at the little shutter that covers the grille, but his hands have grown swollen and stiff this long winter, and the catch will not yield.

'Wait, do you wait, child. Presently, I come, I come,' he tells the gate in kindlier tones, before hobbling in the direction of the cookhouse in search of nimbler fingers – although Sister Felicitas won't thank him for interrupting the final preparations for our Fat Tuesday feast.

Behind me, I hear the lilt and cadence of the closing psalm. Soon, my sisters will emerge. Softly, I cover the twenty paces that separate me from the gate. Softly, I unhook the clasps that hold the shutter in place. With Sophia gone, there is nobody who will care what I may see out there, but still, I think, still I would like to know. I draw the shutter back – and blink at the sudden brightness.

A girl, I see, a girl indeed, a girl holding a torch, its flames weaving this way and that. Beside her is a cart, a donkey and, upon the cart, two cowled figures. The girl – grubby, pretty – is rubbing at her face, tugging at her hair, and at first I think those two figures must be her kin, for the mountain people, when times are hard, do sometimes bring their grandmothers to die in peace and comfort among us. But even as I think it, I know it cannot be so. For the look on the girl's face, as she stares now at the gate, now at her charges, that is not love – even I know what love looks like. The look on her face, that is fear.

I am sure I have made no sound, but perhaps the girl can sense my eyes upon her, for she darts towards the gate, her nose and fingers pressing against the grille. We are so close that I catch the scent of her. Dung-fire, goat.

'Hurry!' she cries. 'For the love of the Green Mary, hurry.'

I look past her, to the women on the cart. The one to the left has lifted her head, and I see a strong face streaked with shadows, a face in its prime, two eyes glittering with reflected torchlight. She squeezes the hand of the woman beside her, who stirs too, and I glimpse lips fallen around a toothless mouth, cheekbones stark as two stones, eyes dark as night's pitch. Those eyes – so it seems – are looking directly at me—

—and I think of Sophia, who died, who left me. She once told me, alone in our library, that when she finally reached our walls, she fell to the ground and wept. 'So many miles, Beatrice, so many moons, so many miles.'

Sophia, weeping! The idea was so arresting, I have never forgotten it. And so, I think, it is this memory, rather than the parlous and particular state of the women, that sets me grappling with the bar of the gate.

Immediately, I discover I am unequal to its weight. That should not, perhaps, surprise me – I pound no dough, porter no water – but I am disconcerted to meet such resistance. I put my shoulder under the bar and push hard, upwards. The metal grinds into my bone, and – yes – I feel it shift.

'Thank you,' says the girl, who evidently can hear my grunts and gasps. 'Oh, thank you, thank you, thank you. I can't understand a word of their talk, but they're suffering, suffering—'

I redouble my efforts and am rewarded with a griping squeal as the bar lifts – a finger's breadth, two fingers – but my sudden access of strength can endure no longer. I give way, and the bar crashes back into its cradle.

That abrupt noise, iron upon iron, recalls me to myself. I look over my shoulder and see that the chapel doors have opened, revealing the dark shapes of my sisters against the candlelight within. Arcangela, our chief warden, our moral preceptress, is standing beneath the portico, on the cold and elaborate stonework that we cross and re-cross eight times a day. I huddle against the gate, a futile effort at concealment, for already her watchful eye is upon me.

'Who is that by the gate? Master Poggio, that is not you, is it? Who can it—?' she is gliding towards me, lantern aloft.

'Sister Beatrice? Sister Beatrice! What are you doing here? Your presence is mandated at the sixth office, yet you were not in attendance? Whatever have you been doing?'

What indeed? I cannot tell the truth. I cannot say I was sitting alone in the library, watching the sun set over the city, letting the darkness wrap itself around me – because Arcangela would ask why, and I would have to say, because I miss Sophia, because I wish she were not dead.

'Beatrice, speak up. Really, I hoped you had outgrown this surliness. What—?'

'Sister, sister!' The girl's voice again, loud and close. 'Don't give up! Try the gate again!'

'Beatrice! Surely you were not attempting—?'

'Leave off of your talking, I tell you, and open the damned gate!' shouts the girl.

Such profanity extracts a bark of appalled and swiftly swallowed laughter from some of my sisters, and Arcangela rounds on the shadowy figures behind her.

'Enough of this dawdling,' she says, ignoring the sound of small fists beating upon the gate. 'To the refectory. At once, do you hear? At once!'

Everyone knows Arcangela disapproves of the carnival feast, considering it an unconscionable licence, but she would rather my sisters were seated neatly about our long tables than witness to some disorder in the dark. The others, some no doubt reluctantly, stream towards the warmth and light now spilling from the refectory door, towards the silhouette of Sister Felicitas, straight up and down as a turnspit, who greets them on the threshold, calling down the Father's blessings upon them all this Fat Tuesday night.

'Now,' Arcangela begins, turning to me – only to pause. The hammering has stopped. Footsteps, running fast, crunch on the stones outside, before fading away across the campo.

Silence. My shoulder throbs, guiltily. Arcangela smiles. 'Well, that's that. Now, Beatrice, I really must say I am—'

'They're still out there.'

'Who's still—?'

'Two women. There's two women. I looked.'

'You *looked?*'

'Is all quite well, Sister Arcangela?' To my relief, I see Mother Chiara walking towards us, rubbing her hands – whether against the chill or in anticipation of the feast, I cannot say. She spies me at the edge of Arcangela's pool of light. 'Ah, Beatrice, you are here too. Some trouble in the library kept you from your prayers?'

'Indeed, Reverend Mother,' I begin, avoiding Arcangela's eye. 'I was hurrying to the chapel, a little late, I must confess' – I hate how timorous I sound – 'when I was alerted by the cries of women in want. Master Poggio being absent, I presumed to see what ailed them. They are outside,' I say, more firmly. 'Two of them. In a cart.'

Chiara frowns. 'Well, what are we waiting for? Bring them in, bring them in!'

'Surely,' says Arcangela, 'we first must ascertain—'

But she has lost Chiara's attention, for now Poggio is returning, followed by Hildegard and Cateline, the two women who have care of our beasts and our fields. Hildegard is carrying a torch, which she upends into the brazier that stands by the gate.

Chiara, her face now lit by leaping flames, smiles and gestures towards the gate. 'Ah, Hildegard, excellent, the very woman—'

'We exceed ourselves,' says Arcangela, barring her path – not a thing lightly to be dared, for Hildegard is a substantial figure, broad and whiskery, with a daunting brow. 'An open gate,' Arcangela continues. 'At night. It is a scandal.'

'Then,' says Chiara, 'we must make sure it is not open long.'

Hildegard presses past Arcangela and puts her shoulder to the bar. It is, as I am still painfully aware, fashioned so as to be beyond the ambition of an average woman, but whoever selected it entirely underestimated Hildegard's strength. The bar lifts. The gate opens. The cart is revealed.

Cateline hurries forwards, seizes the dangling lead-rein and clicks the donkey on. The sudden lurch topples the older woman sideways, and she lolls forwards. I start towards her and prop her back upright, hearing her breath, light and rapid, catch and rasp in her throat.

The cart rumbles past me, and I realise I am, infinitesimally, outside the bounds of the convent. And there – there on the far side of the campo, where the city proper begins, I spy a dozen little lights, milling and circling. I stare, mesmerised, until Hildegard tugs my arm and says, 'Come, come, Sister Librarian. We close up now. First crop of carnival boys is appearing.'

Alarmed, I hasten back inside and hear the reassuring sound of the gate grinding shut behind me. Arriving in the brazier's orbit, I look down at my hands, my front, at where the woman fell against me, and I see my dress is soiled. I hold my hands to my face. That sweet and rusted smell – blood.

'I think,' I say, 'they're . . .' I sway, slightly.

But Chiara is already alive to their condition. 'Cateline, quickly now. Help me escort these unfortunates to the infirmary. And Arcangela?' But already the chief warden is nowhere to be seen. 'Hildegard – it falls, then, to you to greet our other guests. You too, Beatrice – Ortolana will be delighted to find you waiting in the parlour.'

Our guests. Upstanding matrons from the Ten Families – or is it Twelve? – will even now be leaving their palazzos, riding through the city in carriages plump with cushions, armed body-servants jogging by their sides. They'll climb down by the little parlour door, Sister Paola will crank up the grille, and I'll have to listen to my stepmother's assured voice proclaiming how humbled they are to be admitted to the convent to share our feast.

'Mother Chiara!' I turn and start after the cart. 'The women. They are strangers, strangely dressed – are they not? Maybe – maybe they do not speak our Vernacular? Did not Sophia' – I swallow the lump in my throat – 'help you with strangers, deciphering their speech? Perhaps – perhaps I shall be better able to understand them. Perhaps they will better understand Latin – or Greek – or another tongue? That is to say – shall I come with you?'

Chiara smiles. 'You are kind, Beatrice. To forgo the feast and the company of your family. Thank you.'

And I find that, suddenly, I am angry with her, for her obstinacy in seeing me as she would like me to be, not as I truly am.

The Women

Immediately thereafter

THE INFIRMARY, a modest building, lies apart from the heart of the convent, and I cannot remember ever having walked this way after dark. We must leave behind the paved certainties of the quadrilango and follow our little river for a few hundred paces upstream. Mother Chiara goes first – she has taken up Arcangela's lantern, but the pool of light swinging from her hand only makes the surrounding darkness darker. Cateline goes next, leading the donkey, reaching up now and then to fondle its ears. I must walk in the rear. The path is muddy, slippery, the current beside me quick with snowmelt, and I imagine losing my footing, sliding into the water, being borne away in the arms of the river.

I realise I am falling behind and quicken my step to rejoin them as they tread the fringes of the little orchard, which lies shortly before the infirmary. Come summer, it is a rambling, sylvan grove of figs and peaches, of apples and quince, but tonight, bare branches reach towards me, slender fingers caught in the lamplight.

Ahead, I see that Sister Agatha is already standing in the doorway, bidding farewell to three of her helpmeets, who are chattering excitedly about the feast.

Catching sight of us, she starts forwards. 'Why, Mother Chiara – but what has occurred?' She touches the women's foreheads, their cheeks, the sides of their necks, giving swift instruction as to how they are to be borne inside with least distress. Even so, the women groan lamentably as they are lifted down. Their heads droop; their limbs trail down. Discomfited, I remain outside while everyone else passes into the hallway. I watch lamplight brighten behind the shutters of the right-hand room, and I hear Agatha's voice directing the others. She sounds calm, but then she is always calm – even when she is angry.

Often, during the last months of Sophia's life, I felt Agatha was angry with me. She said Sophia should not be working, that it was my duty to persuade her to leave our library, to come to the infirmary, to rest. She was right, of course. Sophia had grown erratic – difficult – muddling manuscripts and reducing our copyists to tears a dozen times a day, calling them plough-girls and dunderheads – but Agatha was wrong to think I had any power over her.

She died during the first week of Advent. A quiet, still afternoon. We were dusting the cabinets where we store our books, sweeping away autumn's relics – the cobwebs and woodlouse shells, the desiccated flies. I was emptying my broom-pan into a pail when I heard a crash, and turned, fearing she had dropped a stack of books, for she was growing clumsy, and we'd agreed, without ever discussing it, that I would carry the ink and the more precious of our holdings. But the books were immaculate, and it was Sophia who had fallen, her limbs awkward, her face awry. I called her name. I called for help. I laid her across my lap and gripped her hand and murmured what I cannot now recall. Prayers, I suppose. But I knew the Father would not give her back. I knew he'd cupped her soul in his palm and taken it for his own.

Cateline now emerges from the infirmary, carrying the lantern. We are not meant to notice beauty, but she still bears its marks upon her face, with long, thick grey hair that she neither cuts nor covers. She gives me a nod, but otherwise pays me little heed, encouraging the donkey to turn around, murmuring to it all the while, telling it to be brave, telling it about the friends it will make – how nice the new oxen are, how sweet the hay, how fresh the water – her foolish crooning.

Soon after, Chiara follows her out. 'There, now,' she says, finding me standing awkwardly in the darkness. 'We must wait while Agatha does what she can for them.'

Were you to believe but a tenth of the stories people tell, you would assume that Chiara, should she choose, could snap her fingers and, in an instant, the women would be hale and whole once more. We, though, who live alongside her, know better than to expect miracles. She comes to stand by me, but does not speak, only hums to herself, looking up at the mountain. Later, the half-moon will rise behind its shoulder, but for now there is only starlight.

'Mother Chiara, Mother Chiara!' Hildegard's voice booms in the darkness.

'Here, Hildegard – what is it?'

'Men at the gate. Asking do we have two women.' I can make her out now, stumping towards us along the path. 'Demanding we should produce them. Poggio and I, we told 'em where to go, but they persist. We are needing you. Do you come?'

'Beatrice' – Chiara's abstractedness is gone – 'please attend Sister Agatha. If the women awake, do what you can to discover who they are – a little history – anything. I should be most grateful.' And away she hurries.

From inside the infirmary, I can hear Sister Agatha telling her helpmeets, 'No – no – run along. You don't want to miss the feast.' Before I can move, the door opens suddenly, and the girls cry out. Their screams summon Sister Agatha.

'Don't be so foolish,' she tells them. She has a clear, high brow atop a long face, with pale grey eyes that appear remote and censorious even at the best of times. 'You can see quite plainly that it is Sister Beatrice. But Sister Beatrice, why ever are you here?'

'Mother Chiara,' I say, my voice perhaps a little stiff, 'said I might be able to assist you. With the women.'

'She thinks *you* can offer these poor souls comfort?' she says, with an unflattering emphasis.

The three helpmeets are still hovering, worried lest they miss more of the feast, and I do not answer until she has shooed them past me. Now I try more fully to explain my task, and I watch Sister Agatha concede to herself that perhaps I might be useful. Have I not helped her puzzle out certain medical texts in Greek? She steps aside to let me pass, only to reach out and stop me with a hand to my shoulder. She peers at my face. I flinch backwards, but she comes on and touches the ragged edge of the scarring on my cheek. I jerk away, and she frowns.

'You have run out of my salve. Why will you never ask for more when you need it?' My hand goes to the old burn, which does indeed weep and crust during cold weather. She sighs. 'In you go. I have settled them as best as I may.'

The room is small and whitewashed, with old-fashioned rushes on the floor, and there is a strong smell of pine resin and rose oil. Small wooden crosses hang above each of four beds. Two are empty, two occupied. A lamp burns low at the window, which is sealed against dangerous draughts. Beneath the window lies a large chest – likely discarded by some rich house – in which their packbags and way-boots lie jumbled. Beside the chest, I can see a mound of shifts, underskirts,

skirts, cloaks. Agatha tuts, picks them up and carries them outside, leaving me alone.

The women, whom I have been avoiding looking at until now, are lying on their backs, under convent blankets, their heads and the tops of their shoulders bare. The face of the older one, skull-like when I glimpsed it before, has shrunk further. Her eyes are hollowed, blackened above and below. Her lips are pale, and her skin is mottled, blue and purple, like a piece of ghastly lace. She looks near death. And yet, even now, she retains something that defies my pity.

I remember the visits I was obliged to make to the oldest sisters when I was a novice. I hated their spotted hands, their sunken cheeks, their clouded eyes. I hated how they drooled over their milk pap, how they told me the same things every week, how sometimes they cried. I can still recall my fear that one of them might reach out and touch me – I kept my hands tucked inside my sleeves. This woman is not like them.

The younger – I say younger, but she cannot be less than forty – has coiling brown hair, threaded with coppers and golds. Even sheened with sweat, her face is strong, definite, the type that is called masculine: the chin, the nose, the mouth, all a little larger than what is thought beautiful. Fleetingly, I decide they are related – mother and daughter.

Stepping closer, I see something I missed in the gloaming at the gate. Their skin – at their brows, their cheeks, their throats – is scored with red marks, deep enough in some places to have bled and scabbed, in others more like pinpricks. I take a step backwards, and another, until I am nearly at the door.

'It is not the pestilenza,' says Agatha, returning to the room. 'Have no fear.'

'I'm not afraid,' I say – although I am, of course I am.

'Those are but superficial abrasions. About their middle parts, the wounds are worse – much, much worse.' She moves to the bed, and I am worried that she is going to show me, but she merely straightens a blanket. She looks at me. 'I staunched the flow, but they've lost a great deal of blood. Too much. I've bandaged them, dressed them, stitched what I could – done what I can – but . . .' She is running a hand up and down her throat, pulling at the sides of her neck. 'This is beyond me.'

I think of Chiara's commission. 'Can you tell what occurred?'

Her shoulders lift in a small shrug – an admission of ignorance, not a lack of feeling. 'As regards their faces – well, you recall when Tamara hid from Sister Arcangela in the briar patch behind the chicken coop? For the rest – I would say that somebody set about them with knife or sword. But who would do such a thing – and why?'

I gesture towards the women. 'Did you find anything among their belongings?'

'My girls undressed them. Their robes were stuffed with all manner of things. Nothing of value though, if that's what you mean.' She gestures towards the packbags. 'They put everything they found in there.'

'Perhaps,' I say, 'we should . . .?'

But Agatha looks uneasy. I wonder whether she scruples to rifle their possessions – or is she anxious as to what we might find? Yet when I take the first bag from the chest, she does not try to stop me; rather, she watches closely as I feed the leather straps, supple with use, one by one through the rusted buckles, and then lift the flap.

A musty, musky smell rises to meet me. I reach inside and pull out pouches of dried herbs, some little glass vials, a thin trowel. A smooth wooden bowl – a mixing bowl, a begging bowl, I cannot be certain. A string bag filled with chestnuts, the cones of an evergreen tree, the cupules of many acorns. The husk of a pomegranate. Pressed poppy flowers. A fly, bound in gossamer thread. A piece of tattered embroidery. Two brown-and-white pinion feathers. A handful of teeth from some animal I cannot name.

These items I spread before me, and Agatha kneels to examine them. She holds the pouches to her nose, unstoppers one or two of the vials, names their contents. 'This, I have in my cabinet. This and this. They are herbalists, I imagine. Travelling women. Village healers.'

I am still on the floor, searching the bottom of the second bag. Velvet, I feel, stretched over something hard – a wooden box, I presume. My mind conjures a cache of coins, gold or jewels, motive enough for a violent robbery. But as my fingers arrive at the edge of what I take to be the lid, they find neither hinge nor catch, but leaves of parchment.

A book.

My eyes stray to their cracked boots, their worn bags. A puzzle. I might expect such women to read a little – a very little – but to possess a book? And one bound in velvet? I am not so sure. I am about to pull it forth, to examine it, but first I glance up at Agatha, who is now standing between the beds, feeling the temples of the older woman. She lifts one eyelid, lowers it. She reaches for the woman's wrist, waits, shakes her head.

'Gone.'

'While we were talking?' I stare about the room, almost expecting to see her soul fretting at the shutters, trying to escape. I have seen other dead bodies – for sure, I saw Sophia's – and we lay our old women in the chapel and so pray them to heaven, but their bodies always looked lamentable – shrunken, weightless. This woman's stillness is freighted, expectant.

Agatha does not answer, but starts to murmur the farewell prayer, hoping that by the Son's grace the woman might enter the Father's house and so dwell at peace. I look over at the younger woman and am startled to find her eyes are now open. She is staring at me, unblinking. The words to the prayer stick in my throat. Her eyes close, but it seems that something has stirred within her, for fresh blood now oozes from the cuts about her face.

'So it please the Father and his Son, let it be so,' Agatha concludes, drawing the blanket over the dead woman's face.

Abruptly, a helpmeet enters, begging pardon, seeking guidance in hushed and hurried tones – one of the novices, it seems, has fainted. Agatha nods, says she'll come at once, but before she leaves, her meticulous gaze shifts to the woman who yet lives. Frowning at the blood, she crosses to a corner table, where she picks up a jug and cloth. She hands both to me, tells me to make myself useful, then hastens out of the door.

As soon as I am alone, I replace both cloth and jug, meaning to pull the book from the bag, but before I do, I glance at the woman whose wounds Agatha would have me bathe. Her eyes are open once more, but the pupils have swum upwards, backwards, out of sight. Beneath the blanket, her arms are moving, stirring, struggling. Perhaps I should help her – pull back the blanket, free her hands, clasp them between my own, say some words of comfort? But even as I urge myself closer, her eyes reappear and find me, and I decide that in no wise does she wish her hand to be held.

Maintaining a respectful distance, I speak my Latin to her, offering concern for her wellbeing and polite enquiry as to her history. She blinks, makes a noise that could be a laugh, or could be a grunt of pain, and shakes her head, one quick twitch – setting new trails of blood winding down her neck.

She reaches up, feels around, blood now smearing her hair, the bolster, the sheet. I beg her please to stop, please to be patient, tell her I will seek help, but her fingers are working, probing, worrying at something beneath her skin. Whatever it is, she must succeed in pulling it free, for suddenly she relaxes, her hand falls open – and I see it is nothing but a thorn. Wordlessly, I pass her the cloth, which she presses against her neck.

I turn from Latin, hurrying through a few phrases of Common Greek, repeating them in the modified tongue of Constantinopolis. I recite some lines I have memorised from the Pentateuch, some words of Aramaic, a Coptic prayer, verses from the holy book of the Surrendered. I attempt other, stranger forms of greeting my bookseller has taught me from his travels, and – in growing desperation – the mournful refrain from a song Hildegard sings as she works.

Finally, I see she is trying to answer me. Her lips part. Her tongue protrudes. She looks to be trying to swallow. Sounds bubble in her throat, guttural at first, turning into a singsong moan, formless long sounds, with no beginning, no end. She grimaces, stops. Draws in a deep and shuddering breath. Whispers. I edge closer. Words – I do now hear words, but words I do not understand, words that bear no kinship to any I have heard before. I stare at her, shaking my head, making gestures of helplessness. Her eyes darken and I watch as with immense effort – sweat beads her brow, her jaw clenches as against some great pain – she raises up her palms and places them together.

And now I do think I understand. She calls to the Father. She knows herself to be near the end – she would entrust herself to his care. In obedience to this, the last wish of her life, I start confidently upon the prayer the Son taught us.

'Pater noster,' I say, 'qui est in cælo—'

I am expecting its rhythm and tempo, the rise and fall of its famous phrasing, to be familiar, to soothe her, to give her peace, but instead her lips curl, her nostrils flare, and I hear a growl fermenting at the back of her throat. I am angering her, and even though she is weak abed, I long to appease her. I put my hands up. 'I am stopping, I am stopping.'

Her face quiets. She closes her eyes. She puts her hands together – opens them, shuts them, opens them, shuts them, opens them, shuts them. Like wings. Like – a rush of inspiration—

like a book.

I fly to the other side of the room and snatch up the pack-bag. The effect on the woman is dramatic, instantaneous. She waves her hands at me, beckoning, commanding. I pull out the book and hold it up to her. She nods and nods and nods. I hurry over with it and place it on her chest. She brings it to her lips – and then pushes it towards me. I frown, confused. Again, she pushes it, imperious, impatient. I reach out. I look at her. She nods. I take it up. She smiles, lifts a hand, runs a finger across my cheek, says two words. Her voice is cracked, her accent strange, but the words are Latin.

'*Mater noster*—'

Our Mother.

'No, no,' I say. 'No, no, no. I am not Chiara. She was here. She—'

But already her hand has dropped away, her head slumps, and although I cannot compass how life can be and then not be, I know that she is dead. I sit heavily on the empty bed beside her, staring down at the book in my hands. It is very small, resting easily inside my two palms. A horned cow, stamped in gold, adorns the rich red cover. It is a lovely thing.

'But have you no conscience?' Agatha has returned with a clay pot that smells of something green – and a look of anger I cannot explain. 'Have you no shred of feeling? Goodness knows I expect little enough of you, but this, this—' She is shaking her head, as though I am to understand that words

24

fail her. 'For shame, Beatrice. I thought – I thought perhaps Sophia's passing would bring about some change, some onset of sympathy. But no. I see you are as you—' she stops, shakes her head again. 'Go,' she says, wearily. 'Go.'

I am confused. Surely, it can be accounted no fault of mine that the woman has— But then I look down and see what Agatha sees. My ink-stained hands, coiled around a book. A stranger dead before me. I stand, flushed, ready to defend myself.

'No, no – Sister Agatha, you don't understand. This book—'

'No, Beatrice, I'm sure I don't understand. She was dying – *dying* – and you were reading – *reading!*'

For a moment longer, she regards me, until, with a last shake of her head, she appears to put all thought of me aside. I back away, clutching the book tight to my belly. She's right. She doesn't understand. None of them have ever understood. I walk out of the room, out of the infirmary, out into the night. I stow the book in the pocket beneath my skirts, and do something I have not done in years – I run.

When I arrive, panting, back at the quadrilango, I intend to pass beneath the cloister, to find the dormitory staircase, to feel my way up to the second floor, where I can count the doors to my cell, shut myself in, and remain, quiet and unlooked for, until the bell summons us for the seventh office. But as I circle the pool of light cast by one of the braziers, I hear Hildegard calling my name from somewhere to my left. I continue on my course, pretending I haven't heard, hoping she'll think herself mistaken, but at once she calls again, louder. I scan the quadrilango, but I cannot make her out, only the outline of the walls and the bulk of our great cedar tree.

'Here, Beatrice! Here!'

I follow her voice to the parlour, to the small, square room, built against the walls, which is all most visitors see of the convent. Its outer door, which leads on to the campo, is locked and barred after dark, although tonight we must open it once more to allow our guests to depart.

'Ah, Beatrice, excellent,' says Chiara, as I enter. By the dying embers of the parlour-keeper's fire, I can see she is shutting the spyhole that gives us sight of the campo. 'You've come to tell us what you've learned about our unfortunate guests?'

There is but one thing I can say with confidence. 'They're dead.'

Chiara reaches out to touch my arm. 'Both?'

'Both,' I confirm.

For a moment she says nothing. Then, she murmurs, 'I am sorry for it. Truly. I only hope they felt they were among friends at the last and so died at peace.'

'Hmph,' Hildegard grunts her agreement.

I look from one to the other. I feel a novice again, wanting to know but not daring to ask. Come, come, I tell myself, you are Sister Librarian now, with a seat in the convent's chapter-house. 'Have the men left?' I venture. 'I mean – what did they want with the women?'

Chiara looks at Hildegard. Hildegard looks at Chiara. Chiara says, 'They wanted to question them. I said they had already been ill-used, and I would not expose them to further insult. They grew – heated.'

'Heated!' snorts Hildegard. 'They started giving it this and that about how the Father did guide their feet, and how we be know-nothing stupid women, promising they'd break the parlour door down if we don't open up. I said I'd like to see them try—'

'But luckily,' intervenes Chiara, 'the guards who accompanied your stepmother to the feast were waiting not far off. They became aware of our trouble and told the men—'

'There was a right huffle-scuffle.'

'—to move along. And now, I'm glad to say, they seem to have left us in peace.' Chiara shakes her head. 'But we must put all this behind us – for the next hour, at least. Everyone will be worrying what's become of us, and that won't do.'

She leaves the parlour and starts towards the refectory, Hildegard keeping pace beside her. I hang back, thinking perhaps, with luck, they will fail to notice I am not following, and I will yet achieve the quiet of my cell. But they haven't gone far before I hear Chiara asking what's become of me.

'Forgive me, Mother Chiara,' I say, when she returns to my side, 'but I would prefer not to attend the feast. The women's deaths – they weigh heavily upon me. Perhaps I will go early to chapel—'

'Now, now Beatrice,' she says, placing a hand on my arm. 'We shall all pray for them later. But first you need food, Beatrice. Food and company.' Her hand gives my arm a squeeze. 'You have not seen Ortolana since your father died. I know you and your stepmother will want to comfort one another in your grief.' Her hand moves to my back, a light pressure, steering me towards the refectory. I resist, wanting no such thing. 'Beatrice,' she says. 'Come, my dear. We do not want to provoke Sister Felicitas, do we? She will already be angry enough with me for making us late. What would she say if we were to miss her pie?'

The Feast

Immediately thereafter

THE REFECTORY, lit by our festive allowance of two hundred beeswax candles, is bright after the dark outside, although our guests, but lately arrived from their palazzos, might disagree. To me, though, it is dazzling – and noisy. Usually, we eat in silence, broken only by readings from the Stories, but tonight we must make merry before the Forty-Day Fast.

I follow Chiara inside, and at once dozens of pairs of eyes alight upon us, full of questions. Finding such attention discomfiting, I turn aside to the water-stand, which Sister Felicitas has placed by the doors in honour of the fine ladies in attendance. My fingers are always blacked with ink but – I wince – now they are also marked with red-brown traces of blood, as well as – I tilt my head – another colour: a richer red, bordering purple. Is it a stain from something I touched among the women's possessions? I scrub my hands in the water, and turn back to face the room.

Many of our guests are still shifting in their seats, wanting a good look at our famous Mother Superior. I watch them watching her, wondering whether those who are visiting for the first time are disappointed by what they see. A woman of middling years, height and looks; cheeks more rounded than not; eyes perhaps a darker brown than is usual. Her chest precedes her by a considerable margin, with little gap between chest above and belly below – surprising many, I imagine, for she was a famed ascetic in her youth, so suffused with holy light that it was said you could see her soul fluttering in her ribcage. Doubtless, they will go home and tell anyone who will listen that the woman who once held the balance of power in the Pontifical Wars is now quite, quite unremarkable.

Chiara, oblivious to this regard, or perhaps simply inured, is making straight for Sister Felicitas, who is standing by the cookhouse door, arms folded, fingers kneading her upper arms. I watch Chiara touch her shoulder, take her hands, no doubt apologising for arriving so late. The tables, arranged in a long, thin rectangle, in accordance with the shape of the room, are currently bare – the soup and the fish must already have been cleared – but evidently nobody could bear to serve the pie in Chiara's absence. Felicitas wags her finger – she is angry, but trying not to be – and lets herself be mollified.

Next, Chiara must make a play of asking where she is to sit, and Sister Felicitas will lead her among the novices, who are worming with excitement. She will have sweetmeats hidden up her sleeves, and will hand them out under the table, signalling for the girls to be careful lest the wardens see – although of course they see, of course they know. I watch Arcangela – sitting between fine-boned women who might be her cousins – tense and look away. She cannot observe without disapproving, and nobody disapproves of Chiara.

At the far end of the refectory, I can see the two Stelleri ladies, the most honoured of our honoured guests. One is my stepmother, Ortolana, my father's widow. The other is Bianca, wed this past year to my brother, Ludovice – or half-brother, I should say, for he was born within wedlock, and I was born without. I had hoped they might not venture abroad tonight, it being only six weeks since my father's death, but there they are, an empty place between them – for me, the Stelleri bastarda.

I walk the length of the room, between the benches and the wall. Ortolana, I see, is talking with her usual fluency to Sister Maria, our disburser, the comptroller of our purse-strings, who appears to be listening with relish. Bianca, on the other hand, is staring ahead of her, fiddling with her spoon. Beside her, Sister Prudenzia, who has the unenviable charge of the boarders, those wellborn girls who bide with us during that delicate period between embarking on womanhood and the safe port of marriage, is attempting to make herself pleasant.

As I pass behind them, I hear Prudenzia assuring Bianca that we have all been – as she puts it – unstinting in our efforts to ensure the timely arrival of the duke's much-mourned and not-forgotten soul at the threshold of the Father's house. Bianca – mute – nods. I wonder how much gold my father allotted to secure these, his posthumous prayers. A heroic sum, I guess, enough he must have calculated, balancing credit – that campanile, those frescoes – and debit – my mother, me – to redeem the sins that smouldered within him when a sudden seizure carried him off on the Eve of Epiphany. The river was frozen two hands thick, and my brother was skating far, far downstream. They say he whooped at the news, but they say all manner of things.

I hitch my skirts to allow me to climb over the bench and take my place, conscious of how the ambrosial odour of their twice-daily toilette must contrast with my unwashed state. My arrival startles Bianca, who looks up at me – I would say fearfully, but what can she have to fear from me?

'There you are,' says Ortolana, reaching out to pat my arm, but I move it slightly so she must tap the table instead. I nod to her; I nod to Bianca. I settle my attention on the portion of dove-and-clove pie that one of the helpmeets has placed before me.

Ortolana sighs. 'Ah, Beatrice. Your manners are my most constant friends. I am glad to find that I can rely on them still.'

Maria tugs at her nose, which, for her, counts as an extravagant display of good humour, and says, 'Come Ortolana, you know better than to value Beatrice for her manners.'

I don't mind Maria. She contests every copper penny I need to fund my work, but she does it with civility – and without sanctimonious comment.

'Oh, I know her value to you,' Ortolana is saying. 'Her charming scrolls. Those immaculate tracts. And the beautiful, beautiful prayerbooks. But the prices – heavens, Sister Maria, the prices! Nevertheless, Bianca tells me her baby must have one. Did you hear that, Beatrice? What do you say to that?'

There are many things I should like to say, but none that will do me credit. I swallow a mouthful of pie, and find that my thoughts are in danger of spoiling its flavour. Why must she patronise my work? If my brother had ever showed the slightest interest in books – and we all know he hasn't, despite the parade of tutors – he would not be copying missals.

I'd always planned to write to my father one day, professing to be a poor student at the city's university – and he would find my thinking brilliant, and we would enter into a correspondence, and one day, my bookseller would tell me all about the clever young man who writes to the Duke Stelleri—

But my stepmother is addressing me again.

'We must congratulate you on your elevation – Sister Librarian! I told your father of it. He was very – very proud. But I am sorry – you must feel the loss of Sister Sophia deeply.'

I nod. I know I should say that I am sorry too, about my father, but I cannot – *cannot* – make the words come. Instead,

I turn to my sister-in-law and say, 'Marriage is treating you well, Lady Bianca,' which is a lie.

A year ago, she was fifteen, newly wed, flushed with her cleverness at having married the heir to the greatest banking fortune in the Peninsula. A year ago, she'd brought a wriggling puppy to the feast, and I'm sure I wasn't the only one who'd looked forward to hearing Chiara say it would have to wait with the guards outside. But no, she'd scooped it up, covered it with kisses, and told Bianca we'd all heard what a beautiful bride she made – for Chiara does not, in the way of many plain women, demean those who are pretty. Rather, she seems to delight in their looks, without attributing any special virtue to them, as you might delight in a flower, without thinking it any better than you.

No dog on Bianca's lap tonight. There isn't room. Her skin is sallow, her flower-bud mouth is pinched, and a baby bulges beneath her belly.

I point towards the protrusion and say, 'Your time must be near.'

She does not, as I might have expected, touch her middle and simper. Instead, she sniffs and prods her pie.

'Tell me,' I continue, 'how does my brother?' I have not seen him for twenty years, but I can picture him easily, the gay young duke, cloaked and masked, laughing beneath the loggia of some low house, an arm about two goddesses – ringlets, goose-feather wings, sandals of gold. 'In happier times, carnival was his especial pleasure, was it not? But with our father so recently lost to us, I am sure he keeps to his chamber tonight.'

She starts to mumble something, but her meaning is not plain. She comes from the extreme south of the Peninsula, and still lacks confidence in our city's Vernacular. Her family told my father's envoys that she was quick-witted and spoke an excellent Latin, but that was shop-stall dressing, yesterday's bread sugar-glazed to make it gleam.

'Forgive me,' I say, 'could I trouble you to repeat that?'

Ortolana, who can listen to many conversations at once, turns away from Maria and fixes her gaze on me. She has black eyes, under black brows, which, unlike most of our guests, she does not pluck. 'Beatrice,' she says.

'Yes, my lady?'

'Stop it.'

'Stop what?'

We regard one another. They say Ortolana was plain even when she married my father, but I would rather call her severe. She is sharp-nosed, thin-lipped. She is small, too, but a smallness that tokens no frailty: rather, it feels as though the strength of a far larger person is compacted within her. That strength is now directed at me, but I do not wilt as once I did. She shakes her head, and I see that her attention has turned to her daughter-in-law's plate, upon which the pie lies, brutalised but uneaten.

'Bianca, dearest. The physicians say you must eat if you want your baby to be strong.'

At the other, less exalted, end of the refectory, a group of younger women erupt into noisy talk, centred about Diana, who has been with us not above half a year. She has a provocative and demotic manner that I understand is very popular. Her neighbours all lean closer to her, while those further off look on wistfully. At the sound of their laughter, Arcangela, already stiff, stiffens further. She would have us believe that Diana, lately a paintress, now a safekeep – one of those come to us to escape some indignity done them in the wider world – is beneath her notice, but of course she notices her. Everyone does.

Arcangela wouldn't, I reflect, make Bianca eat her pie. Arcangela doesn't care for food. She halves whatever is on her plate, pushes half away, and eats the remainder in slow, diffident bites. Others copy her, but they never achieve the same effect. They always look too long, too longingly, at the half uneaten.

'I was surprised' – Ortolana is now addressing Maria – 'to find Mother Chiara absent when we arrived. Whatever can have kept her?'

'You'll have to ask Beatrice,' Maria replies.

My stepmother turns to me. 'Beatrice?'

'A girl delivered us of two women.'

I provide no additional details, but even so, her eyes widen.

'More strays?' She lowers her voice and speaks to Maria with an earnestness that surprises me. 'I have warned you, have I not, that you mustn't allow any and every—'

She breaks off as two helpmeets pass slowly in front of us, rounding up the plates, mopping up the crumbs, readying the table for the finale of the feast. I don't know what more she might have said, but Chiara is on her feet again, making a short and comfortable speech – the same she makes every year – about loaves and fishes, about wine at weddings, about how the Son spent his last night on earth with his friends at table. 'And now,' she says, 'the moment I know our younger friends have all been waiting for.' And Sister Felicitas enters from the cookhouse, bearing a magnificent pudding aloft in majesty.

Everyone watches as she starts to serve, sending great bowlfuls – plump with nuts and currants, dripping with butter and cream – down to the novices first. Hildegard prowls towards them, making believe that she comes to steal their puddings. She does it every year, and every year one of the new girls mistakes her mummery and bursts into tears. My first feast, Prudenzia cried so much she was almost sick.

I look over to enjoy Arcangela's disapproval at this levity – but am surprised to discover she is not in her place. Where . . . ? Ah – there she is, over by the main door, talking to somebody outside. At first I assume it must be Sister Agatha returning from the infirmary to report on the women, until I realise that she would not hesitate to enter. And now Chiara, who has finished defending the girls' puddings, makes straight for the doorway, moving Arcangela aside.

Observing them together, a stranger would be forgiven for thinking Arcangela – remote, swan-necked, forbearing – the Mother Superior, and Chiara a helpmeet bade to explain some misdemeanour, for it is unavoidably the case that she often resembles a woman interrupted in some lowly task: the feeding of pigs, the podding of beans. Arcangela, however, bears comparison to the loveliest images of Mother-Mary, possessing much of her limpid grace. I think of the icon that hangs beside our confessional chair, of that exquisite face turned slightly aside, its eyes blind to everything save the Son on her lap, his head ringed with rays of gold. Regarding Arcangela, it is often hard to believe she is made of phlegm and blood and bile. Indeed, the housekeeps, who must launder our necessary cloths, whisper that she needs them not above once or twice a year.

The conversation by the door is at an end. Arcangela returns to her place and – in what I construe as an angry gesture – pushes her pudding to one side. Chiara, meanwhile, makes her way towards us. She lays a hand on my stepmother's shoulder, apologises for not having spoken to her sooner, apologises moreover for only now being able to offer her condolences. Ortolana places her hand on top of Chiara's and squeezes it. I never can fathom the affection between these two, between our Mother Superior – the girl-anchorite, the holy healer – and the Lady Stelleri, ropes of gemstones swagging her throat. I might expect my stepmother to counterfeit friend-ship, but Chiara – never.

'Everything all right?' says Ortolana, nodding towards the door.

Chiara does not answer at once, instead turning away to stroke Bianca's cheek, saying our pudding is rich, is it not, and carrying a baby must be a heavy burden – should she ask Sister Felicitas for a little bread-and-honey? Chiara's hand now drops on to my shoulder and she is saying, 'Beatrice has been working so hard on the book for your baby. She is so clever. Always her head in—'

'Mother Chiara,' Ortolana's interruption is quiet but firm. 'What's happening?'

Chiara tips her head, this way, that way. 'There's been a great deal of toing and froing tonight.'

'Rowdy boys got up as Dionysus?'

'No – no. Two unfortunate women—'

'Beatrice mentioned them.'

'First, two women. Next, some men wanting to talk to them. And now, Poggio tells us, another man alone, demand-ing – demanding, if you please! – the same thing.' She smiles, briefly. 'He asked Poggio what were his credentials for keeping a convent gate. Dear Poggio was most upset.' Her eyes crinkle. 'The man didn't even know his name. I mean, who doesn't know old Poggio?'

'Who was he then, this man?' asks Ortolana, who isn't smiling.

'Poggio said he claimed to be a holy brother. A Shepherd, isn't that what they call themselves? Dirty-white cloak, no boots, a crook in his—'

'Mother Chiara.'

'—seemed to think waving that crook about was enough for us to do his bidding—'

'Mother Chiara.'

'—Sister Arcangela thought so, too, but I told Poggio to give him coin for some boots and send him on his—'

'*Mother Chiara!*' My stepmother's voice is loud enough for many of my sisters to break off their conversations and stare. She collects herself. 'Did he,' she says, attempting a more measured tone, 'did he give a name?'

'Why, yes! Brother – what was it? – Brother Abramo.'

Ortolana is frowning, drumming the table with her fingers. 'Grief has made me inattentive. He sought to preach in the city before, but my husband persuaded the archbishop to deny him. I wish I had known he'd again travelled north. If I had – but no, it is too late.' Her frown deepens. 'Mother Chiara, what did he want with these women?'

'Oh – a misunderstanding, I am sure. It seems he had himself convinced we'd taken in a pair of dangerous heretics.'

That word – *heretic* – causes pie and pudding to congeal in my stomach. Have I ever heard Chiara use it before? It's a word beloved by the Shepherds, that's for certain. They profess loyalty to Pope Silvio, but everyone knows that they – and the Lambs who follow them – long to deprive him of both the Chair of St Peter's and its Key, thinking him an insufficiently stringent champion of the Father.

My hands have travelled to my lap, and I find my fingers are anxiously tracing the contours of the women's book, which lies concealed within my pocket. Hastily, I return my hands to the table, telling myself there is nothing to worry about, telling myself I have nothing to fear.

The Bench

Deep middle night

THE BELL MUST ALREADY have rung for the night watch, for the sound of the warden knocking on the doors of our cells approaches like a wave along the corridor, rousing me from my dreams. I roll on to my feet, tie my head-cloth, and stoop to tug on my sandals. I am wrapping my mantle tight about me, on the point of opening my door, when I hesitate. I flit back to my pallet and fumble beneath my bolster. The book, of course, is still there.

Out in the corridor, I am about to follow the departing backs of my neighbours filing down the stairs, when I hear Sister Galilea's door opening immediately to my right. Her exact age one can only guess, but she has long surpassed her threescore and ten. Being so advanced in years, she need not attend our night-time prayers, and so I am surprised to see her feeling her way along the passage wall towards me. She's nearly blind as well as old, but she retains a certain acuity.

'Who were you talking to in there, Beatrice?' she says, her lack of teeth rendering her speech curiously sibilant.

'Nobody,' I whisper. 'Nobody. It's the night watch, Sister Galilea.'

'The night watch, the night watch,' she says. 'I know it's the night watch. I could hear you, whispering, whispering.' She has stopped beside me and is all but hissing into my ear. 'I know you don't snuff your candle when you should. I've seen the glow when I go to piss.' She shuffles onwards, chuckling, calling out, 'Good morrow, good morrow,' to the stone-faced warden, who is waiting at the top of the stairwell, her lantern lighting our way.

Outside, the air is cold, the sky is clear, the moon is high, and everyone is hurrying to achieve the chapel's precarious warmth. The flicker of a smouldering brazier lights the line of girls hastening from the novice-house, where I too slept until I made my Promise. Arcangela loves to praise their zeal for nocturnal prayer, for even on the softest summer nights, they all but run across the quadrilango. But, as we who spent our childhoods here all know, it is not fervour for the Father that quickens their steps, but an altogether different compulsion – dread.

Those girls who enter the chapel last must stand by the back wall, before a low archway blocked with bricks, where the light of the candelabra does not reach. Beyond that arch-way, a flight of stone steps leads down to the crypt, and in the crypt – so the older girls whispered on my first night here – lie the bones of the monks who perished in the great pestilenza. I used to be slow to wake. I used to stand at the back. I used to writhe and squirm, praying with a violent intensity so as to stave off the creep of dead men's fingers.

The monks, they say, barred the gate against the pestilenza, pledging to fast and pray for the city's salvation, but when the sick and hungry approached the walls, seeking succour, they heard laughter and smelled roasting meat. They also say – although how can it now be proved? – that particular women were seen crossing the campo and entering after dark. What is certain, however, is that when the sickness passed, not a single monk was left alive, save the one we call old Poggio. It was Pope Silvio who held the monastery's title in his gift, and he surprised some, and infuriated many, by inviting Chiara to found a new house here.

For my part, I owe those long-dead monks a debt – it is thanks to them the convent library is so large. And now my place lies towards the chapel's front, I have come to appreciate the night watch, too. My sisters' faces are blurred, muted; their heads bowed, their eyes lowered. Peace, I feel, or something very like it, as my lips shape the holy words.

Across the nave, there is a small disturbance. Diana jolts, presumably awakening from a momentary doze, her face contorting as she stifles a powerful yawn, and now a warden is moving to reprimand her. Arcangela is watching – I can see her frowning over her shoulder. But Chiara, whose face I can see in part-profile, has remarked nothing and continues to murmur into the knuckles of her clasped hands.

It is hard to reconcile this peaceable woman with the holy child who renounced the world. Her father – a cartwright – was incensed. What use was a daughter who crouched in the cellar and prayed all day? Some say he starved her and beat her. Others say it was she who refused food, she who scandalised her body. She might have died down there, had not the town priest intervened. Chiara, he said, had been called by the Father. The cartwright, he said, must build her a cell, ancillary to the family's house.

From that tiny space, Chiara – already much discussed in her neighbourhood – became known across her little town and throughout the surrounding hills. Women began to visit her, to talk to her through the grille – which her father had installed once he realised his daughter might yet prove profitable. And although she spoke but seldom, often declining to leave off her own prayers to attend to those of her guests, those who sought her, passing little tokens – thimbles, ribbons, flowers – through the bars, went away comforted, relating that such troubles as they had brought with them were afterwards miraculously much allayed.

And then came the pestilenza. The townspeople barricaded their doors or fled, and one by one, Chiara's family sickened and died. But she, now a young woman, abandoned her seclusion to labour without cease among the dying and the desolate, no longer the strange, starved girl the goodwives liked to visit, but the town's heroine, its treasure – its saint.

Our chanting ceases. The night watch is passed. In many houses, the closing psalm spells the start of a new day, but Chiara says we glory the Father with our work as well as with our prayers, and so those whose daily toil must necessarily tax their strength are permitted to return to sleep until dawn. The novices, therefore, along with the safekeeps and the helpmeets, and some number of my Promised sisters, are now leaving, while Arcangela and such women as particularly admire her cluster closer beneath the flickering candelabra.

They drop to their knees and direct their gaze upwards, to where the Son hangs on his cross of wood. His brow is furrowed and his lower lip droops. His chest is hollow, his belly scalloped. His feet fold shyly the one over the other. Soon, as the candles gutter, Arcangela and her intimates will fall to weeping, reliving the grief of the three Marys who mourned the Son's passing upon the hill: Mother-Mary, Mary of Magdala, so young and beautiful, and old Mary, wife of Clopas. Their eyes are wide, their mouths are open – in pain as they partake in his suffering, in pleasure as they bathe in his love.

'Sweet Son crucified,' they say.

'Sweet and holy . . .'

'The cup of your lips – the cup of tears . . .'

'Blood, blood . . .'

'With burning love I run . . .'

'Your death on the cross . . .'

'Spotless lamb . . .'

'Sweet blood – precious blood . . .'

'Eternal Bridegroom – humble lamb – darling child . . .'

Perhaps my prayers might help the women who now lie dead in the infirmary. Perhaps I would rest easier knowing the Son was shepherding them to the Father's house. And so I am deciding whether to depart, as is my custom, to seek the warmth that will yet linger beneath my blanket, or to persevere with prayer, when a hand touches my shoulder.

I turn and see Chiara. She twitches her head in the direction of the door. I frown. She nods, and moves her head again. I follow, as quietly as I may. Nobody looks, but everyone sees.

Outside, beneath the portico, I shiver involuntarily, and Chiara begs my forgiveness, saying we should walk to warm ourselves. 'I find,' she says, leading me away from the chapel, 'that I need to talk to you.'

I make a cautious noise of assent.

'Sister Agatha, who is usually so very, so very – help me, Beatrice . . .'

'Equanimous?' I offer.

'Yes – yes, that'll do – so very precisely that. She told me there was perhaps something . . . *strange* about the two women. She was – she was – a little un-equanimous. Is that a word?'

I shake my head, make a noise of demurral.

'No? Uneasy, then. Anxious, even. Sister Arcangela, it seems, sought her out, questioned her vigorously – and did not like what she heard. Arcangela has also come to me, you see, to lay her suspicions at my feet. She said – she had a very great deal to say – but, in short, she said we have no proof the women are of the faith. She warned me not to – how did she put it? – "rush to accord them the sacred rites of the Father's burial". I thought I would ask you, Beatrice. You were there when they arrived. You, I understand, were alone with one of them when she died. What do you think? Are you of Sister Arcangela's mind? Did you witness anything that gave you pause?'

We have stopped walking. We are now beneath the cedar tree, by the pair of old stone benches where Chiara likes to sit before our evening meal, during our discretionary hour, when we take a little leisure. Sometimes, she lets the novices crowd around her, enjoying their little tales. Sometimes, she waves them away, preferring to sit quietly with one of the older sisters, holding her hand and talking softly, exclaiming over the antics of the cookhouse cats.

A sudden and manic whooping ricochets off the roofs of the city below us – carnival is still in full swing. Rowdy boys, I tell myself, it's just rowdy boys – that's what my stepmother used to tell me and my brother if we awoke. 'It's silly fellows singing and dancing, that's all. Say a prayer and go back to sleep.' But I'd often lie awake for hours, imagining myself a maid of Jericho, stuffing her ears against the roar of trumpets, or a daughter of Troy, trembling as Achilles crashed his spear against his mighty shield.

'Beatrice?' Chiara touches my arm and I come back to myself. 'Sit down, my dear.'

I sit, hunching my shoulders, twining my fingers.

Gently, she asks me again: 'Are you of her mind?'

I hesitate. In truth, I am far from certain. But how to convey what occurred when already it feels so muddled and so strange? And – if once I start to tell, would I have to tell to the end? Would I have to tell about the book, now secreted beneath my bolster, the book I have yet to read? Chiara does not understand books – in fact, Sophia found it hard to believe a Mother Superior could be so unlettered. But at least

Chiara asks no questions. Arcangela, though, she asks – and, with Sophia gone, she is asking more and more.

Sensitive to my uncertainty, but misconstruing its cause, Chiara places a hand, warm and rough, on top of mine. It is too dark, here beneath the tree, to make it out, but I can picture it. The brown stubby fingers. The thick, ridged nails.

'I'm sorry,' she says. 'I should not worry you. How can you know whether or not they were of the faith? It was wrong of me to ask.'

She sounds disappointed – and, at once, I realise a simple tale might serve us both. Attempting to keep my voice light and my hand steady, I say, 'I cannot, of course, presume to speak with any especial authority, but I do not share Sister Arcangela's concerns. I spoke the Father's prayer when one was but moments from death – and I believe I brought her comfort at the end. I pitied them and would gladly pray for their souls.'

So much is true – or true enough.

'Thank you,' says Chiara, after a long pause that makes me fear she doubts my telling. 'You have put my mind at rest.' Beside me, she stirs and stands. 'But I have kept you talking too long. You should sleep.' I stand also, and am about to bid her goodnight when she takes my hand again. 'You need your sleep, Beatrice. Sister Arcangela has been telling me how worried she is about you. The care of the library, she fears, is a great weight on young shoulders.'

I withdraw my hand – sharply. Sister Arcangela has indeed taken to visiting the library unannounced, something she would never have dared while Sophia was still alive. She has also foisted two new copyists upon me, bloodless girls who show no interest in their work, believing only that with their stiff wrists and aching spines they do the Father service.

'The library is not a burden,' I say. 'Sophia prepared me—'

'No, no,' says Chiara. 'You misunderstand me. I know you are equal to the task. But you must feel you can ask for help if you need it. You need not be quite so alone.' She pauses. 'Sophia . . . I know how you admired her. I know how she helped you – and how you helped her, although I am sure she never thanked you for it. But did she not, perhaps, keep you a little apart from the life of our house?'

I shake my head. Sophia and the library, they were my life. The rest, oh, the rest is bells and prayers and squabbles, and from them I am glad – glad! – to be apart. I want to get away – but one cannot leave Chiara.

Her hand finds mine again. 'Goodnight, Beatrice. Sweet dreams.'

I walk away, ducking under one of the cedar's lower branches, feeling its needles graze my cheek. When I reach the cloister, I pause and look back, but of course I cannot see her. She has vanished into the deep dark beneath the tree.

The Library

Grey Wednesday

⌘

EVER SINCE WE LEFT the chapel after the second office, the sky has been filling with swift-moving clouds, and by the time I hurry up the library steps after breakfast – bread, broth, silence – the window panes, no other place in the convent has glass so fine, are streaked with the first dashes of rain, blown across the convent by a rising wind. It is, however, markedly less cold today. For the first time this year, I believe I shall be able to work with no discernible whitening of my fingertips.

I take a seat and look out, and, as always, my spirits rise. The view is as fine as the glass. The quadrilango and the principal buildings of the convent are laid out below me, and, if I lift my gaze, I can see out over our walls, over the campo, over the city itself, with its markets and workshops, its cupolas and campaniles. On the clearest days, I can even see the sun lighting the river where it flows beyond the city, down away to the sea.

Sophia – I still think of this seat as hers, not mine – once told me the evangelists were ever-so verily clever to write how the Devil led the Son up to a tall place to tempt him. 'Too, too well, Beatrice, did they comprehend the vertiginous seductions of height.' Trying to match her jesting tone, which I much admired, as well as her Greek-inflected Latin, I said yes, but the Devil offered him dominion over the whole world, whereas we had only our library.

'And it is *our* dominion,' she said, rapping this desk with her knuckles, 'and don't you dare forget it.' The library, you understand, had been a sorry thing before she came here – the books stacked pell-mell in the furthest corner, while the rest of the room, with its light, its air, was used to dry beans for the cookhouse and grass for the beasts. Sophia changed all that.

My copyists sigh and stretch as they settle to their work – writing, yes, but also pumicing parchment, ruling lines, stitching quires. I, meanwhile, continue to gaze out over the city. The streets will be quiet this Grey Wednesday morning, sticky with soot, spilled wine, meat-fat. The goodwives will be abroad, sluicing, sweeping. I picture the upturned carts. The discarded costumes. The sore heads. The guilty consciences.

When the bell summoned us to the dawn office, I'd removed the book from beneath my bolster, thinking to take a quick look then and there. But the warden was already passing down the corridor, flinging open our doors, and so I placed it quickly in my pocket, which is where it still lies. I am thinking that when the others attend the third office, in the middle morning, I shall remain behind. They will not remark it. I often dispense with certain prayers during the winter months to make proper use of the daylight. Chiara says she trusts me to pray with compensatory devotion at other times – not that she would say *compensatory devotion*, her speech being so obstinately plain.

I trace the outline of the book with my fingers. I could, I suppose, look now – what, after all, is remarkable in a librarian reading a book? – but I am strongly inclined to secrecy. All morning, my sisters have talked – how much they contrive to talk, despite the silence we keep during prayers and meals! – of nothing but the women, and the consensus is not favourable. When Chiara announced that they would be buried today, that she would conduct a short committal, that any whose duties permitted them were welcome to attend, there was an almost dissident stir. Agatha herself is above gossip, and certainly I have not shared what I witnessed, but nevertheless, the strange manner of their arrival, their inexplicable malady, the holy brother's accusation – all have combined to cloak them in suspicion.

I cannot settle. One of the new copyists is whispering too loud, her mouth shaping each word that she must write. It is distracting. I stand and walk about the scriptorium, inspecting their work. I correct a clumsy quill-grip, suggest the redrawing of an erratic margin, caution against the precarious siting of an inkwell, discourse on the proper angle of a terminal serif, before passing through the archway and into the library proper, where I improve the placement of books consulted the previous day.

I stop, as I often do, by the cabinet, where Sophia kept the pair of books she carried with her when she fled the sack of Constantinopolis, fleeing westwards as the Khan King swept all before him. The crystalline love poems of Cassandra, whom she called the tenth muse, and Homer's bloody account of the homecoming of Agamemnon. She showed me how to read them, and although she was an exacting teacher, contemptuous of any failure to grasp what she would impart, she did me a great service – one for which I hoped I should one day find the words to thank her, but somehow never did.

Once, perhaps five years ago, my father had learned what we had in our possession and wrote to Chiara, saying that he would buy both volumes, naming a fantastic sum. Sophia got to hear of it and erupted, storming into the library – I remember how the copyists fled before her – swearing she'd shred the books rather than give them up. Chiara arrived just in time, appearing at the door and saying, curtly as I recall, 'Sister Maria has written to the Duke Stelleri to tell him our books are not for sale. But I wonder' – a smile – 'I wonder how much he would pay for a fair copy?'

For a while after that, Sophia spoke less of holy fools and more of the sound commercial sense sometimes exhibited by simple women.

I resume my seat and write half a dozen words. I am formulating a prayerbook for Bianca's baby – Chiara spoke no lie – but I find myself distracted by the clouds chasing across the sky, carving the quadrilango into light and shade.

Below me, Cateline is accepting a pair of cows from a burly woman at the gate. They are beautiful creatures, large and brown, with gently curving horns. I watch Sister Felicitas come to the refectory door and nod approvingly, seeing extra milk for the weeks ahead, for we will eat no more meat until the Son rises after the Forty Days. Sister Maria, a weighty ledger in her arms, emerges from the chapterhouse and advances on the beasts, a finger raised, doubtless in query as to their cost. Her adjutant, Sister Tamara – wiry, dark, Promised the same year as I – appears behind her and says something that makes the others smile. Probably something crude. She still lapses into the dockside argot she learned during a girlhood spent travelling with her father, a Carthaginian trader in spice. One of the wardens hurries past them in the direction of the bell-post, and the women disperse as the summons to prayer clatters across the convent.

Stools scrape behind me. The shuffle of departing feet fades down the stairwell. From my window, I can see my copyists walking towards the chapel, unrolling their shoulders, cricking their necks, waggling their fingers, but nevertheless

I take myself out on to the landing to satisfy myself I am truly alone. Resuming my seat, I reach beneath my skirts, loosen the drawstring that holds my pocket shut, pull the book forth and place it on the desk before me.

The third office is short – I don't have long.

But now, from the direction of the latrines, I see two of our best-born boarders come running, laughing, late. They skid to a halt when they see Arcangela step out of the chapter-house. She chastises them, and they proceed more decorously. Prudenzia, exiting the schoolroom, has witnessed this, and is already apologising, her hand on her heart. Maybe Arcangela senses my gaze, for she glances up and sees my face at the window. Her expression does not alter, but I feel uneasy, and I think – if only for a moment – that perhaps I ought to hurry to the chapel after all.

The quadrilango empties. The book awaits.

Tomis – my bookseller and, I sometimes think, my friend – once spoke of how he feels when a new book lies before him – his hope, his longing that something rare, something precious might lie between its boards. Always, so he told me, he pauses, and thinks that perhaps he is about to be the first man in a thousand years to read what Dido said to Aeneas when she banished him from the shores of Carthage. Such a find, I remember replying, would be beyond price, but he laughed and shook his head, and said, 'No such thing, Beatrice. You find the lost books of the *Aeneid* mouldering in your crypt, and I'll give you a number.'

We were talking in the parlour, and I could tell from the way Sister Paola, the parlour's keeper, was looking at us that we had been talking for too long. Quickly, I changed the subject to parchment grades. That was last year, before winter came, before Sophia died. He said he was going to take ship from the Lagoon, across the Middle Sea, to the great cities of the Delta. He said he would return by Epiphany. He is late. Perhaps, I think – a quickening notion – perhaps I will have something worth showing him when he does return.

With flying fingers and gnawing teeth, I undo the twine, open the outer boards – and stop and frown. The title page is blank. I turn to the first spread – also blank. I see only that someone has begun to prepare the parchment, marking the left and right margins with an awl, until halfway down the page, the neat line of dots starts to run wild, a melee of pricks, the page stabbed at random, whether out of frustration, or boredom, or some other impulse, I cannot fathom. I peer closer, tilting the book this way and that, and see that what I at first took for small blemishes might, in fact, be scattered droplets. Wine, I think, or dirt – or blood.

A cloud masks the sun, and I run a forefinger up and down the parchment, feeling a coarseness to the grain that speaks of skin improperly scraped, of haste and economy on the part of its maker. The bottom edge is distorted, rippled, so it is possible to guess at the curve of the neck or haunch of a long-dead creature. The bone-white of goat, I judge, rather than the distempered yellow of sheep – certainly not the inviting creaminess of calf that the handsome cover had led me to expect. Were Tomis to offer me this, I would laugh in his face.

I purse my lips and turn the page.

Nothing.

The next. Nothing.

The next. Nothing, nothing, nothing.

I reach the end. The book is short. Three quires, unevenly sewn. I slam it shut, chiding myself. So desperate was I to find something of note, I let fatuous fantasy overcome my wits. It is a cheap commonplace book with a peculiarly elegant binding – nothing more. Perhaps the woman accepted it from some notary's wife in lieu of payment. Perhaps she meant to fill its

pages with scrawls and sigils to dazzle the ignorant. Perhaps –
but I recall her face as she thrust it towards me. Her passion,
her urgency. It makes no sense. I slump down in my chair and
list, perplexed, through the empty pages.

A whispering alerts me to my copyists' return, and I make
haste to conceal the book and assume at least the appearance
of work. But when, after a few moments, they do not enter as
they should, I stand, irritated, and go to the door to see what
they are about. The landing is bright, sunlit, empty. The stairs
are silent. I look out of the window above the stairwell. The
quadrilango is still empty. I ascribe the whispering sound to
draughts of wind eddying about the eaves and return to my
place, resolving to ask Hildegard to send one of her girls up a
ladder to check the tiles.

The wind has blown away the clouds, and the sun's unfet-
tered rays now pierce my window, casting a stripe of light
across my desk. I had placed the book beneath the copies of
Bellum Gallicum with which I give instruction in Empire Latin,
but such discretion now feels foolish – absurd. What, after all,
am I hiding? Testily, I retrieve it and locate my quill-knife,
thinking to nick the stitching, separate the sheets of parchment and turn them over to one of my more diligent copyists,
who might enjoy the opportunity to practise the Old Empire
hand, which Tomis tells me is increasingly sought after.

I splay the book open, pushing the pages apart with my
left hand, exposing the little sinew of hemp that binds them
together. I prepare to cut – and blink. The faintest of faint
lines dance upon the page. My eyes, I think, unused to sunshine, are playing tricks with me. I blink, and blink again – but
still the lines remain.

Perhaps – a dropping feeling – my sight is about to splin-
ter, the familiar but nonetheless sickening prelude to what will
be a day or more's racking head pain. I cover my face with my

hands, fearing to see the same lines shuddering on the backs of my eyelids, but there is nothing – only blackness. Relieved, I open my eyes and consider the page again. The lines – I can see them plainly now – are no incorporeal figments, but lively – or do I mean chaotic? – patterns, traced with the finest silverpoint I ever beheld.

I return to the first page, to the dots, and wonder are they perhaps some code, some cipher? I turn the page. Again, the same delicate silverpoint. I tilt the book to and fro in the sunlight, for here the lines do assume a more definite form. Frowning, I lift the book closer to my face. Little spheres, I see, covered with what could be spikes or barbs. I puzzle over them awhile, wondering what I might be looking at. I sit back and snap my quill-knife shut, and at once the metalled sound suggests a martial object – a weapon designed to be swung from rope or chain. The correct word eludes me, but it wouldn't elude Hildegard. Everyone knows, although nobody quite admits it, that in her youth she fought – yes, fought! – in the army of the Forest Queen in the wars against St Peter's. Our people remember it as a famous victory, but I recall Hildegard saying, 'You know, I am thinking it was more what you are calling a draw.'

I turn the pages once again, and the harder I look, the more I sense there is something there, something on the perimeter of sight – like the sun behind a cloud, like veins beneath the skin. I ponder what little I know of steganography, the practice of hiding writing: how disparate elements can be combined, first to conceal, then to reveal. How is this done? The sap of some tree, the milk of—?

But now, through the window, I see my sisters are finally emerging from the chapel. Immediately, I am alert to some turbulence, some instability in the usual flow of bodies – and then I remember. The women's burial. I had not been planning to attend – very little would part me from the library in the middle morning. And yet – I observe how pointedly Sister Nanina leads her safekeeps back to the workroom, how deliberately Prudenzia shepherds the younger girls to the schoolroom, how she simpers at Sister Arcangela, how superior Sister Arcangela looks.

I jump to my feet, thrust the book into my pocket and hurry down the stairs. 'Come, come, come,' I say to my copyists, who are straggling upwards. 'Have you forgotten? We must do our duty by those two unlucky women.'

The Chestnuts

Immediately thereafter

WE BURY OUR DEAD in a little meadow at the foot of the mountain, where wilder land starts to climb towards the steep scarp, that vast and encircling amphitheatre of rock that forms our eastern wall. To reach it, we must follow the river past the orchard, past the infirmary, past Hildegard's broad domain, the fields upon which she grows our lentils and beans, our roots, our greens. The wind is blowing hard, rattling the branches of the grand shade trees, bending the tops of the boundary pines.

To my left, I can glimpse, but thankfully not smell, the helpmeets forking heaps of ordure, readying the ground for the spring sowing. I remember Sophia once returning in cackling good spirits from a chapter meeting, reporting that Arcangela had suggested we follow the custom of other houses and hire men to do *the dirty work*. At which, so Sophia told me, Hildegard had unfolded herself, all eighteen hands of her, and said she'd emasculate the first bastardo who touched her muck-barrow.

Strung out on the path ahead of me, I can make out scarcely two dozen of my sisters. Maria and Tamara are leading the way, followed by Sister Felicitas and some of the cookhouse girls, their labour necessarily much reduced during the Forty-Day Fast. Behind them comes Sister Timofea, plump and doughty, who has evidently allowed her housekeeps to leave off their toil to attend.

The wind whips and whirls, putting us at pains to subdue our skirts, to secure our coifs, not that anybody – save the crows jeering from the bare crown of an old oak – can see us. Chiara is already at the meadow, standing beside Hildegard, who is leaning on one of the tools of her calling – the puissant offspring, it appears, of an axe and spade.

The city's archbishop consecrated this patch of ground in the first years of Chiara's stewardship, when her fame was at its height and no man dared refuse her anything. Why, the archbishop courteously enquired, did she not wish to inter her daughters in the crypt beneath the chapel – was it that she feared their bones might mingle with those of their brother monks? Why no, she replied, she merely preferred that her daughters' bodies should lie somewhere the flowers bloomed and the sun shone.

I take my place at the edge of the circle of my sisters and look down at the pair of newly dug trenches, the wet mounds of earth. It's still too early for flowers, and the grass is brown and lank from weeks of rain and snow. Mother Chiara will not recite the homecoming prayer herself – Father Michele will do that tomorrow after he has confessed us. Instead, she raises her hands and starts to talk in her unaffected way, as though the women might yet be able to hear her, telling them she is grieved they were so ill-treated, apologising that she was not better able to serve them.

I am standing with my back to the mountain, hands clasped, head lowered, wondering whether someone, somewhere, is lamenting the women's disappearance, or whether they were sufficient each to the other, strangers wherever they went.

I recall Sophia's burial – I can still make out the disturbed ground where we laid her to rest – and with it the uncomfortable knowledge that I alone truly mourned her. She could, I admit, be difficult, especially when seized by a certain blackness of spirits, when everything she did, she did angrily, lashing and lacerating all about her. I know many of my sisters thought her curmudgeonly and cruel – and she was those things, but also she was more – or more to me. And now my thoughts tend dark, and I ask myself who – who will weep when I lie shrouded in the earth?

Thus unhappily occupied, I do not immediately notice that an inattention, a distractedness, is spreading among the others. Belatedly, I realise they are looking at something behind me, and I turn in time to see a white streak, a flash, flitting between the weathered rocks high on the slopes above us. Almost at once, the figure disappears into one of the rocky defiles that leads down to the meadow. I am bewildered. I cannot conceive how somebody could be up there, for unless you are a winged goat – or possess six hundred feet of stout hawser – there is no way down off the vertical scarp.

Chiara cannot have failed to notice that something is afoot, but she refuses to be distracted from her leave-taking. The others try to emulate her, but all are stealing glances upwards. Only Hildegard, standing on the opposite side of the circle from me, scans the hillside frankly. I turn around again, in time to see a slight girl breach the scrubby line of trees, coming now fast and nimble over the broken ground – no, she falls, falls and quickly rises – covering the final stretch of brash and scrub at a frantic run.

When she is but twenty paces away, suddenly I recognise her – not from any particulars of her features, but rather from the timbre of her anguish, the pitch of her desperation. It is the girl from outside the gate, and she is making straight for me. Before I can stand aside for one more suitable, she is upon me, shaking and trembling in my arms. Her breath claws in and out in ragged gasps, and her heart pounds against my breastbone. Helplessly, I take in her torn clothes, her scratched limbs. She sobs and gulps, but does not speak. Helplessly, I look about me, knowing myself unequal to the task of consoling somebody so inarticulate in her misery.

'Mother Chiara,' I say, with rather a forlorn wave, as if she might be unaware of my plight. She raises a hand in return, and starts upon what I hope is the conclusion of her prayers. It seems I must manage a moment longer.

'What,' I whisper to the girl, drawing her a little uphill, away from the others, 'what, in the name of pity and charity, what has occurred now?' But my question secures no answer, only another onrush of tears. Hoping to convey that I know a little of her history, I say: 'It was me, last night – it was me on the other side of the gate. Listen' – I hiss the words into her hair – 'there is some suspicion attached to the women you brought here. For your own sake, I beg you, do not speak of them.'

She moans, her lip twists, her eyes screw shut, and she seems further than ever from speech. When I try to pull back a little, to look at her, to see if she is hurt, she grips me tighter and tighter, encircling me, her thin arms strong, and so I must endure, recalling the accounts of Laocoön gripped by sea-serpents.

Over the top of the girl's head, I watch Chiara take up a clod of earth, raise it to her lips, kiss it and toss a piece into each of the graves. She stands back, waiting, while the others do the same, and then – finally! – they are done. Tamara announces that she'll alert Sister Agatha and races away. Hildegard marches uphill – why, I cannot tell. Felicitas and Timofea round up my copyists as well as their own charges, saying the poor child has no need of a crowd, back to work, back to work, and as they leave, I think how this new incursion will be known to all before the bell sounds for our noonday prayers.

'Thank you, Sister Beatrice,' says Chiara, approaching.

At last, I feel justified in making a more serious effort to disentangle myself. I pass the girl over. As I do so, my hand catches on something – something of an exquisite sharpness – in the fall of her hair. I wince at the pain, astonished to see pricks of blood dappling my fingertips. The girl, I think, notices my surprise. I have a brief impression of bright blue eyes, rimmed red, staring at me fearfully, but then Chiara is tucking an arm around her, leading her away, murmuring, 'Now my dear, you can walk? No, no, don't try to talk. I can see you are too upset. Here, take my hand. We'll soon have you right. Off we go, off we go.'

I stay where I am, sucking my fingers, the pain slowly fading.

By the graves, two helpmeets are coiling the ropes that were used to lower the bodies, piling them to one side, before taking up shovels to fill in the holes. While the wind's fingers dabble the nape of my neck, I watch the earth rain down, little stones bouncing off the taut winding sheets. Hildegard strides back past us, calling out that she'll fix up Beppo for them, and they're to come and find her when they're done. I watch her catch up with Chiara – they exchange a few words – and then she leaves the path, making for a stand of trees at the intersection of what I now see are four distinct fields. After a moment's consideration, I determine to pursue her.

As I draw closer, I can see that she is preparing, with some attendant grumbling, to attach a beast – is this Beppo? – which had been idling beneath the trees, to some sort of harrow. She does not acknowledge my approach until I am half a dozen paces distant, when she turns and says, 'You lost?'

The wind has made her nose run, and she wipes it with the back of her hand, wipes her hand on the red rag tied about her neck. I swallow – determining to take no offence, imagining my consternation should she tramp up the stairs to my library – and say I am perfectly situated, and merely wanted her advice on one small matter. She grunts and turns her back to me, reapplying herself to securing a hank of chain through a catch of metal, sawing it backwards and forwards, muttering what I suspect are some of her native curses, until it jumps home. She grunts in satisfaction and says over her shoulder, 'Still here?'

'It is but a very small matter,' I say, and draw out the book.

She regards it without interest. And then the wind gets beneath my skirts – not hers, hers are lashed ingeniously – and I must wrestle with them, worried all the while that the book is not rigorously sewn, that a sheet might fly free, thinking it is unvarnished foolishness to have brought it out here. Hildegard, meanwhile, with an array of guttural clicks, has encouraged the animal to embark upon a lumbering walk. I am tempted to retreat, but I enjoin myself to persevere and resume my station beside her.

Grabbing at her arm, its flesh unyielding, I say, 'Please Hildegard, please can you tell me what this picture denotes? I believe it has some military connotation, and I thought perhaps—'

Abruptly, she takes the book from me, and I wince as her muddied fingers thumb the pages – none too subtly, it seems, for she fixes me with a level gaze. Standing this close, I am fascinated by how the red veins of her nose ripple outwards, ending in little starbursts.

'You want me to look or no? What is it? These – you would know what these are?' She is holding the book at arm's length, regarding me with no little condescension. 'They are the – how do you say it? – the fruits of the chestnut tree. How can it be you are not knowing this?'

She turns the book towards me, and I see that the spiked balls, once faintest silver, are now a tender green – their identity, once mysterious, now unmistakable. I flush and mumble, saying, yes, of course, *cupule*, the word is cupule, they are chestnut cupules, and she shakes her head, wondering if I be so damned expert, why must I keep her from her ploughing?

I cast about for a rejoinder, muttering something about wanting her to assess the verisimilitude of a design for some new marginalia, but of course I only want to get away – or rather to get the book away. I must examine it. I must find some explanation for how it could have so materially . . . altered. I try to retrieve it, but Hildegard – accidentally or not – moves slightly, putting it beyond my reach.

I watch, cautioning myself against displaying any of my acute apprehension, as she leafs forwards through the otherwise empty pages. She returns to the beginning, to that first ravaged page, and I see at once that – inexplicably, irrefutably – the tangle of silver lines has burst into flower. Each possesses five petals of such a brilliant white that the parchment necessarily appears drab beside them. Here and there, the outermost edges of the leaves blush pink, and at their centres little filaments cluster, tipped a rusted red.

Hildegard is frowning, intent, and my stomach flips. But then a smile tugs at her mouth's corners, and I realise that my anxiety is quite baseless, her frown evidence only of a moment's happy absorption. And, as if in confirmation, she says, 'This drawing – this is very nice. The bramble of the blackberry, I am thinking? Very like to life. Almost I can imagine to taste it.'

She has been tracing the outline of the picture with one forefinger, and now she puts that finger to her mouth, and I see – or think I see – a trace, the faintest hint, of purple staining her lips. The wind has cracked her skin, I tell myself, a spot of blood, that is what it is. Nothing strange – a spot of blood, that is all. She drops the book into my hands with a small nod, as though giving it her approval, and starts bawling at two helpmeets that they must think she is blind if they chit-chat and dawdle-dally so slow when there is work to be done.

I return, very slowly, to the library where I am greeted by a wall of silent hard work, which I know means they've all been talking. One by one, they turn around to look at me. One by one, they try not to look surprised. My skirts are muddy. My sandals slop a wet trail. Wordlessly, one of them stands, collects a handful of the rags, and starts to mop the floor.

I sit down at my desk, close my eyes, press my fingers against my temples and try to conceive what materials, what techniques, could have produced such an effect. That such intricate pictures could have been hidden – then revealed. Buried – then unearthed. I press my fingers hard, harder. Think, I tell myself, think. But I can't. I can't think, because – because suddenly, my sensibilities are awash with the scent of roasting chestnuts. I twist round to look at the others, but their heads are bowed and it is plain that none of them have noticed anything unusual. Slowly, deeply, I breathe in and out. That smell—

Like so many rich men's children, I did not always live in the city. Until I was four, I stayed with the woman who nursed me: on the other side of the mountain, in a valley where the air was good and the slopes were wooded with hundreds upon hundreds of chestnut trees. She must have had a proper name, but I called her Zia.

I remember my last day there quite clearly. I remember lying on my back on the cool earth, beneath a roof of trees, hung with nets like the webs of giant spiders. The women of the village began to beat the chestnuts out of the branches, while my friends and I ran about gathering any that escaped. We were all in wonderful high spirits, because that night we would be allowed to stay up late, playing and eating roast chestnuts until we burst.

Later, to my dismay, I was scrubbed, put in a dress that hurt my arms and told to keep out of the sty – but there were five tiny new piglets to play with, and the tips of their ears smelled so good. When Zia lifted me out of the pen, I cried – cried harder when she pinched me to stop. She told me I was going home – and then she was crying, too. The smell of roasting chestnuts followed me through the hills.

After a long journey, of which I remember nothing – was it two days, or three? – the countryside turned into a city of impossible buildings, one of which was the Stelleri palazzo. There were rows of clipped green hedges in the courtyard and terrifying figures in bronze and stone. From behind one of these, a woman appeared, and I shrank from her sharp face. When she embraced me, her bodice was hard. She wasn't like Zia, who was soft as risen dough. I wriggled, stifled by her perfume.

What happened next, I do not myself recall, but often it was related to me by my stepmother's maids, who liked to torment me with proofs of my ingratitude. Ortolana, they said, greeted me kindly. She promised me dolls, sweet things to eat, a pretty room all of my own – everything a little girl could wish for.

But first, she said, come and kiss your baby brother. She led me by the hand – I do remember that, how her long nails pricked my palm – towards another woman, holding a bundle. This woman, my brother's nursemaid, leaned down to show him off.

'He looks like a pig,' I said.

The maid gasped, but my stepmother hushed her – reminded her I'd had a long journey. She told me her name. She said she was my father's wife. She told me there would be roasted chestnuts later. She crouched down so our eyes were on a level. 'They told me you like chestnuts.'

'I don't,' I said. 'I hate them.'

The Girl

Later that day

⌘

Normally, I pass our discretionary hour as I pass the rest of my day – reading, writing – the only difference being that I choose what to read, what to write, rather than working in the service of the convent. The others tend to gather in the quadrilango, grouping themselves according to age and temperament. Arcangela dislikes this ease and sociability – as did Sophia, who disparaged chatter – but Chiara says, 'Did not Mother-Mary love to visit her sister Elisabetta?', with her knack for misconstruing the Stories of the Son with such a contented air that disagreement is impossible.

But today, I have other plans. Today, I have decided to return to the infirmary, hoping that the girl – who did not, in comparison with the women, appear to be so very gravely hurt – will be enough recovered to speak to me.

I am, I admit, uncertain about how to make such an approach. After all, I am used to consulting books, not people. I have no ease of manner, no affability of address – and never before have I felt their lack. Others of my sisters could wander into the infirmary, full of easy talk, and nobody would wonder what they were about. But as for me – oh, I wish people were more like books, that you could skim their pages until you found what you sought.

As I make my way across the quadrilango, my resolve falters. To arrive at the infirmary, uninvited – I cannot do it. Don't be so craven, I tell myself. She is but a girl – little more than a child. She does not know you. Be congenial. Sympathetic. She will think you a kind sister like any—

'Beatrice, hi, Beatrice! Why are you muttering to yourself?' Sister Paola, her head poking out of the parlour, interrupts my attempts at encouragement. Her warty skin and long-lobed ears, not to mention her avaricious nature, have led generations of novices to compare her – not implausibly – to a gobelyn. 'Listen, your bookseller came knocking earlier, but I sent him packing. I don't know what he thought he was doing, visiting on Grey Wednesday. He tried to sweet-talk his way in – said he'd been on the road, arrived late, forgot the day – but I couldn't do it, not even for him. *She* would have chewed me to pieces. Anyway, he says he'll return tomorrow.'

She disappears back into the parlour, and I stride off towards the infirmary, feeling wonderfully fortified. Tomorrow! I can question him about the book – perhaps even contrive to show it to him. But first, I enjoin myself, if such a conversation is to be fruitful, I must find out everything I possibly can.

'To what do we owe the honour, Sister Beatrice?' says Sister Agatha, who stands in the doorway, as though she observed my approach and was waiting for me.

'I have come to see how the girl fares,' I reply, as agreeably as I can.

'Thank you, but we understand Marta perfectly. Your services are not required. I'll bid you good day,' she says with a polite finality, moving to shut me out. I interpose myself, feeling an unwelcome pressure as I am squeezed between door

66

and jamb. Fractionally, she releases the door. 'Sister Beatrice, I really must ask you to—'

'Mother Chiara sent me,' I extemporise. Usually the will of Chiara is the key that unlocks all doors in the convent, and so it is a measure of Agatha's mistrust of me – or perhaps, it occurs to me, of some precarity to Chiara's power – that she does not immediately step aside, but instead queries me sharply.

'Why? To what end? The child does not need you to recite Latin verbs over her.'

This is not the moment, I know, to tell her that I have, in fact, often found the reliability of Latin conjugation to possess a restorative clarity, and so I opt instead for dogged repetition.

'She sent me. I can return to her. I am sure she will not mind coming here to explain—'

I am walking away, backwards, sure that my stratagem will not work, but then – victory! – Agatha sighs and steps inside, leaving the doorway unmanned. I hasten after her. The girl is in the same room the women were brought to; in the same bed, as it happens, in which the younger woman died – at peace, I am convinced, knowing her book was safely in my hands.

Happily, the girl looks as far from death as it is possible to be: her cheeks rosy, her thick wheaten hair – a type much prized, I know, by girls in the city – brushed and coiled. She smiles – at Agatha rather than at me – luxuriating, no doubt, in the sunny room, the clean linen, the sweet rushes, the tray of milk and bread, and what must be one of the last of this winter's apples. I had hoped, foolishly it seems, that she might be pleased to see me, recognising me as an ally, a confidante, but instead she is eyeing me warily.

'Marta, dear, this is Sister Beatrice. She wishes to have speech with you.' Agatha's tone makes the prospect sound arduous indeed. 'But only if you are well enough,' she adds,

landing heavily on that subordinating *if*. The girl nods gratefully at her benefactor, and it occurs to me that likely she is
trying to put whatever happened behind her – and fears I am
here to remind her of it. Which I am. I sweep past Agatha and
place myself on the bed adjacent.

'Hello there, Marta,' I say. The girl looks pleadingly over my
shoulder. 'Thank you, Sister Agatha,' I say. 'Do not let me keep
you from your work.' I do not turn as I speak, and so I mistake
the sound of footsteps for Agatha leaving, when in fact—

'Ah, Reverend Mother,' Agatha murmurs, and I jerk round
to see – Chiara.

My congenial smile slides from my face. I am tangled in
untruth. What am I going to say when Chiara asks why I am
here? With Agatha watching – whatever am I going to say?
I look away again to hide my confusion, while Chiara bustles
inside, brimming with compliments as to the girl's much-
improved countenance. She is approaching the bed, and I am
still trying to prepare some obfuscatory response to her inev-
itable question, when she clasps my shoulder and says, 'And
Beatrice! How good of you to come and see how our young
friend does. That is very well done, I must say.'

She sounds delighted. She *is* delighted. She thinks me
kind; she thinks me thoughtful. I struggle to renew my smile,
conscious of my duplicity all the while. But I need not worry
– already Chiara's attention has turned from me to Marta. She
is stroking the girl's cheek, dropping a tiny posy of galanthus
into a cup, saying, 'There, now, these made me think of you.'
Now she fusses over Marta's bolster, breaking off only to tell
me how good I am to forgo my work, before returning to her
chief task, namely determining is the girl happy, well cared for,
assured of her safety. 'Do you have a favourite tale from the
Stories, my dear?' she asks. 'Sister Beatrice has a wonderful
memory for them all.'

The girl shakes her head – dumbly, one might say, if one were lacking in charity.

'Well, soon you shall have one. Beatrice will stay here and divert you. Now, Sister Agatha, take me to visit your other unfortunate patients – is Alfonsa back on her feet? Although, forgive me, how can I call them unfortunate when they receive your loving care?'

They leave. We are alone. The girl's eyes flutter about the room, alighting everywhere except on me. My sisters are accustomed to my burned cheek – many others, in truth, have similar defects of person that rendered them ineligible for the city's marriage market – but strangers either look too hard or cannot bear to look at all.

'Why don't you tell me how you happened upon them?' I begin, realising it is for me to break the silence. Too abrupt. What fool, I ask myself, marches up to an unbroken horse and expects it to take the bit. Already Marta has curled herself into a ball and rolled away from me, although from memories of my own girlhood, I know you can still hear perfectly well even with your face to a wall. I try again, with a little more circumspection.

'I am sorry you have been so badly upset.' I leave a pause, an inviting one, I hope, but the girl makes no attempt to fill it. I decide to plough onwards. 'Those poor women. They were in a terrible state.' Silence. 'You do – you do know they have died?' Silence. More profound. 'You showed great kindness bringing them here.' Do I hear a small sniff? 'You are evidently a good girl. A true Samaritan.'

I have lifted my hand to touch her shoulder reassuringly, as Chiara might do, but as I reach towards her, the girl jerks herself upright, emitting a sort of screeching, pent-up sigh, and all but hisses at me: 'I wish I'd never laid eyes on those, on those—' and here she appends a string of words peculiar to her mountain dialect that are too coarse for me to repeat, and thus having delivered herself of her feelings, she flings herself on to her belly and starts to sob violently, her little shoulders shuddering.

Even though most of her noise is dammed by the bolster, I am obviously concerned lest it spill out into the corridor and summon Agatha to decry my heartlessness once more. I hasten to the door, which is still ajar, but it creaks so loudly when I push upon it that, for an instant, it startles Marta from her tumult. She stares at me, her eyelashes a sodden tangle, her mouth curiously formless, while I heave the door closed, only to take up her sorrowing where she left off when I return to her side. This time, I do put a hand to her back, but not to console – rather, to command some silence into her. My touch makes her look round at me, so angry that all her prettiness is gone.

'I'm glad they're dead,' she says. 'Glad, glad, glad.'

'Hush,' I say. 'Do not speak so. You cannot mean to be so unfeeling—'

But now she is crying again, though quietly this time, and I understand she is no longer crying in anger at them, but rather in pity for herself. Her tears drop on to her hands where they lie limp in her lap. I sense weakness.

'Perhaps,' I say, 'perhaps you would feel better if you were to tell me what happened. That's' – I stray again towards untruth – 'that's why Mother Chiara wanted me to stay. She wanted you to feel you could unburden yourself. Freely.'

The room, I notice, is no longer sunlit. The sky outside must be lowering, which is, I realise, to my advantage. It is easier to talk of difficult things in the dark. In confession, after all, one talks unseen.

She rubs at her eyes. 'She did?'

I nod.

'You won't tell nobody else?'

'Not if you don't wish it.'

'And you won't tell me I'm lying?'

'No, no—'

'Swear on the Green Mary?'

At first, I am not sure to what she refers – although I do now remember her using the same words at the gate – and then I suppose this must be the mountain people's name for the little wooden statue of Our-Lady-All-In-Green, which stands in our side chapel. Every year, at summer's end, we place her on a raft decked with lilies and float her down the river into the city. Her celebrants – older women, for the most part – carry her up to the mountain, to a shrine in a cave, there to pass a night in adoration of Mother-Mary.

On moonless nights, the young and the credulous like to tell stories about that place. They say it was once sacred to a goddess of the ancients, a place of keening song and bloody sacrifice. It is guarded, they say, by a mountain bear, which stands ready to kill any man who dares enter. Black-clad Hecates, they whisper, and orange-eyed wolf-women still abide in the shadow of the trees. Dormitory talk, of course – nothing more. The girl, however, is looking at me with such an unwavering intensity, that I understand an oath will carry great weight with her. And so I say, with a seriousness to match her own, 'Yes, by the Green Mary, I swear.'

For a moment she appears to collect her thoughts, and then: 'It was late,' she begins. 'Not far off sunset. It was the first time I'd let the goats out after the snows. We were close by the road that comes down off the high pass. I saw a wagon go by. I kept on walking, and next a cart came on. A donkey cart, driven hard by two – two ladies.' The words are coming slowly but, wary of distracting her, I resist the temptation to offer an encouraging *hmmm*. 'I gave them a wave. Then, not so long after, I heard shouting, hooves – and of course I took myself off the road.'

I nod. Of course.

'Next thing, I heard men calling out, telling the ladies to stop, to give up the reins, to get down. That's when I should of made straight for home.'

That word – *home* – sets her lip trembling, and this time I risk clasping her hand in mine, assuring her that all will be well, but she snatches it away and says, 'It won't be. It won't, it won't.'

I rebuke myself for stemming her flow. She is winding the blanket round her hand, twisting and tightening it. She mumbles something, and I lean in closer.

'I watched through the trees,' she says. 'I saw the ladies climbing down off the cart. One helping the other. There were men all around, half a dozen, more, with proper big horses. Two of them were hunting about in the back of the cart. They were cursing, asking, where is it, where is it? The women didn't seem to know our talk, but the younger one, she pointed her finger down the hill. At that, they all got on their horses, leaving one big man' – her hands show me a barrel chest – 'standing guard over them. He tried talking to them, saying they couldn't fool him, he'd had dealings with their like before, that sort of thing. Then he started looking the younger one over. I thought he meant to – you know—'

'I understand,' I say, but she gives me a long look, as though to say, do you really?

'It wasn't that, though,' she says. 'She was wearing a long sort of shawl, tied crosswise over her chest, and he was telling her to untie it, to show him what lay beneath. She was pretending not to understand him, though his meaning was plain

enough, words or no. Next thing, he grabbed hold of her –
but something made him curse and leap back – I thought she
must have a knife hid – and then the women were off, running
and running away through the trees. That big stupido, he lost
some fine moments yelling after his fellows, but they were too
far gone down the road. So he took off after them – and I followed. Of course, the old woman couldn't go fast, but she was
faster than you'd think. The younger one was keeping behind
her, like if anyone was going to get caught, it was going to be
her. The man, he was crashing into branches, tripping over
roots, but still he gained on them. He got hold of her skirts,
the younger one, and he tumbled her over, and they both tumbled into the older one, and next thing, they all three rolled off
a bit of a ridge and I lost sight of them.'

She pauses. Swallows.

'And then?' I prompt. 'What then?'

'Then I heard screams.'

'The women? The women were screaming? He was attacking them?'

She shakes her head. 'No, no, no. Not them. Him. The
man. He was screaming. I dropped down, crawled along, and
looked over where they'd fell. The land had slipped away and
there was a sort of hole. A well of earth and leaves. I couldn't
see the women. They'd – they'd vanished. But I could see him.
Screaming his head off.'

'He'd hurt himself? He'd fallen badly?'

But she's not listening to me. She is frowning to herself,
shaking her head. 'They had his hands.'

'His hands? His hands, Marta? Who had his hands? The
women?'

She grows at once frustrated, saying she won't speak more
if I won't listen right, before growing if possible less articulate,
telling me not to call her a liar, because she's not a liar and

she won't allow it. I hasten to ask forgiveness, to beg her to continue.

It was dark under the trees, she says. I allow it must have been hard to see. She was much frighted, she says. As anyone would have been, I aver. She was fussing about her goats, she adds, and I encourage myself to persevere in my patience, while suggesting that perhaps she might like to tell me what she thought she saw, even though she might not have seen it at all, the light being so low, and her wits being so affected.

'It was like he'd lain there a whole summer long, and brambles had grown up all about him. He had a big knife in his hand, but the brambles, they'd coiled round and round his arm. He'd tried to free himself – you could see he'd tried – his hands were ripped and bloodied – but the brambles were suckered into the ground, and his arm's strength wasn't near enough. And it wasn't just his arm. It was all of him. He was pierced through and through, long shoots, in and out, in and out. You could see the pain of it – the fear. But he couldn't move. He was pinned. Staked. He stopped moving soon enough.'

She looks up at me. That she didn't, at this point, follow the counsel of rational thought – or the more visceral promptings of fear – and hasten home, speaks, I think, to a great reserve of courage. I am, I admit, in awe, as she proceeds to tell me how she hobbled the chiefest of her goats, scrambled back to the road and calmed the donkey – before casting around to see where the women might be.

'I should of gone then. I should of. Stupid, stupid.' She strikes at her head with the heel of her hand. 'But the women – I thought – well, I wanted to see them right. So – I called. Hallo, I called – but soft and nice – so as not to fright them – hallooo – like that. I heard nothing – and then, I heard maybe a reply. Hallooo, I said again – and again I heard a noise. I followed the sound – and it led me right back to where the man had died. And they were there, the women. The two of them – alive. The man – dead. And the brambles – gone.'

She draws back a little, searching my face, seeing how I might respond. She is nodding, and I believe I am frowning. I need her to admit the absurdity of her words – to retract them, or at least to refine them – to turn them into something more credible – but her expression has settled into one of obdurate defiance.

'Why,' I ask quietly, 'why then did you bring them here?'

'Where else?' she says with eloquent scorn, as though I were deficient – a fool. 'If you or any lady is in trouble, straight you go to Mother Chiara. Mamma told me this. Everyone's mamma tells them this. We all know this.'

For a moment, I contemplate her words. Many women do indeed find their way to us – and some of them choose never to return to their homes. I know it, because I have written the attestations of their vocations, which give Mother Chiara the authority to bid angry husbands, angry fathers, to leave.

'Marta.' I must ask the obvious question. 'Are you now – in trouble? Is that why you have returned?'

Briefly, she closes her eyes. 'I was so tired when I got home. I wanted to forget. My mother was worried. My father – out of temper. Maybe worried, too. I only hoped for some little food and sleep – but this morning, the men came. They asked to talk to my papà. Poor Papà. He is not so young, and usually Mamma does the talking.' She smiles, and I feel the twist I always feel whenever a woman talks of her mother. 'But those men would not talk to Mamma. Only Papà. Poor Papà. He was so confused. They asked was his daughter the girl who'd brought two women to the convent. They showed him gold coins. They wanted to talk to me. To know had I seen something strange. They said a – a holy brother wanted to know.'

'And you told them.'

It is a statement, not a question, but she twitches her head, *no*, and then continues to shake it, a strange affect, as though she is no longer aware what she does.

'I didn't want to tell them. I knew if I told them what I'd seen, they'd think I was like the women. The same as them. Someways wrong. But they wouldn't let up. They said I ought to tell them. I said there was nothing to tell. They called me liar, liar. They said they'd take me to their holy brother. They said he was good at talking to bad girls like me. And then – I ran.'

She is looking directly at me now, fierce and uncompromising.

'I am not stupid. I ran to where there are thicker trees, to where horses would be no good. Deeper, I went, darker, the harder for them. Some men fear the forest. I do not. The wind was noisy in the trees. I knew it was telling me to run – fast and faster.'

'You thought to lose them?' I ask.

'No.' That scorn again. 'I was running to Green Mary. To her cave. Once I am inside her tunnels, I know they will lose their way. The mountain will swallow them up—'

'Wait,' I say, 'wait. The shrine – there is a way down from there into the convent?'

'Yes, yes,' she says, impatient. 'How do you think I came here?'

I ask no more, not wanting to betray my ignorance. Instead, I say, 'So you outpaced them?'

'No,' she says, 'I was not fast enough.' She shakes her head, angrily. 'They came closer and closer. I knew they would catch me. And I was so, so afraid. And then – I found – I found I could not move. I could not move – but they could not see me. You see, I had, I think I had . . .' She throws up her hands. 'Ah, but you will not believe me.'

I protest that I do believe her. I reach out to touch her – flinch. That pain again. I stare at my fingers – again, those pricks of blood. Her hand is already covering the place where mine had been, pulling something from her hair, tucking it into her palm. Her eyes are squeezed shut, but tears leak from beneath her lids. No words follow. The thing lying in her palm, she is rolling it forth and back, forth and back. Her breathing quickens. Tears stream freely down her cheeks. I stay her hands, prise them apart and see—

a chestnut. A green spiked ball. Commonplace, unremarkable, were it the Feast of All the Saints – but not on the first day of the Forty-Day Fast, not when snow lingers on the mountain's peak, not when the boughs of the trees are bare.

The girl looks at me, and I at her. 'Would you like me to keep this?' I ask. She nods and presses it, almost tenderly, into my palm.

The Letters

Later that night

WHEN WE RETURN to our cells after the seventh office, I roll my blanket at the foot of my door, stuff my mantle in the window casement and leave my candle burning in the corner of my cell. I wait until the warden's footsteps fade, before I take both book and chestnut from my pocket and place them side by side.

All evening, at supper and at prayer, I have been confronting myself in passionate debate: what shall I do about the book? I must protect it; I must destroy it. It is wonderful – beautiful; it is dangerous – sinful. It is the best thing that could have come to me; it is the worst. I will be feted and acclaimed if I can unravel its secrets; if it is discovered in my possession I could find myself – condemned?

I do not know. I do not know.

And there is nobody who can tell me.

I could – I could take it to confession tomorrow, and so be rid of it. But I cannot imagine handing it to Father Michele, the elder of our spiritual guardians, a man so large and spreading, he must sidle sideways to arrive safely on the confessional chair. He is a kind man – after Sophia's death, he told me, without prompting, that the Son's followers struggled with their sorrow after his passing, that I should not be ashamed of my grief – but he does not hear well. Tamara claims she once told him she had copulated with a pig, and all he said was, 'Dear me, dear me.' If I tried to give him the book, he would ask why I wanted rid of such a pretty thing.

Nor could I give it to Eugenio, the pale and watery deacon who sometimes comes in his stead. Once I started to confess my pride to him – meaning my pride in my work – and he sighed, misunderstanding me, thinking I meant mirrors and tweezers and creams. He said my body was a vessel of sin and filth – the seat of woman's weakness and man's peril – and other such phrases lifted from his reading, for he thinks himself a great scholar of the church. He bade me pay closer attention when my elders read to me from the Stories of the Son, thereby fanning, not quenching, the flames. My recall of the Stories is near absolute – and has been since I was twelve years old. I could not give him the book and later hear him celebrated as its interpreter. That I could not bear.

I could – I could destroy it. I could burn it. I could set my candle flame to the parchment – here, now – and slowly, carefully, coax each page to ash. It would not be so very hard. I look at my candle. The wax will suffice.

But Sophia would not destroy it. Often, she'd told me how she despised those who burned books out of fear. What, I'd asked her, what about those books that the Curial Court claim are against the Father, against the faith? 'They are forbidden,' she'd told me, 'but only to the weak. The strong – the strong can read such things and come to no harm.' By strong, she meant herself. She meant men such as my father. I wasn't sure whether she meant me – but I remember desperately hoping that she did.

So what am I? Am I strong? No – I am afraid. In all the

time I've been sitting here, I haven't even dared touch the book. Sophia would not fear it. She would—

I open it, sending a few motes – dust from which land? Skin from whose hand? – spinning in the candlelight. A flush rises to my face and my heart speeds a little. I see, to my commingled delight and fear, that the pages have now grown letters: letters that have grown into words; but words I cannot read; words that do not behave as words are wont to do. They weave in and out of a dense thicket of thorns; they trace tall and slender columns between the furrowed trunks of a stand of chestnut trees.

They are a gift. I love new letters – have always loved them.

My stepmother grudgingly owns that within a year of my arrival in the city, I surprised the household by being able to read without anyone seemingly having thought to teach me. *Your little trick*, she called it, after she found me standing on a chair in the kitchens, declaiming recipes from the household ricordanza. Thereafter, I hounded the old chaplain that he might unravel the elementary Latin of the Stories of the Son. He it was who told me those Stories were originally written in another language – Greek – and at first I did not believe him when he said he had not the knack of it.

I was likely seven or eight years old, when I first came upon Greek letters. I was exploring my father's most private cabinet, where I should not have been, not least because of the tapestry of Mars cuckolding Vulcan that hung from the walls. But I wasn't interested in that – I was interested in the books, most especially my father's lavish *Inferno*, of which I was making an especial study, seeking out passages of irresistible horror to relay to my infant brother after dark.

But that day, I remember, I was drawn to a strange book that lay open upon his desk. It was intriguing. The letters were like ours – and yet unlike. Some were friends, some were acquaintances, and some were altogether strange. Turning the pages back and forth, I forgot to listen for my father's approach. If he was surprised to find me there, he did not show it. He neither scolded me, nor sent me away, but smiled, and said words I remember still, they being the only words he spoke to me – truly to me – rather than merely in my presence. He said, 'All men by their nature desire to know. I did not know the same was true of little girls.'

He showed me how this letter was *a* and that *b* and that *g*, calling them alpha and beta and gamma, and I remember watching his forefinger, the one with his red ring on it, as it pointed out the letters, and I remember him praising the ease with which I recalled each one. He told me that just as all men claim descent from one man – Adam – so all letters are descended from the hand of the Father.

He began to quote a verse from the Story of the Escape: '*Et reversus est Moyses de monte—*'

But before I could show him that I understood, that I knew he was referring to Moses's descent from the mountain bearing the Ten Rules the Father had carved into stone, my stepmother entered. She asked me what on earth I thought I was doing. I looked up at my father in the – vain – hope that he might defend me, but he was already absorbed in some papers on his desk. Ortolana towed me away by the tip of my ear. I can still feel it. The shame.

Later, Sophia mentioned the pleasure I took in strange letters to our bookseller, Tomis, and thenceforth he gathered scraps of writing for me on his travels, enclosing them in his letters to her, or bringing them with him when he came.

'Sing, Tomis,' she would say to him. 'Sing to her of the world beyond these walls.'

I have them still. I have not looked at them for years, thinking them a little childish, but loving them too much to part with them. Mostly I could not guess their meaning, and Sophia would laugh and tell me they were likely nothing but an apothecary's bill, a sea captain's cargo list, but I didn't mind. To me, they were precious. I collected them, those scraps, as a physician collects strange diseases or an astronomer distant stars.

In one corner of my cell, behind my pallet, where a summer rainstorm saturated the brickwork and loosed the mortar, I have created a serviceable cavity where I can conceal such small treasures as I do not wish the wardens to find. The small box, a quill-case repurposed, in which I keep those scraps of scripts, lies at the back.

I remove it and spill the contents on to the floor. Each paper I lift in turn, examining it twice, three times over, holding it up to my clandestine candle, comparing the letters with those in the book. None matches, but the more I look at the book, the more certain I am that I have seen the letters before – somewhere. There is one particular letter – the most frequent and distinctive. I trace it on the floor. Two lines up – down. Two lines left – right. And the tops curled.

I shut my eyes. Think. Think.

A memory coalesces.

One day, Tomis sent me a little metalled tube, as long as my hand, and perhaps two fingers wide, sealed at either end. Using my quill-knife, I cut the wax away and peered inside. There lay – well, to be honest, at first I wasn't sure. I upended the tube, shook it a little, and out fell a fragile curl of silvery bark, packed about with dried and crumbling leaves. I was at once enchanted, for I knew that in the Old Empire they preferred to write this way, on scrolls they unrolled, whereas now we stitch our words into sturdy quadrilaterals.

Gently, carefully, I started to open it, knowing that if I attempted to lay it too flat, the bark would crack and split.

Unfurled, it formed a ragged square, about the size of my palm, upon which was inked a rough, red-brown letter. I remember gazing down at it, enjoying the mystery, the pleasure of perplexity, looking forward to Sophia telling me what it signified. To me, you see, the world beyond the convent was as a vast mosaic, but fractionally complete, and I relied upon her to build it for me, stone by stone.

She was busy at her desk, tutting, grumbling – for somebody who was intolerant of others' noise, she was herself surprisingly unquiet. She turned, caught sight of the bark in my hands, snatched it from me, ground it in her fist, and stalked out of the library without a word. From the window, I watched her march towards the river, and that evening I overheard two of the laundry girls discussing how they'd seen her scattering something over the water – although without especial curiosity, for such capricious behaviour was not unusual.

I did ask her about it. Not immediately, of course, for that would have provoked a storm, but a few days, perhaps a week later, when her mood was bright.

'Sophia?'

I didn't need to say any more. She was so sharp; she knew at once what would follow.

'Tomis,' she said, 'is a vexing little devil.'

I waited, knowing nothing I said would influence whether she told me more or not.

She looked at me. 'Some things have no place in a civilised library. That daub was not writing. They peel the – the skin of a tree—'

'The bark?' I interposed, knowing she did not have such words in Latin or Vernacular.

'Yes, yes, the bark. They peel it off and mark it – with fire-sticks or their women's blood or the juice of some poison

83

berry – and that they call writing. *Writing.* Pah. They are like children drawing in the dirt, making believe to read a clouded sky – a spider's web.'

She turned away. I still had a dozen questions, but I knew if I persevered, she would be disagreeable for the rest of the day – and so I let it go. I forgot it. Or rather, I let it sink into my memory's darker sediment – from where I now retrieve that letter, hooking it from the deep on a little thread of guilt.

If Sophia were still alive, I would surely have shown her the book – and then, would it not have followed the bark into the river? But she is not alive, and for the first time, I realise I need not do as she would have done. The thought is dizzying – frightening – enticing.

I tidy my scripts, close the book, wrap both in my mantle, retrieve my blanket, blow out the candle and lie down. As I drop my head on to my bolster, hugging the book close, I realise my eyes are turned towards the place on the floor where my forefinger sketched the letter. The lines I traced, so it seems to me, are lingering silver in the darkness.

I blink – and they're gone.

And then, on the threshold of sleep, I remember one last thing: 'Beatrice, you are discreet. Be discreet in this, too. Do not speak of it. Men do not like such letters. They call them – the letters of Eve.'

The Parlour

Thursday morning

⌘

THE NEXT MORNING I am, for the thousandth time, looking out of the window to see if Sister Paola might be about to summon me, when I am surprised by the slap of quick feet on the library stairs.

'Hallooo! Sister Beatrice! Can I come in?'

I know at once that it is Diana. The unmodulated volume. The throated sound of her voice. Before I can reply, she has arrived at my side and dropped a hand on my shoulder.

'Daydreaming, is it? Not like you.' She looks around. 'What do you do up here all day, anyway? What's this?'

She's fiddling with the tray at the back of my desk on which I keep my knife, my hare's foot, my little crock of bone dust. I sigh and remove them from her, hoping to express my displeasure at the interruption, but she must lack perception, for she neither begs my pardon, nor asks should she return later, but moves to lean against the window and look down into the quadrilango. Before she came to the convent, she was, as I have said, a paintress. But were you to picture a field-hand, you might have a better measure of her physiognomy.

'Nice view,' she says.

'What,' I say, 'do you want? And why aren't you at prayers?'

She grins. 'Why aren't you?'

'I'm excused—' I begin, before it occurs to me that I am answering her question when she should be answering mine.

'I know. That's why I'm here,' she says. I am confused – visibly, it seems. She leans towards me, lowers her voice. 'I wanted to talk to you.'

I frown. 'About the women?'

'No,' she says. 'Why about them?'

I am caught off guard. What else would she want to talk to me about?

'No reason,' I say. 'I thought – only, I know everyone talks about them.'

''Course they do,' she says. 'People like to talk. Well, most people. Not you, obviously. 'Course, if you *want* to talk about them . . .' She suspends the words between us, and I can feel her watching me, amusing herself, watching how I will react. 'No? All right. I want to talk about your book.'

My belly thumps. I place my hands together in my lap, fearful lest the book's outline is visible where it lies in my pocket. 'How do you know?' I say as calmly as I can.

It is her turn to frown. 'Why, everyone knows. Your – what's it called – your *Libellus Mulierum*.'

I collect myself. My account of the lives of great women – certain of the saints, as well as rulers of historical renown – is a much-requested confirmation gift for the daughters of even modest families. It was Chiara's idea. 'Why don't you write something for girls who can't read Latin?' she'd said. I must have wrinkled my nose. 'Do not despise those without your advantages, Beatrice,' she'd chided me. 'There are worthier things to despise.'

'What about it?' I say to Diana now.

'Can I have a copy?'

'Why?'

'To read, obviously.'

'Why?'

She throws her arms up in the air. 'The others told me not to bother. They said you'd be like this. But, honestly, it's ridiculous—'

'Like what?' I say, before I can stop myself.

'Oh, you know – difficult. Hiding away up here, looking down on the rest of us.'

I am stung, but determined not to show it. Sophia had warned me about this. 'You are cleverer than they are,' she'd once told me. 'Sometimes, they will not like you for it. But do not chase their approval. Maybe you get it, but they can take it away' – a snap of her fingers – 'this fast.'

I turn my back on Diana and assume at least the appearance of work. I hear a sigh.

'Listen – sorry. I don't care what you think about me, or anyone else. Only – word of advice. Don't make it so obvious. That old basilisk could get away with it, talking Latin to everyone—'

'Sophia. Her name was Sophia.' I try to say more, but I feel a treacherous tightness in my throat.

Diana grabs a stool and pulls it next to me. 'All right. Sophia, then. I don't know how you put up with her – but you did. You were kind to her, weren't you? At the end. When nobody else would go near her.'

I can't help it. Unshed tears have pooled inside me, and now they overflow, streaming down my face. Desperately, I try to wipe them away – Sophia could never abide tears – but it's hopeless. Diana's arms go round me, easily, and she says – I know not what. Words that are meant to be kind, but I can hardly hear them.

'You all right?' she says, releasing me once I have mastered myself.

I nod. 'Fine, yes. Fine.'

'Do you want to talk?'

'No.' I shake my head. Rub my eyes. 'No.' Swallow. 'Tell me why you want the book.'

She regards me a moment, and I meet her gaze as best I can, feeling my strength returning. She tilts her head to one side. Slowly, her lips twist. She stands up.

'All right,' she says. 'Mother Chiara' – she uses an ironical emphasis, in imitation, I suppose, of the hushed tones my sisters employ – 'Mother Chiara has suggested I adorn the walls of that side chapel. Where that old statue stands. Scenes of holy women. For purposes of edification and illumination.' She makes the words sound puffed and pompous, which annoys me, because that is not how Chiara speaks.

'Don't pretend you're not flattered,' I say.

Her eyebrows shoot upwards. 'All right,' she says. 'You've got me. I am flattered. It's pathetic, really.'

Her face, usually so animated, has fallen, and she turns away. I find the change painful. It looks – wrong. I remember her coiled rage when she arrived here in the panting dog days of last summer. How she stalked and glowered. How the others called her salamander. How everyone feared her, and yet tried to be close to her. How she would not be still. I want to say I am sorry, to say I did not want to be unkind, but she recovers herself faster than I can find the right words.

'Pictures of holy women, I told her, aren't really my – my forte. Nymphs, yes. Cherubs, no problem. Venus . . .' she lingers, unnecessarily I think, over the name of the goddess. 'Anyway, she suggested I ask you for ideas. So here I am.' She spreads her hands.

I am silent, assimilating this information.

'So,' she says, 'can I? Read it?'

I stand up, collect one of the paper copies we have in readiness and indicate a desk.

'Can't I—?' she indicates the door.

'No,' I say. 'If you want to read it, you must read it here.'

'Ah.' She pulls a face. 'Only thing. I can't read. Words,' she says, unabashed, 'not really my—' She shrugs in lieu of completing her sentence.

'Forte?'

'Exactly,' she says, with one of her wide-mouthed grins.

'Then how were you going to—'

'Oh, I was going to get one of those high-class girls to read it to me. In exchange for telling them everything I know about—' She stops herself. 'Actually, never mind.'

'About what?' I ask.

'It doesn't matter, honestly,' she says.

I fold the book in my arms. 'About what?'

She sucks her lips. 'About the . . .' She cups her hands about her mouth and widens her eyes in what I recognise as a tolerable imitation of the boarder Laura. 'About the rites of the marriage bed. See' – I am blushing – 'see, I said you didn't want—' She doesn't say any more, because she is trying – not very hard – not to laugh.

I am discomfited. Everyone guesses, of course, that she is here in consequence of some laxity with a man, but to discuss such things, so openly, is—

'Tell you what,' she says, plumping herself down at the desk closest to mine, 'I'll look at the pictures.'

'Careful,' I say, in concern for my copyist's work. And then: 'There aren't any pictures.'

'No pictures? But I thought it was meant to be fancy? They told me Chiara had one sent down to St Peter's, a gift for the pontifex's daughter herself.'

89

When we were younger, Prudenzia had made the mistake of wondering aloud how Pope Silvio could even have a daughter, delighting Tamara, who'd cried out laughing, 'Why, the same route as any other man. He stuck his—' Prudenzia ran off to tell Arcangela, who made Tamara stand twelve nights' vigil.

I pluck the paper copy from Diana's hands and replace it with an illustrated version, a commission for the Stelleri Bank's agent in the Lagoon, which is waiting to be dispatched.

'Now that,' Diana says, smiling up at me, turning the pages, 'is more like it.' She turns the book towards me, gripping the top with one hand, pointing with the other. 'Who's this?'

'Judith,' I say, taking the book from her and laying it back neatly on the desk.

'Who?'

'You know, Judith. Judith and Holofernes.'

'Holofernes – is that him? Why's she cut his head off?'

'He was her enemy. The enemy of her people. She—'

But then, at last, out of the window, I see the parlour door open and Sister Paola's head peering out. She catches sight of me through the glass and starts to wave vigorously. I am unable to hide my pleasure at her summons, and Diana looks at me curiously.

'What's that about?'

'Tomis – my bookseller. I've been expecting him.'

'*The* Tomis?' she says, gesturing so as to imply long eyelashes and complicated headgear. She sounds incredulous.

I shrug, feigning nonchalance. 'He has always been very good to us.'

She puffs her cheeks out. 'Huh. I thought Tomis was only good to Tomis.'

'Beatrice!' Paola is shouting up at me now. '*Beatrice!*'

'Coming!' I call down to her, hunting round my desk for the list I have ready for him. 'Here.' I turn to Diana and drop the *Libellus* into her hands, surprising her – and perhaps myself. 'Why not keep it for a day or two? Come and ask me if there's anything else you want to know.'

I hasten down the stairs, past the fountain, where a marble shepherd boy pipes to lambs who never come, and push open the parlour door.

'χαῖρε,' says Tomis.

Greetings.

Before I ever met him, I was envious of him – and his Greek. 'So superlative it is to have somebody civilised to talk to,' Sophia had said, after he'd first begged an audience with her, and I remember being rather hurt. 'He's a little flatterer,' she'd said. 'Knew all about me. Called me σεβαστή Sophia.' This was her court title, of which she was unashamedly proud. 'I know his type. The palace at Constantinopolis was full of them. Boys who know how to be nice to old women.'

Well, let him be nice, I'd thought. His visits always put her in a buoyant mood.

'Better late than never,' I say to him now, opting for the Vernacular.

Sophia could talk to him in whatever language she chose, but Sister Arcangela says Paola must be able to understand me. Our chief warden, I reflect, conceded a great deal to Sophia. There was an austerity to her, an asperity, which Arcangela – despite herself – was minded to admire.

'Surely,' Tomis is saying, 'so penetrative a maxim was coined by the great Horace himself – only the relevant epode has yet to be revealed to posterity. Perhaps, even now, an uncouth mouse is nibbling the words to oblivion in the vanquished cellar of a Rhinish monasterium.'

Normally, I would laugh, liking his wordiness, his allusions to things I understand and others do not, but today I am far too anxious. Tomis is the only person I know who might be able to help me understand the book, but our speech is not – can never be – free. Once again, I wish we were meeting on the Via dei Librai, where shop after shop is full of books, set with tables where one can sit and talk, where the pursuit of knowledge is lauded, where – oh, but it's no use. 'You're not missing anything, I promise,' he'd said when once I'd asked – casually, or so I thought – about the men who gather there. 'Strutting cockerels, Sister Beatrice, that's all they are.'

Sister Paola, who is pretending to knit, is eyeing us balefully, although we are standing quite correctly, a good three paces apart, on either side of the line of small terracotta tiles that partitions the parlour. I turn my head away, showing that I care nothing, but Tomis does not shrink from her regard. Rather, he smiles – admittedly, his face is covered, but I am sure I can see the smile in his eyes. We've all told him he is under no obligation to wear a scarf about his face – not on our account – but always he protests that the custom of his people obliges it.

And which people might those be? This is a question I have asked many times over the years, and many answers has he given, no two the same. He was suckled by wolves in the pine forests of Thrace. He was raised by Harmazans in a clifftop eyrie above the Black Sea. He was sold by Barbary corsairs to a witch-princess who lived and died in porphyry palaces of Constantinopolis. I long to learn the truth.

Behind me now, I can hear Sister Paola stirring in anticipation, for she knows what is coming – the sweetmeats that are her perquisite. And, indeed, Tomis is already reaching into his packbag, drawing forth a sizeable bundle, its wrapping of palm leaves whispering of faraway lands where the winter sun is still warm and no snow ever falls.

'Am I right,' says Tomis, 'respected sister, am I right in remembering that you have a particular fondness for dates from the Delta? May I be so bold?'

Sister Paola inclines her head, indicating that he may be as bold as he likes. He hands the package to me, I hand it to her, and she brings it to her nose, inhaling deeply. Wriggling a finger beneath the outer leaves, she draws forth a single date, places it between her lips and starts to chew – a laborious task, for the chiefest of her teeth are little more than blackened stumps. She swallows, carefully licks her lips. The package vanishes beneath her mantle, and her needles click anew, albeit more slowly, as though to remind me – not that I need reminding – that we speak under her sufferance.

I expect Tomis to tell me his tidings, but instead he starts by saying how grieved he was to hear of Sophia's death. He assures me how greatly he admired her learning, her fortitude, her rich reserves of humour. Previously, I might have struggled to respond, but my earlier storm of sorrow has wrought some small change in me, and I find I can tell him how keenly I, too, feel her loss with something approaching calm. It is good, I realise, to hear her spoken of by one who knew her better parts. 'I was lucky to have known her,' I say.

'And she was lucky to have found such an admirable apprentice,' he replies. 'But – forgive me – I must also condole you on the death of your father. A great loss to all who love knowledge.'

This turn to the conversation, which I should have anticipated, is less welcome. Tomis has often spoken of my father, telling me admiringly how broad were his interests, how deep his knowledge, how attentively he listened to others: to the man who swore he could build a flying machine; to the man who could see the future in a globe of glass; to the man who found a new land across the Sea of Atlas; to the man who would prove the Earth turned about the sun. I suppose he told me such things to please me, but instead they provoked in me a cold sort of rage. My father's banquet. My crumbs.

'Thank you,' I say, aware that my voice sounds stiff. 'Although perhaps I should rather be condoling you? You have lost one of your best customers, have you not?'

A taunt – but he does not flinch, merely bows his head in acknowledgement. 'Very true. I was lucky that my personal admiration for your father was complemented by our professional understanding. I fear I cannot hope for a similar rapport with his heir.'

'My brother,' I say, 'has different appetites. Were you a vintner' – I glance at Sister Paola – 'a procurer, or kept a fine pack of hounds—'

'I'd be in business, wouldn't I? But then I'd have to answer to Brother Abramo and his Lambs, and I'm not sure I'm equal to that.' His posture changes, and he leans a little towards me. 'Which reminds me, Sister Beatrice: I'm glad to find you all in good heart. I heard there was trouble here on carnival night.'

Something about the shift in subject makes me wary. Tomis does not normally interest himself in the life of the convent beyond the library.

Lightly, I say, 'Trouble?'

'Did not Brother Abramo come here seeking two women?'

I feel a small chill. 'I – that is to say – I believe he did. Yes – he did. But how do you know?'

'Why – the city talks of it. You know how the city talks. Brother Abramo talks of it, too. He touched upon it – a number of times – during his sermon yesterday.'

'Well received, was it, his sermon?' says Sister Paola, feigning absorption in a dropped stitch.

'Do not doubt, Sister Paola, but that it was.'

'Speaks well, does he, this Brother Abramo?'

'Of that, esteemed sister, you may be certain.'

I glare at him. Tomis knows as well as I do that Sister Paola must be fed news as well as sweetmeats, and it is foolhardy to deprive her of either. Accordingly, he rolls his eyes – which are indeed rimmed by lashes of a surpassing thickness – and adopts a more grandiloquent tone.

'And yet, I fear that *speak* is too meagre a word. I, Tomis, speak. You, Sister Paola, speak. She, Sister Beatrice, speaks. He, Brother Abramo – he exhorts. He extolls. But, most of all, he excoriates – and it seems your lewd and lovely city is much beguiled.'

Paola puts down her knitting and reaches under her mantle to extract a second date.

'The basilica,' Tomis continues, tending now towards the bombastic, 'could not have held another body when the hour appointed for his address drew nigh. The bell sounded. A hush fell upon that holy place. All stared at the pulpit – which remained obstinately empty. Supposition snaked the length of the nave, and soon each man was assuring his neighbour that the bankers and guild-masters, the lawyers and landlords – in short, the rich and the damned – had secured the holy brother's detention. Angry voices began to be heard in the congregation, demanding his liberation, and soon the press of people became unstable, surging now towards the altar, now towards the doors.'

'Where were you?' I ask.

'Good question,' he says. 'I had been forced to clamber atop a tomb, from which vantage I was perhaps one of the first to notice that a cowled man, on his knees, rapt in his devotions, was in danger of being trampled in the southern transept. Those nearest were encouraging him to rise, gently at first, and thereafter with mounting vexation, but before they could lift him to his feet, up he stood, shaping the cross above the brows of those about him.

'Some began to guess his identity and fell back. Soon, those behind did likewise, and so a way was made where you would have sworn none was possible. He mounted the steps to the pulpit. He lifted his hands in blessing. A number of women fainted. And the setting sun, our inconstant companion, blazed down through the high windows, suffusing all hearts with holy light.'

'You hyperbolise,' I say.

His fine eyebrows arch. 'I do not. I document. He spoke of a city beset with sin. He spoke of the Father's wrath, the Son's sorrow. He spoke of our failings, our weaknesses, our faults – only at last to extend a hand, saying it was not yet too late. He was here. He could save us. He could pull us from the pit – but only if we were vigilant. And he fell to talking, forgive me, about what he called the moral frailties of your sex – and then he named this convent.'

I am looking at him in frank dismay, and when he speaks again, his voice is low and serious, kindly and concerned.

He said that you – in your innocence – had taken in two dangerous women from Albion. He said he tried to alert you to your peril, but was rebuffed. He said your stepmother's guards drove him from your gate. The people did not like that – any of it – and that is why I tried to speak to you yesterday. I wanted to let my old friends know a little of the mood of the city. I also thought – that is to say – if the women are indeed from Albion, they are not likely to be versed in Latin, but I speak a little of their native tongue. I thought I could assist you in unravelling—'

'That is kind,' I start to say, 'truly, but—'

'But why not? You know you can trust me, Beatrice.'

He steps forwards, presumably to impress upon me his sincerity, which I do not doubt, and I am about to explain that they are dead, and so beyond his assistance, when I hear Sister Paola standing up with an unusual suddenness. I am thinking, confusedly, that she intends to protest the small movement Tomis has made in my direction, but almost at the same moment I realise that the outer door – the door leading on to the campo – has opened, and that there, on the threshold, stands a man: tall and slender, swathed in a dirty-white cloak, a length of knotted hemp hanging from his waist. His cowl is raised, so I cannot see his face, but at once I feel – that is to say, his presence makes me feel – guilty.

Tomis, not immediately alive to the man's arrival, continues to advance, until my wordless distress communicates itself, and he glances over his shoulder. Only then does he retreat, murmuring, 'ὁ ἀδελφός.'

The brother. This is all the confirmation I need of who stands at our door.

I drop my eyes and fold my hands, while Tomis, his voice light and inconsequential, thanks me for my time, tells me how glad he is to be able to further our holy work, and assures me he will return promptly with my wares – if only I might furnish him with my list of requirements for the convent's library.

My list. Of course. The ostensible reason for him being here. Hurriedly, I reach into my pocket where I discover that it appears to have worked its way beneath the book. I fumble for it – and it is all I can do not to cry out in pain. I delve deeper, feeling the barbs of tiny thorns snatching at my wrist, until my fingers close on the sheaf of paper. I pull it out, trying not to cringe as my skin tears, and hand it to Tomis, letting my sleeve fall over my throbbing hand.

I look up and see that Brother Abramo has raised his right hand and placed it on Tomis's shoulder. The stranger has the advantage of height – but of something else as well. His bearing speaks of great self-certainty, of the completest freedom from doubt. His hand moves – not to release Tomis, for his body still blocks the door – but to twitch my list from his fingers. Slowly, he unfolds it and starts to read.

I know he will find nothing sinful, nothing even questionable. I know even the most suspicious of minds would struggle to find evidence of an assignation in my terse enumeration of so much of this and this parchment, so much of that and that ink. Nevertheless, I find myself growing red. I've read the tales. You probably have too. The choir-mistress and the swineherd. The novice and the pigeonnier. Of course, I should never have read such things, even if every literate man in the city has, and now I feel those dissipated sisters, their eager lovers, pressing about me.

'I had heard,' says Brother Abramo, 'that the Sister Librarian of Mother Chiara's convent is a meticulous worker, whom the Father had gifted with an irreproachable hand.' He speaks slowly, carefully, in a voice that is at once soft and rich and strong, and I cannot help but feel a glow of satisfaction at his praise. 'But this' – he turns the sheet towards me, holding it by thumb and forefinger as though it repels him – 'what is this?'

I stare. What has become of my orderly list? The words I wrote so carefully have grown distorted. They slip and slide down the page, the black ink smeared with streaks of red.

'A – a novice took dictation,' I say. 'She spilled some rubricant. A spill,' I repeat. 'A spill.'

I am about to conjecture further, but Tomis interrupts me, saying mildly, 'Forgive me, brother, the paper?'

Abramo shifts his gaze to him. 'You are young, master merchant, to possess a parlour licence.' He looks him up and down.

'I wonder that the convent's superiors permit you entrance – permit you to receive notes from a sister not yet in her middle years. To me it seems a great lapse in—'

'Oh, he's sound, all right.' Chiara – Chiara! – has entered through the door behind me. So rapt was I in my own confusion, I'd failed to notice that Sister Paola – never again will I malign her! – had taken off in search of her. 'Is that not so?' she adds, turning to Maria, who even now is taking up station at her right hand.

'Nothing wanting in moral character,' says Maria. 'Irreproachable.'

'Sound,' repeats Chiara.

'Permit me to be the judge of that,' says Brother Abramo.

There is a small and exquisitely painful silence.

'My dear.' Chiara is addressing me. 'If your business here is done, why not go and ready yourself for confession. I believe your turn comes soon. And, if you please' – this to Abramo, indicating the paper in his hand – 'that, I believe, is convent business, not yours.'

For a moment, all are still, then he opens his fingers and the paper flutters to the floor. Tomis scoops it up, bows to Chiara, nods to me, and edges out through the small gap between Abramo and the door. As it opens, I glimpse four others waiting outside. Two men with square heads on stout necks, holy garb taut across broad shoulders. Two men of a design more rodentine, skin tending to grey, big nostrils, darting eyes. Before the door shuts, I see one of the heavyset men turn to watch Tomis, revealing a rough red cross daubed the length of his back.

'Beatrice,' says Chiara, a touch sharply, recalling me to myself.

I mumble I know not what and hasten from the parlour, hearing her comfortable voice behind me, saying how nice it always is to greet a holy brother. She suggests refreshment, but Abramo cuts her off, saying he eats and drinks but once a day during the Fast.

'Forgive an old woman her country manners,' says Chiara. 'Your purpose, then . . . ?'

And Maria shuts the parlour door behind me.

I hesitate. I could now clamber up to the parlour vantage – the little nook where the old walls meet the newer parlour roof – but I risk being late for confession, or, worse, missing it altogether. But I must – I must listen. I survey the quadrilango – empty. I look up. I used to make the ascent to listen to Sophia and Tomis haggle and fence, but I was a girl then – nimble. Inelegantly, I start to negotiate the tiered brickwork, its rougher edges chafing my damaged hands.

Hauling myself over the lip, I find five girls deep in hushed talk about their own unfathomable affairs, unaware, so far as I can tell, of what is happening below them. As I come into view, they fall silent. For a moment, I stand awkwardly before them. Some things never change.

'Shouldn't you be in the schoolroom?' I say at last, as grandly as I am able, and they all look to Laura and Giulia, a pair of cousins, the one beautiful, the other clever, who rule over boarders and novices alike in an unassailable duopoly.

Giulia eyes me speculatively. I do not make a speciality of reprimanding the convent's younger members, and so she will be wondering what I am about. From me, her glance strays to the crack in the mismatched brickwork which gives fair sight into the parlour. I do not follow her gaze, only say, 'Now then, girls, make haste,' my voice sounding contrived to my own ears. Giulia signals with a jerk of her head, and, with a grace that verges on the impertinent, Laura rises to her feet. The others stand too, and follow them away.

I drop to my knees and press my eye to the crack. I can

see that Brother Abramo is talking to Chiara, with Maria still standing by her side. His voice is low, their demeanours calm. As a tableau, it might profitably be titled, *Two Holy Women Consult Their Confessor*, or *My Blessings Be Upon You, My Sisters*. Paola's chair is out of sight beneath me, but I presume that her knitting and her dates will both be safely hidden. I swap an eye for an ear.

'. . . expected your convent to be a spiritual oasis in this faithless city. Indeed, I had been thirsting to pray with you – with you, the great Mother Chiara. And yet what do I find? Gates open after dark. Dangerous women admitted. Men insulted. And now I hear of a strange happening upon the mountain: a girl who vanishes. A girl who reappears inside these walls.'

I take a quick look. He is shaking his head, wringing his hands, but I still cannot see his face clearly beneath his cowl. Again, I place my ear to the crack.

'I spoke yesterday to many fine men who are unhappy – suspicious – even angry. You, who lead a cloistered life, cannot know what is said, nor can you defend yourselves from attack, and so I have undertaken to come to the convent myself – to talk to these women, to this girl – and to any who have had dealings with them. I will reassure myself that all is well, hoping thereafter to reassure the city. I come, as I said, in brotherly love.'

I take another look. He is reaching towards Chiara. She is very still, and Maria has a hand, ever so lightly, on her sleeve. I have seen that gesture before – normally when Chiara is talking to Arcangela.

'And yet here, in this very parlour,' continues Brother Abramo, his voice now loud enough to carry, 'I find the mis-begotten daughter of a notorious banker openly treating with a peddler of heretical texts.'

I pull away from the crack, my heart thumping uncomfortably in my chest. I have never heard Tomis so described, but I cannot in all conscience say the description is unwarranted. Instinctively, I touch the book where it lies – smooth, insouciant now – in my pocket. Hastily, I resume listening.

'Ah,' Chiara is saying, 'well, that all sounds very sensible. Let me see, let me see. First, you'll need one of those pieces of paper that allow a man to enter our convent.'

Maria murmurs something.

'Ah, yes – a licence,' Chiara continues. 'You'll need a licence. Sister Arcangela devised a system to – er, authorise – these licences, did she not? How can we go about procuring one for our brother?'

'I'm sorry, Mother Chiara,' Maria says. 'It's not a simple process. I believe I can recall Sister Arcangela's protocol verbatim.' She clears her throat and speaks carefully. 'A sister who has need of a man's services in discharging a matter of vital interest to the convent can write, or cause to be written, an application, to which the petitioner must append a true biography and the proofs and particulars of his professional standing, in addition to which he shall be required to produce three references, including that of his baptismal priest, and finally a confirmatory counter-signature from the Office of the Archbishop.'

'Dear me, dear me,' says Chiara. 'But was not such a system designed for tradesmen, for artisans, not for holy brothers who—'

'Oh no,' Maria says. 'Forgive me for interrupting, but I believe we have such licences catalogued for Father Michele – even for Archbishop Serenus himself.'

'My word,' says Chiara, 'it's more complicated than I thought. That could take – days. Sister Paola – be a dear and go to the chapterhouse and ask Sister Tamara for whatever papers we need?' I hear the sound of the parlour door opening and closing below me, and then, 'I am sorry, Brother Abramo, but I'm sure you understand that our rules in this matter are necessarily—'

The bell clangs for the fourth office and, like thunder restoring a sultry day, I hear laughter – his laughter. I press my eye to the crack. His cowl has fallen back, and to my surprise, I behold a man who, although no longer young, is undeniably beautiful. At once, I find myself thinking: this, *this* is how the Son would have looked, had he lived, had he not bartered his life for our salvation. I stare, fascinated, at his halo of long, dark curls; at his eyes, so heavy, so sorrowful; at the hungry hollows of his cheeks; at his full, almost feminine, mouth.

Maria, I see, has clapped a hand to her mouth, but Chiara – Chiara has not moved. And he – he is smiling now, and what a smile it is. He is open, easy – full of love. My unease drains away, leaving me light and buoyant. I am awash with relief. Whatever wrong we do, however we err, like the Son, he is on our side.

And now he starts to talk once more, this happy impression only strengthens. No longer does he speak in the Vernacular of the city; rather, he uses the homely dialect of the steep-sided valleys that lie on the mountain's far side. The words do not diverge greatly from our own, but the stress lands oddly, so that the vowels advance, while the consonants retreat. It is, in fact, the sound of my infancy – of Zia – and I cannot hear it without a small pang. I cannot speak it, but Chiara can, and does to the oldest of our sisters, for the chiefest town of those valleys was once her home.

He calls her Mother Chiara, speaking her name with warmth and fondness. He mentions, with affection, some details of their old house – Maria, he says, I'd know you anywhere. He asks after Hildegard, Cateline, Galilea. He says how he has missed her. He says he is not hurt that she did not know him, for the years have been long, have they not?

'While I did the Father's work throughout the Peninsula, I always hoped that one day I should be called to this city in his service. And so it has come to pass! How I longed to greet you, to kiss your hand, but' – here, I would almost say he pouts – 'your gatekeeper sent me away. Now, though, I return to you, to this: your new home.'

The angle of my vantage means I cannot see Chiara's face, but I watch her take a step towards him – one, then another, then a third, taking her past the line of tiles, until there is no more than a hand's span between them. She barely reaches his breastbone, but she is never diminutive. She looks up and seems to hold his gaze. Lightly, she touches a finger to his cheek. I expect her to embrace him. To give him her hand to kiss.

'The prodigal son, is it?' Never have I heard her voice so cold. 'Is that the story you've been telling yourself all these years?'

His face, which had been expectant, eager, hardens. His smile thins and fades – and so my fear returns. I long for her to reconsider. Don't, I think, don't refuse his love and duty. Don't make him hate us – please.

'I came here,' he is saying, 'ready to forgive. Even though you drove me—' He stops. Composes himself. Pulls up his hood and strides towards the door. There he turns. 'It is long now since the bell rang. I am surprised you have yet to hasten to the Father's prayers. Although, from what the city tells me of this place, perhaps it is no surprise at all.'

The Chapterhouse

Friday morning

WATCHING THE OTHER principal members of the convent take their seats in the chapterhouse, the mood, I judge, is restive. There was, you see, something of an altercation after the second office, and everyone is still affected, although they're all pretending that nothing is amiss.

Alfonsa, a stolid, ruddy, undowered novice of three years and ten, had another fainting fit – only this time, it assumed a more spiritual character. She dropped like a stone on the chapel threshold, only to start writhing and bucking, clawing at her hands and feet. We had to watch Arcangela bathe the thrashing child with a smile of great serenity, while her followers pressed their palms to their hearts, thanking the Father for allowing his daughter to share in the sufferings of his Son. 'I told her,' said Arcangela, looking happily about her, 'that if she would but unlock the door of her heart, the Son would find a way to enter in.'

Chiara was not impressed. She knelt down, lifted Alfonsa to her feet and told the gawping novices to take her to breakfast. Alfonsa, at the centre of an excited gaggle of her peers, turned and fixed Arcangela with a look of the most abject devotion.

'Sister Arcangela,' said Chiara, not bothering to wait until the rest of us had gone, 'you advised our young friend to fast and keep nightly vigil until the Son spoke to her? Even after she fainted during the Fat Tuesday feast?'

'And the Son has spoken,' Arcangela replied, and her voice, usually soft as a drift of blossom, snapped like dry kindling.

Chiara's anger was unambiguous, and looking at her now, I'd say she still has not recovered. Nor, I must admit, have I.

My hands are torn and tingling, and I am fearful lest anyone should notice. I was, moreover, sinfully late for confession. Worse still, I admitted to no greater lapse than a dislike of the exigencies of the Fast. I heard a rumbling laugh, and Father Michele said, 'If only a sin shared, were a sin halved,' which I enjoyed at the time, but now the magnitude of all I left out makes my stomach churn. I need to talk to Tomis, but normally it takes him three days or more to return with my goods, and I do not know how I shall endure the wait. I entreat myself to be calm, to mind the meeting. I do not want my sisters to think anything is wrong.

The others are busy settling themselves on the narrow benches, which are set against three of the four walls, each taking her place according to the length of her service. Chiara, naturally, is first, followed by Maria, Hildegard, Cateline, Felicitas and Timofea, five of the women who followed Chiara here, any prior distinctions of birth erased by the long years they have passed in one another's company.

Felicitas and Timofea, I guess, are discussing Alfonsa's tussle with the Son's love, communicating to each other with a busy sequence of significant glances. Theirs is an old friendship. They came from the same household in Chiara's old town – Timofea the unhappy daughter-in-law, Felicitas the maid of all work. They are wont to erupt into episodes of misunderstanding and recrimination, requiring their respective helpmeets to scurry to and fro with the fraught solemnity of emissaries between rival courts.

After Timofea comes a space – invisible to a stranger, but like a wall to us – for next in seniority is Arcangela, followed by her acolytes – Nanina and three others of her ilk – women born within the bounds of the city, all possessed of a certain refinement of manner and look, saving only Prudenzia, who has the air of an eager dormouse, at once both prim and fidgety.

And I – I am last, sitting as far removed from Prudenzia as the limited space allows. She does not look at me, nor I at her, and I wonder if she has contrived to tell Sister Arcangela about my late arrival at confession. When we were novices, she endeavoured to make a special friend of me, catching my eye whenever the others stumbled over their Latin. For a while, we formed common cause, until I riddled out that she dealt me double, courting me because of my father's name, then seeking to laugh over my awkward aspect with the Lauras and Giulias of our day.

When Sophia sought an assistant for the library, it was Prudenzia that our old pupil mistress recommended, saying I was sullen and contrary, whereas Prudenzia was 'a diligent little workhorse and neat as a pin to boot', but it was me that Sophia chose. Prudenzia never forgave me it, and I endured years of sniping giggles, spiteful glances.

I am not attending as I ought. Chiara has already offered up her introductory prayer, and we are in the midst of the ambulatory exchange of compliments and commiserations that must preface more serious discussion. The agreeable quality of the new season's eggs is touched upon. The lamentable demise of our bees this long winter. The gratifying size of the dowry accompanying the deaf-and-dumb daughter of an alum merchant. Excited questions from Chiara's friends about

Diana's paintings – what will she choose to paint? When will they be unveiled? Disapproving silence from the rest. Arcangela's preliminary list of those to be honoured with a place in the Vigilate procession, falling – she reminds us – but seven days hence. Excited questions from her friends; indifference from Chiara's.

At last, Maria stands to give us her weekly summary of the convent's business affairs, for we own many dwellings and workshops in our neighbourhood of the city. She reports some few instances of damage resultant upon carnival. A local girl insulted; remedies undertaken. Disquiet among the goodwives about a rumoured levy on unfinished cloth; interventions proposed. A poor widow abandoned; kinder relatives found.

Throughout Maria's crisp and methodical account, Arcangela appears to be growing ruffled. Her blue eyes open wider and wider. The point of her chin lifts higher and higher. And as Chiara starts to thank Maria, saying the day is getting on and she knows we all have work to do, Arcangela coughs slightly – for her, a dramatic abandonment of self-possession – coughs, presses her palms together, and says, 'Forgive me the interruption, Reverend Mother, but are we not to touch more closely upon the more particular events of the past two days?'

A breath of silence follows, and I can see the four women to Arcangela's left nodding agreement, their brows arranged in a uniformity of concern.

'Events, sister?' says Chiara with surpassing blitheness.

'The women, Reverend Mother. This girl. The visit—'

'Aaah. Of course. You are, as ever, quite right.' Chiara smiles at us all. 'Sisters, let us thank the Father for giving us the strength to help women in need, and to his beloved Son for opening our hearts to their suffering.' With that, Chiara stands and turns towards the door, only to find that Arcangela has already hurried across the room to obstruct her exit.

Louder now, Arcangela continues, 'The visit, Reverend Mother, paid to us by Brother Abramo.'

'Eh? Who's that, then?' says Hildegard.

Cateline nudges her and says, 'The one I told you about, silly. The one the butcher's wife says came down off of the mountain. Who spoke so rousing in the basilica. Mantle needed a good going over with a needle and thread, she said. Looks of an angel though, with lovely, you know—' and she twirls her fingers either side of her face, conjuring his curls.

'You consort with butchers?' Arcangela, frigid with horror, is momentarily distracted. 'During the Forty-Day Fast?'

Cateline shrugs. 'It's custom to tip them, this first week – lean times for them, otherwise. And' – she taps her nose – 'a nice tip and a fat one puts us front of the queue when it comes to the Forty-Day Feast.'

'Hear, hear,' says Hildegard.

'You used to like a bit of lamb yourself, Sister Arcangela,' says Felicitas, querulously.

Timofea pats her kindly on the knee, and at once the older women fall to debating which of Felicitas's Son-Rise lambs could claim to be the most memorable – was it the stew of prunes and cinnamon? Or the one roasted entire over Hildegard's clever pit of fire? Chiara is in the middle of happily recalling a sauce of candied orange and plum wine, when Arcangela finally cuts across her.

'May I ask, Reverend Mother, why Brother Abramo honoured us with a visit?'

Chiara turns to where Arcangela still stands in the doorway. 'Why, to be sure you may. He came to offer us the love owed by a holy brother to his holy sisters.'

'I fear it was more than fraternal solidarity he came to express,' replies Arcangela.

'Do you?' says Chiara, folding her arms across her chest.

I look down at my hands. Never before has their antagonism been so apparent. Once, when I'd dared give Arcangela a surly answer to some request, Sophia had warned me: 'Careful now, little γάδαρος.' This was her name for me, a reference not to the stolid humility of the donkey that bore the Son, but rather to the angry passivity of its less exalted descendants. 'That woman will be Mother Superior after Chiara's death – or before, if she can help it.' At the time, I'd thought she exaggerated – Sophia saw scheming everywhere – but perhaps, as so often, she was right.

'I'm afraid that I do,' Arcangela is saying. 'I'm afraid that Brother Abramo came to express sorrow at our shortcomings.'

'Our shortcomings?' Chiara sounds baffled.

Arcangela looks pained. 'Mother Chiara. I fear that your selfless and all-embracing love is blinding you to reality. You must know what people say.'

'I must?'

'We keep a lax parlour. We indulge fallen women. We cleave to families steeped in sin and luxury.' My cheeks start to flush. She does not say the word *Stelleri*, but she does not need to. 'I could continue, but—'

'Dearest of daughters,' says Chiara, 'Brother Abramo did not come to rebuke us.'

'But he—'

'No, Arcangela. He did not.'

'But—'

'No, no. I fear you have been – led astray.' Chiara sounds almost merry. 'Naughty Sister Paola. I've always found she tells me whichever story she thinks I would most like to hear. No, no. It was a friendly visit. We are old friends, the brother and I.'

'You are – friends?' This, clearly, is not at all what Arcangela expected, and her voice has already lost some of its certainty.

As for me, the ground shifts a little beneath my feet; have I ever heard Chiara lie?

'Very old friends,' repeats Chiara. 'Since his boyhood, in fact. He was born, you see, in my own little home town. A poor orphan child he was, back then – back when a few women had first begun to gather about me.'

I look up to see Chiara smiling, while her friends exchange indulgent looks. Our Mother Superior rejoices in her modesty, but 'a few women' takes modesty too far. Everyone – in the convent, in the city, in the entire north of the Peninsula, as far south as St Peter's itself – everyone knows that a quarter of a century ago, dozens of women – barefoot, empty-handed – walked out of their homes to follow Chiara. Rich and poor, young and old, virgins, wives and those the pestilenza had widowed – they all followed her. My older sisters still like to reminisce about the greasy dinner plates they left behind; the cobwebs on the ceilings, the empty bodices, the fine necklaces gathering dust.

As for Arcangela, she – temporarily, at least – is flummoxed. Chiara's youth, its exceptional circumstance, is hallowed ground, upon which the chief warden does not – yet? – dare to tread.

'So you see,' says Chiara, 'Brother Abramo came to pay his respects. To remember old times. Really, sister, you have nothing to fear.' And with that, she walks past Arcangela, pushes the door open, and departs, leaving a complicated silence behind her.

'*Ah-ha!*' Hildegard thwacks her leg and emits a resounding cry. 'Not that nice little boy Tonio, who used to run errands for us? You say that is he? Little Tonio?'

'He wasn't so little, as I recall,' murmurs Maria. 'He was every day of eighteen.'

Hildegard makes a guttural noise, which I take for reluctant agreement, and continues, 'Oh, but he was so devoted, was he not? So eager? Mother Chiara, may I do this? Mother Chiara, may I do that? So he comes to call. His respects to pay? And he is now a holy brother? And he calls himself Abramo? After the First Father? Well, that *is* nice.'

Everyone is standing. The meeting is disbanding. I am watching Arcangela openly now, enjoying – I can admit it – her struggle to accommodate this new information. A mistake. She notices, and rounds on me.

'You met the brother too, did you not, Sister Beatrice?'

I nod, minimally, and the others, mid-departure, pause to listen. Beside me, Prudenzia is jittering with ill-suppressed excitement.

'What,' Arcangela continues, 'I wonder, brought you to the parlour?'

I would like to say that she knows perfectly well what, but of course I lack the courage, and instead mumble, 'I was discussing business with my bookseller.'

'Really, such comings and goings,' tuts Prudenzia.

Arcangela bestows a gracious smile and says, 'Yes, it is a mystery why you must meet that man in person. But many things about yours and Sophia's activities' – she stresses the word most unpleasantly – 'remain a mystery to the rest of us. Perhaps we lack your intellectual abilities. I have often wondered, ignorant as I am, why we have so many pagan writers in our library. Their demonic tales, their obscene subjects, their paeans to false gods – so unsuitable. Can you enlighten me? Can you enlighten us all? We'll do our best to understand you.'

I fumble for an answer. My older sisters are upset, even angry – but not on my account, of that you can be sure. No, they are angry because criticism of the library is criticism of the convent, and criticism of the convent is criticism of Chiara – and that, they cannot bear.

'The texts of the ancients,' I say, 'fill the libraries of the city. They are widely admired. They . . .' I break off. Foolish words. Sister Arcangela has landed me like a fish.

'But we, Sister Beatrice, we are Promised sisters! Do we seek to emulate the mores of the city? What would you have us do next? Whiten our hair? Admire our reflections in plate of gilt? Think more of the appetites of our lap-dogs than the health of our souls? Or perhaps we should follow the example of your brother?' She allows Prudenzia and Nanina's tittering to subside. 'Well, Beatrice?' She shakes her head and sighs. 'I have always said that expanding our library was a dangerous caprice of that woman—'

'Sophia,' I say. 'Her name was Sophia – and she worked tirelessly for the good of the convent.' I look around me, but nobody will come to my aid. Nobody even meets my eye. I feel my face reddening, my cheek beginning to throb, my thoughts becoming erratic. I am alone. Arcangela is a coward, I think, a coward to impugn me only now Chiara is gone.

'A dangerous caprice, Beatrice – and now I fear you would don her mantle. It seems that the library is more important to you than attending the holy offices.'

'I am dispensed. The daylight—'

'And what about the Father's light, Beatrice? What about that?'

'His light is manifest in the psalter,' I say. 'In the testaments, the epistles.'

'Then why do you not confine yourself to such works? Well? Who is this Virgil? This Cicero?'

'I make good money for the convent. Ask Sister Maria. Ask anyone.'

At the mention of money, Arcangela looks like I've emptied my nostrils on to the floor. 'Well,' she says, stretching the word over three syllables, 'you have inherited your father's mercantile instincts, have you not? Now, Beatrice—'

But she is distracted by somebody at the open door. Chiara, I think hopefully, Chiara has returned. Quickly, though, I see I am wrong. It is, in fact, Sister Paola – come to tell me that Tomis is waiting with my wares outside the gate, that I must attend him. I hasten after her, smarting with my sisters' disapproval.

The Ink-Crate

Immediately thereafter

⌘

EVEN COUNTING THE TIME it takes Poggio to open the gate for Tomis's wagon – grumbling, peering at his pass, prodding the crates – I am still sufficiently shaken that I fail to bring my usual zeal to my dissection of his inventory, to the particulars of his pay-note. Tomis, frowning, asks will I be so trusting in all our future dealings, because if so—

'No, no,' I reply, making an effort to smile, telling him I'm lulling him apurpose, to see whether a momentary lapse tempts him to cozen me next time. He laughs, but I sense he is still looking at me strangely.

We are skirting the quadrilango, walking on either side of his pony, which is pulling the wagon the short distance to the foot of the library stairs. Usually, I confess, it flatters my vanity to be seen enjoying such licence, but today I feel exposed, aware that everyone will soon hear a garbled version of what was said in the chapterhouse. I compare myself with Sophia – who, voluble and oblivious, used to harangue Tomis in the middle of the quadrilango – and lament my own lack of boldness. The pony comes to a halt, and I round up my scattered thoughts.

I had thought to fetch the book at once, but a trio of housekeeps is near at hand, listening to Sister Timofea giving instruction as to the proper way to air the storerooms beneath the library. Too risky. I shall have to wait until they move off. Instead, I thank him for his consideration in assembling everything so fast.

'I like to look after my friends,' he says, moving to the back of the wagon and hefting the first crate into his arms.

'Wait,' I say, stopping him as he makes for the stairs. 'I'll take it up later.'

'It's heavy—' he begins.

'Please,' I say.

'It's heavy,' he repeats, but then he understands. He places the crate on the ground beneath the cloister. 'You would rather I remain—'

'Visible, yes. Thank you.'

'In consequence, I assume, of Brother Abramo's visit yesterday?' he murmurs, before returning to the wagon to take up another crate. 'Did he get what he came for?' he asks in an undertone, settling the second crate upon the first. 'Did he learn more about those two women?'

'He did not,' I say, glancing at the housekeeps. 'Chiara refused to admit him.'

He whistles. 'Bold woman. Tell me' – he pauses to straighten the crates – 'tell me, have you found a common tongue with them?'

'No—'

'Well then, it's fortunate I returned. After I've unloaded everything, shall we—?'

'No, no,' I say, 'you don't understand. You see, they're dead.'

'*Dead?*' His voice is loud enough to attract Sister Timofea's attention, and she frowns at us.

'Hush,' I say. 'Yes.'

'But how?'

'They succumbed to wounds they received on the road. We buried them yesterday.'

'And you' – he speaks more quietly now – 'you still know nothing more about them?'

I shake my head. 'Nothing.'

He turns away. I think he must be about to fetch the next crate, and yet he does not stir.

'Tomis,' I say, forgetting myself so much as to reach out and touch his shoulder, 'are you quite all right? Only you seem very—' And then I remember. 'But, of course, Abramo's men! They followed you from the convent, did they not? Did they – have you come to any harm?'

He turns to face me, and when he speaks he does sound more like himself. 'Yes, Beatrice, it was indeed a trying day. His men came to my warehouse. They demanded inspection of my documents, my stock. They thumbed every one of my books with their fat fingers.'

I am aghast, assuming this to be a calamity, but he is quite calm, even giving my arm the briefest pat.

'It's all right. My rarer books – eluded them. Which,' he adds over his shoulder as he moves to lift another crate, 'is lucky, is it not?'

Our eyes meet. Nothing distinguishes the crate he is holding from the previous two, and yet his care in placing it, the way he taps it with his fingers, that tells me all I need to know.

'Forgive me, Beatrice,' he says, and I fear he is about to take his leave, but no, he is telling me that he must attend Sister Maria, must ask her for prompt settlement of his bill. I watch him hasten across the quadrilango and knock on the door of the little annexe to the chapterhouse, where she and Tamara oversee our financial affairs, ordering their chits and quittances. The door opens – Tamara greets him volubly – and he disappears inside.

I wait, recalling the day when I first came across one of his *rarer* books.

Sophia was lying down with one of the agues that tear through the convent during the last weeks of winter. She was still a little feverish, with a rasp to her throat, but slowly mending. Indeed I remember teasing her when I visited her in her cell, telling her she was malingering to avoid her share of the spring clean. She looked up at me from beneath her blankets.

'You see straight through me, child.' A pause, a sly smile. 'I expect Tomis tomorrow. I have spoken to Chiara, and we agree that if I am still abed, you are to be trusted to conduct our business with him yourself.'

I can still remember how I swelled with pride, that lovely tingling consciousness that none of my age-mates were likely to be so favoured. It was no more my nature then than it is now to exclaim my thanks, so I simply said I had our list prepared and would try not to disappoint her. She nodded and said I'd better not.

I made to go, telling her how busy I had been, how meticulously I had assessed our collection for signs of damp or the predations of bibliovores, how particularly pleased I was to have spotted some small indications of silverfish in the old chest where we kept scraps of parchment.

'I dropped it by the woodpile before I came here,' I added.

The effect of my words was dramatic.

'Beatrice,' she croaked, struggling upright, 'what have you—?' She was flinging off her blankets, demanding her shift, her mantle, epithetising me as the daughter of a mangy cow, of a pustulant swine, of a flyblown goat, and I was trying to restrain her, partly because I feared violence, partly because she ought not to exert herself – which was harder than I expected, for all that she was more than thrice my age.

'Stop,' I pleaded. 'Stop, what are you doing?'

Grabbing the front of my gown, she said, 'That chest. Get me that chest. Get it now,' and I felt the full force and fire of the woman who had outpaced the Khan King's armies, clinging to life, until she arrived, beggared, at the doors of the convent. There was no question of delay. Even as she sank, coughing, back onto her pallet, I hurried to the rear of the cookhouse. My timing was poor. Hildegard was there, axe raised.

'No!' I called, but too late. She had splintered the chest down the middle.

'Sorry,' she said, while I babbled that the chest was Sophia's, that I shouldn't have turned it out for firewood. Hildegard shrugged, mopping her brow with her red rag. 'She's not going to want it now, is she?' and raised her axe again.

'It's precious,' I squealed.

'This?'

'It came with her out of her homeland,' I improvised, before remembering she arrived with nothing save two books in a packbag, and I began to blush and stammer.

But Hildegard said, 'All right. Sophia want. Sophia have.' She shunted the chest towards me with her boot, before turning away to square up to a long trunk of pine.

I returned with it to the library, telling myself to move slowly and calmly. For already I could see that where the axe had split the base of the chest, there was a narrow compartment, and within that compartment there lay a manuscript. I placed the chest in what I judged to be the library's darkest corner. I worked. I attended the fourth office – I was not yet sufficiently important to be excused. I worked. I attended the fifth office, I worked, waiting and waiting, until the hour when I could take Sophia her small evening meal. As I entered, her eyes snapped open.

'Well?'

'It's safe. In the library.'

'Good,' she said. 'Good.'

She looked pleased. I handed her the bowl and watched her sniff the contents.

'Sophia?'

'Mmmmmm?'

'What's the book in the chest?'

As I remember it, she choked slightly, so the soup she had been spooning into her mouth spilled. Extravagant Greek curses followed, accompanied by demands that I fetch her a fresh blanket, outrage when I reminded her that fresh blankets came but once a year, deprecations on the idiocy of conventual rules, further deprecations on everything from Felicitas's so-called cooking to the abominable weather of the city. I waited it out.

When she had taken three consecutive scoops of soup without additional insult, I asked again, 'What's the book in the chest?'

She swallowed. Placed her spoon in the bowl. 'You've not looked? You should have had the gumption to look. A scholar is meant to be curious.'

'You say a prentice should respect her mistress.'

'Hmph.'

'Sophia, what's—?'

'Lucretius. *De Rerum Natura*. His account of the workings of all creation. Such profanity! He holds the universe is composed of specks of indivisibility, hurtling—'

'But it's been—'

'Proscribed by the Curial Court. Thank you. I know.'

'But it—'

'Could irredeemably corrupt the feeble mind of any woman who stumbled across it. I know.'

'But—'

'Can you read it? Yes – but you'll have to be quick. Tomis collects it when he returns with our order tomorrow. And, Beatrice, in the name of the Father, check the pages thoroughly for silverfish. No mercy.'

And so it was I discovered that when Tomis had in his possession a book he feared might provoke the censorious attention of the church or – no less a hazard – the rapacious envy of his competitors, Sophia guarded it for him. It was a game for her, but also good business. For Tomis, you can be sure, repaid us in kind, deploying his unequalled negotiating skills on our behalf – good parchment and good ink at good prices. Of course, we also got to read the books, which was the capstone of our deal. I wonder now that I was not more shocked, but Sophia had a way about her that made everything she did seem right.

But now, finally, he is returning from the chapterhouse, apologising for having taken so long. 'Tamara insisted on telling me everything she knew about those women, which it turns out wasn't much.' He smiles, weakly. 'And now—' he starts, but I interrupt him. The housekeeps have dispersed. This is my chance.

'Tomis,' I say, 'I really need to talk to you about—'

But he isn't paying attention. He's pointing at the final crate, saying, 'Listen, Beatrice, this crate. It contains – a new blend of ink. I had – I had prepared it for your father. I was looking forward to presenting it to him, but until I find another connoisseur of – of ink, I would very much like to leave it here. The conditions in my warehouse, you understand, are not conducive.'

I understand, of course. A book – commissioned for my father – and in some way questionable. 'Perhaps' – I run my fingers along the top of the lid – 'perhaps I shall sample it myself?'

'Beatrice, no.' A sharp and warning note. 'It would not suit these – particular times. That is to say, I would not recommend any rash experimentation. Not at the moment. Now, I really must—'

'Tomis – wait, wait. You have forgotten. That – that velvet you brought on your last visit? It's too costly for our use. I need to return it.'

Without waiting for his reply, I hasten up the stairs and into the library, where I collect a bolt of velvet, wrapped in sturdy, unbleached linen. Inside the velvet's azure folds are two books. One is a battered grimoire, scrawled with impenetrable pentacles, purporting to be the *Clavicula of Solomon*. The other is an anonymous treatise, written by a woman who dwells inside one of the Lagoon's more draconian convents, proscribed as soon as it was in circulation. I read it over three nights, cursing my candle stubs. One line I most especially remember: 'A man says submit to the Father, but he means submit to him. And if you oppose him, he says you oppose the Father, and calls you heretic and sinner.'

Next, I take down a large tome with *The Completest Works of Tertullian, Volume IX* stamped across the front. Making sure I am screened by the side of a cupboard, I open the outer boards, take the women's book out of my pocket and nestle it where a deep rectangle of parchment has been cut away.

'What,' I'd asked Sophia, when first she showed me this ruse, 'if somebody wants to read Tertullian?'

'Have you ever read him?' she asked.

I shook my head. 'No.'

'Exactly.'

Approaching the foot of the stairs, I am dismayed to find that Tomis is no longer alone. Diana is sitting on the final crate, asking in familiar tones whether he trades pigments as well as the tools of the Sister Librarian's trade. And he, resting one foot on the crate is saying – easily, so easily – that he could never hope to satisfy Mistress Diana, for are not her requirements famously exacting, and she is laughing, and asking does he often find it hard to give satisfaction, and I see they have met – before, outside – often, and I am scalded with envy. I stand, in the shadows on the third step, listening.

'But how is it,' Tomis is asking, 'that Mistress Diana finds herself . . .?'

'Wouldn't you,' she says, 'like to know.'

'I'd heard a rumour that—'

'Don't believe everything you hear.'

'And naturally I was concerned.'

'Naturally.'

'Diana.' He leans down to speak closer to her ear. 'I heard you'd had some trouble with the Shepherds.'

She pulls away and stares at him. 'Where did you hear that?'

'From Silvia—'

For some reason, this makes Diana smile. 'I say, you *do* have friends in high places. The pontifex's daughter, indeed. What business could *you* have with *her*?' When he does not immediately reply, she pokes his leg. 'Well? Don't pretend my welfare was all you discussed.'

'She – she had an errand for me.' He removes his foot from the crate and takes a step backwards. 'A commission. I was bound for the Delta and—'

'Liar,' says Diana, 'you've not been near the Delta. Your

hands are too pale. And those dates you brought Paola – she gave me one, and they're last season's. Where've you been, eh?'

Grudgingly, I applaud her perspicacity. But before Tomis can answer – or, more likely, evade – the question, Hildegard comes into view, a stepped ladder slung over her shoulder. 'Ah, Diana,' she calls, 'you were wanting one such' – she pats the ladder affectionately – 'for furtherance to your painting work? Yes?'

Taking advantage of this interruption, I emerge from hiding and stow my bundle on the wagon, feeling, I admit, slightly put out. I can never persuade Hildegard to do such things for me. Nor, come to think of it, has Paola ever thought to offer me one of her dates.

'Hello, Beatrice. Adieu, Tomis,' says Diana over her shoulder, before stopping and pointing to me. 'Don't presume upon her innocence.'

To which he laughs out loud and says, 'Believe me, Sister Beatrice is anything but innocent when it comes to the price of ink.'

I realise we are both of us standing, watching her go. 'Please,' I say. 'Please don't talk about her. It's all anyone does.'

'Would you rather they talked of you?' he asks, but before I can decide how to reply, or indeed whether to reply at all, he is pointing at the large volume that I am holding tightly in my arms. 'What's this, then? The lost books of the *Aeneid* at last?'

'No,' I say, unable to join his jest. 'No, something altogether – altogether more . . .' I place the book in his hands.

'Tertullian?' he says, turning it over and reading the inscription. 'If you wish to debate his, I admit, seductive position on the corporeality of the Father, I am, as always, at your service, but – what is this?'

He looks sharply up at me, for by now he has opened the outer boards and seen what lies within. He looks more interested – much more interested – than I ever could have imagined. I swear that his fingers, normally so quick and sure, tremble as he turns the pages.

'The women,' I say quickly, quietly. 'They had this among their possessions. The script – I think you once gave me a sample. On a curl of bark. Can you read it? Do you know what it is? And the pictures, I think they are connected to – that is to say, I think they are depictions of—'

I pull up, realising that in my excitement I am being careless. Quickly, I survey the quadrilango – nobody, or nobody to worry about. When I look back, Tomis has moved a few steps apart and turned away. A back is hard to read, but I can tell you that normally his body is in flux, small movements, foot to foot, heel to toe, unceasing. Now, he is quite still.

'Well,' I say, 'do you know the writing?'

No reply.

'Tomis,' I say. And again, '*Tomis?*'

'Forgive me, Sister Beatrice,' he says, turning to face me again while – I notice with unease – at the same time starting to back away. 'Forgive me, but I have recalled – a commission. I am late – I must hurry. Forgive me. Forgive me—'

His heedless retreat causes him to collide with the pony. Swiftly, he deals it a great thump on the rump – he who is normally so gentle – and the wagon starts to rumble forwards. He seizes the leading rein and steers it round towards the gate, my book now tucked under his left arm.

I run to his side, hissing, 'What in the name of the Father are you doing?'

'Why, I need a little time to study the script, of course,' he says, keeping his eyes on the gate and quickening his pace, releasing the rope for an instant to hail Poggio, who busies himself with the rigmarole that is re-opening the gate. I snatch at the book, trying to wrest it from his grasp. I don't succeed in tearing it away, but I cling on to it with both hands, forcing him to stop.

'Beatrice,' he murmurs, with some of his usual softness. 'Calm down, really, there's nothing to worry about. I'll bring it back. Don't you trust me?'

I jerk hard at the book, but his grip does not fail.

'Give it back,' I say, 'or I'll—'

That *or* rankles. I have no *or*. He is not a big man, but I am a small woman. I feel a breathless anger at my impotence. I want to kick him, but kick the pony instead. It moves, causing the iron wheel of the wagon to roll over his toes. He gives a satisfying yelp, and, with a great grunt of effort, I have the book. Now it is his turn to look daunted. I cross my arms over it, clasp it to my chest and make for the library stairs. But as my foot lands on the first step, one hand seizes the back of my mantle, the other my arm, and try what I might, I cannot shake myself free.

I turn to face him. A little line quivers between his eyebrows and his grip tightens. What can he do? Knock me to the ground, put a foot on my chest, tear the book from me and strike for the slowly opening gate? Yes: that, I realise, is exactly what he could do.

'Tomis,' I say, 'Tomis, Tomis, Tomis.' I repeat his name like a prayer, an incantation, and slowly his aspect changes. He laughs. He says he's sorry. He says he doesn't know what came over him.

'You see, it's – it's writing from my homeland. I feel nostalgia – homesickness. Odysseus, as it were, gazing up at the pines on the heights of Ithaca. The smell of the thyme. Long have I lived in exile. I wanted – a piece of home. Might I – might I look again? Just once?'

Slowly, I shake my head.

'You're heartless,' he says.

'And you,' I say, 'are transparent. Do not lie to me—'

'Beatrice,' he says, grasping my shoulder, all composure gone. 'You do not know what you have there. Beatrice, listen, you must—' and suddenly his hands are everywhere, grabbing, pulling, fighting to take possession of the book.

A dizziness sweeps over me – the shape of him wavers – he is far away, a black dot – he is all I can see, a flesh monolith – a roaring routs my sight – no, my ears – no – but – then – all at once – he reforms. His grip – has slackened. He's gone – where? The floor at my feet. What—? I blink, gasp, swallow – see. Diana is kneeling over him, holding his arm in a way that seems to be causing him immense pain.

'Don't—' he gasps.

'I will,' she whispers, although a whisper that assails my ears. 'I can and I will.' His eyes bulge. 'I will break your arm, then your fingers, then I'll tell Sister Arcangela that you attempted to assault Beatrice, and that – that will be the end of you.'

'Diana – please – the book – it's not—'

'Shut up. Shut *up*. Count of three. I release you. You walk away, you hear me? *You walk away.*'

I look this way, that way. Poggio is standing by the gate, shading his eyes, trying to fathom where Tomis has gone. Hildegard's helpmeets, who've been in the fields since dawn, are assembling near the refectory, waiting for the noonday meal, which we Promised sisters must forgo until the Son rises. The pony still stands in the sunshine. It lifts its tail and defecates.

'Three,' says Diana, 'two, one—' She lets him go and places herself between me and him. 'Go,' she says. 'Go. *Now!*'

He doesn't want to. Oh, but it is plain he doesn't want to. Will he—? Surely, he won't risk a brawl with her? I wouldn't. Her colour is high. Sweat streams at her temples.

Her shoulders heave up and down. I wouldn't fight her. But although he's stumbled to his feet and taken a step or two backwards, he's still there.

His hands go to his face, and I realise the scuffle has caused his mask to slip. He looks away as he fumbles to re-tie it, and in doing so he must see that his luck has run out. Hildegard and Cateline are wandering over to pet the pony, asking Poggio what's become of its owner. Tomis turns back to us. Diana delivers an expressive shrug, and he starts walking. When he arrives at the pony's side, Hildegard thumps him on the back. He flinches – but it's merely a friendly greeting. He passes through the gate. My fingers, gradually, loosen on the book.

'Thank you,' I mumble to Diana and try to start up the stairs, but there is something awry. I cannot walk as I should. I reel, clutch at the wall, and find myself staring at an inviting crack between two bricks. The pulse of my blood – too loud. My breathing – too shallow. I can hear a whispering, a calling. I can hear things in the walls. I crave silence. I crave darkness.

'Come.' A strong arm wraps around me. Eases me away. 'You are not yourself. You are not accustomed to being used like that. Come.'

'If you just—' I gesture, vaguely, at the stairs. She does not, however, lead me up to the library, but rather away towards the chapel, and I find I lack the will to resist. As we cross the quadrilango, Arcangela – who is ordering a pair of housekeeps to clean up the mess the pony made – asks what we think we are doing.

'She's feeling a little faint,' whispers Diana. 'Has she not told you that she is fasting most particularly for her father's soul? She would pray for him. I am helping her.'

Arcangela's eyes narrow – she is sceptical – but what can she say? Diana steers me onwards into the chapel. It is empty now – quiet. I look up at the Son. I have a strange feeling that he is sceptical too, that he would like to raise his eyes and look at me. We walk down the nave, until his feet are almost above my head, and then we turn to the right and pass through some drapes into Green Mary's side chapel, where Diana's painting equipment is now arranged with evident care. The left-hand wall gleams white and even with some undercoat of paint. I glance sideways at Diana, and she grins.

'Welcome to my studio,' she says. 'Do please take a seat.'

Gratefully, I sink to the floor. She has water. She pours. The sound is loud and silvered. She passes me the cup and the taste is an icicle. Slowly, I feel the sense of dissipation itself dissolving. I rub my eyes. Feel my heart slowly stilling. My head grows heavy. I lean back against the wall—

Diana is standing beside me, humming, holding a palette. Has more time passed than I thought? She looks down. Sees me looking up. Smiles.

'You know, you make the strangest noises when you're asleep.' She puts her palette down and assesses me. 'You look a lot better, anyway. Now – you going to tell me what all that was about?'

'I – I hardly know myself.' I sit up a little. 'But I – thank you. Truly.'

'It's alright,' she says, a little roughly. 'I've had to watch enough women taken advantage of and not been able to lift a finger. Today, I could help. So I did.' She kneels down. 'Beatrice – what is it? This book that made Tomis act possessed.' I look around frantically, but she touches my hands. 'You're still holding it.'

My fingers tighten. My first and overwhelming impulse is to lie. I open my mouth to spin some story – a rich widow's legacy, Tomis consulted, his greed provoked. But I meet her gaze, and the lie dies on my lips.

'I – I don't really know.'

Her eyebrows shoot up. 'You don't know – and you were *fighting* him for it?' She touches the book, slowly tracing the letters on the cover with her fingers. 'Tuh-eh-er-T-E-R-T-u-l-l-i-an. Tertullian?'

'Yes, but Tertullian is – just the name on the outside. Inside' – I open the boards a very, very little to show her my book hiding within – 'there's this, but I don't know what it is. At least, I know a little, but I want to know more. And I thought – I thought Tomis might help me, but I was wrong. It's not fair.' I find I am speaking with a fierce and unaccustomed candour. 'He – he has all the books in the world, but I have just this one.'

'And so you didn't want to let it go.' She nods and I follow her gaze up to where the ghost of a picture is starting to appear on the chapel wall. 'I understand,' she says – and I believe she does.

The Ledger

Saturday morning

⌘

ON SATURDAYS, it has long been my duty to make myself available to those who, never having learned to read or write, nonetheless wish to send a letter home – and what letters they are. Enquiries as to the health of Papà, the health of Mamma, the health of sundry relatives, cows and horses. Prayers for the coming season. Prayers, more fervent, for the life to come. Heartfelt pleas for what will doubtless be equally dull letters in return.

When first I came here, my stepmother used to write to me – although I don't know why she took the trouble, for to be sure I never replied. She wrote about the little doings of the household. What my brother did. The cats. Where my father went. It was like a cruelty. We – do this. You – do that. I began to stack them unopened beneath my bolster.

Our old pupil mistress found them and told Chiara, and I was called upon to explain myself. It was our first considerable talk. I stared at my feet until I realised she could tolerate an infinity of silence, and instead seized upon a platitude I had often heard voiced – that we should strive to forget our earthly families. Chiara eyed me beadily and said, 'Nevertheless, you should write.'

And so, every Saturday, I copied out the verses from the Stories of the Son upon which we were to pray that week – sealed them – sent them. And when, after a time, my stepmother's letters ceased, I nonetheless continued, crafting each word more and more beautifully as my skill increased, experimenting with the louche curls of the Hibernian kingdoms, with the dainty Gallic style – until one day Sophia observed me, asked me what I did, boxed my ears and ordered me to stop.

After Sophia died, I asked Arcangela to forgive me my dictation duties, suggesting one of my copyists might benefit from writing out the same dreary commonplaces, week after week. She was, however, unyielding, bidding me to aid my sisters with a kind countenance and forbearing heart. 'But since you feel yourself to be overburdened,' she said, with her matchless instinct for oblique chastisement, 'I shall ask Sister Prudenzia to help.'

A short interval remains until Prudenzia's allotted hour, and I intend to use it profitably. I have, you see, a letter of my own, which I guarantee will not be dull. First though, I must decipher it, to which end my box of scripts stands ready. Let me explain.

Yesterday, after I left Diana working in the chapel, I'd passed an hour carrying Tomis's crates up the stairs and stowing his wares. Paper, parchment. Black ink, and red and white. Pumice stones, metalled pens, goose-feather quills. Clasps and studs and balls of twine. None of what he sells us is luxurious – no gold leaf, no saffron, no lapis lazuli – but unwrapping, handling, settling everything in its proper place did a little to restore my calm.

Come the discretionary hour, I sent my copyists away to do as they would and sought a chisel to lever open the final crate, which I had placed in the library's furthest recess. The lid was nailed down so as to deter casual inspection, and it took me some amount of time and effort to wrench it off. What lay inside, beneath three blameless trays of ink, was not a book – not exactly – rather a modest sort of archive – disparate pages poking out of a leather binding. Crouching down, I untied the knots, opened the cover, an unassuming brown, and skimmed the contents.

I found perhaps fifty sheets, of both paper and parchment, of varying quality, closely written in many different scripts and tongues, mostly accompanied by a Latin translation, mostly in Tomis's hand, but drafted at different times, in different inks and often, so far as I could judge, in haste. Here and there, I met pages which had been ripped or razored from other manuscripts, furbished with Tomis's marginal notes. Finally, tucked at the back, there was a slim metal case and this letter, without address, sealed with a blot of grimy wax.

I broke the seal, hoping it might serve as an introduction to all else, but I found no answers, only a promiscuous screed of symbols. I was certain, however, that Tomis was the author – I recognised his exuberant pen-strokes. Some – ᴐ and ᴔ – were at least familiar, if somewhat strangely written, as for the others, they meant nothing. Putting the letter aside until I could consult my box of scripts, I turned to the sheaf of pages and started to read.

> this was the day of her return the beginning of bountiful
> springtime
> following the torches as they dipped and swayed in the
> darkness
> they climbed mountain paths with heads thrown back and
> eyes glazed
> dancing to the beat of the drum which stirred their blood

I recognised the grace of Old Greek hexameters: Homeric, but not Homer, likely a paean to Demeter, goddess of grain and harvest, of earth and plenty, mother of Persephone, who winters in the Underworld. Unbidden, I found myself thinking of the woman who had given me the book – the strong angles of her face lit by torchlight. The next verses, in more artful Island Greek, were nimbler.

> in the spring twilight
> the full moon is shining
> and girls take their places
> as though round an altar
>
> we know she will walk
> among us like a mother with
> all her daughters around her
> when she comes home from exile

And I thought of our novices, how they crowd around Mother Chiara, showing off their new gowns, when we gather beneath the cedar tree before the Son-Rise feast.

I flicked ahead a few pages and lit upon a collection of writings taken from the Stories of the Father, starting with the tart reply certain women gave to the prophet Jeremiah when he railed against them.

> When we burned incense to the Queen of Heaven and
> poured out drink offerings to her, did not our husbands
> know we were making cakes impressed with her own image?

Thereafter, I found myself reading how Solomon, at the behest of his Seven Hundred Wives, turned his back on the Father to worship their goddess Astarte. I had, of course, read that passage before, but I had never considered its fuller meaning. Now I tried – and failed – to imagine a great king forsaking the Father. How could it have happened? How could the Father have allowed it? And yet evidently it did happen – for the Stories do not lie.

The pages next assumed a historical bent. I met an account of a massacre of the Father's servants in the name of Cybele and her roaring lions; the geographer Strabo's famous discussion of the warlike Harmazans; a dramatic piece evoking Octavian's humiliation by Kleopatra at Actium; extracts from a poem celebrating how the Queen of the Icene put the Old Empire to rout one midsummer's day; and, lastly, excruciate details of the fate of the soldiers of St Peter's captured during the wars against the Forest Queendom.

I was trying not to spend too long on any individual page, for I did not dare neglect the sixth office after everything that had occurred. Nevertheless, I found myself lingering over a letter from a Lagoon merchant. In it, he touched upon reports of certain women of the Indus who – and there I stopped and frankly stared – could transform themselves into birds and trees at will. 'Such tales,' he wrote, 'appear to be an oriental reverberation' – I can't say I cared much for his style – 'of the fashionable fabrications of our more degenerate forebears.'

And at once I remembered asking Sophia why the Curial Court had proscribed Ovid's *Metamorphoses*, an epic that contained no more of love or pagan worship than the *Aeneid*, of which they approved. And she'd told me the Shepherds – it was probably the first time I'd heard that term – believed such tales of change were greatly displeasing to the Father. 'Our Father,' she explained, 'delights in constancy. His power, his glory – it endures, eternal and immutable. Your Ovid, on the other hand, he says we wobble, he says we slip and slide, like the – like the' – she rubbed her fingers together – 'like the sun inside of an egg.'

'The yolk?' I suggested.

'The yolk,' she agreed. 'When he writes of women who change their form to escape the anger of the immortal gods – of flighty Daphne, who became a laurel tree, of proud Arachne who assumed a spider's form – Ovid conceives a world that is inimical to the Father. In the Father's creation, only contemptible things that creep and crawl, only they should shed their skins. Not us. Not people. Not we who the Father made in his own image.'

'But they're just stories,' I said.

'Just stories?' She gave me her most mordant look. 'No such thing, Beatrice.'

Oh, Sophia, I thought, turning over the pages in my hands. What did you know? What did you guess?

After that, but one page remained. It was labelled *Alphabetum Siracidis*.

> Adam and Lilith began to fight.
>
> She said, 'I will not lie below you.'
>
> He said, 'And I will not lie below you, for you belong on the bottom, and I belong on the top.'
>
> Lilith answered, 'We are equal inasmuch as we were both created from the earth.'
>
> But they would not listen to one another.
>
> When Lilith realised this, she spoke the Ineffable Name and flew away into the air.

My scholarly interest in Tomis's ledger had been giving way to restive alarm, but confronted by this exchange, I succumbed to an enfeebling fear. Lilith, of course, is a great and malevolent demon. Her home – No Kingdom There – is an evil place where nothing grows but thistles, furze and thorns. There, goat-demons prowl and buzzards circle. There, Lilith stalks in joy.

I thought of Lilith; of Hecate, of Medusa; of furies, harpies, fates and gorgons; of all the terrible things that bear a woman's face. And then I thought of the old woman at the gate. Those sunken eyes. That black, unforgiving stare.

Telling myself not to be fanciful, I pushed the sheets to one side, fetched the knife from my desk and prised apart the metal case. Inside, I found three squares of rag-paper, rubbed across with charcoal, capturing the shifts and ripples of the graven stone that must have lain beneath. And there, each as large as my hand, were letters from my book. Each square bore a title, written plain – *Glæstyngabyrig*; *Voruta*; *Kleopolis*. The first was unfamiliar, although the agglomeration of squat sounds suggested a connection with Albion. The second, I knew only as a place of rumour, where the Forest Queen does horrible things to naughty girls and naughty boys. The third, I could mark on a map. Kleopolis is the forbidden city of the Upper Nile, the heathen redoubt that neither the Old Empire nor St Peter's ever dared assail.

I had felt safe examining the women's book while its significance stretched no further than the circumference of my candle's flame – a private and personal riddle. But even if I could not trace every connection in Tomis's papers – grasp every hint, follow every lead – I knew I held a compendium of heresy in my hands.

A frenzy seized me then. Stuffing Tomis's unintelligible letter into my pocket, I scooped everything else back into the crate. I ripped the stoppers from bottle after bottle of ink, upending fully a gallon of the stuff over the papers, until nothing but blue-black sodden scraps remained.

Last night, in my dreams, I buried the book beneath the cedar tree, hiding it deep in the earth, only to find myself running like a madwoman around the quadrilango, wielding an axe, hacking down the spiralling shoots of paper that burst between the flagstones. But as I razed each one, lest it betray me, another grew, and another and another, like heads of the Hydra. And all the while, my sisters gathered round me, to laugh or point or jeer, until the shoots grew longer, stronger, greener, and seized me up – and that is when I awoke, sweating sore. Usually, dawn's fingers snap away what thrives in the dark, but something of that dream is with me still – something of drums and darkness and the circling cry of birds.

But now, I tell myself, now for Tomis's letter.

I lay out my scripts, look back and forth – and it doesn't take long to spy a match. Both the addressee at the top and the signature at the bottom start with the symbol ☉, which I find in an alphabet titled *Kartvelia*. Underneath, I have written, somewhat sententiously, *a mountain kingdom lying to the east of the Black Sea*. The symbol ☉ – and, beside it, *T*, for Tiberio, for Tomis – a good beginning. I run my finger up and down, and the ∩ and ♏ reveal themselves to be *I* and *O*. But the other letters? Still they resist.

I pull paper and ink towards me, ready to start the work of unravelling, to mark what I know, what I don't, ready to guess at common combinations, to divine the gaps. Sophia and I, had we not often played these sorts of games? I lift my quill and dip, and in so doing, I catch sight of the letter reflected in the inkwell's silvered side – and thump the table in exultation.

It is a mirror script.

Kartvelian – but backwards.

That hoary trick! I should have seen it sooner.

I rejoice, but only for an instant. I know nothing of this language. But, I ask myself, did my father know any better? I allow myself to doubt it, and apply myself to transliterating the first few words.

T – i – b – e – r – i – o

Yes, as expected.

And then:

kh – a – r – e

I need not say it more than once.

χαῖρε

greetings

My heart crows triumph. The letters are Kartvelian; the language Greek. I am impossibly pleased with myself. A quick glance out of the window, and I start to read.

Tiberio, greetings,

We have crossed the water and prepare to continue south.

You asked me in your letter – I received it from your agent who was indeed expecting us – about my beliefs in this matter. If this answer appears short, do not think I lack faith in your discretion. Rather, the post-rider mounts his horse.

The Father, whom you reverence, desires *imperium sine fine*. Permanence, not change. Eternity, not transformation. I prefer the lines of the blind poet:

Like the generations of leaves, the lives of mortal men.
Now the wind scatters the old leaves across the earth,
now the living timber bursts with the new buds
and spring comes round again.

Your daughter, I must tell you, reads Homer as easily as if she learned it at her mother's knee. Often, I think you would profit from her company, but that is not the way of your people.

I hope to bring them to you by Candlemas, if not before. I have written to Silvia to expect us before Son-Rise. It is a delicate time. The wheel turns. She rises.

In haste,
Tomis

'My goodness, Beatrice, you look cheerful.' My smile warps. Prudenzia has entered the library. My time is up. An hour's dismal letter-writing awaits. 'Don't move,' she says, 'I know where everything's kept.'

The Radix

Immediately thereafter

⌘

Normally, I resent Prudenzia's independence, but now I must be grateful for it. I fold the letter and slip it into my pocket. I tidy my scraps into their box. She, meanwhile, bustles back and forth behind me, finally settling at the desk adjacent to mine, a punctilious trio of pen, ink and paper laid out before her.

'Hello?' I hear a timid voice at the library door. 'I'm sorry, I think I'm a bit early—'

'No, no, come in, come in,' Prudenzia calls.

The novice Alfonsa enters, glancing warily at me, only to look relieved when Prudenzia gestures to the empty stool she has set beside her desk. I always let them stand – quicker that way. It occurs to me that the girl's face, formerly round and ruddy, is drawn and pale, and I wonder whether the Holy Bridegroom will return while they write her letter home. But, no, she is chattering away happily enough.

'. . . and do tell Mamma to make sure she attends Brother Abramo's next sermon, for Sister Arcangela declares it shall be ever so wise and inspiriting. And do beg Papà to please, please write me all about it, his impressions and so on, leaving nothing out – and then, perhaps, perhaps I could read it out to the others. Might I do that, Sister Prudenzia? And – if you don't think it wrong of me – do tell Mamma I am counting off the days until the Vigilate.'

A significant pause. I glance sideways.

Prudenzia is smiling sweetly at her. 'Do you mean—?'

'Yes,' the girl whispers. 'Don't think me presuming, but Sister Arcangela has said in probability I shall be blessed to join the procession.'

I look away. The composition of Arcangela's Vigilate list will provoke incessant speculation in the coming days. The elect few will rejoice in their friends' earnest and envious congratulation, although I have often suspected that taking part in the procession – when the ghostly figures of my sisters radiate through the silent city streets – might, in fact, be something of an ordeal. To re-cross one's childhood threshold, to sit by one's old hearth – but only for an hour – surely that constitutes a consummate cruelty. Three times, Arcangela has written my name on her list. Three times, I have made my excuses, hinting at some lapse that must preclude me. It also gave me pleasure, I admit, to deny my family the honour of welcoming a daughter home at Vigilate. In this one small matter, I was sovereign.

Beside me, Alfonsa is now busy thanking Prudenzia for her help, marvelling over the elegance of her hand, and Prudenzia is saying, yes, yes, she'll make sure Poggio finds a reliable boy to deliver her letter, they'll absolutely have it by noon, it's not far to the Carcere, is it? And the girl is saying she does misgive about Mamma living above the sinners in their cells, and does Prudenzia think sin can perhaps seep upwards, and Prudenzia is saying, well it's a thought, but she's not sure it works like that, and I am wondering whether stuffing my fingers in my ears will serve to block out such nonsense, when they break off. What can have stemmed their flow?

Both, I see, have twisted sideways and are staring out of my window – at Diana, who is crossing the quadrilango. Alfonsa, essaying an air of discreet concern, asks Prudenzia whether it is true that Sister Arcangela is growing very . . . well, she doesn't want to say *angry*, but *angry* is the only word she can think of, that *she* is being allowed to *flaunt* herself about the convent.

'Well, Sister Beatrice, what do you think?' says Prudenzia, and I realise I have failed to conceal my interest in their conversation.

'About what?' I say.

'About *her*, of course.'

'About who?'

'Diana – the paintress.' Prudenzia stands and leans over me, and I remember how, even as a novice, she smelled stale, as though she'd been packed away somewhere damp and airless. 'There' – she is pointing to where Diana is now walking towards the chapel – 'surely you cannot think it right, this commission of hers?'

'She's painting images of holy women, not prostituting herself in the nave,' I snap, and immediately wonder what has possessed me.

'Sister Librarian, Sister Librarian?'

An alarmingly small novice is waving at the door, and my heart sinks. The younger the girl, the longer the letter. Home, mother, the new baby – everything is a recent memory, and they tend to cry when thinking on it.

'Come in,' Prudenzia coos. 'No, no, don't disturb Sister Beatrice. You sit here. Alfonsa and I were just finishing. You take her seat, and we'll write you a lovely—'

But the child is tugging at my mantle. 'Please, Sister Librarian? I'm sent to say you have a visitor. The parlour. If you please, Sister Librarian?'

'Your bookseller again?' says Prudenzia, and I like neither her tone, nor the look she and Alfonsa exchange – nor yet the way they exchange it so openly.

'Oh no,' says the novice, squirming with impatience, 'it is the Widow Stelleri.'

That Ortolana should want to see me is as strange as it is unwelcome. She does visit the convent, true, but only on appointed days, mostly in company, and always attired very fine. So what strikes me first, as I enter the parlour – aside from wishing her away – is how very plain she looks. I have no fluency in the language with which a woman directs her seamstress, but I can say that normally Ortolana's skirts rise up in stiff battlements, glinting embellishments, topped by a veil that is an epic in lace. Today, though, there is little to choose in style between her gown and mine, saving hers is fresh, silken and made to fit.

Don't doubt but that Sister Paola is delighted by her guest. The best chair has been pulled forward. I can see a new log on the fire, although the day is not cold. As I arrive, a second novice, tripping over her too-long hem, is trying to negotiate the door with a covered tray sent over from the cookhouse. But upon seeing me in the doorway, Ortolana stands, clasps Paola's hands, thanks her for her courtesies, begs her to enjoy the refreshments herself, and says she believes she will ask Sister Beatrice to conduct her to the burial ground so she can offer prayers for the two unfortunate women one has heard so much about.

Even for a woman of Ortolana's pedigree, this is highly irregular. Sister Paola opens her mouth – not a pretty sight – to object, but shuts it swiftly as her fingers close around the inducement placed in her palm. Or rather, I presume that's what happened. Ortolana is so skilled in such matters, I didn't see it done. We set off, side by side, in silence.

Once we have left the quadrilango behind, I expect her to stop, to state her purpose – although I cannot fathom what that might be, save only that it is unlikely to be graveside solemnities. But she walks on, her pace quickening, past the cookhouse, past the herb garden, past the fishponds – where Cateline is holding up an eel for Sister Felicitas to inspect – and on along the river. The women we pass observe her curiously, but they seem not to know her, dressed as she is, for none drops the curtsey they might otherwise consider her due. She resembles any ordinary matron of the city, which is all she would be – had she not married my father.

When he was of an age to wed, his father – my grand-father, I suppose I should call him – determined to match him with a foreign principessa – Carthaginian, Occitan, perhaps even Rhinish, if one of the faith could be found. But my father, so I have heard, refused them all, saying he wanted a woman of his city, a gentlewoman of good family, nothing more, for then his neighbours would consider him a friend to be courted, not a dynast to be opposed. Only when the pestilenza took my grandfather's life did my father prevail and take my step-mother to wife. Her triumph, they say, acidulated the grand mammas of the city – for she was full eighteen years on her wedding night and in no wise an acknowledged beauty – and caused the bolsters of their daughters to be wet with jealous tears. But the papàs, the men who sit on the Bench and the Board and forge the course of the city, they often recalled that the Duke Stelleri had not thought himself above them, and so they forgave him more than they might otherwise have done.

When the time came for my father to choose for his son, he must have forgotten his own counsel, for he let my brother bargain for his Neapolitan beauty. And so every mamma in the

145

city said Ludovice was no good, said Bianca was a vain little thing, and Ortolana – who has finally come to a halt – well, let's say they reserved the worst for her.

We have achieved the orchard. Ortolana has wandered from the path towards the apple tree that, come autumn, will bear our sweetest fruit. Its parent, a gift – so the story goes – from Pope Silvio, still stands in Chiara's hill-town. His rival presented her with an edition of the Stories, too beautiful and too cumbersome to read, which sits in our chapel, dusted daily, tethered by a gleaming chain. A few of last year's windfalls lie on the ground, mulched and ugly, and I watch Ortolana poke one with the toe of her boot. Sturdy leather. She has come prepared.

I am used to thinking of her as old, far older than I – her dressed hair, her swooping sleeves, her trailing skirts. I am used, too, to seeing her only in the low light of the chapel or the refectory. She looks different outside, the sun slanting on her face. If she was eighteen when she wed my father, then she must now be little more than forty. Sixteen, seventeen years older than I am? Not old, not truly.

She folds her arms and, without any pretence at preamble, says, 'How came you by this book that has so upset Tomis?'

Not, you can imagine, what I expected. I play for time. 'What book?'

'Beatrice. The book in your pocket.'

'I don't have a—'

'Yes, you do. Your hand went there the moment I named it.'

'Oh.'

'Show it to me.'

'No.'

'I won't try to make off with it.'

'Tomis told you what happened?'

'Everything. He came directly to me after your . . . altercation. Now, will you please—'

'No.'

'Trust me, you do not want this book.'

'You don't know what I want.'

I can see I am trying her patience. Good.

'Do you even know what it is?'

A change in tactics. Brisk plain-dealing is not working, and so now she must belittle me. It will not serve.

'Of course I do,' I say.

'Tomis believes not.'

'Tomis is a coward, hiding behind you, trying to steal something that is not his—'

'No, Beatrice. Tomis is a very dear, very frightened young man who is trying – desperately – to stop a Radix falling into the hands of Brother Abramo and the Shepherds.' She pauses, assessing. 'But you have no idea what a Radix is – do you?' She shakes her head. 'After all, how could you? This is too deep a matter for you, Beatrice. You need to give it to me. Please. Now.'

'Radix? You would call this book a Radix?'

'A Radix,' she affirms.

Radix. *Root*, in Latin. I picture how the roots of the cedar tree buckle the flagstones of the quadrilango. *Radix*. I like the name.

'All right,' I say. 'You can call it that. What else do you know?'

'I will tell you everything, Beatrice, everything.' She steps forwards, puts a hand out. 'But only once you have given it to me.'

I take a step backwards. 'No. First tell me, and then I might – *might* – give it to you.'

She advances. 'Might, might? What is this might?'

'It all depends on what you tell me.' I smile. I can see she is growing angry. Good, again. It is years since I have been able to upset her temper.

'You are impossible,' she says.

I shrug. 'Why should I be easy?'

'You cannot see it, can you?' Almost melancholy, she sounds, but soon enough, she rallies to the attack. 'You – you absolutely refuse to see that I am trying – trying really very hard – to help you.'

Those words, their superior tone, provoke me dreadfully. Blood, hotter than I am accustomed to, rushes to my head. '*You?*' I splutter. 'Trying to help *me?* You – you have never helped me. *Never.*'

'But how can you say that? I have always, *always*—'

'You kept me from my father. You made him shut me away.' She is trying to speak, but I shout her down. 'You did – you did – don't deny it!'

I am jabbing a finger at her, but she slaps my hand away, says: 'Your arrogance and self-pity have always made poor bedfellows. You think I conspired to send you here?' She throws her head back and laughs. No, not a laugh. It is a sound more unbridled, a caw, a hoot. I am stung.

'You did,' I counter. 'You know you did. You deprived me of everything – everything.'

'You insist this – your life – this is hardship? Such bitterness is ugly, Beatrice. Ugly.'

My hand flies to my cheek, covering the place where the warped skin pulls my left eye awry.

'Oh, Beatrice,' she says, starting towards me. 'Forgive me, you are not ugly, only—'

'Damaged,' I say, turning aside, hating the word, hating that the word should hurt me.

For a moment, we are silent. We are both remembering the same day. A long-ago morning, when I was eight and my brother was four. I was different then. Strong, sturdy, plump. He was sickly – cosseted. I wasn't meant to play with him, not the rough games I favoured, but he always sought me out. He liked the games I invented for us. We were wolves, chasing chickens. We were bears, eating honey. That day, we were eagles, flying down the kitchen stairs.

He fell – always, he fell – and twisted his foot. He cried and cried and cried. Ortolana swooped down on us. She was angry, angrier than usual. He was supposed to be resting after his fever. I was old enough to know better. When was I going to learn any sense? I knew I was about to be grabbed, slapped, sent to my room, and so I ran away from her, my arms wide, an eagle still. I flew through the kitchen, skidded, tripped – and upended the stockpot, just as it had come to the boil.

That night, I heard the nursemaids whispering outside my door. They must have thought I was asleep, but my blistering skin screamed in the darkness.

'The physician told them she was lucky not to lose that eye.'

'She was never exactly a pretty thing, but nobody'll want her now.'

'Whatever will the poor duke do?'

I didn't hear the rest. I pulled my blankets over my head.

But now, Ortolana surprises me. She steps forwards. I flinch away, but she proceeds regardless. She takes my hands. An undeniable grip.

'Forgive me,' she says, 'I misspoke. I do not blame you for your arrogance. Rather, I should rejoice in it. It was always your father's chiefest vice.'

I look up. Say sweetly, 'I thought my mother was.'

She releases my hands. 'That tongue's still sharp, I see.' But her manner alters suddenly and her eyes, now narrowed, fix on something over my shoulder. I am about to turn to see what could have captured her attention, but she shakes her head without shifting her gaze.

'Don't stare. It's one of Arcangela's underlings. What do you call them? Wardens.'

'What's she—?'

'Watching us. Showing us we are watched. Wondering whether she has the authority to bid me to leave.' She glances now at me. 'You're worried. Good. I see you have some understanding after all. Move a little to your left. Ah, she retreats. She has thought better of confronting me. For now. Beatrice' – she draws breath, puts up a hand as though to take my arm, but lets it fall without touching me – 'we do not have time to argue. To fence. Much as you enjoy it—'

'I do not—'

'Beatrice, please. You want to know about this Radix? Then, for once, put all else aside and listen.' Without waiting for a reply, she returns to the path and heads right towards the mountain, away from the convent. I hold still – I resent the presumption that I'll follow – but after she has taken a dozen steps I hasten to fall in beside her.

'In matters of trade and statecraft,' she begins, 'your father was a clever man. Prudent. All but impossible to gull. But touching arcane knowledge – lost scrolls, rare manuscripts – he was the veriest lamb.' She looks sideways at me. 'All the dealers knew he had gold enough to slake his thirst. And if some of the books he acquired were heterodox – what of it? He feared neither the Shepherds of the church nor the Proctors of the city. I remember him saying – quite openly – that Apollo could not have been nothing, but it was very disagreeable to believe him a devil.' She looks at me again, perhaps to see whether I am shocked. I find I am not. 'I told him to mind who heard him – but he was right. He was untouchable to the end.'

There is a crack to her voice, which I recognise as the upwelling of grief. Did she love my father? I had never even considered it a possibility. For a time, we walk on in silence. We are now skirting the edges of Hildegard's fields, and I envy her boots. My own sandals are clogging with mud.

'His final obsession—' She starts, stops, chews her lip — she who always knows what to say. Intrigued, I wait. Finally, she says, 'Which Rule did the Father write first?'

'We are to play at catechism?' I am surprised — disappointed, even. But I catch her eye, and relent. 'Rule one,' I say. 'No gods before me.'

'Yes. The first Rule — the one from which the others grow. And yet — and yet — men have always worshipped — do still worship — other gods. We, though, the faithful — we know such men are wrong. We know what they reverence is make-believe, phantasm, chimera. We know their gods are not real — only the Father and his Son. We know that, don't we, Beatrice?'

I nod. We do.

'Well, your father suspected otherwise. He thought — he came to think — that even if a god was no longer worshipped — his shrines destroyed, his followers annihilated — yet still he might exist.' She stops again. 'He, that is — or *she*. That is what interested him. *Who* interested him. She. The Mother.'

I am, you can be sure, utterly bewildered. One thing I know about my stepmother is that she is careful. And this is not careful. This — this is deranged.

'Have I finally said something worthy of your attention, Beatrice?' she says, smiling broadly. 'No, no' — she's actually laughing — 'don't try to deny it.'

In the distance, the bell sounds, and immediately I am in a quandary. I meant to arrive early for every office, but we are now some distance from the chapel. I could take off running

151

– but I'd arrive late and flustered, making myself more conspicuous, not less.

'What is it, Beatrice?' says my stepmother, more gently now. 'Have I unsettled you?'

'No, no,' I say. 'Well, yes – but that is not it. Your visit, you see – I shall miss the fourth office.'

'Surely you are too grand now, Sister Librarian, for reprimands?'

I am about to disabuse her, but already she is correcting herself.

'Ah, no, I see, you fear Arcangela, is that it? She is watching you – your library? She couldn't wrest control of it from Sophia, but now she seeks to undermine you?'

I am – I admit – impressed. That is exactly what I fear, and it is a comfort to hear it expressed with such clarity by somebody else. I don't say that, though – only, 'Yes.'

She puts a hand on my shoulder. 'But you want to hear me out?'

'Yes,' I say again.

'Very well. If there's trouble, blame me – vociferously. Say I dragged you here and would not suffer you to depart. Condemn me all you like. All right?'

I nod, and she talks while we continue towards the meadow.

'I didn't know how far your father had travelled down this dangerous road until shortly before his death. He came rushing into my chamber, very excited, waving a letter from Tomis in some code they'd dreamed up. He was writing from' – she trips slightly over a strange word – 'from Northwich. You know where that is?'

'It's – is it the principal city of Albion?'

'Exactly. Your father strode about, shutting doors, checking closets, making certain none of my women could hear. And then he said, "A Radix, Lana. I believe he's found one at last."'

'And did you' — I realise I begrudge such intimacy — 'did you know what that meant?'

'Did I know?!' My stepmother raises her eyes to the heavens. 'For months, he'd been following leads. Secret messages from a veteran of the Forest Wars, secret meetings with an exile from Kleopolis — but they'd all come to nothing. Then to receive a letter — from Albion itself — well, you can imagine his reaction.'

She gives me a keen look and I make an equivocal gesture. I know less about Albion than I care to admit.

'Their last king,' she says, 'was a great defender of the faith, but he died — suddenly. You remember?'

I nod. 'A hunting accident. Something — gored him?'

'Exactly. St Peter's expected his barons to form a regency until his son came of age, but then the Queen Ana, his widow, seized power. She expelled Pope Silvio's emissaries and threatened to impale any Shepherd found on her island. And to what did the church fathers attribute this defiance? Why, to a cult of Mother worshippers — they said she'd been bewitched. I thought it a clumsy calumny, but Tomis told your father it was true — every word! That was too much for me. I grew angry, and begged him to burn the letter, to direct his energies elsewhere — but he refused to listen. As a man of philosophy — he loved to call himself that! — he said it was his duty to investigate the — how did he put it? — the *ontologia* of the Mother. "You might as well convert," I said. He laughed and said he could hardly worship a woman, could he? "Why not?" I told him. "I worship a man." He laughed some more, as though I'd made an excellent joke.'

We are now approaching the meadow where the women lie buried. Slender bramble stems are already breaking the earth above their graves. Above us, I can hear Marta whistling — her goats followed her down off the mountain. Hildegard loathes them, threatening a grisly end to any mischievous creature whose hoof so much as touches her fields. Marta, however, is mistress of her calling. The goats are grazing well away from the ploughing, their bells a merry counterpoint to the solemnity of our own. Ortolana settles herself on one of the larger pieces of rock that lie scattered about the meadow, and gestures for me to sit beside her.

'But what,' I ask, frowning, 'what took Tomis to Albion? They have no trade in books, in antiquities, only' – I am guessing – 'trees and sheep.'

'Good question. And a strange answer. Silvia sent him.'

'*Silvia?*' I repeat in surprise, but then I remember Diana's question. What business could Tomis have with the pontifex's daughter?

'Herself. She had written to the queen – likely on her father's behalf; he has always placed a great deal of trust in her – asking what led her to renounce the authority of St Peter's. The answer Ana gave must have intrigued Silvia, for they began to correspond – in great secret. Finally, so Tomis told your father, the queen offered to send Silvia a book to open her eyes – a book and two women—'

'Two women!'

'Yes, Beatrice, your two women. Tomis said their names were Janna and Madinia, a mother and daughter from Albion's west. He likened them to apostles, to Peter and to Paul. He said they would tell Silvia the story of the Mother, with such proofs and powers as they possessed. I told your father he was insane to entertain such lunacy, but he said knowledge trumped all. He replied to Tomis, offering an absurd sum for sight of the book, for a chance to talk to the women – money, yes, and an armed escort south to St Peter's.

He was more excited than I'd seen him for years.' She pauses. Her face has softened, but of course I know what follows. 'But then he – he died.'

'I'm sorry,' I find myself saying. 'It must have been hard.'

'Thank you, Beatrice,' she says. 'It was. He died – and in my grief I forgot all about Albion and women and books – until I found Tomis shivering in my chamber after the Fat Tuesday feast. He was in a terrible state, but I, as you know, had good news for him. I told him the women had somehow made their way—'

'Here,' I finish. 'I see.' I stand and move a little apart.

She thinks she has won me round. She will ask for the book again – expect me to hand it over. But it's not that simple. She knows much. But I know more. The book – I do not think she even begins to grasp its power. She thinks it akin to the Stories. Rules and sayings and histories and genealogies. She has no idea what the book can do – what the book has done.

I am right. She is rising, approaching me, her hands palm up, appealing. 'Surely, Beatrice, I have told you enough. Surely, you understand Brother Abramo is not here by chance. He knows something of the book, of that I am certain, and he suspects it is here, in this convent. He suspects Mother Chiara of withholding it—'

'How do you know?'

'How do I know? *How do I know?* Honestly, how do you think I spend my days?'

I have no idea, beyond my imagination's rough daub of complicated dances and dull-eyed fish on silver platters.

'I talk to people, Beatrice. *I talk.*'

'Gossip,' I say, and at once regret it, so withering is her look.

'I had thought you better than that. Men say *gossip* to slight the words of women. Men have their channels. I have mine.

Women hear – and they talk – often for no more reward than the gift of being heard.'

I drop my gaze, chastened. 'Very well,' I say, 'so Brother Abramo is suspicious. But in the end – what can he do? He has no authority here—'

'You sound like your brother. He, too, refuses to take him seriously. He attended this week's sermon in disguise – laughed about it afterwards with his friends. Acted out impressions which I fear he will come to regret—'

'So? What of it? Let Abramo denounce him. Everyone knows what sort of man he is.' I speak to wound, but she does not flinch. 'But how can he accuse Chiara? She's – she's *Chiara*. She raised children from the dead. The pontifex bathed her feet. She's—'

Ortolana throws her hands up in exasperation. 'She's his rival, Beatrice. His *rival*, do you not see? On Grey Wednesday, after she denied him entry, he applied directly to the Bench and the Board, to the Office of the Archbishop, seeking urgent admittance. Believe me, it took every last shred of my influence to thwart him. You are safe – for now. But I do not know how much longer I can protect—'

Quick as light and shade, her face alters. Her right hand goes up in a wave. I spin round. Arcangela is not above a dozen paces away, approaching fast. Ortolana must have been able to see her. I am flustered, anticipating trouble for having strayed so far, but my stepmother greets her seamlessly, taking her arm, drawing her aside, her manner confidential, girlishly confiding:

'Ah, the very woman I need. Can you help me? Sister Beatrice sent word that she has finished the prayerbook for my much-anticipated grandchild – but now she tells me she is not happy with it. She has it with her, tucked in that pocket of hers, but she refuses – absolutely refuses! – to part with it. I have every faith that you will be able to persuade her.'

I am cornered – outmanoeuvred – acutely aware that any protest will draw attention to the book. I hate her – *hate* her. Worse still, I had – almost – started to like her.

Arcangela sighs, says, 'Beatrice, I have business with the Widow Stelleri that cannot wait. Please give her the book.'

'But—'

'Beatrice. Do as we ask. The book is not yours to keep, it is yours to give. Such perfectionism, I must say, smacks of a most unworthy pride.'

Again, Ortolana touches Arcangela's arm. 'She is so stubborn, Arcangela, is she not? I am wonderfully grateful for your support.'

My stepmother holds out her hand to me.

'Beatrice,' says Arcangela, 'do not make me ask again.'

I give it up. She turns it over, runs her finger down the velvet, murmurs, 'Ah, the Stelleri red, so thoughtful,' and then it vanishes inside her cloak. She takes Arcangela's arm and walks away, saying, 'It has been too long, my dear—'

But I, trailing behind, am so foul with rage – seething with wild plans as to how I can stop her leaving – that I do not at first attend them. Only when we are nearing the infirmary does some shift in Arcangela's inflection make me listen.

'Now,' she says, 'I really must tell you that while you were enjoying your visit with Sister Beatrice, your escort sent into the parlour to ask that you be found.'

'Oh, indeed? You see how it is – the cares of my household follow me even here.'

'It appears to be a most serious matter.'

'Dear me, dear me. How vexing. Well, I had better await their report, had I not?'

Arcangela knows and is yearning to tell, that is plain. But whatever the news may be, Ortolana does not want to hear it from her, for immediately she diverts the conversation. As we retrace our steps, she discourses brightly upon the blessings of the Forty-Day Fast, the clarity it confers, the greater depth of one's prayers, topics from which Arcangela cannot, in all conscience, deviate.

It is only when we are back within the quadrilango, almost at the parlour door itself, that Arcangela takes Ortolana's arm and says, 'Before we part, remember that we are always here for you, should you need us. I fear' – she lowers her voice – 'that your son has been hunting—'

'Young men! They are such a trial.' Ortolana is shaking her head, the indulgent mamma, but I fancy I detect a tightening in her throat. 'We beg them to hawk less, to curb their passion for the races, and as for their obsession with their ball-game—'

She is trying to part company, but Arcangela is determined to finish. 'Hunting, yes, which is ill-advised, but after all, no sin. No – what I understand the city is most upset about, what your escort most urgently desired to report to you, is that he, in this, the first week of the Fast' – she leans closer, enunciates with cutting clarity – 'ate the flesh of his quarry.' Arcangela leaves a little pause, which my stepmother does not fill. 'At this precious time, when all men and women of the faith practise holy abstinence – a little, a very little sacrifice on all our parts, in memory of that greatest sacrifice of all. And for your son to flout it so! Such a grave insult to the authority of the Father. Such unfeeling disregard for the suffering of the Son. One would almost think that Ludovice Stelleri was taught to think himself above the laws that bind other men.' She lays a hand upon my stepmother's arm. 'I am sorry to have been the bearer of such bad tidings. If you will allow me to make a suggestion? Your son should hasten to the basilica and there do public penance. Thus the people might yet be appeased, otherwise I fear his reputation for – ah – a certain faithlessness will count against him, especially now, that Brother Abramo has opened all hearts to the Father.'

'Thank you, sister, for laying out the ramifications for me so clearly,' says Ortolana, holding herself very still. 'Your grasp of affairs without your walls remains acute.'

'I would hate for the sins of the son to redound upon the mother's head,' replies Arcangela, gazing sorrowfully at my stepmother, and I am wondering how Ortolana can bear it, this condescending compassion, until I remember that I have no reason to pity her – that I despise her, that once again she has stolen from me.

But now Chiara, too, is hurrying towards us. Dispensing with any preliminaries, she removes Ortolana from Arcangela's gossamer grip and says, 'I've had word. I'm so sorry. It will go ill in the city, will it not?'

My stepmother – despite everything, I cannot fault her composure – nods. 'It will. Very. Thank you, Mother Chiara, but I must go. Sister Arcangela, you've been too kind.' She kisses Chiara's hands, Arcangela's cheeks – whereupon she turns to me. 'Pray for your brother, dear Beatrice.' And I realise, too late, that she intends to embrace me as well.

Her hand closes about my arm, so I cannot think to pull away. Her lips touch first my unscathed cheek, and then the other. Two words she whispers into my astonished ears. She releases me and passes into the parlour. I watch her go, my hands now folded once more around my book, which she pressed to my belly while she held me tight. The words she spoke: 'Safer – here.'

The Cedar Tree

Sunday evening

IT IS THE FATHER'S DAY, the short hour between the sixth office and the seventh, which in the darker months we pass in private prayer in our cells. Often, I struggle to pray alone. Often, I feel I am slipping downhill on the scree of baser thoughts, while my sisters ascend higher, ever higher, towards the Son's embrace. But tonight, I do not feel alone. Tonight, every one of us – I'd wager even Arcangela herself – is struggling to pray as she ought.

The evening should be quiet. The Father's peace should reign. Yet all afternoon, the relentless rumble of civil ferment has been rising from the city, and we are all afraid.

During our evening meal, noises testament to riotous unrest grew so loud that they could even be heard – dim but menacing – from inside the refectory. Alfonsa, who stumbles over the thornier passages of the Stories of the Father at the best of times, was growing more and more anxious, pausing after every third word to stare helplessly about her. My sisters listened, distracted, spoons suspended between bowl and mouth, wondering was the violence yet far off, or did it advance upon our walls. With each surge of sound, I found my soup, eagerly awaited, growing less and less palatable.

Chiara, Maria and Hildegard quietly took themselves outside, presumably to survey the campo and the outskirts of the city. While they were gone, Arcangela – having taken her customary ten sips of soup before putting her bowl aside – continued to listen, as though rapt, to Alfonsa's miserable tussle with Deuteronomy. Following the unignorable blast of a cannon, several of my sisters started to their feet, but Arcangela frowned and indicated they should resume their seats.

Sister Felicitas was hovering, reluctant to clear when so little had been eaten, but aware the bell for the sixth office was not far off. Finally, she sent her girls scurrying up and down the tables, some stacking the bowls, others tossing spoons into basins, whereat Arcangela stood and thanked Alfonsa, complimenting her much-improved diction. At this point, Chiara returned, and everyone stopped what they were doing to listen.

'Dear sisters,' she began. 'There does seem to be some trouble down in the city, but nobody is to be afraid. We shall be quite safe here.'

Those words, uttered with calm certainty, were enough to reassure all but the most fearful, and we proceeded in better heart to the chapel, where the thick stone walls did something to dampen the noise. And yet now, confined to our cells for this period of solitary devotion, the shouts and screams, the clang of bells, still carry from across the city.

My door is open. A warden has been walking up and down the corridor. She passes once more, her pace quickening, and I hear her talking urgently to somebody on the stairs. Perhaps there is some news. I rise softly to my feet, to move a little closer, to hear a little better.

'Beatrice.'

A curt reproof. She has spied me lurking at the door. Reluctantly, I sink back to my knees. I can hear the whispered prayers of my sisters in the cells upon either side. Louder than usual, they sound, and more urgent. They are right to be afraid. Everyone knows what happens to convents – to the women in convents – in times of chaos. The whispering grows louder. Almost, it seems my sisters are crouched behind me in the darkness. Almost, I can feel their breath on my—

I turn around.

My cell. Dark. Empty. It is not my sisters. I can admit that now. It is the voice of the book. It is – agitated. Something moves it. Something moves. Yesterday, after Ortolana left, I hid it in the cavity behind the loosened bricks, but now I long to take it up. To see it stir and wake. But I cannot – the wardens, the wardens. I close my eyes. I run my fingers back and forth over the stones beneath me, the cold stones, and I fall to thinking of my brother.

I try to imagine what hubris set him on his foolhardy course – but wasn't he always easily led? I have never met the man, but I remember the boy well enough: how readily he acquiesced to all my schemes; how poorly he acquitted himself when the need arose to conceal our childish purposes from adult eyes; how quickly he traduced me if those plans went awry.

Yesterday afternoon, as news of his transgression sped about the convent, I had found myself the object of much unwelcome interest. The bolder of my sisters even presumed to climb the library stairs and peer inside – although, honestly, to what end? Did they expect to find me slavering over a haunch of venison? But as for my thoughts – they, I fear, were at least as wicked as my brother's deeds.

The Mother. In a reverie, I'd shaped her name in my mind. Would the Father's retribution swiftly follow? No boils bloated my fingers. No frogs hopped across my desk. *The Mother.* I formed her name with my lips. A thundering!

No – not the Father's wrath, but Diana charging up the library stairs.

'Ho, Beatrice.' She poked her head around the door, waving the *Libellus* I had lent her. 'Want this back? Want to come and see how I'm getting on?'

'Won't I disturb you?'

'Wouldn't ask if you would.'

When she parted the drapes screening the side chapel, I saw an extraordinary thing upon the wall. A man lay slumped on a bedstead, a cup of wine spilled on the floor. A woman, knife in hand, leaned over him. He was only a rough outline, a sketch, an impression of neck and shoulders. But she had form, expression. And her face – her face was *mine*, and yet not as I had ever imagined myself. I looked strong; intimidating.

'D'you like it?' said Diana. 'It's just the underdrawing, but' – she stood, assessing – 'I've made worse starts. Judith – she would've had to've been pretty fierce to saw off a man's head.'

I didn't know what to say, and so was relieved when Tamara fought her way through the drapes. 'Oh, hello, Beatrice,' she said. 'Hey' – she was pointing at the picture – 'nice one of Sister Librarian. When you going to do me?'

Diana pointed at the empty space. 'Don't worry. You'll all get a turn.'

'Oooh,' said Tamara. 'Who'll Arcangela be?'

'Mother-Mary ascending into heaven,' I said quickly, before I could think better of it. I saw Diana grin to herself and heard Tamara emit the snorting and gulping that has always been her way of laughing.

'Ugh,' she said. 'Imagine having *her* as your mother?' She removed her head-cloth and ran her hands through her short, bristly hair, standing it on end. 'Have you got one, Di?'

'Got one what?'

'Mother.'

'Mmm. Yes.' She was considering her picture – adjusting the angle of Judith's knife.

'Where is she?'

'St Peter's. Minding my brothers and sisters. She doesn't much like me.'

Tamara caught my eye, made a face. 'Jealous, is she?'

Diana frowned, looked round. 'What makes you say that?'

'Well – there's you, being you. And your Pa teaching you to paint. And she's up to here' – she levels a hand against her oddly delicate eyebrows – 'in children. Who wouldn't be jealous? Now, I was always jealous of Beatrice here' – she points – 'me being a ruffian off the ships and her so high and very mighty—'

'That's not fair,' I said. Suddenly everything felt sour.

'Suit yourself, Sister Beatrice.' She elbowed me in the ribs. 'You always did, right?'

'Hey!' Diana aimed an only halfway friendly kick at Tamara. 'Leave her be. And don't you run off, Beà.' I had indeed been about to go. 'Tamara's got report of what's going on down in the city.'

And with that, Tamara – whose moneychanger, it turns out, is a garrulous source of news – painted her own grim scene. Abramo's men, so he told her, had been rounding up penitents – women mostly – dressing them in burlap, shaving their heads, hanging placards from their necks, saying jezebel, babylonia, whore. Come Saturday morning, the Lambs were marching them round the basilica.

'And that, Sister Librarian, was when your brother and his gang of idiots, drunk from the night before, thought it would be a good idea to go a-galloping through the streets, waving their bows in the air and belting out psalms. Apparently, a bunch of Lambs followed them. And what did they find? Only your brother sitting pretty in a forest glade, a dripping dead hind strung up, and him stuffing his face. The city's up in arms, and Enzo says worse'll follow come the Father's day. Brother Abramo's going to preach, which'll be like poking a wasp's nest with—'

Now, the uncompromising retort of an arquebus – not near and yet not nearly far enough – startles me in my cell. Tamara's moneychanger was right. Whatever Brother Abramo thundered from the pulpit this afternoon, he has set the city aflame.

Again, the warden approaches my cell, and I hear her take a step or two inside. She lifts her lantern a little higher. My shadow fills, billowing before me. I am where I should be, on my knees, at prayer. She withdraws; my shadow fades. The whispering grows louder still. Whispering – and a skittering, a scratching – as though some creature possessed of sharp claws were fighting to escape. The bell clamours for the seventh office and I scramble to my feet, pressing my back against the wall. I watch the dark shapes of my sisters file past, down the corridor, down the stairs, out into the night.

'Beatrice, Beatrice.' The warden is at my door, lantern aloft. 'Beatrice, hurry up now.'

She stands aside and watches me leave, following me down to the quadrilango, which flickers in the light of many braziers. Sisters, novices, safekeeps, all should be making for the chapel, but the smell of smoke and the sight of flames reflected against the clouded sky has turned all to muddle and confusion. The warden hangs her lantern on its hook and hurries to admonish a knot of frightened girls who have frozen by the fountain, marbled versions of their daytime selves.

I take my chance.

The lantern is in my hands, and I am rushing back up the stairs, back to my cell. I close the door and stand a moment, still and listening. Has anyone followed? No. Nobody. No footsteps. Only the whispering, which has assumed a different character. It is harsher, more menacing. The lantern is on the floor, and I am on my knees, working the bricks free, fumbling for my book. Blood, hot in my ears; breath, loud in my throat. The book is in my hands. The book is—

open. The brambles have ripened with berries, plump and purple. The chestnuts have split. Through each scission, brown nuts gleam. And over the page: a new image.

It is wild, erratic, formless. I turn the book, this way, that way, trying to impose sense, to make meaning. What am I looking at? A streaking bewilderment of brushstrokes, splaying outwards from a dark, dark centre. It is dizzying, vertiginous. I—

I wrench my eyes away. Steady – I steady myself.

Slowly, carefully, I look back.

Now, I see it.

The lines are feathers – flared pinions – and the curve of empty talons. The centre – a raptor's unrelenting eye. It is a bird, a great bird, seen from below, a bird in a storm, a bird whirling under angry clouds. It is happening. It is happening again. Somebody else has—

A loud cry outside, followed by answering shouts. Alarmed, I cram the book back into its hiding place, wedge in the bricks and run to the window, fearing that I am missed. But I am being absurd. Nobody is thinking of me. My sisters are crowding beneath the walls, seventh office abandoned. I hasten down and hear Hildegard's voice calling from atop the parlour vantage.

'Some ladies – they do come!'

From the midst of the press of women, I hear Chiara ask, 'Who is coming? Who?'

Arcangela, lantern in hand, is pushing forwards. Normally, my sisters fall back before her, but tonight she must elbow them from her path. She seizes Chiara's arm, tries to lead her away, to talk more privately, perhaps more frankly, but our Mother Superior will not be moved. The lantern's light reveals Chiara's dislike, manifest on her face. She points one finger at Arcangela, then slashes it sideways: no, enough.

'Hildegard!' Chiara shouts once more. 'Come down, come down – help Poggio open up.'

My sisters forsake discipline and surge towards the gate which, once unbarred, reveals shadowy figures, some two dozen, maybe more, thronging the campo outside. Already they are hurrying inside, their tearful voices crying out against the wildness that has gripped the city. The woman last to enter clutches at Hildegard as though otherwise she might fall.

'Ah, but it's good to see your face. That man! What's to become of us? They've torched it. They've torched my lady's house. We saw it behind us as we ran. Burning, burning.' Her face crumples, and – but I know her! It is the cook from home. I ransack my memory for her name—

'Benedetta!'

'Why, if it isn't Beatrice – Sister Beatrice, I should say!' At once she is embracing me. 'Well, I never, well I never, well I never.' But before I can ask her anything, she is tugging on Hildegard's arm, begging her not to shut the gate. 'Wait, wait! We've tried to hurry the poor lass along, but she's that far gone, she can't move any faster—'

And from the campo comes an almost inhuman wail.

'Hah,' grunts Hildegard. 'What a time to choose.' She disappears into the darkness, calling out, 'Take heart, take heart, I come, I come.'

When she returns, she is flanked by a pair of sturdy women, with one other, slighter, bundled in her arms. She strides past us, yelling, 'Agatha? Agatha? This one's not got long to go.'

The wail redoubles in volume. Benedetta and the other two cross themselves, kiss their knuckles, hurry after. Only then do I realise the bundle is Bianca, and her baby is on its way.

Alone now by the gate, I must contend with a strange and sudden shame. Once, I might have wished to see Bianca humbled – to see her approaching our gate in need. But now the moment is come? It tastes bitter as hyssop in my mouth. Once, too, I might have wished my stepmother—

But Ortolana. Where – is she? Where are you?

Where?

I career around the quadrilango. My sisters are hard at work – running for blankets, adding fuel to the braziers – one holding a bawling infant, another settling a tottering grand-mother. Each little group, I approach in turn, but I cannot find her. I hasten towards the guesthouse, whence Bianca's cries are clearly to be heard, and meet Benedetta coming the other way. She is smiling, happier, saying, 'Well, she's in good hands now, praise be. Sister Agatha and dear Mother Chiara will see—'

'Benedetta, Benedetta. The Lady Ortolana – is she with Bianca?'

'Why no, child, she—'

But already I am running back across the quadrilango – out through the gate and into the campo. I have travelled a hundred paces, two hundred, when I stop short. What in the name of the Father am I doing?

'Beatrice, Beatrice.' Hildegard has followed me, has hold of me. 'What is this?'

'The women – the women – Ortolana isn't with them—'

'It's not safe out here,' she is saying, tugging me back towards the gate.

'But she's out there – and he's burned my house – and – and—'

'Hush, hush. Listen, listen. She's an able woman, your step-mamma. She'll be safe—'

And now Benedetta appears at my other side, taking my hand, adding her voice to Hildegard's. 'Yes, yes – don't you go fearing for her. She wanted to get that brother of yours away, that's all. She could hardly bring him here, could she? She has our guards by her and they're good men. She'll be safe, don't you fear.'

I try to nod, to disentangle myself, but she keeps hold of my hand.

'You're upset,' she says.

'I'm fine, really,' I reply.

'No,' says Benedetta, refusing to release me. 'You're not. My word' – an aside to Hildegard – 'she hasn't changed a bit. You, young Beatrice, you never would admit when you were hurt. Now, come and sit by me. No, no – I'm not discussing it.'

Unable – or unwilling – to resist, I am led to where her friends are gathered beneath the cedar tree. She names them – women who work in the Stelleri house or live in the streets nearby. One or two have children clutching at their knees, twining bits of skirt round fingers and thumb. Somebody makes room for us on a bench. Benedetta keeps an arm about me, rubs my back. The women, I realise, are complaining unrestrainedly.

'—acting like they own the place, when our street is none but pious houses—'

'—boys that don't reach my chin, knocking on my door, asking me—'

'—what we're eating—'

'—what we're reading—'

'— what we're wearing—'

'—and if we argue, they set up shouting—'

'—we come in the name of the Father—'

'—as if we have stuffed peahen in the pantry—'

'—or any book other than the Stories and the *Libellus*—'

To which Benedetta calls out, 'This one here wrote that! She's the one I told you about. No taller than a goat and sat there on my kitchen table reading aloud from my ricordanza. Baffled it all out all by herself. She'd write my lists for me – and read us the Stories when we had a thousand and one beans to pod.'

The others start to exclaim over me, and it feels – oh, but it feels wonderful. I am back there, in the kitchen. The rattle of the beans. The stockpot bubbling. Benedetta slipping me spoonfuls of honey cream. Sitting this close to her, I can breathe in her flour-and-butter smell, and I almost feel a child again.

Sister Timofea, I see, is now bustling towards us, saying she's sent the novices to room with the boarders, and you ladies are to go and make yourselves comfortable for the night. Why bless you, they tell her, we don't want to make work for you, we'll sleep here, we've blankets, it's a mild night. But Timofea says she won't hear of it, and they're to run along before she gets cross.

The others stand, grumbling a little as they gather bags, children, shawls. Benedetta touches my arm. 'I missed you, Beà. You promised me you'd write, but you never did. I told myself you were busy, and then we started to hear of you taken up in the library. Our lady couldn't have been prouder. She gave us all one of your books. My Matteo reads it to me. Coming, coming,' she calls, and, with a last squeeze of my hand, she hurries after her friends.

I remain where I am. A faint shout and an answering cry rise above the city, but the turbulence is otherwise much abated. Dark shapes are exiting the chapel – Arcangela and her intimates evidently refused to forgo the seventh office.

Now the wardens are fanning out, bidding everyone return to their cells, to sleep until the night watch. The quadrilango empties. The braziers's light dwindles. I do not move.

I can hear something – something coming from the other side of the tree. A whispering in the branches that is not the wind. I summon what courage I have and edge around the trunk, which is so broad that some four of my sisters would need to join hands to circle it. Above me now, almost within reach of my outstretched hand, one long, low branch stretches towards the walls. It is from there that the whispering comes. I creep forwards, feeling my way along the branch. As I approach, the whispering becomes words, words spoken in a voice that cracks and croaks. The sounds are familiar. Fractured and disjointed they might be, but I have heard them before. Five nights ago. In the infirmary. I compel myself to advance the final steps.

Something, someone, is huddled on the branch. I put a hand up, and feel a body's warmth. A limb, I think, an arm or leg: soft, slight. A woman's. At my touch, it jerks away. I hear a low moan and the sound of slipping, sliding. I move to catch her, or at least to break her fall, and I do at least partly succeed, for when we crumple to the ground, I am underneath. I am jarred, but not nearly as winded as I might expect. She twitches and quivers, her legs kicking a little on the ground. I find myself stroking her hair, murmuring, 'Shhhh, ssshhhhh.'

Voices, footsteps – I stiffen. Two women, walking slowly, murmuring. Their tread starts and stops, but they are definitely coming this way. I am sitting awkwardly, trying to support the woman's body, willing her to remain silent. The faint glow of a lantern spills around the tree.

A happy exclamation: 'That's it, sister!'
'Shhh.'

'Sorry.' A husky whisper. 'We thought we'd lost her. My littlest can't settle without her Bambolina. Thank you, sister. She's been crying so hard I thought she'd . . .'

Her voice fades. Their footsteps retreat. Sharply, I exhale.

I drag the woman backwards, as gently as I am able, and prop her against the tree, my hands lingering on the strange cloak she wears about her shoulders. I feel – I feel – a hunched mass of feathers, as though she wore a costume, a priceless carnival disguise. Kneeling now before her, I try to speak some quiet words of comfort and encouragement. I try to raise her head, which is slumped forwards on her chest. I am starting to wonder what in the name of the Father I should do next, when her hands jerk upwards and seize my wrists. The grip is tight. Sharp nails press into my skin. And out of the darkness, harsh and cracked, speaking words that are no words, comes my stepmother's voice.

The Son

Deep middle night

⚓

WE SAT THERE for a long time.

Slowly, she softened into my arms, and I felt her assume a heavier weight, as though what I held at first was not all of her, but only part, and now she did renew herself. I do not need to wonder what happened. It is plain – she was pursued, attacked, at bay, until the power that is in the book released her, delivered her, brought her here. I think of the bird I once found trapped in the library, how Sophia and I cornered it and I scooped it up, how it felt like an angry soul caged in my hands, its featherlight fierceness belied by its tiny bones.

'I sent her away,' she whispers, the first words she speaks that make sense.

'She's safe,' I say. 'She's here.'

She turns, clutching me. 'I sent her away. I sent her away.' Her eyes are two rounds of deep and shining dark.

'Bianca,' I say. 'She's safe.'

'Bianca?'

'Safe,' I repeat. 'Safe. Her baby is coming.'

She stands and teeters, still lacking strength – or, perhaps, lacking knowledge of standing altogether. I pull her down.

'You mustn't,' I whisper fiercely. 'You can't be seen like this. You'd scare her. You're—'

'Frightening?' She stretches an arm out and I see pinions tumbling from it. She stretches another arm out and I see a sweep of black dress. I look back. The feathers have resolved into silk. I reach for her hands. Dry and fidgety fingers scratch at my palms. She turns her hands over and over in front of me, her eyes peering blackly at me.

'So,' she says. 'This, then, is the Mother's power. Her mystery, her mastery. You knew?'

'I—'

'You knew and did not tell me.'

'You would not have believed me.'

'No. I would not. But now – I believe.' She stands again, and this time her feet hold. 'Please,' she says, 'take me to her.'

Circumventing the light of the braziers, we come to the guesthouse, where Hildegard had borne Bianca. As we climb the stairs, we pass one of Agatha's helpmeets carrying away a whorl of blooded sheets and cloths. Ortolana stays her – asks the question – and is rewarded with a tired yet jubilant smile.

'Both alive. A son.'

She clasps the girl's hand, thanks her, and stands aside to let her descend. I expect us to continue up the stairs together, but at the turn of the landing she sinks to the floor and seems no longer able to move. 'A moment, Beatrice,' she says. 'Give me – a moment.'

I crouch beside her, trying not to think of woman's parturition struggles, of the dolours of Eve. The Son, they say, eased out of Mother-Mary's womb as a ray of sun passes through a pane of glass – effortlessly. No cries of pain, not even a muffled moan, disturbed the rumination of the cattle. It can't have been so for my mother. She must have suffered and cried – or I can only assume she did – for, certainly, she died. That fact of her death – the one thing I know about her. The rest is a blank page.

She cannot have been a gentlewoman, for she came unwed to my father's bed. Nor, proofed by my own reflection, was she a beauty. And if she had neither consequence nor looks, I wonder what my father wanted of her, those being the two qualities men value, alongside chastity – and that, he wrested from her, leaving her nothing to call her own.

Above us, a door opens. I look up and see Sister Agatha coming down the stairs. She spies us, startled. 'Lady Stelleri!' She kneels beside my stepmother, her voice full of concern. 'What is wrong – are you hurt?'

But Ortolana will say nothing of herself, only pressing her to repeat what the helpmeet has already told us.

'Yes, yes,' says Agatha. 'Both alive, both well. She is exhausted, wrung out, to be sure, but that's no surprise.' Gently, Agatha lifts my stepmother to her feet. 'She says you saved her – and her baby. Come, you will want to see her. Mother Chiara is with her.'

Together, we help her up the stairs and Agatha indicates which door we are to go through, before heading back down, saying she needs some things from the infirmary. I want to follow her – I feel this is no place for me – but my stepmother does not release my arm.

'Aaah,' exclaims Chiara when we enter, moving swiftly to embrace Ortolana. 'I was so worried, you have no idea – but enough of that. Look what clever Bianca has done.'

We turn to the bedside. The whey-faced doll is gone. A fierce young woman is propped up on bolsters, a tiny baby clasped to her chest, and I see at once that the images of Mother-Mary are all wrong. Bianca, staring down at her baby, looks more savage than serene. Wind, earthquake and fire could whirl around her, and yet still she would grip that thing.

I find myself wondering – though the thought is very painful – did my mother live long enough to look at me that way?

Ortolana pulls a chair forward and sits by her side. 'Well done, dearest,' she says, almost humbly. 'It's quite a thing, is it not?' She glances round at me, and I wonder – although I realise at once that the idea is absurd – whether she can guess what I am thinking.

Bianca smiles, without looking up. She smiles and traces the baby's earlobe with the tip of her finger. 'He's perfect. Is he not – perfect?'

Ortolana leans forward to look. 'He is.'

'I do not want to let go of him, not now, not ever.' She looks up at Ortolana. 'And yet I am so tired, and I fear – I fear I shall drop him if I go to sleep.'

'I could sit by you and hold him,' she replies. 'If you like.'

'Here? You will not move?'

'Here. I will not stir.'

'And if he cries? If he needs me? If he misses me?'

'I shall wake you.'

Bianca shifts slightly to pass the baby. The bit of blanket that covers him falls briefly aside and his frog limbs startle outwards before he curls into a ball once more. Ortolana tucks him under her chin, caressing the back of his downy head. Bianca lays her head sideways to watch, and her eyes close and open, close and open, close – and then she sleeps.

The bell sounds for the night watch – I fancy that the warden has rung it more gently than usual for the sake of the sleeping children – and Bianca does not stir. Chiara stands.

'I must go,' she whispers. 'They will worry otherwise. Such a night.' She reaches out and touches Ortolana's arm. 'Was it bad?'

'Very.'

'But why – why did you not come with Bianca and the rest?'

'My son.'

'Of course. You were—'

'Trying to find him. Yes. I left it too late. I thought I would be safe in our chapel. But those men – those Lambs – dragged me from the altar rail itself.'

'Your guards—?'

Ortolana shakes her head. 'Outnumbered. I told them to put off their livery and slip away.'

'How then – how did you come here?'

She does not immediately answer, but continues softly to stroke the baby's head. 'They bore me into our courtyard. Once there – it seems – it seems that our sharp-witted steward loosed Ludo's hunting birds – his darling raptors – which affrighted them sufficiently for me to make good my escape.'

Surely, I think, surely Chiara will question such an implausible account – although, of course, the truth is yet unlikelier still. But she only nods and briefly lays the back of her hand against the baby's cheek. 'I'll return when I may – I imagine the coming days will be difficult.'

'Not least with Arcangela?'

'Not least with her.'

'I'm sorry to have brought trouble to your door.'

'Don't say that,' says Chiara. 'Never say that. I've always been glad to share your troubles.'

She leaves, squeezing my hand on her way out. For a long moment, my stepmother and I are silent. She looks at the baby, while I look at her. She glances up at me.

'What do you make of your little nephew?' she says.

I don't think she expects a reply, and I have none to give, but the question recalls me, uncomfortably, to my childhood. I remember standing, uneasily, in the corner of a room. Ortolana was dandling my brother, my pretty little brother. He had tiny ears, fuzzy white hair and brown eyes as soft as a calf's. She was singing to him, nuzzling him, nibbling the tip of his nose, all to make him laugh. She turned, saw me, smiled and reached out, but I was certain she did not want me there – or anywhere.

I spent a lot of time watching them. I peered around doors; I crouched under tables; I dodged behind drapes. Sometimes, a nursemaid or sweeper, carrying a long-poled duster, would chance upon me before I could dart away, and I was ashamed when they asked me what I did. But I could not stop myself. It was a strange hunger, spying on their love, but one I could not sate.

Ortolana's eyes shift from the sleeping baby back to me. 'What is it, Beatrice? You look even more serious than usual.'

'Where's Ludo?'

She sighs – a deep, unhappy sound. 'I believe he left the city.'

'Without you?'

'Yes. Without me. Without his mother, without his wife, without his unborn child.'

'Are you not angry with him?'

'Would it make you happy, Beatrice, if I was?' The baby stirs, its whole face frowning. She stands, sways a little, and it settles.

Of course, the answer to her question is yes – yes it would. That my brother might do something to blunt her love. That vain and cherished hope.

'Your brother,' she says, still moving, gently, from side to side, 'is a very unhappy young man. The things your father loved – knowledge, power – they mean nothing to him. Always, he'd rather be in the stables, rubbing down the horses, not discoursing about ideas, politics. He'd have made a loyal companion to an older brother, a good prentice to a patient man, but there was only one path for him – to be his father's son – and for that, he had no skill. Worst of all, they both blamed me for their disappointment in each other.' She looks at me. 'I love him, though. Don't think I don't.'

And there it is again. Envy's green and ugly tug.

I stand to leave.

'That's the real curse of Eve,' she tells me as I retreat. 'To love our children. Even if they do not love us in return.'

The Packbag

Monday morning

I LAY MY QUILL DOWN. I am at my desk, but I cannot even begin to think of work. I've sent my copyists to help Timofea and Felicitas, who are preparing bundles of clothes and food for last night's guests. This morning, at breakfast, while they ate our bread and milk, and we sisters sipped a much-diluted broth, Mother Chiara had reassured Benedetta and the rest that Ortolana had arrived unharmed, that Bianca and her baby were doing well. The news cheered them, but when Mother Chiara begged them to stay until we could gather news of how matters stood beyond our walls, Benedetta shook her head and said it wouldn't do. So many of them in the convent, it'd cause too much trouble; they'd talked it over, and they would leave this morning.

'Not to us,' said Chiara. 'You're no trouble to us.'

'No,' Benedetta had replied. 'Trouble in the city. Trouble with *him*.'

I hear footsteps on the stairs, and it takes me a moment to recall that every Monday at this hour, Laura and Giulia present themselves in the library. Their fathers – two brothers – have expressed a desire for them to acquire Empire as well as Vulgate Latin, and I have been deputed to teach them. I greet them distractedly – I had forgotten they might still be coming – and hand each a copy of the *Bellum Gallicum*, which we have been using as our primer.

As I search for our place, steeling myself to resume our faltering pursuit of Julius Caesar across all three parts of Gaul, I frown. In places, the edges of the paper have begun to crumble and brown, decomposition threatening the conqueror's redoubtable prose. I brush a stray hair from one of the pages. It does not move. I repeat the gesture, realising as I do that the hair is in fact a mark of scintillate silver. Attempting to preserve my countenance, I turn to the next page and the next, where I see that, here and there, Caesar's letters have grown kinks and curlicues. It is then that I recall how, briefly, I concealed the Radix beneath my copy – but, no, I must pull myself together. The girls are starting to stare.

I am not, I admit, a patient teacher – and Laura, at least, is not a zealous student. Nevertheless, I had started to think that Giulia, for all her defects of person, possessed a certain quickness of mind. She affects resentment and boredom, but only last week – which now seems impossibly long ago! – she proved herself more than mistress of the sequence of tenses after the subjunctive, and I had hoped she might yet do me credit. But today, she is as dull-witted as her cousin.

They mumble. They lose their place. And rather than attending to the syntactic clues provided by the elegant inflections of the Latin, they guess wildly. I am preparing to chide them for their inattention, when I remark their red eyes, their blotched complexions, and it occurs to me that they are overtaxed by all that has occurred. I recall with what charity they played with the grimy and unprepossessing children, tickling them to make them giggle, riding them about the quadrilango on their backs, and I decide to show some charity of my own by way of return.

'I shall read and translate while you attend me,' I say. 'Although perhaps we should take up one of Virgil's pastoral lays.' I am thinking this little sally might entertain them. 'After all, perhaps we've had sufficient of fire and fury for one night?'

At my words, Giulia turns white and Laura, who is the meeker of the two, bursts into tears.

'Come,' I say. 'Come, what is it?'

But Laura is inconsolable, and Giulia is tight-lipped. I look from one to the other with bewilderment, until it dawns upon me – perhaps my wits, too, are a little sluggish – that their homes lie hard by the Stelleri palazzo, and it's possible they have not yet been reassured as to their families' safety.

When I put voice to some of this, Laura flings her arms around Giulia's neck, who pats her back and glares at me. At first, I take this unblinking fixity of gaze for rage, but then I recall myself at a similar age and recognise a fierce battle against treacherous tears. Such determination recommends her to me, and so I take to my feet, at which Laura turns anxious and starts dabbing her eyes and promising to listen quietly, but I hush her, and say I am going to the parlour to ask for news. Surprise causes Giulia to blink, and two tears fall. Hastily, she whisks them away with the back of her hand.

I stand up, and am about to leave, when something unexpected – incongruous, alarming – snags my attention. I stare down from my window. A man – I recognise the red-and-black trappings of the city guard – is standing in the middle of the quadrilango. Four more men are walking through the open gate, pursued by Poggio, who is snatching at the cloak of the hindmost in a vain attempt to make him stop.

The first man, who has been looking about him, his right hand resting on his sword's hilt, pulls a paper from a packbag slung over his shoulder, and hands it to him. Poggio shakes his head, unrolls the paper, holds it at arm's length, appears to read it, shakes his head again. Now the man is asking him something, and Poggio is dithering helplessly.

Suddenly, his face brightens, and I see that he is waving frantically at somebody. Arcangela – Arcangela is approaching. Graciously, she acknowledges the stranger's courteous bow. Calmly, she accepts the paper. I watch her read it, at one point appearing to check some point with the guardsman, who inclines his head in confirmation. Finally, she too nods, apparently in reluctant agreement, and returns the paper.

She moves off, and they follow her, so that soon the cloister beneath my window screens them from view. I fear the paper is some subpoena relating to my stepmother, and I am thinking that Sister Arcangela has chosen a strangely roundabout route to the guesthouse, when I hear the tread of boots upon my stairs. I turn to Giulia, to Laura, who is clutching her cousin in alarm.

'Go,' I say, 'go before—'

But already the guardsman is at the door. The shock of him, of a man standing there – the dazzling white shirt, the stiff embroidered jerkin, the black hair curling beneath his helmet – sends me stumbling backwards into my desk. He bows low to the girls as they hurry past him.

'Forgive me,' he says to me. 'It was not my intention to cause alarm.' His voice is elegant, nicely modulated. 'Am I addressing—? That is to say, are you—?'

'You are addressing Sister Beatrice. I am the Sister Librarian.' I hope I sound indignant. 'By what authority do you—?'

But the guardsman is not listening to me. He is moving aside for—

'By the Father's authority. Is there any other?' Brother Abramo is crossing my threshold – with Sister Arcangela two paces behind him.

His face is shaven raw. There are nicks of dried blood about his jaw and throat. Blunt razor, I think. Water unwarmed. He looks even thinner. Bones pronounced. Tired, I think. He's tired. The sins of the city are wearying him. You can see it in his eyes. Which are fixed upon me. Such an unlikely colour, they are. The delicate blue of noonday pools, of wayside flowers.

'You seem to be at a loss, Sister Beatrice,' he says, walking slowly towards me. 'I am surprised. You must know why these gentlemen are here. No? Can you not at least guess?'

I stare at him. I am mute – frozen.

'Perhaps,' he says, softly, 'perhaps you would feel more comfortable if you saw our licence? Would you please, captain?'

The guardsman steps smartly forward and hands me the roll of paper. I look down. Careless penmanship, I think. Smudged ink. You can't hide haste. But although the red seals are smeared, I recognise the devices of the Bench and the Board and the Office of the Archbishop.

'All in order, Sister Librarian?' Brother Abramo retrieves the paper with a smile. 'I must commend you, Sister Beatrice,' he says, looking about him. 'You keep a well-ordered room.' He walks from desk to desk, holding up some samples of my copyists' work, nodding approvingly, repeating such phrases as seem particularly to please him. 'And what is this?' He has picked up the cut-out one of my sisters had placed over a manuscript. Haltingly, I explain it permits the inexperienced copyist to focus on a single line at a time. 'A most worthy contrivance,' he says.

The captain coughs, begs forgiveness, says hadn't they better start – but Abramo holds up a hand, commanding silence. He passes now through the archway to wander among my books, running his fingertips along their spines, murmuring the names of certain of the authors. I glance towards the door, where Arcangela stands, very still, watching.

'Ambrose, Augustine, Bernard, Boethius, Gregory, Jerome – such riches. Glory be to the Father, but you keep great company.' He smiles at me, expansively. 'And you do not, I understand, scorn to excerpt some of the more illuminating passages, translating them into the Vernacular for the edification of your less lettered sisters?'

My mouth is unspeakably dry. I nod. Swallow.

'But why, Sister Beatrice,' he says, beckoning me towards him, to where he stands before the cabinets that house texts from the Old Empire, 'why must the Doctors of the Church consort with fools who grovelled before false gods?'

His sneer is a cup of small courage.

'The wisdom of Aesop,' I say, 'the probity of Cicero, the grace of Virgil, have long been recognised. The poet Dante—'

'The faithless,' he says, a harsher note entering his voice, 'have nothing to teach us.'

'Father Augustine himself,' I return, 'contended that Plato and his master Socrates would have been good men of the faith, had they not had the misfortune to die before the Son was born.' He stills, absolutely. Perhaps unwisely, I start to quote the relevant passage, before breaking off and saying, 'But, what am I doing? I am sure you already know—'

'Sister Beatrice!' Arcangela has left her post and inserted herself between us. 'Sister Beatrice, that is quite enough.' She turns her back to me. 'Forgive us her insolence, brother. Often have I warned her that such pridefulness is displeasing to the Father, but she will not listen. Too long has she been indulged by one – I do not think I need name her – who knowing little of books is too readily impressed by them.'

But he is not looking at her. He is looking at me.

'Yes,' he says, gently. 'Yes,' he says, with greater feeling. He indicates that Arcangela should stand aside, and closes the distance between us, coming nearer, far nearer than any man ought. He bows his head until his mouth cannot be more than a finger's breadth from my left ear. I feel his breath on my skin. I catch its scent. It is sour – hungry.

'Books have voices of their own, do they not, Beatrice?' I flinch and try to draw away, but he seizes my shoulder so that I cannot move. 'They coax, they seduce. They' – his voice drops even lower – 'they whisper.' He pulls back, regarding me, and this time I cannot meet his gaze. 'Your friend, the little bookseller' – my eyes fly to his, and he smiles – 'I have enjoyed making his acquaintance. He was attempting to leave the city last night. He thought he had bribed the gatekeeper sufficiently, but my righteous friends are everywhere. They brought him to me. I am so glad they did. Do you know what we discussed, Sister Beatrice?' His voice is light, almost conversational. He prolongs the pause. 'Tertullian.'

My head snaps up. I am appalled. Brother Abramo is shaking his head, sorrowfully.

'Come here,' he says. 'Come, Beatrice. Come, I said.'

I take one faltering step towards him. He reaches out and touches the place where my skin warps, looking warmly at me as though he had found something to love.

'You are, one hears, a curious young woman. Have you never wondered why that young man covers his face. No? He bears a most peculiar mark. Like so.'

Slowly, he traces a shape on my good cheek with one cold forefinger. Two lines up – down. Two lines left – right. The tops curled.

I cannot even begin to describe my consternation.

He takes my hand and pulls me close. 'You think, Beatrice, that because you do not have the begetting sin of physical beauty, you are safe – but you are not. The Devil has set other traps for you. Talk to me, Beatrice. Talk to me and you will discover that the Father forgives all – but the quicker the confession, the lighter the penance.'

Behind me, an ugly crash. I turn and see my desk overturned, ink spilling, parchment skidding across the floor. The guardsmen have fanned out across the room, but there is one close by my desk, looking at me, fish-eyed, insolent.

'You're an ungainly fellow, aren't you?' says the captain, who is lounging against the door-jamb. He does not order the man to right it.

Arcangela, I realise, is nowhere to be seen.

'It is a long time,' says Abramo, as though nothing has happened, 'since I read Tertullian. I'm ashamed. I set such store by him in my youth.'

He walks away, and I know he is going straight to my hiding place, straight to where Tomis must have told him the Radix is hidden. He will not find it – it is in my cell – but he will find a holy book with its insides cut out, a holy book despoiled. And he will ask what and he will ask why – and I do not know how I can begin to answer him.

'Ah, *Volume IX*.' He glances at me, all too aware, I fear, of my distress. 'An old favourite. It contains, does it not, the master's clear-sighted views upon the lamentable weaknesses of your sex?' He has the book in his hands. He pauses without opening it. 'I wonder, can I recall his exact words?' He casts his eyes heavenwards as though in thought. 'Ah, yes – you are the Devil's gateway. You deserved death, but it was the Son who had to die.' Keenly, he looks at me. 'When I pray, I sometimes imagine myself to be a woman, wondering how it feels to bear such weight.'

He places the book on a table before him. He looks at me once more – and then gently lifts the outer boards.

But instead of tampered pages—
a carnival of woodlice.

I bow my head, meek – exultant. Her creatures have eaten the evidence. Abramo sweeps them on to the floor with a hand. Grinds them under his foot.

'You have been lax in your attention to your books,' he snaps.

'I confess I am greatly at fault,' I say, giving inward thanks to the power that lies within the Radix. 'These first warmer days – their nests come alive. When you leave, I promise to be exceedingly thorough in my efforts to uncover more depredation.' I seize a broom and cover my joy with an industrious display of sweeping.

He comes behind me. Grips my shoulders. Leans close. 'When the serpent spoke in the garden, Eve listened – Eve obeyed. That is the voice you hear in the book – the book I know you are hiding from me. The voice of the serpent. After the first Fall, the Father trusted Eve's daughters never again to heed that voice, but still it whispers to them – it has been whispering into your ear, Beatrice, has it not?'

I am quite, quite still. I dare not look round. I no longer feel exultant – I feel cold.

'I know you are not a sinful woman. I know it must be very frightening. It is frightening, isn't it? The Whore of Northwich sent this serpent among us, hoping it would slither into the bosom of Silvia, the Succubus of St Peter's, and so destroy us all.'

I grip the broom as though it might keep me from falling, for I can feel not only the weight of his body bearing down upon me, but a pressure more moral and absolute, a pressure that constricts my chest, compromising each breath I try to draw.

Into my ear, he murmurs, 'You are too young to remember

the pestilenza. For a time, it was as though a pit of hell had opened here on earth. But those days of horror will be as nothing compared to a second Fall. I will not have the little children crying out for their mothers. I will not let you force the Father's hand. I will not let it happen, Beatrice. I will not.'

I think he senses some hesitation – some receptivity on my part – for now he turns me gently to face him, and when he next speaks his tone has markedly softened.

'Tomis knows what the book is. He has confessed all. But he also told me – compellingly – that you are innocent. That you lacked all knowledge; that you were enchanted by it as a child is enchanted by a toy. He begged me not to hold you to account. I am not heartless. I am willing to believe this is the truth. But now, now that you know what the book is, give it to me freely, and I promise no blame shall attach to you – or your sisters. Give me the book, Sister Beatrice. Give it to me now.'

Should I? Wait, I could say. Wait, it is in my cell. Let me get it for you. Here it is. I'm sorry. Forgive me, brother, I knew not what I did.

And yet, instead of speaking, I find myself thinking of the women hunted through the forest; of Marta's slight body shaking in my arms; of the mob of men tearing my stepmother from the alter rail – and I know I cannot. Maybe I am wrong, and maybe he is right, but I will not surrender it.

I look up at him. He is still smiling at me, warmly, expectantly, with certainty. I realise he is caressing my hand, running a thumb up and down my palm, as though to coax me onwards. It sends a dart of revulsion to my core. I tear my hand away and step backwards.

'I fear you are mistaken,' I say. 'I know nothing of this book of which you speak. It does indeed sound fearful. Tomis is a great teller of tales, is he not? For years he has diverted us. But if you would like to reassure yourself – my library is at your disposal.'

From the moment I started speaking, he has been shaking his head: almost imperceptibly at first, and then with more and more force, until suddenly his composure shatters.

'Your library? *Your* library? This is not *yours*. Nothing is yours. Poverty, chastity and obedience – they are your only possessions. All else – is the Father's. All else belongs to him. Wait outside while we discover how you have insulted this treasury of his wisdom. Captain, if you please.'

The guardsman extends his arm, palm up, a mockery of a gentleman offering polite precedence to a lady. I do not move. My reluctance, you understand, is not born of fear. My cabinets are comprehensive, yes, but there is nothing in them that contravenes propriety. Nothing proscribed. No, I do not move because I do not like being ordered from my own library – from my domain. What would Sophia do were she ordered from here? She would stand firm.

I stand firm. I square myself. I find words: 'I am happy to help you search, brother, but I cannot permit unschooled soldiers to—'

The captain emits an exaggerated sigh, drops his arm, and says, 'Tell me, brother, what's the Father's position on the compulsion of sisters that do not do as they are told?'

Brother Abramo's lips thin. 'He is – amenable. When circumstance demands it.'

'Right, then. Come on, you.' The captain grabs my upper arm and pulls. I try to resist – I do try – but, within moments, I find myself outside the library, with the door closing in my face.

I pace the landing, listening to Abramo ordering the search, rubbing my bruised arm, but then it occurs to me that somebody peering through a crack in the door might read pacing as the disquiet of a guilty conscience. I stop. I listen. The sounds of the search grow louder, more violent. The rending of wood, the smash of glass. I start to fear for my books themselves. The miniature Horace; our beautiful *Aeneid*; Sophia's precious manuscripts. What might he do to them out of spite? How dare he? How dare he?

I am angry – oh, yes, I am angry – but I am also afraid. Have I – have I forgotten something? Is there some pamphlet I neglected to return to Tomis? No – no. There is nothing – nothing to find. I wait – I wait and wait – gnawing my thumbnails, raging at my impotence, until the waiting grows worse than the fear, and I go to push the door open – but it does not move. Something is wedged against it. I call out, demanding to be let in, but my library is shut against me.

'What are you doing?' I cry. 'What are you doing?'

And then I remember something. Something which had seemed so banal, so incidental. The packbag slung over the captain's shoulder. The floor beneath me lurches. I beat upon the door.

'Let me in,' I scream. 'Let me in.'

The door opens. I rush inside. My library has been turned over – *desecrated*, the word resounding in my head. Everything I have tended is heaped in sordid piles. Mauled and trampled. Boards broken. Pages adrift. I feel anguish, and a terrible guilt – how have I let this happen? The first brute shock passes. Worse, I see, is to follow.

Brother Abramo and the guardsmen are arrayed in varying aspects of triumph, amusement and sorrow. The captain advances towards me, proffering two books in his black-gloved hands. For some reason, his pose recalls Principessa Salome with the head of Baptist John on its salver.

'Care to explain these, sister?' he says.

'How can I explain them when I don't know what they are?' I say.

'Funny,' he says. 'She's funny, isn't she, brother?'

'I think, Beatrice,' says Abramo, 'that you know very well what they are.'

I do. They are the books I returned to Tomis three days ago. *Letters from the Lagoon* and *The Clavicula of Solomon*.

'They're not mine,' I say, truthfully – pointlessly. 'They're not mine – and you know it.'

The guards laugh, and Abramo shakes his head. 'Perhaps one of your copyists acquired them and hid them here? Is there any you suspect? We are not barbarians. You may speak in your defence.'

I shake my head, and repeat, 'They're not mine.'

'That's what they all say,' says the captain, chuckling. 'Not me. I didn't do it. Same old story. But here's a big bag of gold and my virgin daughter – just to make sure you believe me. What next, brother, seeing as the sister's not got gold nor daughters to bargain with?'

Brother Abramo is standing by the window. The weak sunlight illuminates the side of his face, revealing its hollows and angles. 'Nothing to bargain with? Oh, but she has, Captain – she has.'

I hear a great trampling on the stairs. More men, I am sure, more men coming to drag me away. But – no. Not guards. Chiara. She has come. She stops on the threshold, flushed, out of breath, propping herself with both arms on the door-frame.

'Reverend Mother,' says the captain, approaching her. 'We were apprised of—'

'Out – out – *out!*'

' —dangerous and heretical works within—'

'Ah, so it's you, is it, Cesare?' she cries, seizing him by the collar of his coat. 'Polished boots and a starched shirtfront, but you're still the same boy who cried to his grandma that the Devil had possessed his you-know-what and was making it stand on end. If I can't make you sorry for what you've done this day, I know she will.' She wags a finger in his face, which is now a scalding red. 'You were happy enough to send that lovely wife of yours to Agatha to convince her the doings of the marriage bed were no sin. Would you have your two handsome boys else? And this – *this* – is how you repay us?'

She has backed him out on to the landing, where he stands, looking rather dazed, still clutching the books to his chest. And now she turns, sweeps back into the library, and accosts the youngest and burliest of the guards.

'And you, Pietro! You ought to be ashamed of yourself. After all we did when your poor father was struck with the pleurisy and couldn't work his forge. Your brother's apprenticeship! Alfonsa's dowry! What would your mother say if she could see you now? Eh? What? What?' He is silent, pink and nonplussed, shifting from foot to foot. 'No? Nothing to say for yourself? Shame on you. Shame, shame, shame.'

He holds his hands up, unequal to this determined assault, and hurries out to join his captain. Before Chiara can say another word, the remaining guardsmen follow him.

Only Abramo remains.

His eyes are lifted. His lips are murmuring in what I suppose is meant to be – or perhaps even is – prayer. She strides towards him, raises her hand as though to strike a sharp slap across his cheek, and he flinches backwards from the blow that does not fall.

'Get out,' she growls.

'There will be consequences,' he says. 'You must understand that. I shall turn this matter over to the proper authorities, to the Tribunal. They will—'

'*Out.*'

He leaves. He does leave. We both listen to the men's footsteps descending the stairs. We watch them cross the quadrilango and go out through the parlour door. When they are out of sight, I sink to my knees. I close my eyes. From above me, I hear Chiara's voice.

'What have you done, Beatrice? Oh, what have you done?'

The Sister

Tuesday morning

⌘

TWO OF ARCANGELA'S wardens are seated outside my cell. One bulky, the other hunger-ravaged. They shift and whisper and huff. One of them opens my door a finger's breadth. I hear creaking, heavy breathing, as she presses her eye to the crack. Whatever she hopes to see — perhaps a demon suckling at my breast — she will be disappointed. I am lying on my pallet, on my back, staring at the ceiling, as I have been ever since they brought me here yesterday.

'Who's that in the corridor?' My neighbour Galilea's voice. 'Skulking novices, is it? I know you're there, don't think I don't. Out of my way, out of my way.'

'Mind your stick, sister,' cries one of the wardens.

'Oh, it's you, is it? What are you—?'

'You remember, Sister Galilea, Beatrice must keep to her cell until—'

'What? Little Beatrice. What?' she exclaims. 'What's she done, eh?'

'We told you, sister, she had books—'

'Books? Books? But she's the librarian. Don't be absurd. Books, indeed.' I hear her voice still grumbling as she descends the stairs.

Outside the door, I hear the wardens settling back on to their stools.

'To think, in our very midst.'

'So distressing.'

'But then, I always said—'

I jam my thumbs in my ears and screw my eyes shut. They're enjoying themselves, playing jailer. They probably wish they had a real Carcere, like the one down in the city – damp cells, iron bars, rats. Why am I thinking about that? Don't think about that. Don't—

I don't hear them opening the door again. I only realise they are inside my cell when one of them prods my side. They loom over me. Would it, they ask, ease the burning of my conscience if they were to pray with me? My silence they take for acquiescence. They kneel beside me and bow their heads. I stare at them. The bulky one – no doubt elated by her proximity to real sin – is sweating hard. The other one scratches feverishly at the desiccated skin of her neck, a red collar of scabs and scurf. Together, they contend for my soul with a commanding intensity.

At first, they beg the Son to reconcile me to the Father – to guide me, his meek lamb, back into the fold. They steal a glance at me. They observe that I am unmoved – that I neither tremble nor weep – that I am, in short, insufficiently lamblike. And so, the bent of their prayers darkens. Let Sister Beatrice confess her sins, and let her do so soon, lest she need be persuaded to confess. The nature of such persuasion they leave unspoken, but their ominous hints, their tortuous circumlocutions are enough. Sometimes, they whisper, it is necessary to trample the grapes to make the wine flow. I hold still. I will not let them know how keenly their words affect me. Brother Abramo – surely – would never sanction the excruciation of—

A knock. The gaunt warden unpeels herself from the floor and slips out into the passageway. The other follows, laboriously. I hear them saying, 'Yes, yes, Reverend Mother, she has refused every morsel,' and, 'No, no, Reverend Mother, not a bite, however much we beg it of her.'

Untruths, both. Last night and again this morning, they brought me bread and milk and set it beside me, only to whip it away before I could reach for the spoon, saying, 'There now, we know you're far too mortified to eat.'

But now I hear Chiara bidding them return to the cookhouse, to ask Sister Felicitas to prepare me food. 'And not milk pap,' she says, 'but something that'll land in her belly – off you go, off you go.'

Footsteps fade. The door opens. She approaches, but I do not stir. She lowers herself on to my pallet and takes up my hand.

'There, there,' she says, that is all, and yet it is more than I can bear. My chest tightens and my head clouds. My breath quickens, and from some sunless place deep beneath my ribs, a gasp, a sob, escapes. I am engulfed. I roll away, convulse into a ball, and cannot stop.

Dimly, some time later, I become aware the wardens have returned, that Chiara is telling them she will mind me while they attend the fourth office. No, they need not trouble Sister Arcangela, she is more than equal to the task. Yes, she is very well aware at what time the Proctors of the Tribunal are due to present themselves. And then they are gone, and we are alone once more.

'Beatrice? Here.'

I twist my neck and look at her. A small bowl of soup rests in her hands.

'Eat,' she says, 'before anything else, eat.'

I am utterly spent, and yet wolfishly hungry. She coaxes

me upright, and waits beside me while I spoon it clumsily into my mouth.

'Give me that.' She takes the bowl and sets it on the floor. 'Now – look at me.'

Her tone is not admonitory. She speaks as to one a little touched, as though she fears I might crumple, fold in upon myself like a box with its nails plucked out. I glance towards her and look away.

'No,' she says, 'really look.'

It is hard, but I obey, and she takes hold of my face, searching my eyes, and I – I cannot meet her gaze. She lets her hands fall. Keenly, I feel the loss of their warmth. Fearfully, I see a frown darken her brow.

'You are troubled, Beatrice. If you have done wrong – even if you did not think it wrong at the time – tell me now, and I shall try to soften what must follow. Presently I must answer to men from the Tribunal. You may have to be parted from your library, but you need not – I hope – be parted from us. It will hurt, I know. I can only promise to help you bear the pain.' She pauses. 'This is no small matter, Beatrice.'

'They're not mine. The books he found. They're not mine.'

For a moment, she regards me. 'All right. If not yours, then whose?'

'Tomis's.'

'If we are to play at logic, you know you will best me. Tomis's, then – and not yours. But you took them from him. You took them and hid them in the library.'

'I didn't.'

'Then who?'

'They did. *He* did.'

Chiara stands up, shaking her head. 'This is serious, child—'

'I know it is, I know.'

198

'Then you must be frank with me, and not make up—'

'But it's true – it's true. I swear, it's true. *I did not hide those books*.'

She sits back down, heavily, and for a while appears to be deep in thought. She reaches out and takes up one of my hands in her own. 'You didn't hide those books?'

A light stress on *those*.

She squeezes my hand.

'Not those books, no,' I say, and then in a smaller voice, 'I'm sorry. I'm sorry.' I look up at her, and, again, the tears are coursing down my cheeks.

'No,' she says, 'no, Beatrice, no, no. Stop this. Believe me, if anyone is to blame, it is me. I thought I'd never see him again, that my dealings with him were past, but . . .' She pauses, rubbing her face with her palms.

'But I *am* to blame. You see—'

'No, no, I will not – *will not* – have you blaming yourself.'

'But—'

'No. Listen – *listen*. It concerns my past. And his.'

Any confidence of Chiara's, however minor, is accounted a small fortune in the currency of the convent. Absurdly, I find myself remembering how Prudenzia, back when we were novices, whispered triumphantly to her particular friends that Chiara didn't favour Sister Felicitas's quince tart. And so I wait – almost greedily – as she draws breath to begin.

'I said in the chapter meeting, that I'd first met him in our hill-town, in the days after the *pestilenza*, when we few women were living together. It was hard, Beatrice, harder than we often admit. There were men in the town who wanted to put an end to it. They wanted to find us out, to catch us in sin. They couldn't believe we were living chaste and honourably. They said it was impossible.'

'Abramo,' I say, eagerly, feeling we are on firm ground. 'He was one such?'

But already she is shaking her head. 'No. By no means. He – he admired us. His family were all dead, but the priest – a good man – had taken him in. He was a bright boy, after all. Father Fredo taught him his Latin, a little reasoning, something of the world. I remember asking Father Fredo, did he intend Tonio – that's the name we knew him by – for the priesthood. He tilted his head, so' – a credible mime of a contemplative cleric – 'and said Tonio wasn't cut out for the work.'

She catches my eye and smiles ruefully.

'Father Fredo encouraged him to study for the law, and Tonio seemed content with that. Still, when he wasn't bent over his books, he continued to accompany the priest. He came to us often. He begged to be allowed to serve us – to run our errands, to write our letters, to split our wood. He'd do anything. I saw no harm in it. And it seemed to make him happy.

'By then he was seventeen, eighteen. He – he was a fetching youth. Beardless. Curls. An – an Adonis, is that not the word the young people use?' Briefly, she smiles. 'You know he was the first person to call me Mother Chiara? I was not yet five-and-twenty. I told him not to. I said it was not a title I deserved, but he persisted. He said I was as all mothers should be. Always, he wanted to sit with me, to pray with me. I was but newly in the world, Beatrice, and at first I let myself be flattered. But then – it palled. I found him stifling. I kept him more and more at a distance. I hurt him, I think. And then – he seemed to fall in love.'

'With you?'

Chiara laughs – a swift, uproarious bark. 'No, bless you, Beatrice. No!' She pauses. 'No. He turned from me – to my sister. She was a pretty child, very sweet, very shy. Very easy to love. She had long, heavy, dark brown plaits, strong enough to moor a ship, we used to say. I was so relieved he no longer followed me about, that I allowed myself to think there might be a happy ending in sight. I told myself Tonio was young, handsome, hard-working, upstanding – a man any woman would like for her sister. I ignored my own misgivings. I ignored his hard eyes.

'And of course, it was not love they found together, in the end, but something quite different. They prayed without cease. Hours, they spent in the town church. Hours, at our little shrine. I tried to deflect her. But why, she asked me, why was she not allowed to do as I had done? Because, I told her, this fervour only began with Tonio. She glared at me. Did I accuse her and Antonio of unseemly behaviour? No, I said, no. "He says I am pure and faithful," she said. I told her she was. "He says I am modest and good." I agreed she was those things too. "He says – he would no more touch me than he would the Mother-Mary. He says the Son loves girls like me. He says the Son is a Holy Bridegroom who visits us at night and pours his love into our hearts."'

My heart is beating fast. Even I can hear how strange those words sound, but it takes me a long moment to pose the question: 'He – he wasn't speaking metaphorically?'

'I do not know what that means, Beatrice, but if you're saying what I think you're saying, then you'd be right. Many a man has found his way into an honest girl's bedroom by calling himself a god. I do not know when or where or how – but I do know that he got her with child.

'I confronted him – and, of course, he denied everything. He would never – *could* never do such a thing. "Ask her," he said. "Ask her!" I already had. She'd denied it all. Only stared at me with round, dreamy eyes, asking me why, oh, why must

I spoil her happiness with nasty questions. I had never told her how a man comes to a woman. She was thirteen, and in all ways innocent.

'He came to me. He said he would marry her – like a second Joseph. I said I had little enough scripture, but as far as I knew, Mary and Joseph were married long before the Angel Gabriel came to Nazareth. I told him to leave. He wouldn't. So I told Father Fredo, and he ordered Tonio out of the valley, never to return. I don't know what threats or bribes he used, only that Tonio finally agreed. So help me, I let him bid her farewell. I let him say he was going on a pilgrimage to the birthplace of the Son.

'I was a coward, Beatrice. I should have denounced him. Back then, I would have been believed. But I feared – for our reputation. We were trying to live without men – and it was hard. Better, I thought, to manage it all quietly.

'After he left, she stopped eating. The baby became a hard stone in her belly. She said the Bridegroom brought her milk and honey at night, and she needed nothing more by day. We could not make her eat.'

Her silence is hard to break.

'What happened?' I say at last. 'Did the baby—?'

'No. It didn't. It stopped moving. It fell to Agatha's mother to explain the baby had died inside her, but my sister refused to believe it. She told us the Bridegroom had taken her child back to the Father's house – that she didn't deserve it – that some other lucky girl would bear it.' A pause. Her face is bleak. 'Even though it was dead, still the baby tried to come, but my sister, by then she was too weak. It was – terrible. I cannot tell you.'

Even as I am trying to find the right words – any words – Chiara is pushing her hands down on to her thighs and standing. For a moment, I am confused, but then I catch Sister

Paola's voice, coming from somewhere below us. She's asking will somebody please, please tell her where Mother Chiara is to be found. She's saying the Proctors have arrived. Already, Chiara is hurrying towards the door. Before I have time to think, I seize her arm to make her stop.

'Mother Chiara, wait, I have something – that is to say – will you do something for me?'

'Before or after I convince the Tribunal of your innocence?'

I am abashed, and start to say, 'I'm sorry, I didn't mean—'

But she hushes me. 'I'm teasing, child – but then, you never did like to be teased. Ask – ask. Honestly, Beatrice, in all the years I've known you, this must be the first time you've wanted anything of me. Oh,' she says, noting my face, 'things for your library, I'll admit that – great, big, long lists of things – but never anything for yourself. After what – twenty years?'

'Eighteen, nearly.'

'Is that all? Well, then.'

'Thank you,' I say. 'Thank you. Wait.'

I dart to the corner, pull my pallet from the wall and loose the stones. Quickly, I withdraw my book and press it into her hands. She looks down at it, speculatively. Up at me.

'What is this, Beatrice?'

'A book.'

She raises her eyebrows.

'Sorry,' I say. 'I mean, obviously, it's a book. Will you look at it for me?'

And now she's laughing. 'Bless me, Beatrice – why would you want me to look at a book? A book, of all things!'

'Please. Please, do look. You see, I cannot tell, whether it is good or – not. I thought perhaps you could tell me.'

'*Me!* Tell *you* something about a book? A book! Brother Abramo has truly addled your wits. Come, now. Do I tell Sister Felicitas how to – to jelly a pike? No! So how can I tell you – you, Beatrice, you of all people – anything about a book?' She turns again to leave, chuckling to herself.

Again, I seize her arm. 'Please – it came to me. It came – the women brought it. They – that is to say—' I take a great leap into the dark. 'Have you heard tell of the Mother?'

She stills. Turns. Looks me up. Looks me down. I wait for her to say, what do you mean, the Mother? Or, I have heard of this heresy, why do you speak of it here? But she says neither. Only, quietly, thoughtfully:

'So. She has books, does she? I did not know. But then, why not? It is the age of books, after all – or so Sophia was always telling me.' She smiles a little. 'If I'd known, perhaps I'd have attended better when the poor woman tried to teach me to read.' She holds out her hand. 'Let me see it.'

She opens the book and slowly turns the pages. Anxiously, I watch. Down in the quadrilango, Paola is shouting at some unlucky novice that I can't find her simply isn't good enough.

'Brother Abramo is searching for it,' I start to tell her.

She glances up at me. 'Is he, now?'

'Tomis was taking it to the pontifex's daughter.'

'To dear Silvia?'

'Yes, yes. But Abramo says it's dangerous – evil, he calls it.'

'Now, Beatrice' – she turns the book to face me – 'tell me, where's the evil in a beautiful thing like this?'

'He says – he says – it's against the Father.'

She puffs out her cheeks. Sniffs. 'Oh, the Father. He's all very well – in his way. He and I sometimes get on very well. But if I've learned anything in my life, it's that he oughtn't to have everything so always and absolutely his own way. After all, some people have a good understanding with their mothers – others with their fathers – some both. How do we say it when we pray? *Et in cælo et in terra*? So on earth, so in heaven. That's what I think. Simple, no?'

I am tongue-tied, tongue-struck, struck-dumb – and Chiara takes the opportunity to put the book down and embrace me – fondly, I tell myself. It is definitely a fond embrace. She's done it before, a few times, over the years, and previously I stiffened, kept my arms tight by my sides, and held my breath until she released me. But now, before I even realise what I am doing, I am holding her as tightly as she is holding me. And for once, I do not want her to let me go.

'Beatrice,' she says, easing her arms out from beneath mine. 'I know how you've chafed at our walls. But higher still are the walls you have built about yourself.' She touches my cheek. 'Thank you for letting me see over them today. Now' – she glances out of the window – 'I'd better go. Let me rid us of these – Proctors. I shall have to mind my temper. I grow tired of men telling me how to run my house.'

She smiles, pinches my cheek again.

'You can tell me all about your book later.'

The Quadrilango

Tuesday afternoon

⌘

AFTER CHIARA LEAVES, I go to my window. I watch her enter the parlour; watch Arcangela try to follow; watch Maria block the doorway, keep her out. I can make out Diana, Tamara, a few others, all scaling the parlour vantage. Good, I think. They'll hear Chiara defending me. I find I am happy, almost joyful. Chiara has banished all my doubts. Soon, I am sure, she will dispatch the Proctors, and I shall be exonerated. I return to my pallet. I lie down – wait – holding the book in my arms. It is whispering to me, but the sound is more than voices. It is the sough of wind, the rush of water, the sibilance of leaves, the brittle hum of the stars—

Shouts. I jump to my feet and look out of the window. A strange sight by the parlour door. Maria and Arcangela, all but wrestling. Arcangela's arms and legs are stretched across the doorway, and now it is Maria fighting to squeeze past. She gives up – no, she doesn't – she retreats a few steps and lowers her head to charge. Arcangela's grip breaks. Maria is through. But where is—?

I hear footsteps running back up the corridor, and I fling my door open to tell the wardens I refuse to be cooped up any longer. But it's not them. It's—

'Diana! What's happening?'

'She's gone! Chiara's gone! Maria's running after her, and—'

'But, where, where – where's she gone?'

'To talk to *him*. To Brother Abramo. She said if he could barge into her house, there was nothing stopping her—'

'But *why*? What's happened? Didn't she tell the—'

'Oh, she told them all right. She vouched for you – said she'd stand witness, have pins stuck in her, whatever they wanted. She said those books weren't nothing to do with you, and that was that. But they – ugh, they were a bunch of shrivelled old lizards – they said her word wasn't enough. *Wasn't enough!* They said you were to be removed – but she planted herself in the doorway and said they'd have to come through her first. Obviously, they none of them wanted to be the man to knock Mother Chiara down, so they backed up, saying she'd regret it – saying Brother Abramo would be angry. That lit her right up. She threw them out and then off she went – and Maria's gone after her – and—'

At that moment, we hear a bellowing beneath us and rush down to find Hildegard returned from the fields. She's yelling to her girls, telling them to hurry up, there's no time to lose, Mother Chiara needs them. But before she can lead them out into the campo, Ortolana comes running from the guesthouse, begging her to stop, to think.

'Please Hildegard, please – don't play into his hands. Women, running wild in the streets? No, no, no! It will prove everything he says. Who has already gone? Maria? Good, good. A calm head. A wise head. We must wait – hope. Be patient. All will be well. All will be well.'

She prevails. Grudgingly, Hildegard retreats to the parlour vantage to keep watch. Diana follows, but I am too numb to move. A cold, grey, empty feeling spreads within me. I sink to the ground. My head hangs between my knees. Nobody comes near me. I am tangled up in guilt and defiance. It's all my fault; it's all his fault. What have I done? I haven't done a thing.

The waiting that follows is – oh, very bad.

Ortolana is pacing the quadrilango. Once, she stops by my side.

'Is this serious?' I say.

'Maybe,' she says. 'Maybe very.'

How long passes, I do not know. An hour, at least. More. At last – a shout from the vantage. Somebody is coming. Maria – it is Maria! She staggers through the parlour, into the quadrilango, and at once Arcangela is there, trying to steer her away:

'Sister Maria, I do believe the chapterhouse would be a more appropriate place—'

She can believe what she likes, but Maria is not moving. She is desperately out of breath, puce with exertion – distressed, undone. Her mantle is gone. Her head-cloth – gone. I've never seen her hair before. Black curls, shot with white. Her head looks tiny. Her eyes gape wide. Everyone is crowding round her. Tamara is at her side, yelling for water, for space. Hildegard drives everyone back, ungently. Maria looks up, finds Hildegard, and although I am not close enough to hear the words, I can see them on her lips.

'They've taken her—'

Hildegard's wrath ignites. Her neck turns red. 'Who has? Taken – what is this? Taken where?' She reaches down, shakes Maria once, twice, trying to wrest an answer from her, but the poor woman is beyond speech. Tamara is pounding Hildegard on the back, telling her she's hardly helping. Maria puts a hand up, accepts a cup of water. Slowly, drawing ragged breaths, she recovers herself. She presses her temples. We all gather closer. Silence falls.

'She—' Maria starts, and stalls. Tamara rubs her hand.

'Chiara – she was making for where he lodges. I was running after. She stormed, she raged. I have never seen her so. We arrived. There were many of his men about. Those Lambs. And others. Boys with clubs and guardsmen with swords, standing about a fire. She strode to them. Bade them bring him out. I – to my shame – I did not stand by her. I – I who have always been by her side. But they were so many.' She looks round, needing us to understand. 'They told her to go away – called her ugly names – but she kept shouting up at the house, asking what he was so afraid of – was he feared he might forget himself and try to c-c-couple her like a dog in the street.'

My sisters gasp, exclaim. They bury their heads in their hands. Prudenzia, pink with scandal, tries to hustle her girls away. She has hold of Laura, but she, voluptuous already at fourteen, is impossible to move. She tries Giulia, but she pushes back – with interest. Only Alfonsa and two or three others make a show of hastening towards the dormitory, but they quickly turn to listen. We are all listening.

'One man made to strike her – no, no, I swear it's true. He tried to hit her, but she blocked the blow. Grabbed his wrist. "How dare you?" she said. But he shook her off, laughed in her face, told her to go on home. That's when I realised they did not know her. They thought her a cracked old woman, roaming the streets. "Who does this old hag belong to?" one shouted. She grabbed his collar, told him she was Mother Chiara and belonged to no one but herself. And, like it or not, she said, she was going to wait for Tonio – the bastard son of the town whore.'

Alfonsa shrieks. Laura clutches Giulia. Hildegard puffs and blows out her cheeks. Even Ortolana looks a little winded.

'Oh, he came out then. He was frenzied. He had not meant to come, that was plain. He had meant to leave her raging on his doorstep. But those words, they brought him out in a mad, mad rush – like he would wring her neck with his bare hands – but he stopped himself in time. All those people watching. And he a holy brother.

'He gripped the balustrade and rocked a moment, mastering himself, I think, becoming once more cold and still. He said he was disgusted, horrified. He said she should leave at once. And she said *his* disgust and *his* horror were nothing compared with hers, and she would not leave – not until he'd dropped his baseless accusations against – against' – her eyes seek me out, find me – 'against Sister Beatrice and the convent. And he said he would not. The matter was serious, he said. It was already with the Tribunal. And what's more, he said, the library was only the first step. The archbishop, he said, had ordered an investigation into Chiara's spiritual leadership.'

My sisters cry out and lift their hands to the sky in prayer. A giddiness sweeps over me, and I reach for the rim of the fountain beside me.

'Chiara said if that was the case, they'd better go to the archbishop at once, and he said, "Gladly," and she said, "Let's go," and then – it was like a nightmare – a nightmare. The men, those Lambs, more and more had been arriving from nearby streets, and some started to – to insult Chiara, and they began to jostle her and push her away down the road. I tried, I swear I did try to go to her, to follow her, to stand by her, but the crowd had got between us, and they were moving her away too fast. I saw her, one last time, and then she was borne away.'

A rough hand grips my right arm. My mind floods with chaotic images of steel and sackcloth. I flail and turn, my heart pinched, expecting to see the smiling guardsman's face, but instead – Hildegard. My relief is short-lived. She pushes me to the ground, and I cry out in shock and pain.

'You!' she roars. 'You and your accursed books. What have you done? What have you done?'

I cower beneath her, my arms above my head. There is a great noise of voices, calling out, telling her, 'Stop, stop, stop.' I curl into a ball. I fear she will hit me – kick me – and then somebody comes between us. I see black skirts. I see—

'Get away from her,' cries Ortolana, standing above me, warding Hildegard off. 'Get away from her, I tell you. You want to hit somebody – find him, hit him. Not her. It is not her fault.'

And now Tamara and Diana are each heaving on one of Hildegard's arms, pulling her backwards, while Maria begs her please, please to remember what Chiara always says, that violence never serves.

Into this pitch of turmoil walks Sister Arcangela, who I realise has been absent since shortly after Maria's return. She asks for calm. She says we are all upset. She says we must be patient. She says that is what Chiara would want. Ortolana confronts her: what makes her the authority on Mother Chiara's wishes in this matter?

'Ah, the Widow Stelleri,' says Arcangela, and I expect her to challenge Ortolana's right to speak, she being a convent guest of uncertain status. But instead: 'I'm glad to find you here. Your son has been found. There are representatives from the Bench and the Board in the parlour who urgently need to speak to you.'

My stepmother's hands fly to her face, and she gathers her skirts to run to the parlour. Only when she is nearly there, does she remember herself and slow her pace. When the door has closed behind her, Arcangela resumes.

'Now, dear sisters. The men upon whom the Widow Stelleri now attends also have questions for us, but I think – by speaking to them reasonably – I have bought us all a little time to order our thoughts, to prepare ourselves. But do not doubt that they will have questions – very many questions – for us all.' She starts to number points upon her elegant hands. 'About the library, yes – but also about Maria's accounts; the provenance of our safekeeps; the lack of evidence for all vocations—'

'What is this? What is this?' Hildegard is rumbling back to life. 'All we want to know from you, Sister Warden, is what you might be doing to bring Mother Chiara home safe. You be telling us that, if you please.'

Arcangela touches her steepled hands to her lips. 'Dear Hildegard, I have been trying to tell you how cruelly we all have been deceived.'

'Deceived? That means lies? Is that what you mean? Who has lied unto me?'

'Chiara— '

'Is a better woman than—'

'—is not all we thought she was.'

Hildegard lunges. Diana and Tamara are trying to pull her back down, but the effect would be the same if they were to attach a rope to a tree and heave. They swing. The tree stands.

'I have been knowing her – she has – you – you are knowing nothing—'

Excess of feeling has robbed Hildegard of all coherence, but her clenched fists are emissary enough. Arcangela, however, maintains her inviolate calm.

'I urge you to do nothing rash, Hildegard. It is hard for you, I know. Where would you be without Chiara? Who else would permit a woman such as you – unbaptised, unconfirmed, a woman who has taken no Promise – to live so long among us? Not only unchallenged, but honoured – a place in the chapterhouse, the charge of impressionable girls. No, sister – and yes, still I call you sister, for all that you have no claim to that title – it is no surprise that you cannot hear the truth spoken about your protector. But it is as a sister that I urge you to listen. Our patrons, the wise archbishop and the valiant brother, are – so far – unaware of – how shall I put it? Your complicated spiritual history. Shall I enlighten them? Shall I? No?'

While Arcangela spoke, Hildegard seemed to hunch, to shrink, to wither. Now she sits down, heavily, on the fountain's edge. Cateliné tries to touch her hand, but Hildegard whips it away and bends over her balled fists, silent. What a triumph for Arcangela – quelling Chiara's most devoted friend while we all stood and watched. And so gracefully done. With such barbed love.

'So be it,' says Arcangela, brightly. 'You fled the Forest Wars. Mother Chiara sheltered you. You work hard in our service. And that is all anyone needs to know.'

And now she turns to address us all.

'We need not pretend one to another, sisters. We all love and admire Mother Chiara – her warmth, her strength, the power of her youthful story – but we also know she is stubborn, headstrong, heedless of the realities of the city.

'We know she permitted Sister Maria to borrow heavily from the Stelleri Bank to expand the convent's holdings, installing tenants whom she saw as loyal. We know she accepted many, many safekeeps against their families' wishes, separating daughters from fathers, wives from husbands, mothers from sons. We know she sold the sacred relics our brother monks left behind – such an insult to the martyrs of the Son. We know she encouraged Sister Beatrice, while still a child, to copy pagan texts for profit. We know—'

But I have stopped listening. I look up, away. Above me, birds ball and stretch in great waves, tiny silhouettes against the dying light. Every word is false – and yet every word is true. It is a fair portrait – and vile deceit. She is not stupid. She must know she lies, and yet she persists, so graceful and serene. But she is like a slug: a slug crawling all over Chiara, a slug glistering slime. And now she is preaching on about rocky paths, steep ravines, precipitous slopes, all with a hateful look of perfect piety on her perfect, hateful face.

My control cracks. 'Shame on you!' Words erupt. 'How can you? How dare you?' A great heat has risen to my face. My arms and legs are shaking. Everyone is staring at me, open-mouthed. Arcangela alone wears a frown of cool surprise. 'Shame on you,' I am repeating, 'shame, shame, shame,' but with diminishing force. Nobody else speaks. Arcangela's expression is resolving into one of compassionate concern.

'Please will somebody attend to Sister Beatrice? She is overwrought. We all are. In fact, I think now is the moment for us to repair to the chapel. Already, we have neglected one holy office. To miss another – no. Let us hasten there and pray to the Father that Chiara might be allowed to return to us.'

Plain Chiara. And that judicious conditional – that *might*. To my consternation, my sisters start to obey her. I call them craven – pusillanimous – but only to myself. I tear away, not knowing where to go, only that I will not follow *her*. The cedar tree looms up in front of me, and I fling myself on to a bench. I wrap my arms tighter and tighter around my head, trying to block everything out. A cool fingertip touches the nape of my neck, and I start violently.

'Beatrice,' says Arcangela.

'Go away,' I say.

'Really, Beatrice.' She brushes a few needles from the bench and sits down. I stand up. 'Sit down, Beatrice.'

'No.'

'Beatrice, sit down.'

'No.'

214

'Sit down, or I will ask the men currently talking to your stepmother to remove you – without delay – that you might join Chiara in the Carcere.'

I sit. I hate myself for it, but I sit.

'That's better. This is a delicate moment, Beatrice. Both for our own souls, and for the more figurative soul of our convent. The authorities, both the civic and the ecclesiastical, are concerned – very concerned – and I think we can agree with good reason. It is absolutely imperative we convince them that our faults stem from the pride of one woman. One woman alone. Do you follow me?'

'Yes,' I say, rejoicing as the burden of guilt lifts. 'Yes, of course. I can assume responsibility. I can say the books were mine – the responsibility mine – all mine. They'll return her then, won't they? They'll return her – and I'll – I'll face whatever sanction is my due.'

Arcangela is looking at me strangely. I have surprised her, I think, by my readiness to confess, and I wait for her to instruct me. But she does not speak. Instead, she lets out a small sigh, reminding me curiously of myself when I am irritated by a clumsy copyist.

'I do not,' she says, 'in this instance, refer to your pride – but to Chiara's. You may admit your guilt, yes, but it would only serve to illuminate the greater guilt of your preceptor. Such testimony, along with the testimony of others of your sisters, will show Chiara as a woman who has overreached herself in every particular, who has long aspired to meddle in matters beyond our woman's estate. My understanding, Beatrice, is that the archbishop and his spiritual advisers—'

'You mean Brother Abramo.'

'—will look sympathetically upon any of our younger sisters who have erred. Provided, that is, they are prompt in the admitting of their faults. Their faults, and those of their superiors. Otherwise . . .' She reaches for my hand and places it between her cool white palms. 'Beatrice, we have had our differences, have we not? But trust me when I say I do not want you to suffer needlessly.'

I reclaim my hand. I stand. 'Speak plainly. I must betray Chiara or suffer the consequences?'

'I would not put it like that.'

'How, then? How would you put it?'

'I only ask you to tell the truth. For your own sake – and for the sake of your sisters.'

I am shaking my head. 'This is wrong. Wrong, and you know it. I want nothing to do with it. Nothing, you hear me? Nothing.'

I start to walk away, but her hand flashes out, grips my wrist and pulls me close. 'Beatrice, let me be quite clear. If you ever want to set foot in that library again—'

'And what if I don't? What if I don't?'

She removes her hand. 'That,' she says, 'will be very easy to arrange.'

The Pots

Wednesday morning

⌘

WHILE WASHING THE FLOOR of the latrines, I learn I am
as slow with a mop and pail as Laura is at locating the match-
ing halves of an ablative absolute. The water flees. The dirt
remains. I have turned dry, dirty boards into wet, dirty boards.
And now my skirts, my hands, my feet – and the walls! How
did I do that to the walls? – are dirty too. I hear Timofea
approaching and ready myself for reproof. She cocks her head,
clicks her tongue, and considers the mess I've made.

'You'll improve,' she says, taking the mop from me. 'Now' –
she indicates a pair of buckets – 'slopping out time.'

I don't need to ask what is to be slopped. The smell tells
a succinct story. If we need to use a pot during the hours of
darkness, we visit a niche at our corridor's end. I had never
given much thought to the pot's removal, but evidently, it must
be removed.

'Don't' – she wags a finger – 'wrinkle your nose at me,
young lady. I was born into the best house in town, and if
I'm not too proud to porter my sisters' piss—'

'No, no.' I must stop her before she works herself into one
of her famous lathers. 'Honestly, I don't mind one bit.' That

isn't quite true, but I seize up the buckets with what I hope looks like valiant enthusiasm. 'Where do I start?'

She nods, appeased. 'Reformatory first, cells second, dormitories third, guesthouse last. And Beatrice?' she says.

'Yes?' I say, pausing to get a better grip on the handles.

'Well said. Yesterday. What you said. I'd like to have said the same and more, but' – she looks uncomfortable – 'Arcangela knows I send more than the Green Mary down that river. Women who want to avoid those ruinous tariffs at the city gates, well, they leave their goods in the cave, and we float them down at night. Makes all the difference.'

'You're' – I'm not sure whether I'm shocked or impressed – 'a *contrabbandiera*?'

She shrugs. 'I'm a washerwoman who doesn't like the Bench and the Board taking more than their fair cut of poor women's work. But if Arcangela reported it, I'd be out on my ear, and—'

'Where would you go?'

She nods. 'Where indeed? And listen' – she's pointing now at the buckets – 'don't take it personally. It's what all my new girls do.'

I set off, trying to stop the buckets rubbing against my skirts, wondering how I'll cope when they're full. I glance up at the guesthouse. I told my stepmother, over a whispered conversation in the latrines, that we needed to talk. We agreed she would leave her window open to signal when she was in her room alone. She was deft, too, in her acknowledgement of my peremptory banishment. In fact, all morning, others of my sisters have shown me similar marks of sympathy. Sister Felicitas filled my bowl almost to overflowing. Giulia made an impudent face behind Arcangela's back. I have found my hand squeezed, met a few quiet smiles. It is strange.

But none of it helped when, after breakfast, I saw Arcangela leading Prudenzia towards the library. I knew – obviously, I knew – that my position would be given to her. I had been telling myself she was welcome to it from the moment I awoke: that with Sophia gone, I no longer loved my work; that Abramo's violation had spoiled the place forever. Lies, lies, lies. As they vanished up the stairwell, I could feel the pitch of each step beneath their feet; I could hear the clack of the latch, see the light-striped room, savour the fathomless smell of many books living side by side. And then Prudenzia's face showed at the window above my desk. A mouse staring out of its hole. My hole. My library. I swayed a little, buffeted by loss, only to stumble forwards as Tamara – whose physical gestures are poorly controlled – cuffed me on the back.

'Hard luck,' she said. 'Wouldn't stand and stare though. Only make it worse.' She nodded towards the parlour. 'Boarders've gone too, you know.'

'What? When?'

'Their mammas pitched up around daybreak. On foot, believe it or not. Dressed in sackcloth and ashes. Or good as. Told Sister Paola to be so terribly, terribly kind as to fetch their girls.'

'Did they say why?'

'Didn't need to. It's obvious. They think we're a bad bet. Convent's reputation going down, down, down. Got to go. Me and Maria are cooking the books best we can before Holier Than Thou turns them over to the Bench and the Board.'

'Tamara.' I reached a hand out to stop her leaving.

'What?'

'Why are you, you know – putting up with all this?'

She twisted her face. 'Because it's better than having to bed half the sailors in the Lagoon to buy a one-way ticket back to Carthage, all right?'

Passing beneath the library now, carrying the buckets to the reformatory, I heed her advice and don't look up. I fix my eyes on the ground and plaster a beatific smile across my face. Only when I'm inside, out of sight, do I groan softly to myself. My arms hurt.

Through the workroom door to the left, I can hear Sister Nanina reading from the Stories in a thin but fluent voice. I turn to the right and search along the corridor until I find the night pot. Mastering my revulsion, I tip the contents into my bucket and mount the stairs to the first floor. Another corridor, another pot, then onwards to the upper floor. I have miscon-strued each bucket's capacity, and the one in my right hand is now overloaded. Sighting the final pot, I put on an ill-advised burst of speed. The bucket brims and spatters my legs with excreta. I cry out in vexation and wonder how I can wipe it away. A door opens nearby, and I look up, conscious again of my humiliation, but I am relieved – pleased, even – to see Diana emerging from her cell. I smile at her ruefully, expecting her to greet me with warmth, but instead she leans back against the wall, folds her arms and regards me with a cold contempt.

'What?' I say.

'Chiara's protected you, right enough. The others don't blame you – they even seem to think you're some kind of martyr for speaking two words against that Judas of a woman. *Shame, shame.*' Her words are an unkind but accurate mimicry. 'They don't blame you, but you can be sure I do. He's after that book, isn't he? The same one Tomis was after?'

I open my mouth to deny it, but she jabs a finger at me.

'Don't lie to me. I spoke to Giulia. She didn't hear everything that happened in the library – and she didn't understand everything she heard – but it's plain as day you've got something he wants. I wish I'd let Tomis take it, then at least he'd be banged up, not Chiara.'

'But he is – he is banged up. He told Abramo about the book. He betrayed me—'

'*He betrayed me.*' The same mocking tone. Do I really sound like that? 'And if he told, why d'you think that was? Because Abramo asked him round for a cup of wine and a cosy chat? Don't be so naive! What that man spouts from the pulpit – thumbscrews and firebrands – those aren't stories. They're the Shepherds' bread and butter.' She pushes herself off the wall. 'Beatrice, what in the Father's name were you doing with that book in the first place?'

'It was – a sort of accident. The women gave it to me. Before they died.' I had thought thereby to excuse myself, but my words are fat on her angry flame.

'You took a book from those women? When you knew the Lambs were after them? When we already had Abramo hammering at the gate? How could you be so foolish. How?'

I blink. The guilt uncoils in my belly.

Diana is shaking her head. 'You are so blind – so selfish—'

'Stop,' I beg her, 'stop.'

'—if he wants your stupid book, you give it to him.'

'I can't. I can't. Diana, you don't understand—'

'I understand enough – I understand you care more about that book than—'

'But Mother Chiara, she told me not to give it to him.'

'Hah.' She stares at me. 'That's handy. Too handy. It doesn't wash – why would—?'

'No, you must believe me. You see, I showed her the book – just before she met those men in the parlour – and she said, "Don't let him have it." She said—' I pause, trying to reassemble her exact words. 'She said, "The Father shouldn't have everything his way."'

Diana grasps my hand. Covers my mouth. 'Beatrice, stop. What are you saying?'

We stand like that, very still, very silent, listening. I was not guarding my voice. I was – bawling heresy. I think we are both expecting Arcangela and Abramo to come galloping up the stairs. Finally, she releases me. Leans close to ask, 'Beatrice – what is this book?'

'You remember,' I whisper, 'you remember what you said, when Tomis was trying to take the book from me, what you said about wanting to help, when you could. Well, this book – helps. When it can. When women are threatened – in danger – it helps.'

'How – how can a book help? Beatrice – *how?*'

I lower my voice to its absolute minimum. 'It is possessed of the power of – of – the Mother.'

She lets out an extraordinary and explosive string of curses, and immediately we hear the voice of Nanina on the stairs.

'Diana, whatever are you doing? Your presence is required this instant – this instant, in the workroom, do you hear? Sister Arcangela has said I am to brook no more excuses. Diana? Diana! Is somebody up there with you?'

'Nothing!' she calls. 'Nobody! I'm coming.' She grips my arm. 'This is dangerous. Beatrice, this is – I need to tell you something. Find me later – find me—'

'Di-aaaaa-na!'

'Cooooom-ing!'

'What?' I hiss. 'What do you need to tell me?'

'*Diana!*'

'*Coming!*' And with an apologetic backwards shrug, she is off, leaping down the stairs.

The Guesthouse

Immediately thereafter

⌗

I DESCEND MORE SLOWLY, lopsided, lugging the buckets.
Standing now outside the reformatory, I squint against the
sun. Ortolana's window is open. Gingerly, I cross the quadrilango and climb the guesthouse stairs. In the first two rooms
are two ladies, antique and immeasurably grand, who are passing the Forty-Day Fast with us, shoring up additional credit
for their – surely imminent – journey to the hereafter. I knock,
creep inside, empty their pots. Both are motionless, humming
in their chairs. I creep out again. The third door is ajar.

Through the crack, I can see Ortolana, seated at a little
table, writing what I take to be a letter. The window casement beside her is wedged open, and a breeze lifts her hair,
which is uncovered and unkempt. Her face is unpainted. She
appears – raw, skittish. I knock on the door, and hear a brisk
call: 'Come in.'

When I enter, she does not look up, only waves a hand and
says, 'Thank you – it's in that corner.'

I clear my throat, which makes her flinch with irritation. I
have distracted her. Her pen, which previously cantered across
the paper, slows to a crotchety trot. She stumbles over a word,
crosses it out with great vehemence – slash, slash – before

thrusting the pen into its stand and turning to frown at the tactless housekeep. Her expression lightens only a little when she realises it is me.

'Beatrice,' she says, arranging her papers so as to cover whatever she was writing.

'Yes,' I reply, rather absurdly.

She does not look well. The whites of her eyes have yellowed with tiredness. Her pupils are strangely large. Possibly it is the darkness of the room, but the effect is uncanny. She fidgets with the papers before her, pulling one back out, hiding it again.

'I was – that is to say – I fear my days here are numbered. They told me yesterday – you heard? Yesterday, they told me that your brother is found. He had ridden to one of our villas. He was found drunk and debauched. They are escorting him back to the city. My poor boy' – a feverish laugh – 'he couldn't even run away properly.'

'Ortolana—'

She waves me quiet. 'I wish I could save you from a life hauling slop, but I'm sorry. It's too late. Brother Abramo is the Father's besom, and we are all dried leaves and cobwebs at his feet.' Her head drops into her hands. 'I'm sorry,' she repeats.

I go to her, touch her shoulder. 'Never mind about that. I didn't want to talk about me. Chiara told me something. Something important. About him – about Brother Abramo.'

'Gossip, Beatrice?' A tired smile. 'I'm all ears.'

And so I proceed to tell her everything Chiara told me. My account is neither orderly nor composed, but rather a headlong rush, so keen am I to arrive at the end – to say, 'So you see – knowing this – were we to make this known – could we not undo him?'

When I have finished – and I acknowledge she has listened with acute attention – she does not stir, and I think perhaps she does not believe me, and so I begin to insist on my knowledge, my truthfulness, touching – I admit – a little on her shortcomings for not trusting me, only ceasing when she unfolds her arms and raps the table in front of her.

'Knowing this,' she says, slowly, 'knowing that Brother Abramo has long nurtured a profound and personal animus against Mother Chiara, that this animus has informed his targeting of the convent, what action would you now advise?'

'Tell the world. Tell everyone that he is a seducer, a charlatan, a hypocrite. That he is bent on vengeance, not salvation.'

'Such a course,' she says, 'would be death.'

'And does he not deserve to die?'

She emits a great peal of laughter, a merry sound at odds with everything else. 'Bloodthirsty Beatrice! But alas, no, I do not mean his death – but mine. Mine and Chiara's. Let me see, what is it you would have me do?' She picks up her pen, pulls forward a fresh sheet of paper, makes to dip it in the ink. 'Write to the best men of the city, to the Bench and the Board, to the chiefs of the guilds, the heads of the corporations, alerting them to Brother Abramo's youthful transgression? What would they do? Throw up their hands in horror, muster the guards and drive him beyond the city's bounds with his wrists knotted behind his back?'

'Why not?' I say, for that is a fair copy of what I had in mind. 'Why not?' I repeat.

'You sound like Ludo when I denied him comfits.'

'I didn't know you denied him anything.'

'There's a lot you don't know, Beatrice – as I think this conversation is proving.'

For a moment, there is silence between us. I had thought mothers were blind to their sons' faults, each thinking herself another Mother-Mary, cradling an immaculate boy-child.

225

Perhaps, I am mistaken in that, too. I return, nevertheless, to the attack.

'You're afraid to denounce him. You're a coward,' I say, but the word does not land as emphatically as I had hoped.

'A coward?' she says, thoughtfully. 'Very possibly I am. But it is not courageous simply to climb a tall tower and leap to one's death. If I thought I could save Chiara and damn Abramo with such a leap, I might do it.' She winces. 'Might.'

'Chiara would. She'd do it.'

'She would. But I'm not Chiara. And even Chiara could sacrifice herself and yet save nobody. Accept it, Beatrice: it won't work.'

'Why not?' I say again.

She rubs her forehead with the heel of her hand, digging her fingertips into the hair on the crown of her head. She grimaces. 'Because the people admire him.'

'So tell them – tell the people. They won't admire him once they know the truth.'

'And how would you do that, Beatrice?'

'I don't know. Write an annuncio. Have it cried in the piazzas . . .' I trail off.

She is watching me. 'Would you do that? Knowing the regard in which he is held? Would you walk the streets, handing out pamphlets attacking him? What would happen? Can you not guess? You were there to hear Maria's tale.'

I picture the Lambs, their white dirty cloaks, their yellow teeth, their certainty. I picture paper flying, scattered, trampled – and my own end, fast or slow.

'But,' I say, incapable of relinquishing my plan, for a fervid sense of its rightness still burns within me, 'but is there not some great man of the city – you know them, their qualities – surely one of them could—?'

Already, she is shaking her head. 'Oh, Beatrice,' she says, a little despairingly, but not unkindly. 'Towards the end of his life, your father tried to draw the teeth of anyone whose wealth and power rivalled his own. Such a course now appears – short-sighted. It fostered resentment.'

She sighs and spreads her hands on the table before her.

'Abramo would claim he was summoned here by the Father, but he was also made very welcome by a confederacy of your father's enemies, by the other rich men of the city who have long felt themselves slighted. Perhaps now they regret the extent of his success – or perhaps not. Abramo has thrown the Stelleri down. Our name is trampled in the dirt. And they, in return, they will raise him up. They will raise him high, perhaps as high as the pontifex's chair in St Peter's itself.'

'He – he wants to go to St Peter's?' She is running too fast for me. 'But – but he hates it. He calls it debased. The – the whore of Babylon. The—'

'The rank sty. The suppurating pit. Yes, yes, all that and more. But if you wish to rule over a thing, first it can serve to despoil it. That's what he's doing to Chiara – to the convent. You know what men in other places like to call our city? Men in St Peter's, in the Lagoon, in Herculaneum?'

I shake my head.

'The City of Women,' she says. 'And they do not mean it as a compliment. You, Beatrice, you have only known Chiara. Her position – her influence – perhaps you think it commonplace? I can assure you it is not. This city is full of men – women, too – who would delight to see that influence broken. They think it wrong. Sinful. Dangerous. Against the very will of the Father. You do not need me to elucidate further?'

I shake my head. I have read the texts. It is hard to avoid them. I know too well how women – from Eve onwards – are thought of.

Ortolana has fallen silent. She is gnawing a thumbnail. She rips it, winces and stares as it glistens with blood, before placing it in her mouth again. When next she speaks, it is with sudden violence. 'I wish your father had never heard of the damned Mother. I wish that damned book was at the bottom of the sea. I wish you'd never got your hands on it.'

'Don't say that—'

'I can say what I damn well like. You don't know what it's done to me. I'm always hungry. I can hear the mice in the walls. I can see little trails where they run. And I – I want to eat them. And the sun is too bright, and the fountain is too white. And I – I feel strange.'

'But you should see it – what happened to you. It – you – you look magnificent. The picture. It's so beautiful.' I reach into my pocket, bring out the book, but she slams the table with both her hands.

'Put that thing away.'

'It saved you,' I cry. 'And it'll save Chiara – I know it will. Look at it. Please,' I beg her, pushing the book towards her. 'Don't be afraid—'

'Have you?'

'Have I what?'

'You know. *Changed*.'

'No,' I say. 'No. I haven't.'

'If you have not, then please do not tell whether or not to be afraid.'

The book sits on the table between us. I think she is going to push it away, but I see she is now looking at it. Slowly, she reaches for it. I watch her open the boards. I step forwards, ready to tell her what she is seeing, but she holds a hand up. She traces the trailing brambles with the index finger of her right hand, traces the letters as they twist and twine. I hear a hushed whispering, and I assume, of course I assume, that it is the book. But I am wrong. Her lips are moving.

She can read it.

She can read it.

I am so consumed by envy – that of all things, she should have this, this too – that I do not at first see that she has turned to the next page, and the next. She is staring, stricken, at where the great bird soars across the parchment. Her teeth lock about her knuckle.

'What?' I say. '*What?*'

'You can't read it?' She laughs, wildly. 'You – you can't read this?'

'No!' I cry. 'But how – but why can you?'

'Because, child, because I'm hers. Because I – changed.'

'But that's—'

'Not what you want to hear? Sorry, Beatrice. Does your learning have its limitations, after all?'

'But what,' I say, ignoring that gibe, 'what does it say? Is there some key to its power? Something we can use? What – what?'

'No, no, it's me. It's all the things I've never said. What I've never been able to say. What I've yet to find the words for. It's – it's me.'

'*You?* Is that all?'

Her laughter has a yet more hysterical edge. 'Yes, yes, that's all. But you don't want that, do you? You want the Ten Rules, all over again. A great revelation written with the Mother's finger. And then you could come down from your mountain and tell everyone all about it—'

'No,' I say, 'no, that's not what I – no.' Although, of course, she's right. Of course, that's exactly what I want.

'You – want something lofty, something grand. You don't want my grief, my pain, my love—'

229

'I'm sorry,' I cry. 'I'm sorry my father died. I'm sorry that Ludo ran away. I'm sorry.'

I reach towards her because I find the words are true. I reach towards her, but she pulls her hands away, and I hear what sounds like knives dragging across the table, and I see great scratch marks, scored into the wood. She watches me, unblinking, her hands beneath the table, until one by one, her eyes fill, brim, spill.

'What is it?' I whisper.

'The night. The night Bianca gave birth. When you left, when I was holding him, my hands changed – like this.' She holds them up, and I glimpse great hooked talons, before she hides them once again. 'I had to wake Bianca. There was blood running down his back where I'd caught him. I had to pretend the blood was mine. My own hands returned, but each time I try to hold my grandson, I feel it happening again – and I have to give him back. And I – I think it is a punishment. I think the Mother – I think she is punishing me. Because I never held my daughter. As soon as they cut the bloody rope, they bundled her up and removed her. No – no – that's not true. I *told* them to remove her. "Don't you want to hold her?" they said. "Just once?" No, I told them, no. I never held her. And I think, somehow, she remembers, and I think that is why – why she has always hated me.'

'Your daughter?' I am confused. Why is she staring at me like that? 'But you don't—'

'I do, Beatrice, I do, I do, I do. You really want to know what's written in your book? Well, I'll tell you. What's written there. It tells how I've felt every day since I gave you up.'

She is looking at me fiercely, so fiercely. She holds still – then turns away, with a gasp, a pent-up cry. I sway. What do I say? Do I have to speak?

Why – why did you—?

I feel a keen pain between my temples. Words are jumbling and muddling in my head, a knotted mess, tangled black threads. I can't straighten them. I can't – I am so angry. Am I angry? I put my hands to my face, as though my fingers, tracing there, might read how I feel and inform me. No, no. Not angry. I am so—

hurt.

'I had no choice,' she is saying. 'I regret it, body and soul, I regret it, but I swear I had no choice.'

One word, I summon. 'How?' I say – for *how* seems easier than *why*.

'Love,' she says. 'It made me – and your father – behave in a way I can no longer understand, in a way I can hardly now recall.' Her words are coming fast, and I sense I am listening to a speech long prepared. 'I was little more than a child. We had met, but never spoken. But I knew he burned for me, even as I burned for him. It was carnival. My father allowed my sisters and I to go to watch. I was dressed as Minerva. I saw him across the street. I pretended to get lost. We found one another and – and then the pestilenza came, and, by chance – although we called it fate – our families sent us to the same valley in the hills. Up there, the rules were different. We walked, we worked, we helped with the harvest. It was a time of great joy. And the night before he was to return to the city – we forgot ourselves.

'I knew almost at once what had happened, what was happening, and I was in despair. I confessed everything to the woman I was staying with – the one you know as Zia. She told me there were ladies in the nearest town who would help me. I walked there alone. Fifteen miles. And that's when I first met Chiara. I cried and cried and cried, and she said I wasn't to take it so hard. She said I wasn't the first girl nor the last to get in trouble. She said I should write to my parents and say I had been invited to pass six months with them, serving the poor and needy. I thought my parents agreed because of Chiara's fame, but now I think maybe they guessed, and were glad I'd found a solution. As my time grew near, I thought maybe I'd stay. I loved Chiara. I loved them all.

'But then a letter arrived from your father, saying he'd won his own father round, that everything was arranged, that I had but to finish my madcap devotions and we could be man and wife. And so after you – after you were born – I left. I returned to the city, I married your father, and when enough time had elapsed that no questions would be asked, when Zia said you favoured your father most especially in your looks, I brought you home.'

I have no name for the hollowness inside my chest. 'Had you already told him? About me?'

She nods.

'Before or after you were wed?'

She cannot meet my gaze.

'Before,' I repeat, 'or after?'

'After. Beatrice, I—'

But the sound of footsteps climbing the broad stone stairs silences us. Neither of us moves. I am sure we are both hoping the feet are bent on some errand that does not concern us. I will them to pass, but they do not. They stop at the door. A light tap.

'You will permit me to come in?' Arcangela's voice.

'One moment,' calls Ortolana.

I snatch up the book and scramble without dignity across the bed, dropping into the gap between it and the wall. I am trying to level my breathing, when I hear Arcangela enter.

'Forgive me,' says Ortolana, who is arranging blankets above me, 'while I set things to rights.'

'Surely you have not been abed?'

'I was resting. I have a bad head.'

'I trust nothing serious? You will forgive me, but I cannot think you look well.'

Ortolana makes no reply, other than to say, in a voice flat and weary, 'What do you want, Emilia?'

Emilia – not Arcangela. A tussling silence follows. When a woman wishes to indicate a particularly overwhelming vocation, she can choose to assume a new name upon making her Promise. Emilia, then, is Arcangela's birth-name, the name she wished to leave behind. The silence continues. Who will speak first? Suddenly, I feel stifled, a little delirious, imagining hours of this stretching ahead.

'I'm surprised,' says Arcangela, at long last, 'that you should wish to recall the days of our girlhood.'

'Would you rather look to the future?' Ortolana already sounds more like herself. 'Mother Superior! Was that what you had in mind when we used to sneak into your mamma's cabinet to paint our faces? I've been wondering – did it exist back then, your famed vocation?'

'I was very relieved when Papà finally gave permission for me to withdraw from the world.'

'Oh, so it *did* exist? It's just that you hid it so well. How I envied you. Your hair – I remember it fell like a waterfall to the backs of your knees. And those clever dresses your mamma had made for you. That trick you had, of tying your ribbons so as to hoist, so as to elevate – well, you remember, I'm sure. When you suddenly vanished behind these walls, the very month of my marriage, I wondered, was there some disgrace, some lapse? And then I thought, you never could bear to be second best—'

'Enough. You forget yourself.'

'—but perhaps I was wrong. This convent is quite a prize. What else are you prepared to—'

'I said, *enough*. It is no longer wise for you to speak so.'

'How should I speak? Meekly, humbly, modestly? Please, Sister Arcangela, please tell me why you are here.' I hear what sounds like Ortolana sitting down at her table.

'The Proctors,' begins Arcangela, 'have now spoken to your son at length, and I understand it was a most – productive conversation. He had a great deal to say, only sometimes he struggled to order his thoughts into a useful coherence. Nevertheless, he has helped shine a light on the crooked relationship between your family and this convent. He has already hinted that he plans to make the larger part of his wealth over to the Shepherds, that they might further their holy work. Indeed, it seems that, as with so many others, the time your son has spent with Brother Abramo has much improved both his moral and spiritual character.'

'The horses, the drink, the dice – they were but a – a costume? I see. And he needed Brother Abramo to help him find the right path.' A pause. 'Bravo, Emilia. Bravo.'

'You, too, can choose the right path, Ortolana, and I am here – in my own modest way – to help you take the first step along it. Your son has requested that you join him at the archbishop's residenza to prepare yourself for penance. Brother Abramo plans a great Day of Remorse, that troubled souls might acknowledge their shortcomings, beg forgiveness of their fellow citizens, and renew their commitment to the Father.'

'Those troubled souls being?'

'You, your son and Chiara.'

'And if we are deemed insufficiently remorseful?'

'The city's anger – you must understand – is near to boiling point. You can only provoke Father-fearing men for so long. It is lucky, I think, that Abramo is here, to lance their rage, else who knows what might have happened? I must add that—'

'I know, I know. I am a widow. In law, Ludo is my guardian, and you could not possibly obstruct his will. I will not resist. I do not want to give that man further cause to pervade this holy house. Give me a moment to gather myself, and I shall come to the parlour.'

'I am sorry, no. We are to go at once. The Proctors have been waiting long enough.'

There's a pause, during which I can hear the sound of Ortolana pulling on boots, and likely a cloak and shawl.

'Your son,' says Arcangela into the silence, 'also requested that his wife and son join him, but Sister Agatha reports them still in such ill health after the delivery that they cannot possibly be moved. I continue to pray for their recovery.'

The door opens and closes. Footsteps fade. Stillness. I am, I realise, hiding from nobody in an empty room. I unbend arms and legs, cricked and complaining, and squirm free of the blankets. I shove the bed aside and stand. I dart to the open window and watch them disappearing into the parlour. A few moments later, I can just make out Ortolana's small shape, surrounded by guards, crossing the campo.

For a moment, I find I am pitying her, but then – *how could she?* How could she – for *years* – pretend? Ah, I say to myself, but it wasn't so very many years, was it? She left you in the hills for as long as it served. She brought you to the city when the fancy took her – and sent you away as soon as she realised her mistake. I wish she'd never told me. I wish I didn't know. But she'd never have told me – would she? – had it not been for that book.

Seized by a sudden upwelling of hate, I smash it down on to the table: once, twice, three times. If this is its knowledge,

I do not want it. Wandering witches, an ignorant dirty goat-girl, a selfish old woman: the book is nothing but a tawdry witness, ogling us and spattering its pages with a scrawl of fear and dread. No wonder her temples are dust, if this is all the power she can muster. Turning women into trees and birds. Making beasts of us. As if men don't do that already. And why – *why?* – have I risked so much to protect it when it can do nothing – *nothing* – but tell me what I suffer? I hate it. I despise it. I want it out of my head. I want my old calm: quiet library, dip of pen, straight lines.

The book. I stare at it on the table. I nudge it. Shove it.

Are you in there? Are you there?

Why – why are you doing this?

I pound it with my fist. I pick it up and shake it. I – I have dislodged Ortolana's papers. Sheets skim across the floor. One – a letter – addressed to me.

Dear Beatrice,

I have tried to write this letter a hundred times, but I never knew how to begin. A hundred times, I begged Mother Chiara to tell you the truth, trusting she would find the right words, but she said it was my tale to tell. Now she is locked away, and I fear I am to follow, and so I must speak before it is too late. Beatrice, I am—

My anger finds a new target. I tear the letter to shreds.

The Light

Immediately thereafter

✠

I STUMBLE DOWN THE STAIRS with no real idea of where I am going, and all but collide with one of Hildegard's help-meets. I try to dodge around her, but she is frustratingly intent on detaining me.

'Sister Beatrice? Sister Beatrice! *There* you are.' She sounds querulous, plaintive. 'I've been looking for you *everywhere*.'

'I can't talk now, I can't—'

But she moves to block me. 'Have you not heard? Arcangela says, after everything, we're to confess a day early.'

And I understand. Confession proceeds from youngest to oldest, a rigid order, long established. Her place falls three before mine and so, newly shriven, she bids me to the chapel. I stare about me wildly. How can I go to chapel? A horrible hiccupping laugh escapes me. *Honora patrem tuum et matrem tuam.* The fourth Rule. But how – tell me how – how can I honour my mother after this?

'Sister Beatrice,' says the helpmeet. She still has my sleeve, and is looking at me warily. 'I should tell you – that is, you probably should know—'

'Theophila!' A passing warden. 'What's this dawdling? Hildegard will be wondering what's become of you.'

The girl gives me an apologetic shrug and races away towards the fields. The warden doesn't tell her to slow down. She's too busy glowering at me. I grimace. Very well, to confession then. Dear Father Michele, all my life I have mourned a woman who is not dead. Dear Father Michele, all my life I have hated the one woman I should love the most. What'll the poor man make of that?

I throw myself on to a stool at the side of the chapel – beside Prudenzia, who always has preceded me. She is trying to ignore me, staring straight ahead, her hands folded in her lap, but she can't resist one quick, disdainful glance. I feel my dislike of her almost as a balm. Leaning back against the chapel wall, I stretch my legs before me, digging my heels into the dirt.

'Congratulations,' I say. 'On your elevation. Don't hesitate to ask if you need any advice.'

Ever so slightly, she turns away.

'Sorry,' I say. 'To disturb you. You must be trying to think of something to confess. It must be hard – you being so very good.' I click my fingers. 'There now, I have it! *Invidia.* That means envy.'

Her head snaps round. 'I know what it means,' she hisses.

I shuffle infinitesimally closer. '"All had their eyelids stitched with iron wire like untamed falcons." That's Dante,' I whisper. 'Thirteenth canto. But I expect you knew that, too.'

She stands up, sharply.

'Prudenzia,' I bleat, leaning forwards to tug at her mantle, 'aren't we supposed to sit here quietly?'

She tugs back, putting another couple of steps between us.

'"Their eyes,"' I continue, '"were ghastly seams, remorse from envy forced their weeping through them."'

'Why,' she says, and her eyes shine with sudden tears, 'why

have you always been so unkind to me? Why? What have I ever done to you? I try to live here, the same as anyone. I try – try to be nice and sisterly. I *try*. And, since we were novices, you – you are like this. I think you are arrogant, hateful, and I hope you get everything you deserve.'

At that moment, another woman from my first dormitory, all nose and chin and mindless fervour, comes round the corner of the chapel, her confession done. She gives me a cold look and says to Prudenzia, 'You are to go straight in, sister.'

She does, without a backwards glance.

I sit in silence, frowning. Am I those things? I do not think I am. I summon all the reasons I have to dislike Prudenzia. There are many, I am sure. Her mealy-mouthed niceness, her relentless fawning – but then, until yesterday, when did I ever dare displease Arcangela? Before I can answer myself, Tamara slides down beside me and grunts a greeting.

'Pleasant morning?'

I hardly know how to reply, but I don't have to. Tamara is leaning closer, talking fast.

'We've had the Bench and the Board all over us. Gathering evidence. Demanding accounts. Receipts. The works.' She glances at me. 'Saw your stepmother being marched out.'

I nod and swallow.

'Arcangela gloating, the—' she adds a coarse word, which I believe means both runty piglet and shrivelled pouch. She looks towards the chapel door. Sniffs. 'I told Maria I wasn't going to tell him nothing. But she told me nothing was dangerous-er than something, and a dog with an empty belly is dangerous-er than one fat and fed, and if we clam up too hard, he'll dig harder, and – well, she told me more besides, but the meat of it is, this is a fight, and she's not afraid of a fight, and there's others who aren't, neither. The pontifex won't like it, she says, nor Silvia neither – but we're not going to win here and now, not by ourselves, not with the city minded as it is, so she said I wasn't to stir up more trouble than we've already got – and she said you weren't to neither.'

She wags a finger at me and assembles her face into an unflattering mirror of my confusion.

'But what – whatever are you talking about?'

'Just don't get him more riled up than he already is, all right?'

'Who, Father Michele?'

'No!'

'What? The deacon?'

'No, Beatrice, you dolt, no. Him. *Him.* Brother Abramo.'

I look around me, bewildered.

She jabs her thumb behind her. 'There. He's in there. That' – another word, coarser – 'that Arcangela, she's let him come hear our confession.'

'She's – she's what? He's—'

I am lost for words, but not Tamara, not by any measure.

'That's right. Special dispensation from the archbishop. Burdened souls needing expert confessor. Where've you *been* all morning? The tinies all came out in tears, but Alfonsa looked like she'd had the time of her life. Like she'd smoked a pipe or three of papaver.' And she does an impression of Alfonsa's face in bliss, which, at another time, might have been very funny.

'But why – why does he want to hear our confession? He cannot make use of it. Surely, the sanctity of the—'

'Oh, grow *up*,' she says. 'Whatever he can get on Chiara, he'll use. He's working up his case, his *inquisizione*, his *denunciatio*, his – I don't know – whatever the Shepherds call what they do when there's somebody they've got their crooks into.' She cranes her neck round again. 'Pah, she's been in there a long time.'

She's right. I've sat here — how many times? — while Prudenzia examines her soul, and normally she seems to do it briskly and efficiently, as though confession were no more bothersome than dabbing one's face with a napkin. But at that moment, she rushes out, hurrying away without looking back.

Tamara joggles my stool. 'Best hurry, Beà,' she says. 'Don't want to keep him waiting. Over and done with, right? Right?' She gives me a bracing shake. 'Off you go. No more trouble, remember?'

I follow the wall around to the chapel door. I push it open. It creaks. I step inside and the day's warmth fades. Slowly, I walk down the nave. I pause. *No trouble.* Didn't I fail to bow when I entered the chapel? Fail, too, to shape the cross? Did he notice? I drop to the ground and press my head to the grille that lies before the altar steps. I stand and touch my fingertips to my head, to my heart, to the point of each shoulder. And only then do I turn to my left, towards the northern transept, towards his confessional chair.

It is open to the front, so I can see his bare feet and the outline of his legs beneath his robes — but with a high back and sides, so I cannot see his upper body, nor his face. A hole has been cut in the side closest to me, the side that acts as a screen between us. Below the hole, a step, a little ledge, upon which I now go to kneel. Father Michele smells of frying onions. The deacon of sweet lime-soap. Abramo — of his own unwashed body. I clasp my hands and close my eyes.

Have mercy upon me, I beg of you, for I am a sinful woman. The words, the worn old words, rise up in my throat, but I cannot make myself say them. I cannot — not to him. A stillness follows, during which my resolve grows, if anything, stronger — and then he speaks.

'What is this? Silence? Are you, sister, already in a state of grace?'

Until this moment, I would have said that his power came from his bearing, his countenance – but now, listening to his voice, shorn of its body, I know I was wrong. While I could yet see his face, he remained a man, fallible. Now he is voice alone, he is something more. Honeyed, that is the word the poets use for a voice such as his, and it is apt, capturing the longing it provokes in me, an unfamiliar desire to permit myself to sink into something rich and sweet. I think of the wasps, circling the cookhouse traps in high summer. What a way to die, honey closing over your head, drowning in everything you ever sought.

'Beatrice,' he says again, and I feel a heightening that is, I confess, some parts elation and some parts fear, for he should – of course – not name me during the sacrament of reconciliation, and in doing so he appeals to my vanity, my pride. 'You are so unlike your sisters.'

Again, that same ugly thrill.

'I have spoken to Sister Arcangela about you.'

My breathing hitches.

'Beatrice, you are such as the Son most loves. The lonely, the outcast. One who is little loved by their fellows. The motherless, fatherless. The lost.'

I thrill no longer. I refute him in my head – no, no, *no* – even as my heart mewls, yes, yes, *yes*. The intolerable weight of all that is unlovable about me lands on my chest, stealing my breath as surely as though I were prisoned in a vice of diabolical devising, to which the Devil had given him the handle.

'Beatrice,' he says, his voice softer, closer. 'You should feel no shame if you have so far failed to secure the goodwill of your companions on earth, for there is but one reckoning that signifies – the account we give of ourselves to the Father. He looks deep, deep into our hearts. I wonder, Beatrice, what does he see in yours?'

And there he pauses and lets the silence grow. The world shrinks. The vice tightens. The vaulted ceiling, the high windows – gone, all gone. Only the steadiness of his breath and the puling of my conscience remain.

'Beatrice, come now. I cannot let you continue down this path. Long ago, I promised myself I would never let a woman tread the road to hell without devoting myself, body and soul, to calling her back – to saving her. And I would save you, Beatrice.'

I find my voice. 'Like you – like you saved Chiara's sister?'

I hear a long, low sigh.

'Oh, Beatrice.' He does not sound as I expected. He does not sound angry. He sounds sad. 'That poor girl had – forgive me – had so many lovers. When she found herself with child, Chiara was the only person who was surprised. I do not know why she chose to blame me, the one man who never looked at her sister that way. I no more lusted after her than I would lust after you, Beatrice. I had seen too clearly what a man's lust does to women. I had seen what it did to my mother.'

He shifts in his chair on the other side of the screen, and his voice now comes from a little further away, and I think he has leaned back, tilted his head up.

'As a little boy, I thought my mother very beautiful. You could say I worshipped her. When I was old enough to ask who my father was, she told me the Son had no Father on earth, and he was a good boy who loved his mother just as dearly as I did. But as I grew older, I learned what she was. A woman who kept lovers. Lovers who paid her well. Lovers whose money allowed us to live as we did, who bought my books and boots, who patted my head on their way up our stairs. When I was older still, I told her what she did was wrong, that it was not too late, that she could repent, that the Son would forgive. She refused. She said she did it for me, and

243

one day I would understand. I grew angry, and in my anger I failed to reconcile her to the Father until it was too late.

'She was one of the first in our town to die of the pestilenza, and in her terrible suffering, the black and bloody dissolution of her body, I saw but the precursor to the suffering she would endure after death. The priest did not come – he could not come to all. Alone, I tried to make her confess, to repent, to submit to the Father at the very end, but she refused. She said she had done no wrong. She died, and it was Chiara who found me by her side; Chiara who convinced me to bury her; Chiara who persuaded me that my mother, in her heart, when she was beyond speech, had begged the Father's forgiveness, and so found her way to his house.

'But, Beatrice' – his voice now comes closer – 'she lied. I know where my mother is, and every day I suffer her pain. I love women. Your gentleness, your softness. Hell is no place for you. And so I must protect you: from yourselves, from the world, and from the Father's wrath.'

He leaves a silence that I cannot fill. My foolishness, my recklessness, are now laid bare to me. No, speak plainly. My *sin*. What have I been doing? In all conscience, what have I done?

I have heard Arcangela say that in the ecstasy of prayer, she sometimes finds herself in the lowest hallways of the Father's house, within sight of his sweeping stair. And sometimes, she even hears a footfall, glimpses a shadow upon the landing, and knows that he listens, knows that he is there. Such a smile plays upon her face when she speaks of it, that I have often wondered how it feels. But when I have tried, in prayer, to find my own way there, I have always failed.

Now, though, all too clearly, I can picture myself standing on the threshold of the Father's house. The blinding light of his grace pours from the upper windows, while I stand outside, in the shadows. This moment, I realise, is hell's subtle prologue, one upwards glance at everything I might have had – before the trap-door opens to the vaults below.

'Forgive me, Beatrice.' Brother Abramo is now so close that I can hear when his lips part. 'When we spoke before, in the library, I was angry. Perhaps I even frightened you. But I know you fear the path you have taken – the path you take. And yet, there is another road – and it leads upwards.' There is a smile and a lift to his voice. 'I know you love Alighieri Dante. Perhaps you don't know that I love him too. Recall how he follows Virgil out of the darkness. You know the verses? "We bore an easy load – the task of getting back to the sweet light. And up we went, he first, I second, to the point where I could see an opening." I would have you follow me, Beatrice. I would have you see the stars again.'

The book, I realise, has found its way into my hands. I am gripping it tightly to keep my hands from shaking. Slowly, I move it sideways – to my left, to where he must be able to see it – but he does not take it.

I say, 'Here. Here it is. It's yours.'

Still he does not reach for it. He says, 'I do not care about the book, Beatrice. I care about you. Tell me, are you ready to return with me to the Father? Will you walk in his light by my side?'

I feel words welling up, lovely words, words that will put an end to doubt. I want to be a good woman: one who deserves a place in the Father's house, at his table, by his side. I can picture her, this good woman. I could be her. I could climb inside her, fit my limbs into hers, feel our hearts start to beat as one. Together, she and I will step out of the deep places, out of the darkness, out of fear, and return to his light. But when I open my mouth to speak, I hear only the whispering of the book, filling my head with its noise and shadow.

I look down.

My sight is – blurring.

My hands—

I can see hands, hands layered over hands, hands holding the book, and each hand is threaded with black and silver.

My sight.

It shatters, it splinters. I—

I make one last great effort.

I hammer on the door of my heart and beg for help, and for the first time I hear a reply. For the first time, a voice comes from that place inside me, the place that has always been empty and dusty, a cold and shuttered room. But now, at last, there is light under the door and the warmth of a body inside, and a voice that says:

'HE IS NOT LISTENING. BUT I AM.'

Where?

When?

⌘

I—

I am—

I am not—

I am not myself.

The Wall

Deep middle night

⌗

I AM ON MY SIDE, my knees drawn to my chin, my shoulders hunched to my ears, my fists clenched against my brow. My jaw aches. My head aches. Everything aches.

I stare at a point of light, and wonder what it means, whether I should drag my heedless body towards it or shrink deeper into the dark. I lift my head from its bolster of stone and the light resolves into a single lantern burning in the darkness of the chapel. I try to sit up, but I am numb, ragged with exhaustion, and can only pull myself on to my elbows to stare bewildered about me.

The chapel is empty and the windows above the nave are almost black. I am, I realise, wedged into the corner of the northern transept, between the wall and the altar of Green Mary. I look up at her. By my right hand, between two bars of the rail that surrounds her shrine, stretches a spider's web – perfect, empty – shifting in the unseen breath of the chapel. I lift my hand and see silver threads weaving in and out of my fingers. I try to tear them off, but as I do, more come – more and more and more.

My skin crawls and my bones shake. I feel my face with hands that are sticky, gluey, grimy. The rest of the world feels at once both very loud and very far away. I am seized by wave upon wave of nausea. I try to stand, but even as I roll on to my knees, my sight fogs and fractures, the ground wavers and I collapse.

I lie still. I can hear water trickling in the crypt below, the drip of the candle's wax, the tide of my breath. I can feel footsteps outside. Outside – men's voices. They boom and dwindle, and I understand, dimly, that all day these men have sought me. Sought – and not found. Like a thunderclap, I hear the gate clanging shut.

How much did he see? Is it a thing one can – see? Or does this, the Mother's metamorphosis, happen outside of our understanding – the way the Father turns our bread, our wine, into his Son's body and blood?

My memory is scraps and fragments, and something in me recoils when I try to order what remains. I remember – what do I remember? He had been talking – talking – and I was afraid. And I had been about to give him – no, where is it? No – I didn't. I have it. I have it still. I am holding it. She would not let me give it up.

I fear to move, to leave the chapel, but soon my sisters will come for the night watch – and when they do, there is nowhere here to hide. The chapel is the Father's house on earth, and I no longer feel safe here. I imagine him striding along his corridors, looking for me, opening doors, slamming them shut, yelling and yelling, his voice booming, the marble corridors echoing. I imagine the Son tearing his hand away from the cross above the chancel and pointing down to where I lie.

'There she is. There she is. Get her, Father, get her.'

I struggle to my feet, steadying myself with a hand against the wall – the wall is wet. I pull my hand away and stare. It is white, all white. White paint – whitewash. For a moment, I am confounded, and then I realise the drapes that had screened the side chapel while Diana worked have been taken down. I can see them bundled in the corner. I look up – her painting – gone, all gone. I look down – the stones beneath my feet are splashed with white. Brother Abramo must have searched the chapel, seen her work, and made her white the wall.

Something stirs within me. I lift my hand and trace a letter in the paint. Two lines up – down. Two lines left – right. And the tops curled. I step back, admire how it shimmers silver, and go to seek Diana.

I press myself against the outer wall of the chapel, contemplating the immensity of the quadrilango. The fountain's statue looks crueller by moonlight, as though the shepherd boy played upon a pipe of bones. Further off, the cloister's spectral columns. The cedar's lowering branches near at hand. I hear the first owl – a screech, no gentle hoo-hoo – and yet I find myself undaunted. We sisters are creatures of the day, trespassing but lightly on night's dominion, but now I, too, am a creature of the dark places.

At that moment, the full moon soars over the mountain, lighting the night. Some impulse makes me reach my arms towards it. As my arms rise, my sleeves fall back, revealing my skin, which is threaded with black veins. I marvel at the forks and branches, twisting my arms this way and that, the better to admire them, which motion – so my eyes assure me – traces silver lines on the face of the night.

The reformatory is the closest of all the buildings to the chapel, not above two hundred yards away. I sidle round to the chapel's northern wall, keeping its bulk between me and the windows of the chapterhouse, where a warden sits unsleeping, marking the hours until the night watch.

Sister Nanina, I know, sleeps in a cell that opens on to the entrance hall, and keeps her door ajar. I cannot enter that way.

And so, after I cover the short stretch of open ground between the chapel and the reformatory, my shadow whisking after me, I make for the building's rear, for its unfrequented side. There I stand, my back to the wall, telling myself I have not been seen.

Come summer, when grasses, brambles and sticking weed shoot up seemingly overnight, this strip of ground grows impassable, but the months of rain and snow have flattened what once grew. And there to my right, is a little run of steps and a small door, used by those who seek a moment's solitude. This shall be my way inside.

I know where Diana's room is – the far corner of the uppermost floor. She will – I am certain – be fast asleep. In a matter of moments, I will – I am certain – be waking her. I push upon the door, but it does not move. I put my shoulder to it. Perhaps, bloated by snow and rain, it is simply stuck, perhaps a fulsome shove will dislodge it. I try, I try again, and a third time I hurl my inconsequential weight against the timber. It avails me nothing. I stand back. I rub my shoulder and curse Arcangela. How like her to deny the safekeeps access to this private place; how like her to commission bolts and bars.

And suddenly, whatever bank held back my fear is breached. I press fingers to my lips to still the wavering of my mouth. Tears prick my nose and eyes. Hopelessness pinches my throat. What can I do? In all this wide world, where can I go? Doubly, am I trapped. Impossible to stay, impossible to leave. I have nothing, nobody – no knowledge of the world. Rage and impotence circle inside me, two hackled dogs, snapping and snarling. Why are you so angry when there's nothing you can do? Why do you do nothing when there's so much to be angry about? I scrabble at the wall. A sob, a wail beats up inside me. I rake my fingers against the unrelenting stone.

And then—

> I am   climbing   against nature
>   many   hands sticking   thread trailing
> air speed   air   cracked   crumbling
> more hunched downdown crouch   which is
>   impossible

—I am inside a moonlit room. There is a woman, lying on her belly on a pallet, and for a moment I feel I am looking at myself, but I see she is sprawled magnificently crosswise. Her blanket is on the floor. Her shift is rucked even to the backs of her knees. One leg is raised high, crooked. It is Diana. I am in her room. I am—

I feel at my torn palms, my ragged nails. Experimentally, I move my arms and legs, and find they answer as I would expect. I unstick my tongue from the roof of my mouth, moisten my lips. I – I am myself. But I know the Mother helped me. She helped me climb the wall.

I prepare to reach forward, to lay a hand on the part of her closest to me – an elbow – but she must have been less deeply asleep than I supposed, for as I stretch out my arm, her eyes snap open like twin locks on a strongbox. Up she bolts, and I see her eye-whites in the darkness, blinking to banish the nightmarish creature crouched beside her.

'Diana,' I whisper, 'Diana, it's me.'

But I am still in some wise awry after my unnatural ascent, for only a parched croak emerges and, accordingly, she shrinks backwards. I reach towards her, to beg her have no fear, but – as I could have foreseen – a limb extending from a night-apparition brings little comfort. She springs – not for the door and escape, but rather for my person, pinning me down. I try to speak, to say, 'It's me – it's me,' to persuade her I am no devil, that she need not wring my neck. But instead of the words

I intend, I hear only the book's voice on my lips, a formless whispering, broken, rasping—

'Beatrice?' she whispers, and, '*Beatrice?*'

I nod, drained suddenly, wearied, unable to do more. But it is enough. She lifts me up and places me on her pallet, puts a blanket on my knees, a cup of water in my hands. I drink and she speaks me small words of comfort, an arm about my shoulders. I feel – safe. But when presently she stands and crosses to her door, at once I ready myself to hear that it is too dangerous for me to stay, that I must go. Almost, I begin to push myself to my feet – but I am wrong. Softly, she returns and sits by my side once more – although perhaps not quite so close.

'I stop my door at night. A wedge of wood. It is undisturbed. Beatrice – how did you get in?'

I grip the cup tighter and point towards the window, a line of silver trailing from my finger.

'But—' she says, and of course she needs say no more. The window, although bright with moonlight, is small and its iron cross-pieces make it even smaller. Small – and far, far above the ground. Again, she draws breath to speak. The words catch, and I think, even you do not know how to begin.

'He accuses you,' she says at last. 'He accuses you of – he said much – much that I did not credit. He said much, and he implied more. At first, I thought he talked a pack of lies. I thought he had taken you and would torment you until you told the same lies as him. But Tamara swore she saw you enter the chapel – enter and not come out. Did he not take you, Beatrice? Beatrice? What did he do to you? Where have you been?'

I clutch the edge of the pallet. I press my feet into the floor. I try to array the words, but I fear that anything I say will sound like delirium, hysteria, like nightmare. Instead, I fumble under my skirts, draw out the book and place it in her lap. Her hands go to it.

'Your book?' I hear a little huff of air in darkness, no more. A laugh. I welcome it. It is familiar when all else is strange. 'Of course.'

Haltingly, I begin to tell her, in a stumbling whisper, about the power the book unleashes. And Diana, who disdains circumlocution, despises euphemism – not that she'd name them as such – heeds my faltering exposition. I come to my own part. I assure her that she will not – that she cannot – believe me, that she will think me demented, a liar. Desperation is starting to overwhelm my voice when she says:

'I believe you.'

'Truly?' I seize her hand. 'Truly?'

'If Beatrice, sober, unfanciful Beatrice, assures me she scuttled up—'

'Don't,' I say, dropping her hand, recovering my book, bundling it away. 'Don't mock me. Anything but that. Just say you don't believe me, and I'll—'

'But I do believe you. I said I believe you, and I do. Sister Nanina was reading to us from the Stories today. The end. When the Son rises. The women, the three Marys, come back from the tomb and tell the men, his friends, what happened – but they don't believe them. But it did happen – and, if you say so, so did this. The two women became brambles and killed; a girl became a chestnut tree and escaped; Ortolana grew wings and lived; and you . . .'

Her fingers are on my arm, and I realise she is scrutinising me, searching my face, and for a moment I forget to hide from her regard. And then I remember I don't like people to look at me, and I turn away.

'Show me,' she says. 'Show it to me.'

I return the book to her hands, and she takes it up and moves to the window, to where the moon's light is strongest. I hear the creak of the boards, the whisper of the pages, the soft stroke of her finger on the parchment. My soul watches over her shoulder, wanting to marvel over it with her. Surely she – of all people – must be rapt by the pictures. Their freedom – how they dance about the pages, dive into the margins, run over the folds. The chestnut's prickle, the celerity of the feathers, the bite of the thorns. And then, of course, I remember that I have not looked – not since—

I move to stand beside her. A veil parts. There is no boundary, no barrier. I can hear – see – feel – be. I am stumbling through a pathless forest. I am hiding behind a crumbling goatpen. I am gripping the polished oak of an altar rail. Shouts, faces, hands, dirty-white cloaks. My leg skews, my heart fails, my belly pools with fear. I run, I run, I run. I stumble, I am dragged, I scream, I cry out, I am alone, forsaken, lost – my wings brush the clouds, my branches claw the sky, I am—

'There you are,' she says.

A line, a filament, a tiny thread circles and circles and circles the page: a silver thread, so fine it's hard to believe it's there at all. And letters: tiny, perfect letters. And I – can read them. Although is read the right word? I have no agency. None. Rather, I feel as though I am standing at the confluence of two rivers – one the letters, the other my mind – and where they meet, that turbulence, that rush and roar, that is my understanding.

Abramo was wrong. The voice of the book does not whisper, does not coax. It makes no promises. Instead, it shows me how, for years, I have hidden. Clinging to the shadows; feeling unwanted, unloved, invisible; lingering in corners, at the tops of stairs, high up, out of sight; snatching at knowledge, weaving words, trying to make a picture of the world, but never daring to be a part of it. *Hide hide hide hide hide hide hide hide hide.* The words wind round the page, round my mind, until they fade to nothingness, until the page is still.

'Beatrice,' Diana whispers, turning around. 'The letters.' She points at the page. 'Are they words? Can you read them?'

I nod. 'But only since' – I lean over and touch the place where the silver thread weaves its intricate patterns about the page – 'only since then.'

'Will you read me what it says. There?' Her finger traces the letters that spiral outwards, twining in and out of the radial arcs.

I shake my head.

'No?'

'No.'

'Why not?'

'Because,' I whisper, not looking at her, but at the book, at her fingers, 'because, what's there, it's me, and I don't . . .' I trail off.

She nudges me. 'What? What? It's you? And so?'

'Not everyone,' I fumble for words, 'not everyone is as – as easy with themselves as you.'

Another huff of laughter, but unhappy this time. 'Not been feeling very easy today, I can tell you—'

'I saw, I saw. Your painting. I'm sorry. I'm so sorry. Was it—?'

'Miserable? Yes. Worst was Arcangela made me do it myself – stood over me while I did it. I wanted to wrap my brush round her face, but I couldn't, not with him and all his men everywhere. "Your shameful daub." That's what she called it. "A simple white wall is much more suitable, much more to the Father's liking." That's the whole point, isn't it? All the colour and beauty in the world, and all we get is bastard, scumbering white.'

She turns to the window, looks out. It is deepest night, when the watchmen doze, when the stars sink into the sea, when even the restless find sleep.

Diana sinks to the floor and stretches her legs out before her. 'I'd started on the head. Holofernes's head. Staring up out of the basket, a lovely bloodless moonlit grey. It was coming up really well. Really like to life. You'd have known him any-where—'

'Him?'

'Him. Brother Abramo.'

'But – surely – you've never met him?'

'Not so. I spent the worst night of my life with him, back in St Peter's. That's why I'm here.'

I wait, expectant, but she says no more. I cannot make out her face – it now lies in the deeper dark, beneath the casement, where the moonlight does not reach. I kneel down and wait. Still, she does not speak.

And then, suddenly, she leans forwards and pokes me with a finger. 'You know why I like you, Beatrice – why I came to like you?'

I shake my head. The thought – that she likes me, when I thought she might hate me, blame me for the loss of her paint-ing – fills my head, momentarily occluding all else.

'Everyone,' she says, 'everyone was always asking me why I came to be here. What had happened? What terrible, ter-rible thing had I done? They all found their way of asking. Grubbing around. Trying to dig up the dirt. Even Tamara. "What'd you do, Di? Go on, tell us, I love a good story." At least she didn't pretend she was worried about my soul. Not you, though. You only cared for your library – your books. I understood that. I – liked it.'

'But I – I did want to know.'

'You did?'

'Yes. It's just – I lack boldness.'

'You can ask now. If you like.'

'What – what happened?'

She pats the ground next to her. 'Sit. You're unsettling me. Perched like that.'

I obey, shifting to join her against the wall, lowering myself, extending my legs parallel to hers. For a moment, we are still. Outside, two of the cookhouse cats yip and yowl.

'You know,' she says, 'you know my father was – is – a painter too? A very bad one. No,' she corrects herself, 'not bad. Middling. He knew it, too. It ate him up inside. But I didn't know that. Not at first. I thought he was sun and stars. And he loved me. He let me play in the studio. He taught me to paint. He took commissions and I painted them. We were busy. Always more commissions, more clients. And then, about this time last year, somebody new approached us, somebody very, *very* eminent, asking that I figure his private cabinet with a frieze. Atalanta, he wanted.' She has been looking forwards, but now she turns her head towards me, so she is almost whispering into my ear. 'Of course, I didn't have you to ask who the hell she was, and by then I hated to ask anything of my father – so I asked a bookseller I knew.'

'Tomis?'

'Tomis. He told me all about her – the race, the apples – and asked whose walls she was to grace. When I told him, he was concerned – pretty much told me to refuse. I laughed at him. Said I was no meek virgin—'

I twist and stare at her. I can't help it.

I hear her chuckle. 'There. I've shocked you.'

'No, you haven't.'

'You're an awful liar, Beà.'

'It's just—' I drop back against the wall. 'Well—'

She shunts her shoulder into mine. 'Don't worry. I'm all confessed. Shriven. I can hardly do it again – can I? Old Poggio? Do me a favour.'

I do my best to laugh as I am meant to.

'Anyway,' she continues, 'like I said, I wasn't worried. Even when the man started to call by to watch me work. He was a person of – standing. A senior – *very* senior – father of the church. The vicar general or the curial deacon – the man, anyway, the Shepherds would have made pontifex if Chiara hadn't backed Pope Silvio.

'I didn't much care for it – the way he sat behind me, watching – but I thought, very well, look if you must. I thought of the gold. One day, he stood closer. Only this far' – she picks up my hands to measure the distance for me – 'behind me. He pointed at Atalanta. Said, "I have always thought she wanted to get caught." I told him I thought otherwise. And he said – oh, never mind what he said. The usual lechery. Innuendo he thought was playful, clever. Some little joke in Latin I didn't understand. The usual – you know?'

I shake my head. 'No. I don't know.'

'No. Sorry. You wouldn't. Count yourself lucky. It is so – so tiresome. I wanted to paint. But there was this man breathing and chuckling and talking behind me. A few days later, he thought to tug at the strings of my coveralls, to suggest I had a little rest – an apple tart and a glass of Vin Santo. I said, "Illustrissimo, you've bought the painting, not the painter." I thought that would put him off, but he was delighted. Delighted. Said, "Oh, call me that again." He thought I was – *flirting*.'

She makes a low noise, eloquent of her disgust.

'He lunged. He wasn't a big man. I was taller by half a head. He had hunched shoulders, a pot belly. But even small men can be strong. When I found I couldn't shake him off, I stopped trying and' – her voice lightened – 'you know, he was so sure of himself, he probably thought that his passion had broken down my defences. Anyway, he smiled – hateful – and leaned forward to kiss me, his pink tongue poking out – and I sank my teeth into it. He let go of me then. He was red, an unholy mess, yelling, "Bitch, bitch, witch, whore," which didn't surprise me, but then he roared another word, one that was new to me. *Morpha.* He said it two or three times, jabbing his fat finger at me, before his aides, half a dozen scurrying deacons, broke the door open – he'd barred it – and swept him away. I realised I'd been foolish. Worse than foolish. I tried to leave. I nearly made it out. But a pair of guards scooped me up and locked me in a little room. I thought I was done for.'

'But, Diana, did you – had you—?'

'Changed? No, *no.* I just bit the bastard. I waited a long time in that room. There were two stools, nothing else. No window. No light. And then, finally, he came – Abramo. He propped his crook beside the door. Stuck a smoky lamp on the ground. Of course, I didn't know his name, but I saw at once he was a Shepherd. And that made me afraid. I was – am – many things, but no heretic.

'I could feel his disgust for me. He was writhing all over, almost shimmering with it. He knew all about me. All about my life. He said I had deliberately set out to seduce Father Augusto. I said, in this instance, it was rather the other way around, and that his Father Augusto was a vain satyr, a pompous lecher. He said he was the Father's much-beloved servant. In my experience, I told him, the one didn't rule out the other – but that was the last brave thing I said.

'What's this, he said, did I make a habit of it? Had I made it my life's mission to entrap blameless men of the church? What was my motive? Who had put me up to it? Was it Silvia? What had she paid me? What was she planning? Was not I friends with Tomis? Where had Tomis gone? Silvia had sent him somewhere, but where?

'A great big pit was opening up before me, and I grew scared. And he knew it, and he liked it. He did not curse or rage. He never touched me. He never even came close – but

I felt as though he crawled all over me – as though his fingers groped inside of me. Father Augusto, I knew how to deal with him. I'd been dealing with men like that since I was twelve years old. But Abramo – I didn't know how to make him stop.'

For a moment, she is silent, then:

'Later – more of them came. More Shepherds. They had metalled boxes with strange things inside. Pieces of tapestry. Stale old biscuits. Twisted reeds. And each was marked with letter shapes – the same ones, Beatrice, that are in your book. But back then, of course, they were unlike anything I had ever seen. They poked them under my nose, asking what does this mean, how about this, how about that – tell us, and we'll let you go. I told them I had no idea. I told them I could scarcely read our own St Peter's speech – but that seemed to make it worse.

'They began to threaten me. With awful, awful things. They'd threaten – break off – watch me – threaten again – stop – watch. I don't know how long it went on for. Hours.

'Later – much later – there was a knock on the door. Just one quiet knock. They looked at one other. I could see they didn't want to open it. The knock again. One of them asked who was there, and I heard a voice say, "Me." That was all, but they opened it all right, and I saw there was a woman outside. There was a pale light in the hallway, so I knew it was dawn, that they'd been at me all night. She came in. Dropped her hood back. I remember how her arms jangled with bracelets. She looked like she was returning from a wonderful party. Her cheeks were flushed. Her eyes were black with belladonna. Her face was white with lead. I saw the medallion at her breast. A suckling wolf. It was Silvia.'

'Herself?'

'Herself. The pontifex's daughter.'

I muster a gasp. 'Oh.'

'Yes. *Oh.* I was never happier to see anyone in my life. The way she filled that doorway. They none of them could look at her. She is – luminescent. Magnificent. Not young, not old. Not beautiful, not not. But she has this – power. Like Chiara's – although I doubt Chiara ever wore a dress cut to show seven fingers of her chest.

'Abramo was sitting on a stool in front of me. She leaned over him. Said, "You putting words in young women's mouths again?" He didn't move. Not even his eyes. He stared ahead. She straightened up. "Thank you, gentlemen," she said. "I'll take it from here." He tried to resist, they all did – the law says this, the Father says that – but she brushed it all aside.

'She led me away by the hand, like I was a little child. There was a carriage. Inside, I broke down. Sobbed like a child. She held me close. She smelled divine. She gave me a silk handkerchief – crimson, same as her dress – and said I was in big trouble. I said, thank you, but I'd worked that out for myself. She raised her eyebrows at that, but I ploughed straight on, demanded to know what a *morpha* was, and why the Shepherds were so keen to make out I was one.

'"I hope you'll find out soon enough," she said, and wouldn't say no more. But she told me it was enough to know I'd made the Shepherds angry – that they'd come at me again. She said I needed to lie low, and she knew just the place. I told her I wasn't going to no convent. She shrugged and told me where to find her if I changed my mind. She was right, of course. Three days later, they knocked at my door, and if my mother hadn't kept them talking – it doesn't bear thinking about.

'In the end, Silvia brought me here herself. Before she left, I remember she pulled Chiara aside, to speak to her alone. I wasn't meant to hear, but I did. I didn't know what it meant, but somehow it scared me half to death.'

'What – what did you hear?'

'"The wheel turns. She rises."'

At that moment, the bell for the night watch sounds. Diana groans – extravagantly loudly – and I don't hesitate to hush her.

'It's all right,' she breathes into my ear. 'I often complain a whole lot louder.' With that, she jumps to her feet, feels about for her skirts and mantle, discarded in a heap on the floor, and stuffs her hair haphazardly under her coif. She reaches down, pulls me to my feet, nudges me on to her pallet and covers me with a blanket. I hear the door open, hear Diana murmuring an illicit greeting to her neighbours, hear two or three women replying in kind. A warden calls up the stairs, saying, 'The Son loves women who go *quietly* to their prayers.'

As their footsteps recede, I let my limbs slack and sink. Despite everything – or do I mean because of everything? – it feels improbably good to lie down, to be still. Diana seems to have three blankets on her bed, all of them softer and sweeter-smelling than my single one. I burrow deeper, into their alien warmth, drawing my knees up, hugging the book tight to my belly, running my fingers up and down its spine, pressing my thumbs on to each of its corners, feeling their imprint on my flesh. Perhaps, I think, perhaps I will shut my eyes until she returns.

The wheel turns. She rises.

Tomis's final words in his letter to my father.

I hold those words tight.

And, of course, I sleep—

dreamless

necessary

sleep.

It must be approaching dawn when I awake. At the window, a sky of clouded pearls. Moans of birds returning to the meres below the city. When the Forty Days end, men will go with nets and dogs and sacks, and there will be bird pie. I don't like bird pie. I don't like the little bones. A kiss of cooler air from the window blows across my face. I shiver. Blink. Rub my eyes. Loose my lips. Sit up.

Diana is sitting on the floor, watching me. She's taken one of the blankets from her pallet and wrapped it about her shoulders. I start to apologise, but she waves me quiet. She rises to her feet, mouths, 'You hungry?'

I nod. I am – very – and she comes closer, feels around beneath the pallet, produces a wrap of honey wafer. I recognise the maker's mark from feast-days in my childhood and round my eyes to show I am impressed.

She smiles, moves to sit beside me, and whispers, 'From Laura and Giulia. Payment. I sketched their likenesses. Laura was thrilled. Couldn't take her eyes off herself. Said she'd give it to her betrothed – when she had one. Giulia said she'd keep hold of hers. Said she was going to enjoy looking at it in her cell when she's older and uglier than Galilea.'

I was only half attending – the wafer is so good, so sweet – but hearing that, I splutter up the crumbs I'd been licking from my fingers.

'Giulia wants to be a *sister*?'

'Yes – she likes it here.'

'But doesn't she want a husband – a family?'

'Do you want that? Husband? Family?'

'No – but—'

'If you don't, why should she?' She leans forwards, wipes a fleck of pastry from my cheek with her thumb. 'She told me that after her oldest sister bore her sixth child, they had to truss up her' – I look away when I realise she is gesturing towards her woman's parts – 'lest her insides tumbled out. Can't say I blame her. I'd rather stay here than face that.'

'But you – you hate it here.'

She shakes her head. 'No. At first, maybe. No, definitely. I'd decided to hate it. The bells. The walls. But then – then I saw that Chiara welcomed all, shamed none. I saw that no man cuts our wood nor counts our coin.' I have finished the wafer, and she roots out another. 'I saw Maria explaining a marriage contract, the rights due a widow. Tamara showed me our loan sheet. We've given money to half the women in the city. I saw Prudenzia – don't scowl – learning all those girls their letters, a little history, a little arithmetic. And you – I saw you were allowed to work yourself as hard as any scholar. It's a good place.' She seizes my hand. 'And that's why Abramo wants to destroy it, Beatrice. He's drawn a line between Chiara, Silvia, the Mother, the book, and what happened in the chapel yesterday that sent him running like that what's-its-name hell-dog was at his heels – and he's going to wrap that line round all our throats and squeeze and squeeze and squeeze.'

'Cerberus,' I whisper.

'What?'

'The hell-dog. He's called Cerberus.'

She's still gripping my hand, which is sore from the vehemence of each *squeeze*, but now she loosens her hold. One of her fingers touches the veins at my wrist.

'What?' I ask.

'If I cut you, would you bleed ink?'

I smile, and she smiles back.

'Beatrice,' she says, 'while you were asleep, I've been thinking. We can hide you for a day, a week, but sooner or later one of the wardens is going to spot you – and then, well—'

'The Carcere, with Chiara.'

'Or worse. We need to get you out of here. Tonight. And I think I've worked out how.'

The River

Thursday evening

⌘

DIANA REPEATS HER INSTRUCTIONS for the hundredth
time, while I pull on my mantle, cover my hair, cover my face,
wrap the book in oilcloth and return it to my pocket. She
opens the door a crack and checks the passageway outside.
Together, we descend the back stairs, and she draws the new
bolts on the rear door. Again, she assures herself that the
way is clear.

'Good luck,' she says. 'The washhouse steps.'

'I know.'

'Timofea will be waiting.'

'*I know.*'

And before I can thank her, or ask her what'll happen
afterwards, or whether I'll see her again, or any of the thousand other questions that suddenly fill my mind, she has
embraced me, pushed me through the door and shut it swiftly
behind me. I hurry along the back wall of the reformatory,
glad to be moving after a long day spent hunched and fretful,
startling at every sound, grateful only that the bells allowed me
to mark the passage of time.

When I reach the end of the building, I peer cautiously
to my right. Everyone is gathering in the quadrilango in the

failing light. Standing a little apart, their faces covered, their mantles spotless, the lanterns in their hands as yet unlit, are those of my sisters whom Sister Arcangela has chosen to perform the Vigilate. Soon, Poggio will open the gate, and, when the sun sets, the procession will move off across the campo.

But I, you can be sure, am not going anywhere near the gate. I – as Diana put it – am to float away like Our-Lady-All-In-Green.

When she first explained the details of the plan she'd cooked up, I basked in the warmth of conspiracy – *con-spiro*; *with-you-I-breathe*. Joint fortifications: a lovely feeling. But now the enormity of what she proposes threatens to unhinge me. I feel querulous, almost tearful. This is an escapade for her, or Tamara – for somebody stronger, bolder – not for me.

I see Poggio advancing on the gate, and I tell myself to hurry. I cover the ground easily enough, passing first behind the storerooms, with my library up above, next our cells, then the schoolroom. Finally, I circle around the guesthouse and strike towards the river.

I am briefly in the open now, but my face is covered, and Diana promised me that if anyone saw my passing, they would assume I was making for the latrines, and attribute my unseemly haste to a desire not to miss the opening of the gate. Even so, I do, of course, at every moment fear discovery, but when I pass a pair of Felicitas's helpmeets, hurrying the other way, they only murmur, 'Blessings on the Vigilate, sister,' and continue without a backwards glance.

Once I gain the latrines, I run down two further turns of stone steps to the washhouse, where I find copper pots and lumber stacks roofed and walled on three sides. It does not lie open to view from the quadrilango above, but my presence would attract notice if anyone chanced upon me. Luckily, none of Timofea's charges would have cause to find themselves here at this hour.

I could count on the fingers of one hand the number of times I have stood here over the years, and on those occasions it was always busy – fires blazing, river-water sluicing in and out of culverts, washerwomen bustling to and fro with great paddles and jars of lye. The sound of their laughter rising up from the river often makes Arcangela freeze like an elegant hunting dog, nose questing, paw raised in question, considering should she descend the steps and remind them of their duty, but of course, when she does, all she finds are dutiful workers, hymning in unison.

Now, though, all is scrubbed and silent.

No, not quite.

Faintly, in the distance, I catch the sound of the city's watchmen clanging their gongs, clearing the streets of beggars, drunks and schoolboys. It is nearly time.

But where is Timofea?

I draw myself into the gap between two pots, and there wait, experiencing all the tumble of feeling when a necessary but dreaded endeavour might have to be foregone – disappointment, relief, thankfulness, despair. In preparing me, Diana made much of the river's reduced flow now the snows have melted, but from this vantage I can see the river has by no means assumed the stately rate of late summer, when we embark Green Mary's statue. Busy and brisk it yet appears, running deep and cold before ducking darkly beneath the convent walls.

So lost am I in fearful contemplation that when Timofea's hand lands on my shoulder, the river having muted her approach, I all but cry out in alarm – until my eyes latch on to her round and reassuring face.

'Good, Beatrice, good,' she says, rubbing at my arms, hoping maybe to transfer some of her body's warmth into mine, for I am, I realise, shaking in anticipation of the cold water. Or perhaps that is simply what her hands do – perhaps it is their very nature to take what is limp and bedraggled, and make it plump and billowing anew.

'Come,' she says, 'off we go, off we go, no time, no time to waste,' and other words, spilling one over the other without cease, meaningless enough on their own, but merging into a reassuring stream.

She leads me down the last little flight of steps that disappears into the water, sitting me down before returning with what I understand is to be my means of escape: a raft of washboards. I am, I imagine, failing to conceal my trepidation, for she wags her finger at me, and says:

'Now then, my dear, I've not lost a raft these twenty years or more. I know when it's safe and when it's not. Send one at the wrong time and you'd spin, tip and sink faster than a sinner on his way to hell, but you'll be safer than houses, you'll see.'

And now she repeats everything that Diana has already told me – that the river bends left after the walls, following the line of a last spur extending from the mountain, with the campo's embankment providing cover to the right – that after a quarter mile, no more, the river turns, shallowing as it does so, around a spit of land that is much used by the poorer women of the neighbourhood to wash their household things.

'That's where one of my friends will fish you out,' says Timofea. 'She'll have a pair of lamps with her. She'll see you safe to Giulia's house—'

'Giulia?'

'Yes, yes. She's talked her mamma into getting you away from the city.'

'Her *mamma?*'

'Yes, yes. A very great lady. She was here herself when she was a girl. Near as clever as her daughter. Worse even than you with a mop.'

I'm meant to laugh, but I can't. I'm staring at the river again.

'You promise me you've not lost one?' I ask, and she has to make me repeat myself twice before she can hear my strained voice above the swirl of the water. Once she understands me, she blesses me, and says she didn't think I was one to make such a fret.

'I promise you it's safe,' she says, dropping the raft into the water and securing both ends with what looks like practised ease. She pats my back, wishes me luck – only to look at me, surprised, when I do not immediately sally forth.

'Have you ever—?' I ask.

She does not reply, only winks and touches a finger to her nose, and I wonder what else I do not know.

I sit down to make the attempt, but as I stretch my feet out on to the raft, I feel it skitter on the water's surface. I decide she was only jesting to give me courage – nobody could manage this – and I pull my feet back on to *terra firma*, ready to say, no, no, I can't do it. But then I remember Abramo's cold fingers and Diana's face as she told me about her night with him in a St Peter's cell.

And so, compelled by fear, not buoyed by courage, I fling myself clumsily forwards, belly-down, on to the raft, sending splashes of water surging about me. I grip at the gaps between the boards, feeling Timofea tuck some sacking about me. I hear her speaking some final incomprehensible words of encouragement, before she unhands the ropes and – my heart jigging in my throat – shunts me out into the river.

First, I feel a mighty surge of relief that my vessel does not immediately submerge and sink – but the respite is brief, for the waters speed up as they pass beneath the walls and into the tunnelled darkness. As the way narrows, a turbulence skews me sideways and I bump into the sides of the tunnel, which feel cold and greenly slippery as I push myself back into the main stream. The twilit circle that marks the tunnel's end grows swiftly larger and, daring to raise my head, I see what I assume at first are my sisters setting out – only for the shapes to resolve into three men in long dark cloaks.

I grab at the tunnel's sides, its end and thus my summary exposure being but twenty paces distant, but only succeed in snagging my nails on plaster and slime. An impulse to flop down into the water, thereby rendering myself less visible, all but overwhelms me, but some scrap of remaining sanity induces me to cling more tightly to my craft. As I sweep out of the tunnel, I flatten myself, squeezing my eyes shut, anticipating every moment shouts and discovery – but nothing, nothing. And so I open my eyes, lift my chin from the boards, and see the bend and the spit that is to be my harbour.

Nobody is waiting for me, and frantically I begin to debate with myself. Should I abandon my raft and strike for land? Soon it will be too late; soon I will pass the bend and sail on through the city. A storm of indecision assails me. I have no way of knowing if the river is deep or shallow – I know only that finding myself in water in which I cannot stand is a prospect too dreadful to—

A grinding crunch. The riverbed has shelved. I beach upon a spit unseen. Briefly, I rejoice, but I am not yet safely come to anchor. The oncoming water, speeding now over the shallows, promises at any moment to dislodge me, and so I struggle to my feet, the river snatching at my skirts, and watch the raft, deprived of my weight, accelerate away downriver.

Out of the torrent, I feel some command of myself return, and I congratulate myself on surviving what felt like a desperate battle with forces elemental, akin to the wreck of Aeneas on Dido's shores. Although, as I now watch a branch bump over the spit and spin gently after my raft, I acknowledge that perhaps my fear heightened my sense of peril.

I am distracted by a woman waving at me from the shadows beneath the embankment – this must be Timofea's friend. As I splash ashore, she gestures at me to lower myself, and so, even though the water yet laps about my calves, I drop to hands and knees and flounder forwards. She emerges briefly to pull me into a sort of hollow, where floodwaters must have washed the brickwork away. She holds one forefinger to her lips, the other pointing up behind her, to enemies unseen.

'What's happening?' I whisper, pulling aside my sodden face-cloth. But the woman, who has not let go of my wrist, increases the pressure, warning me plainly that even a whisper is too unearthly loud. Above us, I can hear men's voices. They are too far away for me to catch their words, and yet far too close for comfort.

The woman puts her mouth to my ear and breathes, 'City guards. They've been clearing the campo. They're leaving.'

It is then I realise Timofea's friend is not the homely matron of my imagining, but Ortolana.

'What are you doing here?' I hiss.

'Shhh. What does it look like? Getting you out.'

I rip myself away, feeling that I have been tricked, managed, manipulated – treated like a child. And what's worse, that's how I feel – fretful, sulky, childish.

But she's not attending me; rather, she's craning her head upwards, trying to see over the lip of the embankment. To our left is a worn and slippery track, with steps cut out of the earth. She moves a little way along it, presumably to survey the campo. I wait, squatting on my haunches, feeling wretched. I know what she is risking. I know I should be grateful – but I'm not. I feel – I feel exactly as I did when she pounced and ended my games with Ludo. Already, she is stealing back down the slope.

'The guards have all gone,' she whispers, crouching down beside me. 'The gate is open. Your sisters will be leaving soon. We must wait—'

'I thought he'd locked you up, the same as Chiara.'

'Your concern overwhelms me. I *was* locked up – but not with her. Your brother was so lavish in his cooperation, they spared both of us the Carcere. He's in guarded rooms in the archbishop's residenza. I was in a room adjacent – until I got out.'

'But how did you – you didn't—?' The possibility she can conjure the Mother's metamorphosis at will makes me feel worse even than when she read her letters.

'No, no.' There's a smile in her voice, almost as if she guesses my thoughts. 'It was a more prosaic departure. As far as Abramo is aware, I'm passing a long night at prayer, preparing to abase myself in the piazza tomorrow morning. Unluckily for him, the archbishop's cook is sister to our Benedetta. She – Bartolomea – borrowed one of the gardener's ladders, laid it against the larder roof and sent her littlest pot-boy to my window to guide me down – brave fellow. Abramo thinks women can be saints or sinners, but he can't imagine us clambering across rooftops. Or floating down rivers. He won't miss me until dawn, and by then we'll be far away.'

'I'm not going with you.' I sound infantile – absurd – but I can't help it.

'Oh please – please don't be ridiculous. Where else are you going to go?' She fetches a pair of shuttered lanterns from a hollow in a bank and holds one out to me. 'Beatrice?'

I take it, hating how powerless she makes me feel.

'Now – listen. We'll follow the Via Santa Croce from the campo towards the basilica, and then turn north towards Giulia's house. You'll know it when you see it – an angel's wings are carved above the gate. Remember, follow me twenty paces behind—'

The convent bell rings out to our right, echoed by a louder clanging from across the city. Without a word, we cover our faces, creep up the slope and watch. My sisters are processing out of the gate, solemn figures gliding across the campo, lantern-light bobbing before them – a holy tide of grace.

The moon – she is waning now – has not yet risen. The sky is low. The lamplight in my sisters' eyes means they do not remark our dark shapes rising from the river's shadows to join their tail. Ten, twenty, thirty paces we walk before Ortolana unshutters her lantern. Light gleams through its wooden slats – my beacon. I fix my eyes upon it and advance.

The vanguard of the procession is now nearly at the campo's edge, and there it divides, each woman following her own path towards home. Not a soul is abroad, but every house, every workshop has left something burning on their doorstep: a candle stub on a window's ledge; a brazier at the gate. I stare about me, captivated by the silent city, the beckoning lights. Only then do I remember to unshutter my own lantern, and for a moment I find myself night-blinded, fearful I am following the wrong cloaked shape. But, no, there – I have her – the pattern of her lantern's light is subtly distinct.

We are halfway down the Via Santa Croce, the broad thoroughfare that leads to the basilica. At every major crossroads, rude crosses stand atop makeshift altars, testament to the Lambs' zeal. Everywhere, I spy vestiges of violence. Here – a shopfront smashed. There – a ransacked studio. Down one side street, I glimpse the painted signs of many, many booksellers. I am passing the Via dei Librai, where I so often longed to be. But the handsome alley's gutters are clogged with books mangled, books maimed, and I understand that others have suffered – not just me.

Now we are skirting the piazza, where the light from four blazing bonfires plays upon the basilica's walls. Before it, a crude platform stands: Abramo's public confessional, where sinners come to attest their faults before the hating crowds. Tonight, though, all is quiet. I can hear the crackle of the flames.

We have made our turn to the north, and there remains but one lamplit figure ahead of us. Whoever it is, she keeps glancing back over her shoulder, trying to work out who we are. But who is she? Prudenzia, perhaps? No, her father is a theologian; their home is near the seminary. Not Nanina – she has a slighter frame. One of the wardens? No – they tend to remain behind.

Before I have my answer, childhood memories intrude. I know these streets. We are near home. And then I see it – to the right – the road that should lead to the Stelleri palazzo – but at its end, a hole, a gap. A dozen houses gone. A flurry of wind – a dash of rain – darkness – a charred smell.

I turn away in time to see Ortolana douse her light and vanish. I do likewise and gingerly inch towards where last I saw her, my skin prickling in the darkness. Her hand pulls me under cover – into some shed or booth. Her mouth goes to my ear: 'Nearly there.'

I look ahead, I see – torches flickering in sconces on the facade of a great house, carved wings above its gate. Our sanctuary, scarce two hundred paces distant. But in the road ahead, closer still, the woman we've been following has come to a standstill between us and safety. If I peer round the edge of our hiding place, I can see the building she means to enter.

Its outer walls are windowless, forbidding, but the frontage is lit by a welcoming run of lamps. A gate opens in an archway, and a second figure appears.

'*There* you are!'

'Oh Mamma, you *know* you're not meant to come out on to the street. And please, please do not talk so loud!' That voice – Alfonsa. Unmistakable. And now, of course, I realise where we are. The building – it is the Carcere. We are standing in its sentry-box.

'What's the difference?' her mother is saying, lowering her voice not one jot. 'Out here – in there? I can greet my big girl, can't I? Now, your sisters have been rehearsing a little surprise for you – wait two shakes and they'll signal us inside. How *are* you, little one?'

'Oh Mamma, such events. Sister Beatrice – she vanished – disappeared in the middle of confession. I heard Brother Abramo telling Sister Arcangela she was *borne away by devils*. Can such a thing happen, Mamma? I do not want to be borne away, but sometimes I *am* very sinful – and there were two figures behind me earlier, and I feared – oh, Mamma, I feared—'

'Hush, child, hush. You shouldn't go working yourself up.'

'Sister Beatrice isn't here, is she, Mamma? Only some of my sisters are saying it's not true about the devils, and that Brother Abramo arrested her.'

'The Stelleri girl? Why no, only—'

'Mother Chiara? Is she – is she here?'

A pause. 'Yes, she's here.' A grimmer tone. 'Although I say it should be that man behind bars, not her.'

'Oh *hush*, Mamma,' says Alfonsa. 'How can you speak so? We've all been praying so hard for her to return to the Father's light.'

'You can leave that to Brother Abramo. He's been at it with her for hours.'

'He's here?' Alfonsa gasps. '*Here?* Oh, Mamma! I – I – was blessed enough to receive the holy sacrament from him yesterday, and never, never have I felt closer to the Son. Truly, he is—'

A handbell tinkles.

'Let's not talk about what he is or isn't,' says Alfonsa's mother. 'They're ready.'

And together they disappear through the archway, whereupon a trio of squeaky voices starts up a round – some verses about the Bridegroom set to music – with somebody picking out the notes on a wheezy ciaramella. My nose twitches. I can smell custard torta on the damp night air.

'Finally,' murmurs Ortolana. 'Quickly, now. Giulia will be anxious.'

She travels a dozen paces before she realises I haven't moved. She returns, takes my arm, tries to tug me along the street.

'Beatrice,' she says. 'Be brave now, one last effort—'

'He's in there,' I whisper.

'I know, Beatrice. I heard the same as you.'

'He's in there with her.'

'Beatrice—'

'We can't leave her.'

'What precisely do you think we can do? He's in her cell, talking—'

'All the more reason to—'

'Beatrice – it won't just be him. The Carcere has its own guards – a dozen of them at least.'

'It's Vigilate. They're all inside.'

'*Beatrice*, we're not going in there.'

'I am.'

'I won't let you.'

'You can't stop me,' I say, wriggling past her.

277

'Wait,' she hisses after me.

'No.'

'I mean, wait for me.'

'You're coming?'

An angry grunt in her throat. 'Of course I am, you fool.'

We hasten through the archway, where we find ourselves briefly illuminated, before passing into the courtyard beyond. We fumble to the right, squeeze behind a water butt, pause to take stock. In the courtyard's centre, a single brazier glows dimly. To our left, muffled voices, easy laughter. Light bleeds around a door-frame. A sword-stand, boots. That must be the guardroom. The tuneless singing comes from our right – Alfonsa's family's quarters, cookhouse smells, and, further on, I glimpse what must be the embers of her father's forge. Where the cells are, I can only guess. Perhaps on the far side of the courtyard.

'What are you planning to do?' whispers Ortolana.

It is a straightforward question, without mockery.

'If we work out where Chiara is, one of us could distract him, then maybe—' I fall silent, miserable. Patently, it is impossible. I am about to admit defeat when the singing comes to an end. There is loud applause, a man's voice saying, 'No, no, you take my chair, daughter. My word' – two extravagant kisses – 'but it's good to have you home. Now, Manu, where's that wonderful torta of yours?'

'Still cooling in the cookhouse, gobble-guts.'

A door opens. Alfonsa's mother stands a moment in silhouette, holding her daughter's lantern, before shutting the door behind her. She is very close. Ten paces, no more. Beside me, Ortolana starts to hum a tune. I grab her arm to stop her – I think she's lost her mind. I try to cover her mouth, to silence her, but that doesn't stop the sound. The woman raises her lantern, advances.

'Who's there?' she whispers. Her pool of light finds us. 'Sisters! Why – Lady Stelleri!' I expect her to cry out, to rush to her husband, to hammer on the guardroom door, but instead she touches Ortolana's hand, says, 'So it worked. They got you out. I'm so glad.'

'Emmanuella – there's no time. One question. Will you help Mother Chiara?'

Silence. And then, 'Yes – yes.'

'We need to get Abramo out of her cell. Can you do that?'

'Yes – but how?' Doubtfully, she says, 'I suppose I could invite him to share our torta.'

'I know,' I whisper. 'Stand there, in the courtyard's middle, by that fire, and scream – scream like you've never screamed before. And say – say you've seen demons, devils – a feathered harpy – a many-legged and hairy beast. Giant. Monstrous. Hell-beasts – stalking the street. That'll bring him out—'

'Yes, yes, yes,' says Ortolana. 'Perfect! You can do that, can't you, Manu?'

'Why yes!' She opens her mouth wide—

'Wait!' I beg her.

'Yes, wait.' Ortolana grips her arm. 'We must be in position by her cell. And – is there another way out, save this archway?'

'Yes, yes – through the forge.' She points. 'There's a door on to the side-street.'

'Locked?'

'No, no. Two bars, this side. I'll do it now.' Quickly, she moves away. The noise she makes is unbearably loud—

'Mistress Manuella? Where are you?' Her husband is standing in their open doorway. He is large, bearded, peering into the darkness. 'Our girls are getting hungry!'

'Coming, coming,' she calls. 'Have you cleared a space on the table? No, you haven't, have you?'

Clapping a hand to his forehead, he retreats inside.

Emmanuella, meanwhile, returns out of the darkness, thrusting something heavy into my hands. 'Croppers,' she whispers. 'For her chains. She's in one of the upper cells. Two along from that back corner. You'll see his lamp. Hurry. You don't have long until the Nox bell.' Loudly now, she says, 'Right then, who's hungry?' and back to her family she goes, taking her torta with her.

As quickly as we dare, we start to feel our way along the courtyard's right-hand edge: past the cookhouse, past the forge. At the corner, we pause a moment, a few drips landing on our heads where the guttering comes down. A sour stench rises up to meet us – excrement, putrefaction – we must be standing by a vent that gives light and air to the prisoners down below.

I can make out Chiara's cell quite clearly now – a small, barred window, a faint orange glow. Now and then, the light is obscured. Abramo, I guess, walking up and down. Once my breathing stills, I can also hear his voice: his low and rhythmic tones.

As we stand there, waiting, I feel for the book. I have become attuned to its voice, whether a whisper on the edge of hearing or a roar in my ears, but tonight, it has been quiet – until now. Now, I can hear it, grumbling, rumbling, like something large awakening—

Emmanuella's screams rend the night.

She is surpassingly good. Truly, a performance exceeding any expectation. She screams and whirls and whirls and screams and, as she draws breath to launch another salvo, the cell door bangs opens – Ortolana grips my hand; our plan is working! – and Abramo strides outside.

'What is this? What is this?'

Emmanuella runs at him, full tilt. I can see the black hole of her mouth, her eyes' dark sockets, her flailing hands; she is the model of a woman beset by an unearthly power. She seizes his arms, buries her head in his chest, cries out thanks to heaven above that he is there – and drags him towards the archway, gulping, 'I saw them, I saw them, oh, oh, oh! Bid them begone – fiends! fiends! – oh, save us, brother, save us—'

We, meanwhile, slip neatly around the open door.

I am unprepared. I had thought Chiara would look as she ever does, but these days of isolation and insult have much diminished her. I do not want it to be so, but it is. Worse, I see her face, lit by Abramo's lamp – I remember how Diana said it, *his smoky lamp* – and I see how she tries to erase the marks of strain – to smile – to give us her usual welcome, as though we were the ones in chains, not her.

Ortolana, though, still has her wits about her. She takes the croppers from me and hurries to the back wall, where the chain is looped around a strut. I hear her grunt; I hear the metal snap. Next, with another gasp of effort, she parts the fetters between Chiara's wrists. Recovering myself, I start towards her, meaning to seize her hands, to say, let's go, let's go, but in my haste, I trip over something, some crack in the stones, so I all but fall at her feet.

Out in the courtyard, Alfonsa is screaming too. 'I see them! I see them! There – there in the darkness!' Her terrified sisters cry and sob. Her mother still wails like one possessed. The shouts of guards, the stamp of feet. A colossal crescendo of noise.

Ortolana is at the doorway, looking out. She turns, holds out her hand. 'Come, Mother Chiara, now's our chance. We can get you out of the city. But' – a new and anxious tone – 'are you hurt? Can you not stand?'

'No, dear Ortolana' – a rueful smile – 'I'm afraid I can't.'

'Has he hurt you? Has he dared to—?'

'No, no. You are very good – so very, very brave – but there is only one place I am going, and that is back to my convent.'

I grip her hand. I try to drag her to her feet. 'Please,' I beg, 'please. Tomorrow – he will make you do public penance.'

'So he has told me.' A chuckle, as though my words have cheered her. 'I must stand on a platform. People will shout. Throw things. I can survive that, Beatrice.'

'But you know it won't end there.' Ortolana is at her other side. 'If he has yet to hurt you, he will. You know that. He'll get an Order of Excrucation from the Curial Court. He'll torment your body until you say what he wants.'

'My body indeed! For years – *years* – I shamed it and hurt it and hated it, all to honour the Father. No, my dears, there is nothing he can do to me that I have not already done to myself.' She takes both our hands. 'I must say, it makes me happy to see you two together—'

'Mother Chiara.' Ortolana is almost weeping with frustration. 'Please, please get up.'

'I cannot.'

'You can, you must.'

'No. I *cannot*. The Mother bids me stay.'

The crack in the stable floor. I put my hand down. A single root, the thickness of an arm, disappears down through the ground, surrounded by shattered stone. Chiara remains upon her chair, her feet hidden beneath her robes.

She smiles. 'I cannot fight, and I will not hide, and so I must endure. Come what may – I will endure. Go, now, go – before it's too late.'

Suddenly, Ortolana leaps up and kicks the lantern over. 'They're coming.'

She is dragging me forcefully out of the door.

'Chiara,' I gasp, 'we must—'

'Too late,' she replies.

Ortolana is pulling me left, left, away from the door. We cower in the courtyard's corner, watching black shapes running fast towards her cell.

'The lantern's out,' one man shouts.

'Where is she? *Where is she?*' Abramo roars.

'I'm still here, Tonio, don't fret,' Chiara calls. 'Although' – I hear the knell of metal striking the floor – 'my chains have broken. I prayed for help. Someone heard me – who? I wonder who it was—'

'Silence,' I hear him cry, followed by the sharp retort of flesh striking flesh.

I can hear his laboured breath, and then her voice: even, unperturbed. 'What was it the Son said – the other cheek? Enjoy it, Tonio. That's all you'll have of me.'

The Crypt

Deep middle night

⌘

WITHOUT WARNING, from beneath the courtyard's paving, fingers snake about my ankle. I gasp – all but cry out – tear my foot away.

'Who's there?' a subterranean hiss. I whimper and flatten myself against the wall, too frightened to move. '*Who's there?*' The voice again – only this time I know it.

Tomis! It is Tomis.

I drop to my knees, scrabble on the ground, find a grate, bricked-edged and barred. Our fingers touch – but his skin, his nails, they are wrong, all wrong. Cracked and crusted. Bloated, burning. Doubt vanishes. Diana was right. He's been horribly used.

'Tomis,' I breathe. 'What has he—?'

'Beatrice?' he whispers. 'Oh, Beatrice! How—? Please. Help – in the Mother's name. He says he'll – he says he'll – please. Help, Beatrice, help.'

I am about to speak, to say we'll try, to say we'll think of something, but already Ortolana is pulling me, almost angrily, to my feet.

'Wait,' I begin, but she clamps a hand over my mouth, gripping my jaw, turning my head towards the archway. It throngs with the shadows of many, many men. The night's boldness seeps from my limbs, and I stand, trembling, in a palsy of confusion, even as the Alarum begins to sound.

At once Ortolana is dragging me, ungently, through the forge and out on to a dingy road. I am utterly disorientated. I have no idea which way to go – but Ortolana does. Keeping hold of my hand, she sets off at a run. I try to keep pace, but my legs are leaden, the cobblestones treacherous. My sandals snag. I skid – fall. She hauls me up.

'How far?' I gasp.

'The next, the next—'

But ahead – two bobbing lanterns on poles. Men. We slither to a halt, veer down a yet smaller, darker alleyway. It narrows around us, above us. We stand, gulping and panting, our backs pressed against a slimy wall. My face-cloth is slipping. With shaking fingers, I re-tie the strings. The lanterns pass – return – loom.

'Dear sisters.' Voices. 'Be not frighted!' Men approaching. We are seen. I cannot hear their words, only the terror resounding in my ears. But Ortolana is talking – she has my hand – she is calling them saviours, Samaritans – and I understand that they have come from Giulia's household – to find us – to help.

Onwards, we go, no longer running, but moving swift and sure, flanked by the men, guarded by their lights. My breath steadies and I steal glances at them, daring to hope. Household servants, they look to be: a majordomo, sleek and round; a beardless hallboy; a wiry groom; a clerk with a leg that drags. A left, right, left, and there it is again – the house we seek. Not far, I tell myself, not far to go.

But ahead – appearing at a crossroads between us and sanctuary – more lights. Our companions slow their step. *Come on, come on, come on,* I urge them silently. The lights draw closer, and I see a dozen men, all in dirty-white, carrying torches, crooks and cudgels. One of them advances to block our path. He is big, thick of brow. A broken nose juts out and down.

'Greetings, brothers,' he says. 'It is forbidden to be on the streets.'

'You're on the streets, pal,' grunts the groom – but too quiet for the man to hear.

Says the majordomo with calm courtesy, 'These sisters, much frighted by this disturbance, were crying out for help. We, of course, were honour bound to—'

'All right, all right,' the big man replies. 'Spare me your frighted and your honour. Jog on home and polish your pots. We'll take it from here.'

'Surely it is dangerous for women to be abroad? Our mistress can keep them safe until the city is settled,' our brave friend tries again.

'I said' – the big man walks towards us, leaching violence – 'we'll take it from here.'

'By what right?' our friend replies, retreating even as he speaks.

'What's that? What's that, eh? You want them for yourself? You seen something you like? You dog, eh?' The man laughs, pleased with himself, and gives the majordomo a shove that is both play and threat. 'No, you're all right,' he laughs again. 'You don't look the type.' He turns away to share the joke, but when he turns back all mirth is gone. 'Still here?' he says, and lifts his crook.

I shut my eyes before he strikes, but I can hear the thud and crack as each blow lands. When I dare to look again, the majordomo is crawling, groaning, blood dripping from his mouth. And then he's up, stumbling, and he and his friends are running, running. I don't blame them. I wish I was running too.

The big man comes closer. He bows low and my stomach churns. He shapes a cross, kisses his fingertips, says: 'There's forces of darkness abroad tonight. The holy brother says we're to keep you holy sisters safe. That bitch – pardon my language – that bitch you call Mother Superior, is cooking up some devilry. You be good girls and come along with us.'

There can, of course, be no refusal.

The men start to escort us back towards the convent, rounding up others of my sisters as we go. We leave the city's streets behind and enter the campo, a score or more of us, herded together, and I hope there might yet be some proximate safety in numbers. For by now, a raucous gang of youths is running alongside, calling crude things and cruder from the shadows, growing bolder when the men make no attempt to quiet them.

How do we look beneath our robes? Would not a visit from their *bastoni*, their *pipi*, their – oh, so many words – much improve us? Do we know what it pleases them to do to Chiara – to the Widow Stelleri – to Lady Silvia? To every jumped-up whore who doesn't know her more proper place? We bear the onslaught in stricken silence, bunching closer together, terrified lest we somehow provoke our tormentors to match words with deeds.

Ahead of us, I can see the gate opening, and two familiar silhouettes – Hildegard and Poggio – backed by the brazier's orange blaze. We all quicken our step, Ortolana and I along with the rest. But there, on the threshold, another silhouette intrudes – Arcangela. By the fire's light, I can see she holds something: a piece of paper. Her list – her precious list. She plans to tally us as we enter. Disaster. Lambs and jeering boys and Sister Arcangela. There is no way forwards. No way back.

My sisters are almost running now, frightened chickens scurrying to their coop. I slip to the rear, until I am last save one. Ortolana stands close behind me. I am in danger of bolting, wildly, desperately, but she holds my shoulders, whispers, 'Steady now, steady,' in my ear.

Hildegard has advanced a few steps from the gate, as though to shield my sisters with her bulk, and the boys now shift their attentions on to her. What, they ask, did she do for the Father to curse her with such a face? Is she a gargoyle fallen from the chapel? They smack their lips and thrust their parts. They grunt and gasp and groan. And I am sure, so sure, that our dauntless Hildegard will shout them back, but she is silent, and so my own fear grows.

Arcangela has started to usher my sisters through the gate, as fast as she can reckon them, but there is a delay when Alfonsa comes to the front. The girl clings to her, babbling of demons, devils, monsters, and Arcangela can neither hush her, nor hurry her inside. My desperation rises in pitch, and perhaps I give out a strangled moan, for the woman before me turns, takes my hand and says, 'Trust the Father, sister, this nightmare will soon be over.'

I know Prudenzia's voice at once and withdraw my hand in alarm – a foolish instinct, for it only elicits a greater solicitude.

'It's me – Prudenzia,' she says, drawing closer, pulling her own face-cloth aside. I am breathing hard – too fast, too hard – and she reaches up, says, 'You are stifled, sister, let me, let me—'

I bat her hand away, pushing her with a sudden violence that sends her stumbling into Alfonsa, who screams, 'The monster! It's attacking me!'

Already, Prudenzia has collected herself, and she advances upon me, tears my cloth aside – gasps, grips my arm, raises her voice: 'It's Beatrice! Sister Beatrice is here!' But in the next instant, she cries out and releases me. Somebody – my mother! – has barrelled into her, knocking her to the ground.

Arcangela springs forwards, pleading, 'Stop, stop!' but then she sees, then she shouts, 'It's the Widow Stelleri! Quick, quick! Seize her!' Whereupon somebody inside the gate – by accident? By design? – kicks over the brazier.

Out of the darkness, I hear my mother calling, 'Run, child, run.' And I do. I run. I dodge sideways and dive for the gateway, trying not to yelp as my feet skim the burning embers, losing myself amid the turbulent melee of my sisters.

From there, from that place of provisional safety, I watch the Lambs advance. Two of them set upon Ortolana, but she is fighting back, twisting, biting, kicking. I will her to tear free, to take wing, to fly, to soar – to save herself. But a crook comes down, hard, upon her head, and she stops moving. 'No!' I cry, but my voice is lost beneath my sisters' screams. I stare, helpless, while they carry her away. She is taken, and I, for the moment, I am saved. But I have time for neither grief nor gratitude.

The Lambs have ordered the jeering mob aside, and now it is they who crowd the gateway, torches flaming, demanding entrance. 'The Stelleri bastarda!' they shout. 'She was here! She's escaped inside!'

Arcangela attempts to deny them, saying the darkness, the wildness, it is inappropriate, improper – but they do not heed her. She retreats before them, begging them to send for Brother Abramo, for the archbishop, for one invested with the Father's authority. The big man has been leering at her, and at that I hear him laugh and say, 'We not good enough for you, are we?'

But now Hildegard intervenes. She pulls Arcangela behind her and says: 'You heard the holy sister. It's late. It's dark. You're not coming in.'

He doesn't like that. He steps forwards, but she won't give way. He tries to step around her, but she steps with him. I can see his face, angry, disbelieving. His crook goes up, but still she will not yield. Her back is to us. Taller she seems to grow, taller and taller. Her shoulders drop and droop. Her arms swing lower. Her legs bow. Her right arm flashes out. Something – unmistakable, unforgettable – catches the light. The glint of five curved claws.

The man howls, drops his crook, clutches his face and staggers backwards, colliding with his friends. In that confusion – the man roaring pain, the others asking what the hell's that troll done – my sisters unite to haul the gate shut. I hear the bar crash into its cradle. I back away, looking frantically about me, trying to make out Diana, Tamara, Timofea, a friend who might yet conceal me.

But choice is removed. Arcangela is calling upon us to seek the chapel's shelter, and everyone is hurrying to obey. For a moment, I think to fight free of the women pressing around me, but I fear to betray myself. As we flock inside the chapel, a band of rain sweeps in across the campo, and the onrush of wind blows out the single candle. Loud and tearful voices complain about the darkness, about those still jostling to get in. Tamara is shouting that she'll run to the cookhouse for a light, but could everyone please, please calm down.

I extract myself from the confusion of bodies by the door and grope sideways, shrinking against the stones. Wasn't this back wall always the darkest place? No, I tell myself. No, you're wrong. There is one place darker still.

Feverishly, I find the bricked-up archway – run my hands over its cold cold stones – feel the breath of the crypt below. Darkness waits, deep and unassailable.

I ask the Mother to
        take

            me

               there.

For a time, my reason is – confounded. Darkness, noise – that is all I know. But gradually, I become aware of fingers probing my temples, my cheeks, my lips. I fear their intent is hungry, malevolent, and I bite into them, feel the pain. The pain is mine, the hands are mine. I am me.

Of that first time, when I changed, I remember almost nothing. Of the second, some impressions of my ascent do yet remain. Now, this third time, I find I can retrieve a little more. There was a great chasm, vast towers rearing up on either side. Sharp squalls snatched at my limbs and the earth thundered and shook. I strung ropes about me, to stop myself being borne away, until I came to a cliff edge, the ground gaped, and down I dropped, down down down—

To where I am now.

I am lost, lost in the darkness of the crypt, while a storm shrills up above. Rain spatters and gulps. Hinges rattle. Latches bang. It is an angry sound. And, closer, more tormenting, I can hear my sisters' low and mournful lament. Frightened women, a vernal storm, and a sharp *clack clack clack* – my teeth, chattering with astonishing violence. My entire body is shaking. River's water, night-chilled streets, sweat of fear drenching my clothes—

In anguish, I send my mind groping backwards: hand over hand I go, following the thread of memory. I tried – did I not try? – I tried to leave the convent. I thought to escape. I thought to bear the book to safety. I thought – I thought to rescue Chiara. And in doing so, I thought – I think – I thought to save us all. But I failed. Of course I failed. I knew I would when I set out. I knew – did I not? I knew it was not something that I – Sister Beatrice, Sister Librarian – could hope to do. All I have done is weave my sisters into a web, trap them there like helpless flies. Selfishly I wove, to sate my ambitions, my desire. And they – they are suffering for it.

Where do I – where *can* I – go from here?

When Persephone left the sun behind, forced by Hades to live with him in the dark below, Demeter raged across the world until she brought her daughter forth. I know – I do now know – that my mother would do the same for me – if she could. But she cannot. She is chained, I am sure, chained and suffering. I am alone. Nobody will come for me. I will die down here—

Or not. The stones are damp. Tiny things scuttle and creep. If I let go, if I loose myself, I could hunt – eat, drink. I could feast. But again I think of Persephone – the pomegranate seeds she ate in the Underworld stuck in her teeth – condemned to live half of every year below. That's what I fear. I fear that if I lose myself once more, I will not return. I will remain, forever, a thing of fear – a thing of skin and teeth and bone. I will become what I am. A thing that hides and skulks and pries. But I can't stop myself. I can feel it. I am – I am slipping—

The book. Open the book. You will hear – her voice. Their voices. Your mother – Chiara—

With fingers stiff and jerky, I fight to unravel the oilcloth, and the book drops on to my lap. It is wrapped around and around with clinging threads. I sweep them away, but they gather and stick in my hair, my nose, my eyes. I try to tear them away, but more come, more and more and more. I fight, I sweat, I struggle – I wrench the book open – and hundreds upon hundreds of tiny *somethings* cascade from between the pages, spilling over my hands, running up my sleeves, down my neck. Horrible, horrible – and yet—

I can hear Chiara's voice. For a heartbeat, my spirits soar, but – no. She – she blames herself. She grips the floor. She will not move. She is distressed – in pain. Dreadful, dreadful pain. She blames herself. No, I shout at her, you didn't do this. You didn't. No. Not you. And then her voice blurs with my mother's. She is hooded, battered, chained. She blames herself. No, no, I cry. You did what you had to do. It wasn't your fault. Not your fault. No. I am sobbing, weeping, for her, for me, for motherless years, for death, for life, for her for me for her.

And then, above: a crash, the sound of the wind chasing through the open door, a sharp bang as the door slams shut. Angry footsteps measure the length of the nave.

'Where is she? Where is she?' Abramo's voice, distorted and malign. 'Two women I have in hand – where is the third?' Threats follow. Vile and violent. 'Where is she? Give her to me or—'

I am seized by a manic, ludic joy. I can save them. I can! I can give myself to him. I can give him what he wants. Me, the book. The book, me. All his heart's desire. I cry:

Take it take me. Take me take it.

At least, that is what I mean to say, but my own voice is gone. Only the voice of the book – louder and louder and louder – only that remains.

The Robe

Friday

⌘

My MIND AND SENSES converge. I am in a little room awash
with light. The infirmary – I am in the infirmary. To my right
– the door. On the bed to my left, a body lies, slumped or
sleeping, I cannot see a face, but the hair – Diana. She is here.
Ahead – somebody has opened the shutters – I can see birds
flying. Swallows, maybe, or do I mean swifts? The ones who
look to be flying for no other reason than joy. For a moment,
I am flooded with relief to find myself no longer in the crypt
– but hard on its heels comes fear. What happened? I try to
lever myself upright, but my head swims and I sink. I touch
my head – bandaged. And then, beyond the door, a voice.

'Everything is prepared. She is awake?' His voice.

'No, brother.' Arcangela's. 'They gave her a second draught
before dawn. To avert a further – paroxysm, you understand.'

'Very well. We shall meet again at noon.'

'Brother Abramo?' she is calling after him.

'Yes? Quickly, I am in haste.'

'Why are you permitting Mother Chiara—'

She stops, gasps.

'You dare question me?' For what seems a very long time,
I hear nothing. At last, he speaks. 'The Father burdened you

with great beauty, did he not? I know you fought to hide it. You shaved your head, shrunk your figure. You mortified your flesh. You think you have a modest glance – but you do not deceive me.' She must try to answer, for he snaps: 'Silence. You wear your obedience with the same vanity that other women wear their furs. Some birds are drabs, but the males dance for them, nonetheless. Would you have me dance for you? Hop, hop – hop. Should I spread my wings and dance?'

'I beg your compassion.' Her voice is low – pained. She speaks a few words more, but too soft for me to hear. And then, 'You see me as I am.'

'I do?' His voice is softer.

'Unerringly.' Her voice comes a little thicker now. 'Nobody else has such sight.'

There is a swollen silence, which I cannot interpret. I feel revolted for as long as it endures.

'Noon, then,' he says. 'Farewell.'

I close my eyes, expecting to hear the door opening, to hear her entering. Nothing happens, but I am sure she still stands outside. I hear what could be a hand striking the wall – once, twice, three times – and then her footsteps, hurrying away down the path.

Again, I try to sit. This time I do better. I find I am wearing a clean shift. A shift. No skirts. No skirts – no pocket. No – my book! My hands root around beneath the blankets. Nothing. I flail about, trying to kick them off, to stand – but suddenly Diana is there, leaning over me, trying to make me lie back down. She takes my shoulders, she holds me to her, she grips me tight.

'It's gone, Beà. Gone.'

'No, no.' I cover my face with my hands. I press my fingertips into my temples. I feel – shame. Why am I ashamed? I ought to feel anger, despair, not this – not this shame.

'I'm sorry,' she says. 'I know how you—'

I shake my head, violently. 'No,' I say. 'No, you don't.'

'Sorry,' she says again.

'What happened?' I say. 'How did I come—?'

'Agatha said if I was to stay, I wasn't to excite you.'

'It doesn't matter. What does it matter? What happened? What happened?'

I am fighting upright, breathless, pounding the bolster, but Diana is no longer looking at me. She is looking towards the door, to where Agatha stands, surveying us, steadying a bowl on a tray. I brace myself for asperity.

'Tisane,' she says, advancing past me and handing the tray to Diana. 'See she finishes it.' She comes to my side, touches my brow, my wrist, peers into my eyes. 'Please don't do this to yourself, Beatrice. It won't serve. He's done enough harm without turning your wits as well.' She rests her hand briefly upon my head. 'You were very far gone, last night. I thought I was going to lose you, as I lost the women – but I did not. And for that I give thanks.'

'To whom?' I ask.

'Enough,' she says, giving her head a quick shake. She hands me the bowl. It smells green, herby – good. I blow on the surface and watch it ripple before taking a couple of sips. She nods, says to Diana, 'No excitement, I mean it,' and leaves.

'She's furious,' says Diana, watching me drink. 'None of the girls will eat. They keep saying they're so full of love for the Son that there's no room in them for anything else. And Alfonsa turned up here before dawn. Prudenzia had found her babbling in the chapel, her hands all over blood. Holes like eyes in the centre of each palm. Who knows how she did it. She'd only swear she dreamed of the Son, hammers and nails, hammers and nails – Arcangela said it was a sign the Father was ready to forgive. I thought Agatha was going to bash her brains out.'

'Is that why she's letting you sit with me – because she's angry?'

A sudden grin. 'No! Because everyone else is much too scared.'

'Scared? What? Of – me?'

She nods.

'But you're – you're not?'

'Well—'

'What happened?'

She moves to sit beside me on the bed, tucking her legs beneath her. 'Where d'you want me to start? After you left? Well – I thought it was bad already, standing in the darkness, waiting, waiting, everyone reciting the Vigilate prayer. I was longing for the Nox bell, for it all to be over, to know you'd got away safe – but then the Alarum sounded instead.' She pauses. 'I honestly thought the Lambs were going to break in – and that would have been—' She doesn't finish that thought. 'I saw what they did to Ortolana – and I knew they were after you too – and there was nothing I could do.' She looks up at me. 'And then, in the chapel, the girls at the back, they started saying they could hear – noises.' My face falls into my hands. 'I thought they were just – you know – heightened. Scared. Arcangela told them it was their consciences plaguing them, and to think on the Son. But soon we could all hear it. Beà, it was the book, wasn't it?'

I feel her reach out and try to pull my hands away from my face, but I don't let her.

'What happened?' I say. 'Just tell me what happened.'

'Well – he appeared. The way he came crashing through the door – I'm not sure what he was planning on doing. Actually, I'm not sure he was in his right mind. But once he realised everyone was looking at him like he was their saviour, he went straight from awful, awful rage to – euphoria. He shouted for his men – he must've had them crawling all over the convent searching for you – pointed at the archway, and one of them brought it crashing down with a sledgehammer. The man started up saying, "Wait while I fetch you a lamp, brother," but he said the Father's light was all he needed. Down he went. No hesitation. Do you remember?'

I shake my head, dumbly.

'We all stood there, silent, until he came up, carrying you in his—'

I groan.

'Shall I stop?'

'No,' I say, swallowing. 'Tell me.'

'He was carrying you. Tenderly. Like he was raising you from the dead. Your skin was torn, your face was grey, and your eyes were white, all white, and – you – you seemed to trail great warps of dust and shadow, like there was something beneath that didn't want to let you go. Everyone screamed and ran and clustered beneath the Son, begging him to save them. And his men, they were trying to look – manly – but they were every bit as frightened. Abramo, though, he was gazing down upon you with – love, with this radiant, shining love. He dropped to his knees, he pulled you on to his lap. He cradled you and stroked your hair – touched your head where the blood ran down. Your head was slumped. You were far, far away. He – *sorry* – he kissed your forehead, your fingers. Ran his hands the length of—'

'My book!'

'Yes. I could see when he touched it. It was tangled in your skirts. I saw his eyes – blaze. He pulled it forth. Tucked it beneath his robes. "Quickly," he said, and I swear there were tears streaming down his face. "Bring her a robe, a good one. Put a ring on her finger," he said, and—'

'Sandals on her feet,' I finish.

'So you do remember?'

'No, no.' My hands drop away from my face. 'They're the words of the Son. She was lost' – I close my eyes – 'and now she is found.'

There is a silence between us. My eyes overflow. I don't even know why I weep. Yes, I do. Diana's tenderness, her caution. They are like candles, showing me how dark things are. She draws breath as if to speak, holds it, lets it out in a rush.

'Everyone's saying it's an exorcism. A miracle. He told us the Devil stole Chiara's soul, Ortolana's too, leaving them in diabolic garb, but he has them safe, and with the Father's blessing, in time he shall redeem them. You, though – you he has already saved. And that's evidence of his, I don't know – righteousness? Power? He says it's not your fault. That you were possessed. That he has returned you to the Father.'

'That's a lie – a lie.' Better words do not come. Only: 'I wasn't – he didn't—'

'It's better this way. People will understand.' I realise she is pleading with me. 'It makes sense. They'll forgive. Please, agree – please.'

'You do not believe him? Tell me you do not.'

'You – you did not see yourself. Perhaps – perhaps it is for the best.'

'How can you?'

'How can I not, Beatrice? In all honesty – how can I not? He is – he is like a rat-catcher. He needs bodies to hang from his cart. Chiara – Ortolana – they must have – you know, *changed*. And he has them in his keeping, but he lacks the power to return them. He cannot show them. He cannot point to them and say, look, look what I did. But you – he can point to you.'

I feel cold – sick. I will be famous as the young woman Brother Abramo saved. Silly Sister Librarian beguiled by an evil book. A lesson for other foolish girls. Sick. Humiliated. This – this is to be my fate? I reel. Diana moves to prop me. She keeps her arm about me, and after a moment, I tip my head sideways and let it rest against her shoulder. We sit – merely sit. I didn't know stillness like this was possible. So many things I never knew.

Through the window, we both see her at the same time. Arcangela is walking up the path, holding a bundle. For a strange moment, I think she must be carrying Bianca's baby, but as she draws closer, I see it is nothing but a pile of clothes. Sister Agatha pushes open the door.

'Diana, hurry, Arcangela's—'

'I know, I know, I've seen her.' Diana turns back to me. 'Listen, Beà, I was meant to tell you. There's to be a celebration. Of your dispossession. Today, now. We are to give thanks. You – you are to give thanks. Please Beà – please, please be careful, otherwise we all shall—'

'It's all right,' I say. 'I understand.' And I do. I really do.

Arcangela enters. She looks surprised, I think, to see me upright. Relieved, perhaps. Curtly, she dismisses Diana and Agatha. Reverently, she holds the clothes out. Shift, skirts, a mantle. When I do not move, she comes and places them on the bed. They are clean. More than clean. They look new – newly woven, newly stitched. For years, I have had nothing new. I hold the bundle to my face. Meat and wine for the prodigal son. For the prodigal daughter – lanolin and lavender.

'He saved you,' she says. 'He saved all of us.'

I stare at her, wondering, do you believe – do you truly believe that? I long to take her hand, to whisper, Come now,

300

sister, let's not pretend any more, we both know what he really is. But I don't. I say nothing while she explains – with a most fulsome enthusiasm – how, at noon, the foremost men of the city will stand witness to our collective act of contrition. How, as proof of our penitence, everything that divided us from the Father – every little thing – will burn.

'Chiara permitted us to hoard worldly things, tokens from our lives before we took the Promise. This is our chance to purify ourselves. And you, Sister Beatrice, you will be able to thank Brother Abramo—'

I make a noise, anguished and inarticulate both.

'Beatrice – this is mercy – this is his mercy. Take it, Beatrice, take it.'

I push the clothes away from me.

'Beatrice—'

'Tell me, Sister Arcangela, what will you put on the fire?'

She lifts one admonishing finger. 'That's between me and—'

'Brother Abramo?'

'The Father!' She points that same finger in my face. 'Beatrice, you have done enough. More than enough. If you think this is the moment for foolish – for wilful—'

'What will you put on the fire? Tell me – tell me that – and I'll do what you ask.'

Her knuckles whiten on something in her left hand. She turns it palm upwards. Her fingers uncurl. Inside – a sleeping baby, carved in alabaster. Her hand closes. I look up. Her face has a new pallor.

But all she says is, 'Get dressed.'

The Rag

Immediately thereafter

⌘

I WALK WITH Sister Arcangela from the infirmary to the quadrilango. She is taller than me, her stride longer, and I struggle to keep pace. Every few steps, she glances at me, as though to make sure I am still there. Otherwise, she stares ahead, chin up, jaw outstretched. The day is bright and brisk, the wind blowing hard, and the sunlight hurts my eyes.

The quadrilango opens up before me, and I see it – his bonfire of our vanities. It stands on the open ground between the chapel and the gate, a great pyramid of planked wood. Square at the base, it builds to a point that all but surpasses the height of our walls. Platforms, several layers in all, stretch from edge to edge. About the bottom rim lie sacks of straw, stacks of twigs, armfuls of brushwood, and, in the middle, beneath the apex, a number of large and rough-hewn lengths of timber.

'There,' says Arcangela, pointing to where a brazier smoulders near the pyramid, a line of smoke twining and twirling into the sky. 'Wait there.'

I obey, and she removes herself to the chapel, to where, I assume, the remainder of my sisters are gathered. The gate, I now see, is propped wide open. Outside, our audience assembles. Abramo's Lambs stand hindmost, aping a sober respectability. In front of them, I number some score of black-clad men, chains of silver about their necks, the members of the Bench and the Board. And foremost, surrounded by a number of lesser clerics, waits the archbishop himself. I might not have recognised him without his gold-stitched mitre, but the way he clasps his hands over that portly stomach – that, I'd know anywhere.

He visits us once a year, on the birthday of Mother-Mary, giving us communion with dainty fingers that reek of almond oil. Afterwards, he takes a turn about the quadrilango with Chiara, his fingers interlaced as now, puffing a little with effort, expounding upon matters spiritual while casting covert glances at the prettiest girls. Before he leaves, we gift him a ribboned basket containing the first of Pope Silvio's apples – with our tithe nestled among them. Usually, he is beaming and beneficent, but today he tugs at his wattle, worries at the rings on his fingers. He must be wondering when the mob might come knocking on his door.

The Lambs part, and Abramo comes forward to stand by the archbishop's side, placing a hand on his back, like an apologetic host, neglectful of his guest. He starts talking, pointing at the pyre, at the library. The archbishop is nodding, shaking his head. Every so often he seems to murmur something, without actually interrupting. Yes, yes, I see – no, no, dreadful – dear me, dear me – I had no idea, no idea. And then Abramo points at me, and I feel the archbishop's scrutiny. Ah, yes, the Stelleri bastarda, the foolish girl. Don't move, I tell myself, don't cringe. You can withstand this. You can.

The bells above the city cry noon, at which signal Arcangela and my sisters start to file out of the chapel. Slowly they come, singing as they walk. Their faces are covered, so I can only guess who is who, but as they pass by me, I see each one is holding some little thing. I see:

packs of letters
lockets strung on silver
coral necklaces
carved spoons
little ivory rings
needle-cases
pretty handkerchiefs
rocks and stones
wooden animals
pewter hairbrushes
painted boxes
scarves that, years ago, smelled of home.

Such tiny, tiny things – and yet each one, I guess, I know, holds worlds.

Last in line comes the unmistakable shape of Hildegard, empty-handed, grumbling, 'I told them this morning, if they want a bonfire, I build it. No no, they say. They build it themselves. What do they know? Those logs there at the bottom – there – they are greenwood. Too much alive. They will not burn.'

Arcangela indicates now that I should join my sisters as they process towards the pyramid, each laying her treasure upon the platforms. As I approach, I realise that somebody has anticipated me. High up, almost out of reach, my books – mine and Sophia's, our books – they all lie, tumbled. I recognise them. I know them all – they are my oldest friends. This, too, I tell myself, this, too, I can withstand. But then I catch sight of it – a flash of red – and I lose my composure. Unthinking, I start towards the pyre. I have no idea what I will do once my book is safely in my arms, only I cannot – must not—

But before I can attempt to scale the scaffold, arms tighten about me. I struggle – but it is pointless. Hildegard has me in her grip.

'The book,' I gasp. 'You don't understand. I must—'

She pulls me to one side, screening me from the men outside the gate, while my sisters – glancing fearfully at us – continue to advance. Tighter, Hildegard holds me, speaking urgent words into my ear. 'I understand all. You worry if it burns – that is an end? Beatrice – there is no end. What is a book? Skin cut from a dead beast. Let it burn.'

'No – no.'

'Each year, I burn my fields. Is it the end? No, the poppies come again.' Her grip loosens, and I jerk and try to free myself once more. 'Beatrice.' She shakes me hard and growls. 'You are not listening. Stop this – what is it, the word? Stop this, your vanity. So – you had something precious of the Mother? You think it is her only thing? That you are the only one? That you are somewise special? Everything, you hear me, everything your sisters now put upon that fire – whether they know it or not – every little thing holds something of her power.'

I stop struggling. I stare up at her.

But before I can speak, Arcangela is upon us. 'What is happening? Beatrice, you—'

'It's all right,' I say. 'It's all right. You can let go, Hildegard. It's all right.'

And somehow – it is.

Hildegard releases me, and together we are about to join my sisters, who now all wait at a safer distance from the fire – but Arcangela stays her. 'Sister,' she says, and says it sweetly, 'I did not remark your offering to the Father. What was it?'

'My offering?' Hildegard snorts. 'You want I burn my seeds, my tools? I have nothing – nothing to put on your foolish fire.'

Arcangela points to the tattered 'kerchief about her neck. 'That – you have that rag.'

'If it is a rag, why must it burn?'

'If it is a rag,' Arcangela returns, 'why should it not burn?'

'You,' says Hildegard, 'miss nothing.' She pulls the rag from her neck and shakes it loose. 'Not much to look at, no? But you are right – as well as cruel. It is precious.'

The rag, I realise for the first time, is stitched in green. Some threads are ragged, some are lost, but even where they are missing, I can see the holes the needle left. The design is more angular than I am accustomed to – like the spiked shape of northern forest trees – and yet unambiguous. Two lines up – down. Two lines left – right. And the tops curled. Hildegard meets my eye – does she wink? – then balls the 'kerchief in her hand and tosses it high, high on to the pyre.

'It's only needlecraft, Sister Librarian,' she whispers as we join our sisters. 'I can figure it anew.' She pats my back, as though by reassuring me, she reassures herself. 'Her letters, you know, they are not meant to last.'

The bonfire is prepared. We stand, a neat, meek line.

Abramo takes up a stout branch, its tip swathed in cloth, and advances through the gate. He plunges it into the brazier, and it ignites into twisting ribbons of fire. Holding it carelessly, so all might know he fears neither heat nor pain, he beckons me to him. I shrink and quail, but my sisters' hands push me forwards. I tumble to the ground, press my head to the earth.

'You goose.' A voice in my ear. Diana. 'Get up, you must get up. He bids you light the fire.'

I raise my eyes. Abramo is before me, his feet gripping the earth, the flames pouring into the sky. He lowers the brand towards me. I pull myself to my knees, to my feet. A swirl of wind licks the flames towards me, and I recoil. The fire is between us now. The air palpitates. His features ripple. I reach out to take the brand. I should plunge it into his face, watch his skin scorch and crackle, his curls crimp and fry. He smiles, invitingly. He knows that is what I want to do. He knows I do not dare. I take the brand, and he steps aside.

I approach the bonfire and I look for my book, I look and there, there—

my book

the book

a book

whose book?

her book

our book.

I set it all aflame.

A rush – some of my sisters shriek – a great and vaunting rush of fire. The brushwood must be doused in oil. The fire leaps platform to platform, racing to the summit, there to dance. I stumble backwards, into Brother Abramo, who grips my arm and bids me:

'Watch.'

Already, books are vanishing. Pages red, pages glowing, pages gone. I can still see the corner of my book. The flames have yet to reach it. I look sideways, at him. He does not look at me, but his fingers tighten, and again he says:

'Watch.'

Another gust agitates the fire, and when it abates, the book is fire and fire is it, and then it is gone, and only fire remains. He drops my arm and looks at me.

'You thought it would not burn,' he says – and smiles.

'And so did you,' I whisper in return, but I do not think he hears me. He has turned away, is leaving. The time when he feared me – or something, somebody, within me – that time is past. He sweeps through the gate, and his men push it shut behind him, leaving us alone.

We no longer have to watch, but of course we do. My sisters come closer, to stand beneath the crackling sparks, to watch the glowing planks, to watch their treasures subsumed, one by one, to witness this, his mounting conflagration – his inferno. Black smoke writhes upwards, wreathing the chapel tower. The logs at the base are starting to catch. I can hear the green branches hiss and spit. My eyes blur with smoke. I can feel the heat on my face. Women weep – and I know it is not from loss, but from the release of fear. I know, because I am weeping too. The book's long song is silent. It is over – the worst is over. And so I am about to turn away from the fire, from everything, when I see her—

Chiara.

Her face in the flames.

The Body

Saturday

⌘

I'M IN MY CELL. I begged to come here. Yesterday. Afterwards. Agatha argued, said I should be with her in the infirmary, but Diana said, 'What the Devil does it matter now? Do as she asks.' So I'm home, near as.

I miss the Beatrice who used to live here, who sat up late, greedily hunched around this book or that, her thoughts busy, the furtive candlelight the tiny circle of her world, that flame the limit of her understanding. I miss her, but also I want to shout at her, 'Open your eyes, open your eyes!' She can't hear me. She only turns the pages back and forth, back and forth, gnawing her knuckles, intent on what I can hardly now recall.

Last night, I dreamed of the ice-parlours beneath my father's house, the dripping caves packed with mountain snows. In my dream, I lay on my back, unclothed – such felicity – but then my burning body began to melt the ice, and it was cracking, and I was falling, falling, when I awoke.

I am awake now. My hands are bandaged, and my feet. The pain is – pain. They've been calling me brave. I've heard them, outside my door, whispering it. Diana – she didn't call me brave. She called me, *you fool, you jackanapes, you you you insanity*, but I know those words mean brave, too. I am not brave. I am guilty. Blistered raw and weeping with guilt.

I pulled her out – her body. That much, that little I achieved. The others can make no sense of it – how came she there? Surely, she had not been there before? We'd have seen her – did you see her? But I know. I wish I didn't, but I do. The new-felled tree at the base of his fire – that, that was her. Abramo – he hewed her down, he laid her out – he left us to watch her burn. But as soon as the book turned to smoke and ash, she returned to herself – her face—

So help me, at first I thought it was a vision – an intimation of hope, from her, from *her* – but at once, my senses reproved me. It was no vision. It was *Chiara*, her lined and living self. The others had seen her, too, and frantically they screamed and pleaded, they wrung their hands, they reached for her – in vain, in vain. She lolled and sagged. She did not move. One cry we heard, one rendering, sundering cry, and that cry parted me from sense – from fear – and I plunged into the flames.

I remember crouching over her – afterwards – once I had her safe beyond the ambit of his fire. I grasped her shoulder, I shook her, I implored her to open her eyes, to breathe, to live. Meanwhile, my sisters were trying to drag me away from her – pummelling me when I resisted. I twisted round in protest, only to see they were wielding hanks of underskirt to stifle the flames that leapt about my back. I felt no pain – not then.

I took up her arm, only to find her robe had meshed with her flesh. I went to kiss her hand, but found her palm was scorched, her fingers fused. I remember looking the length of her, and seeing that she – that she ended, ended where her legs should rightfully begin. I thought, Oh, I see, her legs are gone, so that's why I was able to lift her. And then I gagged and choked, not in horror of her, no, but in revulsion at myself, that I had contrived a thought so lucid.

Diana was beside me, and propped me as I started to fall. She held me, and I looked up at her while she stared down at Chiara. I remember the unshed tears blazing in her eyes. Her bared teeth, her nostrils flared. And I remember her shaking and shaking, as though some great beast inside her was fighting to get out. Some of my sisters fell upon Chiara's body, clinging, sobbing, wailing, while others stood further off, stunned and trembling. Hildegard, Maria – her dearest, oldest friends – I would like to forget their faces. I would like to forget it all.

Outside my door, my sisters are still whispering. They are telling one another that Chiara refused to accede to his lies, that he murdered her in a fit of rage, that having done murder, this was how he chose to dispose of her body. That is true enough. A good portion of the truth. Is truth divisible? But I have more – more truth. I know that inside my book – on the last page, the last page before it burned – I know there will have been a glorious cedar tree.

I close my eyes to picture it. A stout initial trunk, splitting and shooting skywards, before spreading into a dozen dancing canopies. I try to feel it. The rough bark. The scratch of the needles. The cool beneath. And around the tree, there will have been words, but I am glad I will never read them. I do not want to know what she suffered. I do not want to know her doubts, her pain, her fear. I would rather think of her as I used to – as something giant, unassailable, supreme.

Agatha comes to change my bandages and apply a salve that smells both sweet and foul. She has very cool hands. She gives me a tincture she says will numb the pain. She kisses my brow. She smells of woodsmoke, and I turn my face away. She tells me not to weep. I tell her I am not, but wordlessly she touches a finger to my cheek and brings away a tear. She says Chiara will be at the gates of the Father's house, where she will assuredly find welcome. I try to explain that maybe there is another house, that maybe Chiara has gone there, but she hushes me and says I am to sleep. I object. I say the Father doesn't deserve Chiara. I say it's his fault that she is dead. She hushes me again, more urgently. She tells me she will give me something for my fever. I tell her I am not feverish, I am speaking the truth, I will tell everyone the truth—

The door opens. It is Arcangela, shuffling and neatening a sheath of papers in her hands. She looks tired, I think. It must be tiring, holding that smile in place. What does she look like, I wonder, before she assembles that smile?

'Sister Agatha. Your ministrations to Sister Beatrice – they are complete? I do not think I can wait any longer.'

'To speak truthfully,' says Agatha, kneeling at my side, a hand soft on my shoulder, 'poor Beatrice is making little sense. These days have been hard on her. I think, perhaps, you should return—'

'Hello, Sister Arcangela,' I interrupt. 'Have you come to bathe a sinner's feet?' I point down to where my bound toes protrude from beneath the blanket. 'You and Brother Abramo – you could take one each.' I laugh, wildly, irrepressibly. It feels good – too good to stop. I see the two women exchange a look above my head. With effort, I gulp my laughter down. 'What is it, Sister Arcangela? Or should I say, Mother Arcangela? It cannot be long until your ascension is confirmed?'

'You see, sister,' says Agatha, standing up and trying to usher Arcangela out of the door, 'she needs rest. I am sure you have others yet to—'

'I see no such thing,' says Arcangela. 'Leave us, sister. Leave us. I know you have urgent business to which you must attend.' She all but pushes Agatha out of my door, closing it fast behind her. 'Sister Beatrice, I am here to tell you the location and disposition of your new house,' she says.

'What?'

'Your new house.'

'I'm to leave?' I had thought no other blow could fall.

'We all are. The archbishop has issued the order. We are to be broken up. We are to join new houses. It's all arranged. Tomorrow – all must depart.'

'Tomorrow?'

'And why not?' she says. 'Poverty, chastity, obedience – they are our only possessions. They are easy to carry.'

'Tomorrow,' I repeat. And then: 'Get out.'

'Beatrice,' she says. 'You must believe this was not my end.'

'Liar,' I say. 'Traitor,' I say. 'Have you told the archbishop – told him what that man did? That he *burned* Chiara?'

'It wouldn't do any—'

'Any good? And what will? What you're doing? *This?* You placate and conciliate and submit and submit, and think if you play it his way, it'll what – turn out all right? Even now? Even now – you still do his will?'

She has been standing as far away from me as possible, but now she comes a few steps closer. To say I am surprised when I see that tears are standing in her eyes is to tell the truth, but not the extent of it.

'What I did,' she says, and the tears are quickly brushed away, 'what I have done, I did for all our sakes – I did it to protect the convent. I feared the path Chiara walked would destroy us – and so it has. So it has! She was so naive, Beatrice, so unschooled in the ways of the city, in the ways of men. Her insistence on our independence ran so counter to the current of our times. I tried to warn her. Nobody can say I did not try – but she minded the pot-girls more than I.' She nods and blinks, her poise returning. 'I am sorry, Beatrice, truly sorry, but you must see that she brought this end upon herself, upon us all – and now it is we who are to suffer for it.'

'That's what you tell yourself, is it?' I say. 'That you did everything right? Everything for the best? In that case, thank you, Sister Arcangela, thank you, thank, you thank you.' The pleasant smile I had set upon my face contorts. 'Get out,' I say. 'Get out, get out, get out, get *out*.'

I take no pleasure in watching her retreat. I hear her enter the room adjacent, where she now must tell blind old Sister Galilea that it is true, that all must leave. And yet Arcangela will rise again, wherever she goes, I am sure of it: sloughing off her association with Chiara, with this convent, with all of us. But Galilea, and all the others for whom this convent is their life, their home – how can they leave?

My guilt, which has been circling at a distance, like the cats that haunt the cookhouse door, comes slinking closer. Once, I remember Chiara reproving Sister Felicitas – who tries to rout them with curses and poorly aimed copperware – saying weren't we all the Father's creatures, and Sister Felicitas, protesting, affronted, saying, 'But dear Mother Chiara, they're after the sisters' milk pudding,' and Chiara laughing, saying, 'I see, I hadn't grasped quite how naughty they are,' and proceeding to take up a pan and shy it most adroitly at an oncoming tom.

When she used to sit beneath the cedar tree, even the flightiest of the cats would leap into her lap, there to purr and writhe. The other novices, seeing it as a mark of her holiness, tried to achieve the same effect – with the cats, but also with pigeons and lizards – but without success. I used to watch them and laugh – for I knew Chiara's secret. I had glimpsed the little crumbles of cheese that lay in her hand. She had seen me looking, put a finger across her lips, and smiled.

I hear running down the corridor, and this time it is Diana who enters. 'Where is she? Where is she?'

'She's gone – gone. It's all right – she's gone.'

I want to tell her about Chiara and the cats. I want her to sit quietly by me, hold my hand, call me Beà, but she will not settle. She paces, like a wild animal. She swishes and she growls.

'We can't let him,' she says. 'There must be a way,' she says. 'If I see him again, I swear I'll – I'll—' She flings her hands into the air. 'Why are you so calm?' She reaches out to touch my arm, but remembers my bandages and withdraws her hand. 'Are you not angry?'

'Just because I'm not raging—'

'I'm not raging,' she rages, her fists now clenched above her head. 'All right, all right. I am.'

'Maybe I should try to rage. It's an escape,' I say. 'As good as any. A way out. We could run howling up the mountain and tumble off a precipice.'

'You're hardly doing any running today.' Her voice is light. She's humouring me. I hate to be humoured.

'I'm not mad,' I say.

'I never said you were.'

'You think I am, though.'

Crisply: 'You are not party to my thoughts.'

'You blame me. You all blame me.' I start to struggle to my feet. 'I want to see her.'

'Don't be ridiculous.'

'I'm going. She's in the chapel, isn't she?' I have swung my feet around. I must put them on the floor, but I do not think I can stand unaided. I look up at her. 'You can help me or not. As you choose.' Our eyes lock. 'Please,' I say. 'Help me.'

For a moment longer she holds my gaze, and then: 'Very well,' she says, and places an arm around my waist. I loop an arm over her shoulder, and together we hobble – or rather I hobble, putting my weight on my heels, which are less badly burned than my toes – along the passageway, down the stairs and out into the quadrilango.

I had assumed – because anything different was unthinkable – that my sisters would be faithful to the convent's cycle of work and prayer, the unsparing clock-craft of our ordered days. But I am wrong. Whether singly, or in pairs, or in little groups of three or four, my sisters are engaged in multiple acts of dereliction. Felicitas has propped the cookhouse doors, and I can see women coming and going as they please. The schoolroom door, too, is wedged open, and the novices are huddled on the threshold. The safekeeps have dragged the workroom benches out of the reformatory, and are sitting together, talking quietly. Diana follows my gaze.

'They're all to be put out. Other houses do not take such women.'

'Out? Out where?'

'The streets.'

'You?'

'The same. All of us in the reformatory.'

'But how will you—?'

'Live? Sell myself to the highest bidder? Crawl on my hands and knees to my father? I don't know which is worse.'

'And Hildegard? Cateline?'

'The same. The same for all of us who are not Promised to the Father.'

We are standing by the fountain, its sides grimed with ash. Yesterday, after the first shock of discovery passed, Hildegard had scooped me up and plunged me into its waters. I thrashed and howled, but she held me down, her great hands scooping water over my head, talking to me, saying, 'I saw her, too. In the fire. And I loved her. I loved her. But I was not moving. I could not make my body move. My spirit was weak. Your spirit served. I am glad. I am glad.'

Above us now, the grey sky is veering towards a fine drizzle. I tilt my head upwards, thinking the drops might soothe my smarting face, but instead they sting like needles.

We continue our halting progress towards the chapel, our path bringing us close to the charred heap that had been the fire. My eyes are drawn to it. I can see blocks of unburned wood. I can see pieces of parchment, decomposing in the rain. I don't realise it, but I must be trying to steer us towards it, for Diana holds me back, saying, 'It's gone. Gone. You won't find it. And – and you'll soil your bandages, and that will upset Agatha. Come on.'

As we pass, the smell – the smell of burned, wet wood – turns my stomach. I stumble.

'Beà—'

'I'm all right. I'm all right. Stand a moment.'

'Come on,' she says. 'They're all looking at you.'

'Are they? What does it matter?'

'You're scaring them. They're thinking you'll start raving again.' A pause. 'Will you?'

'No,' I say, 'no. All that's past. All that's gone.'

Together, we enter the chapel, exchanging the sullen day for the glow of many, many candles. There is a strong fug of olibanum, a pungency of sweet rushes and the dried herbs of summer, potent enough at this distance to mask the smell of death. She lies, wound in linen, upon a bier before the altar, with Agatha and two helpmeets at her side. This, of course, was her urgent business – to ready Chiara for us to say farewell. We approach slowly down the aisle and come to rest before her. I do not think I can look at her – not yet – and so find myself looking at Agatha. Her expression is peculiar. It is lively – inviting, joyous. And then Diana grips my shoulder. 'Look,' she whispers, 'look.'

I look down, and for some moments I see nothing through my grief – but then something tugs at my understanding. Chiara's face. It is pale and bruised, but in no other wise does she resemble a woman dead. I reach out a hand to touch her cheek. Her skin is not quite cold. I lean down to kiss her, and my nose fills with – a good smell. Sun-warmed earth; the floor of a forest at summer's end; something ancient, dark and powerful. My heart contracts.

'A prodigy,' I breathe, transported.

Behind us, others are starting to enter. Maria, I see, and Felicitas and Hildegard. Cateline and Timofea. Paola and Tamara and Nanina. Marta running; Poggio hobbling. Prudenzia, propping Galilea. Everyone, safekeeps and help-meets, Promised sisters and novices, is coming to say goodbye. I step back and watch, a little aside, as one by one, they look and see – and understand. A body that does not spoil. The surest sign there ever was of grace.

When we are nearly gathered, Arcangela enters, all but running the length of the nave, slowing only at the altar steps. She approaches Chiara's body, leans over it, a frown wrinkling her brow, eyes darting this way and that, her lower lip gripped by her little white teeth. With my hands and wrists bound into unwieldy stumps, I could not easily take hold of her, but I could use an arm as a wedge and drive her backwards, never mind the pain. But I remember something else Chiara used to say: we mustn't always be following the cart's ruts. A homely enough message, but from her lips, the homely always sounded new. I turn away to allow Arcangela's conscience to conduct whatever transaction it must. I turn away and take my place among my sisters.

The Cross

Deep middle night

☦

THAT NIGHT, we stand vigil. Or rather, I determined to stand vigil, but I must have fallen asleep, for I wake to find myself unable to move, lying upon the floor. At first, in my confusion, I think I am still in the crypt, and I begin to struggle – but, soon enough, I understand somebody has wrapped me in blankets and propped me in the side chapel, laying a mantle beneath my head. I unravel myself, take up the pair of staffs Hildegard had thought to fashion for me and shuffle towards the nave.

Chiara lies as she ever did, candles bright about her, but my sisters are crowding outside, pushing one another through the door, with much attendant, 'Where? I can't see – Let me—'

I follow in their wake. The rain has stopped. The air is cold and clear. Everyone is looking up at the mountain, its dark slopes visible against the attenuated black of the night. The moon, now missing a piece from its right-hand edge, is high, so only the brightest stars prick the sky. And yet stars do seem to prick the mountain – stars that have slipped from heaven's face, burning a darker orange than their pale cousins up above. I watch them fall lower and lower, until reason finally chases fancy away, and I know them for torches.

Some people – some large number of people are coming. We fear thieves. We fear impudent youth. But most of all, we fear Abramo's Lambs. We return inside the chapel, seeking the bolstering effect of the soft pool of light around Chiara's body. Hildegard favours setting out across the fields to see what's afoot. Oh, no you don't, replies Cateline. Surely, suggests Felicitas, brigands would never come so bold. Timofea asks since when was Felicitas so expert on brigands. Tamara says it's not brigands, it's Lambs, come to take her body. No mountain woman would of shown them the way through Green Mary's cave, protests Marta. And why, says Maria, would they not come through the gate? We could hardly prevent them.

The chapel door still lies open, and through it appears a dark figure and a loom of light, which frights those who first perceive it – but light and figure become Arcangela, still with her warden's lantern, her warden's manner.

'Sisters, sisters, calm yourselves,' she says, 'we can be in no danger with our brothers watching over us. I believe Brother Abramo asked a number of his fellows to spend the night upon the campo, to ensure nothing should befall us, this our last night. Return to your cells and I will undertake to alert them.'

'You'll do no such thing,' says Maria.

'Leave those bastards out of it,' says Tamara.

More might have been said, much more, but at that moment the women closest to the door call for quiet, saying they can't be sure, but they think they can hear something – come, come quick – and out we all hasten, back into the night. At first, we hear nothing save the faint rush of the river, the soft soughing of the wind, but then, as if in counterpoint to these, comes the sound of singing.

'It is perfectly clear,' says Arcangela, 'Some young men of the city have drunk themselves into a knavish state. I will invoke our brothers' protection at once.' And away she hurries, towards the gate, but Hildegard overtakes her and blocks her way.

'It's women's voices,' says Hildegard, 'as well you can hear. Women's voices in the night. They sing the song of their Green Mary. What is the bad in that?'

'If we are not in peril, then assuredly they are. To be abroad at night at this uncertain time. Please obstruct me no more.' So saying, she steps smartly around Hildegard, and moves, fast now, towards the gatehouse, calling upon Poggio to awake, awake.

The darkness of the gatehouse vanishes as Poggio uncovers his lantern and stumbles out, his uplit face composed of fire and shadows, giving even this least threatening of men a brief and diabolical splendour. 'Bless me, dear ladies,' he begins, holding up his light and peering irresolutely at the scene before him.

'Poggio,' says Arcangela, 'you need to—'

But he is not listening to her. 'Why, bless me,' he says. 'What can that singing be?'

'Poggio, it's imperative that you – Poggio – *Poggio*—' She repeats his name with increasing exasperation – or maybe I mean incredulity – for he all but pushes her aside, turns his back on her and walks, slowly, as if one raptured, towards the singing. 'Poggio,' she calls, one last time, but he waves a hand behind him as you might hush a child.

'That song,' he says, 'Mamma sang it me, to me and my sisters when we couldn't sleep. When Papà was at the wars, when we had no food nor fire. I haven't heard it since – I never thought I'd – I've tried to remember its tune, but I never, I never—' and he weeps, suddenly, violently, and I behold the long loneliness of his life. And if I know not how to comfort him, it appears Hildegard and Cateline do, for they take an arm apiece and say, 'Poggio, dear man, dear fellow, don't weep, don't weep,' and their kind words set him sobbing the louder.

And suddenly, I am thinking, Diana, Diana, where are you? – for I realise I have not seen her since I woke, and I am looking around, growing worried, for she should not be hard to find, but then come footsteps running across the quadri-lango, and there she is, approaching at great speed, skidding to a standstill before us.

'Ah,' she says, 'you're all – but why is he? – no, never mind – you'll never guess – ah, but you can hear it here now, too. I've been – I've seen – that is to say—' By our candles' light, we can see she is smiling – more than smiling. She is jubilant, hot-eyed with glee. 'The women of the city, they're coming. They're coming! Down through the cave and across the fields, to honour her – to honour Chiara. I ran ahead. They'll be here soon—' she breaks off and swiftly moves to stand by Arcangela, who I now see is edging away from us, bent on some purpose of her own. 'And you – you shan't stop them.'

Arcangela opens her mouth, and I have a brief moment to think, come now, surely you don't think you can brow-beat us now – but she does not speak, rather executes an extraordinary feint. She hurls her lantern down and moves at first as though she would run for the gate, causing Diana to follow her that way, and then – quick and lithe – she skews towards our bell, which, if rung, would assuredly summon the Lambs standing guard. She is fast, and has all the advantage of momentum and surprise – and only once does she need to sound the bell to bring them to our gate.

Diana, you can be sure, starts after her, leaping for her trailing scapular, but it eludes her grasp, and she tumbles to the ground. Such of my sisters as possess the necessary dispo-sition to knock her flat are yet too far off, and so I find myself straining to intercept her on the perpendicular. So bent is she upon her object, that she does not see me until I collide with her, overbalancing her, landing atop her, and so she falls to hissing and pounding me about the head, my bandaged hands helpless to stop her. Now Diana is trying to haul her from me. Tamara, too, is grabbing at her kicking legs. One moment all is confusion and pulsing pain – my feet! my feet! – and the next, we are no longer wrestling Arcangela, but—

a swan, rearing up, hissing, white wings beating, neck out-stretched, hissing hissing, running now, running and climbing into the sky. Slowly, its forlorn cry fades.

Above us, the bell hangs silent in the moonlight and my sisters must test the fractious bond between seeing and believing.

Tamara whistles. 'So it is true.'

'Told you so,' says Diana.

And it is then that the first of the city's women start to cross the quadrilango. A few I recognise – Benedetta, Emmanuella! – but most, of course, I do not. There are so many. Fully a hundred, two hundred – more – and still I see them coming. And suddenly, it seems the easiest matter in the world for me to approach them, to greet them, to tell them Mother Chiara awaits, to say we rejoice from the bottom of our hearts to see them here. As I turn to lead them to the chapel, Diana comes to my side and says, 'Hark at you and your princely manners,' and I tell her to mind my battered pride, and she says, 'Peace, Beà, I am in earnest. That was a fitting welcome.'

Our progress to the chapel is necessarily slow, for my feet are crying out after my exertions. At first, I hope everyone will flow around me, but then I start to enjoy our stately progress. The chapel fills and, with neither plan nor order, the women resume their song. While I listen, my heart lifts and fills, as it has never yet done in prayer. I breathe deeply and look upwards, thinking only, thank you.

All at once, I see lines and shapes, dancing against the chapel's walls. I blink, and the shapes remain, imprinted on my eyelids like lightning behind a cloud. I blink, and now they fade. It's nothing, I tell myself. You're overwrought. It's nothing but the cracks and shadows of the chapel's age.

And now the song comes to an end, and there is a silence, which three or four women attempt to fill at once. There is a little comfortable laughter, and then one voice begins alone, telling how when she was fourteen, her parents sought to marry her to their rich and widowed neighbour, who everyone knew to be a cruel man, and how Chiara intervened on her behalf, and although she never knew exactly what passed between Chiara and her father, he relented, and a year later she wed a good man of nine-and-twenty, who has proved a loyal husband and a kind father these many years.

'She gave me my life,' she says, simply. 'And when I heard her life had been taken from her, I decided to come and pay my respects. I set off with my daughter and these my neighbours' – proudly, she indicates the women standing at her side – 'for what woman in our city does not have reason to be grateful for Mother Chiara's care? But when we came to the convent, those Lambs turned us away. And so' – a sideways grin at her friends – 'we decided on this little adventure, but it seems these other good ladies had the same idea.'

She has finished, and another woman takes up the tale, and another, and another, and I listen, delighted, to all the voices, the speakers unnamed, overlapping, one breaking her story off, another taking it up, some loud and confident, some tentative, the shy ones encouraged – 'Go on, you tell the nice sisters what she did for you' – and the louder ones, too – 'Go on, go on, we've heard it once, we've heard it a hundred times, but we'll hear it again, just this once. We'll hear it again tonight.'

She gave me my life. That's what we hear, over and over again. *She gave me my life.*

And I think, as I listen, ah, I should write all this down. But even as I think it, I remember it is too late, that tomorrow we must be gone, that tomorrow Abramo might decide that even to speak her name is to blaspheme. A few of us will whisper about her, remember her, remember this place, but for the rest, I imagine how, one day, children playing on the campo will point at our abandoned walls and whisper, 'Oh yes – didn't you know? Evil women lived there once upon a time.' Or maybe they won't call us women, but some other word – meaning monster, meaning fiend. And they will tell each other that a brave man drove us out, that the city is forever in his debt. Deeper and deeper, my spirits sink. This moment – soon it will be over. We will be gone – and he shall remain. For his is the kingdom, the power, the glory – for ever and all time.

I look up in despair.

Again, I see cracks forking the ceiling, but now they bring to mind not lightning, but the roots beneath the earth, the veins beneath my skin. I stare, and the cracks grow, and I am seized by a premonition of the roof collapsing upon us, burying us all with Chiara. The others, too, begin to point and exclaim, so I know that what I am beholding isn't the wilful wandering of my own mind, but a collective vision. The chapel fills with shouts of alarm – even as my heart begins to swell.

'You've come,' I cry aloud. 'You've come.'

But I am – as you can imagine – almost alone in my exultation. My sisters and our new friends are spinning around and around, stumbling into one another, likely at any moment to rush out of the doors, out into the night. I fight my way forwards, climb the altar steps and call, 'Sisters, friends, listen. I beg you, listen: there is nothing to fear.'

At first nobody remarks me – I am not remarkable – but then, by ones and twos, they do. I see Tamara yelling for quiet. I see Diana by the door, bidding the fearful to stay. Hildegard bangs things together and shouts and points. Finally, everyone is attending me – me – and I am seized by a sort of vertigo, as though I stood not five feet above the ground but five hundred. I am newly aware of the smell of so many bodies, unwashed and overwashed, scented with woodsmoke, pan oil and the richest pomades. I can see furred mantles and tattered shifts and the whites of many pairs of frightened eyes.

To begin with, I am flustered, careering from thing to thing, trying only to make them listen, to make them stay, for how to explain it all – the book – the writing – the Mother – the stories – our stories – our lives. How he wants to destroy her, to make us hate ourselves for loving her – how he thinks he has succeeded – but you cannot destroy her – you cannot destroy us – cannot destroy her stories – never, never. They might lie dormant, but snatches are blown by the wind, fragments take root: they change, they grow, and even after the longest, hardest winter, branches blossom pink and white and gold.

I'm not making much sense, I know, but they are listening, they are still listening. Breathless, hoarse now, I point at Chiara's body, lying immaculate among us.

'She,' I say, 'she was our mother here on earth. Her branches sheltered us all.'

The chapel darkens, not the dark of night, but the green-domed dark of the forest, and such is the silence, I find I no longer need to shout.

'She sheltered us and protected us, and when Abramo tried to humiliate her, another Mother, even greater than she, pitied

326

her and released her from torment and gave her sanctuary inside a cedar tree. But he saw no miracle, only a threat to his ambition, and he cut her down and burned her in our home, before our eyes – and yet the Mother returned her to us, so we could honour her and grieve. Now though, he wants to drive us from here, to drive us from our home, but I say we shall not forfeit what is ours. For Chiara's sake, for all our sakes, for the sake of those to come, we must resist. This place is ours. Our lives are our own.'

Behind me – why are they looking behind me? What are they—? I look over my shoulder – and my knees buckle. I drop to the ground, steadying myself with trembling fingers and look up – stare up – mouth agape, soul aflame.

The cross, made of scoured and varnished oak, grows knotted now and gnarled. The bars are long and leafy branches, the trunk is furrowed, old and whorled. Windows crack and flagstones shatter, as the tree seeks sky and earth. Vines now twine about its boughs, cradling the body of the Son. The gash in his belly closes, thorns bloom about his brow, and before he can raise his eyes to look at me, I see that he and the tree are one. The roof over our heads has roughened, the walls turned crude and cragged, and instead of barren whitewash: letters – her letters – gleam stark and brash and proud.

'The cave!' one woman shouts. 'The mountain cave! It has such marks. Didn't we always say they were Green Mary's secret shapes?'

I squeeze past many bodies, to the chapel, to where her statue stands. I take her up, and marvel at what is in my hands. Her head-cloth is no longer paint, but linen, dyed a dark and leafy green. Some prescience tells me to untie it, and this is what I see: a shrewd old woman looks left, a bold young girl looks right, and in the middle, looking outwards, there she is, our own Green Mary. Others reach out to take the statue from me – with reverence and a little fear. They pass her hand to hand, this holy trinity.

'Let's have her, then,' says Galilea, batting novices aside with her stick. 'I knew she was coming. I'd heard her voice growing stronger and stronger. I'd hoped she would come before my time was done. I am glad to welcome her. Glad indeed.'

The tree has settled, growing now at the rate of all trees – that is to say, invisibly. Hildegard and Cateline are standing side by side, contemplating it, asking each other, now what kind of tree do you reckon that is? Neither, it seems, has a definitive reply. Maria gazes up at the roof, and Tamara asks is she reckoning the repair bill – asks what price she'd put on one of those branches, and Maria tells her to hush this instant.

Looking up through the broken windows above the altar, I can see dawn is in the eastern sky. What, I wonder, what can possibly come after this – but I am worrying needlessly. Sister Felicitas has the answer. 'Ladies, ladies!' she calls. 'If you'd all like to wash, we'd best have our breakfast. I'm sure *he'll* be along shortly, and—'

'And we'll be damned well ready for him,' yells Hildegard, to great and collective cheers.

I wait until the others have gone and clamber up and over the roots to reach Chiara's body. I brush away a few leaves that have settled on her face. I'm sorry, I tell her. I wish you had not suffered. I wish you could see all that has happened here. I wish you could see us now. By which I really mean – I wish you could see me.

I kiss her again and make to leave, but at the bottom of the steps, I stumble over something on the floor. A tumbled book. Our most ostentatious edition of the Stories, which was always too grand to read. I scoop it up. Its chain has turned to plaited ivy. Flowers, not jewels, stud its boards. And inside? You know, of course, as well as I do, how the Stories start.

In principio—
In the beginning—
But instead: a blank page.
A blank page.
Imagine – imagine what we could do with that?

The Forest

Sunday

⌘

WE LOCK THE parlour door, we bar Poggio's gate, and behind each we mound up such barrels and chests, such benches and trestles, as we can carry, pausing only to eat the bowls of food pressed upon us by Sister Felicitas. While we labour, we can't help but be aware that some women of the city are now choosing to slip away, their daring exhausted, and after them trail such of our sisters as cannot endure the course upon which we are set. I do not begrudge them their apprehension, for we who remain are no more fearless than they – only perhaps more desperate.

I say *we* mound, *we* carry – but of course I am incapable of such heavy labour, with or without my bandaged hands. Instead, I am trying to stack the breakfast bowls, when Felicitas takes one look at me, asks me what I think I am doing hobbling about like that – do I want to smash the lot? If I want to make myself useful, she says, I can go and sit quietly in the cookhouse and dry the dishes. I am about to ask what it matters – plates dry, smashed, filthy, whole – but then I realise obedience to custom, for her at least, is a kind of hope.

I am a little sorry, though, to find Alfonsa and Prudenzia up to their elbows in washing-up – all the younger, stronger

330

housekeeps having been requisitioned by Hildegard for her defensive schemes. But I was wrong to worry. At once, Alfonsa turns to me, shaking dirty water from her hands, and says:

'Is it true, Sister Beatrice? What they're saying? That a great Mother dwells here with us? That she loves us – and always has, and always will? That she's wise and kind and beautiful and knows all our hurts?'

I am about to say, *it's complicated*. I am about to explain – to quibble and to hedge – but time is short, and sometimes a simple answer is best, so I smile and say, 'Yes, yes. It's true. Every word.'

'The Mother,' she breathes. 'How I love her.' And away she sails, humming the women's song.

Unwittingly, I catch Prudenzia's eye, and we are both about to look away, when she rolls her eyes and smiles at me – and I smile back.

'You've not left,' I say.

'Evidently not,' she replies. Silence, a moment. I want to ask why – perhaps even to say I am glad she is here – but she speaks first. 'I saw them. Together. In the chapel. That night. After he found you.'

'Saw who?' But, of course, I know. 'You mean – Sister Arcangela and—'

She nods. 'Yes.'

'Ah,' I say.

'She was lying, face down, on the floor. Her arms outstretched. He stood above her. I cannot swear it, but I think she kissed his feet. I left. After that – I could not see them as I did before.' She shakes her head, banishing it all, and says, 'I want to apologise. About the books. I was wrong to put them on the—'

I touch her arm, shake my head. 'It doesn't matter. Honestly. I'd have done the same thing.'

She nods. 'Thank you.'

'I'm sorry, too—' I begin.

But at that moment, the novices who have been deputed to keep watch from the parlour vantage, shout, 'We can see him – across the campo – he's coming!'

Prudenzia drops a bowl – it smashes – and together we run into the quadrilango. Everyone is still. Are they all as scared as I am? Will our plans, our resolve, amount to nothing more than moon haze, than morning dew? What were we thinking? What—?

But then a stout lady, who has climbed one of the ladders Hildegard set against the walls, calls down, 'Oooh, look, there's Old Pietro with him. What's he doing with that big stave? Hoping it'll make up for his leaky old tap? I don't know who he thinks he's trying to fool!'

And, of course, we all laugh – and we're laughing still when Brother Abramo, in the company of two dozen guardsmen and an even greater number of Lambs, presents himself at our gate and calls up, 'Master Poggio, I bid you good morrow. Why does the gate stand closed? Were you not told to expect us at this hour? These gentlemen are here to escort the sisters to their new houses.'

Poggio is standing behind his gate, rubbing his hands in an excess of what I can only call boyish glee. He cups his mouth and calls at the top of his voice, 'Begging your pardon, holy sir, but the gate's jammed – seems as though the heat from your dirty great bonfire swolled its hinges.'

Abramo speaks again, 'Hasten then, if you please, to unlock the parlour door. Word has reached me that some errant sisters inveigled certain good matrons inside these walls last night. We are here on behalf of their menfolk to return them to their duty.'

Poggio, grinning broadly now, nudges Tamara, who yells,

'Grille's jammed too, you – you donkey's shit-hole,' which bravado turns Abramo's ashen complexion a fulminate purple, and makes all but the most delicate of my sisters shriek with laughter. He withdraws before his dignity suffers further affront; but smile as my sisters might, we all know laughter alone cannot keep him out.

The women up the ladders report that he is in discussion with the guard captain, who now orders an assault. Men try to force the gate – to batter down the parlour door – but both hold firm. They attempt the walls with ladders, but their climbers are met with flaming jars of Sister Felicitas's best olive oil. A quartet of lissome youth tear off their cloaks and, much encouraged by their fellows, attempt to swim upriver, but Timofea sends pitch-soaked washboards down to meet them. They try the spot where the mountain scarp meets our walls, but the brush is thick and Hildegard and Cateline await them, armed with bows.

After a long wait – during which Felicitas, delighted to abandon the Fast, tries to feed us a noonday meal – they try Green Mary's cave, which might have gone ill, had not Marta been ready for them, a triumph that she recounts to us with relish.

'They were sneaking inside, ropes round their waists, so as not to lose their way. Well, I got round behind them, undid their ropes, and, sure as sure, they went to pieces. I crept after them in the dark, listening to them sob and cry, begging the Father to save them, save them. I whispered down the tunnels, told them they were asking all wrong. Said if they were good boys and asked the Mother nicely, I'd fetch them out later – otherwise, the mountain'd swallow them whole.'

Finally, as the sun turns westward and the shadows lengthen, I watch from the parlour vantage as Abramo sends his men behind him. Alone now, he advances, his long, thin shadow reaching out towards us. He lifts up his voice and starts, by way of a prologue, to paint in bloody red and pitiless black all that will befall us if we do not open the gates by sunset – before warning us in yet uglier tones that failure to comply will cause us to forfeit the lenient treatment we might expect as members of the gentler sex.

Now he touches upon the forms of lonely incarceration and more public punishment that are a matter of record on the city's statute books, before climaxing with an account of those trials to which none living have borne witness. His description of cruel talons raking our scalps, of fanged jaws snapping at our heels, of the rending sound that demons make when peeling skin from bone are – vivid.

He turns. He walks away. A dozen paces he travels, then pauses, turns, returns, and those with better eyes than mine swear his face is wet with tears. And now he speaks gentle words of contrition and apology, such as we must strain to hear him. He has failed us, he says, falling upon his knees. We have been perverted and ensnared. Our diabolical enemy, he says, has come among us like a hyena and so devoured us. He, Abramo, has abandoned us on a hillside that was the haunt of wolves. The serpent has whispered to us, and he has failed to stop our ears.

'Forgive me,' he says, 'forgive me, oh my sisters, I who should have protected you.'

And he takes up a flail, made of fully a dozen strips of hide and chain, all dangling from a brutal rod. He holds it aloft so all can see, then bares his torso – pale, ribs prominent, back and sides striped red – and proceeds to scourge himself. The knots bite, the skin splits, old wounds open, blood flows. Again he raises his flail, again and again, his vigour undimmed.

'*Et livore eius sanati sumus*,' he cries.

By his wounds, we shall be healed.

More and more women are creeping up the ladders to look. More and more are crowding onto the parlour vantage to stare. In vain, Maria suggests everyone ignore him – but it is hard to ignore such a visceral manifestation of the Father's retribution, which may yet await us all.

All day, the guardsmen have held back the people of the city, preventing them from approaching the convent's walls, but now they permit them to advance. Fathers, brothers, husbands, sons – they fall to their knees before us, their arms extended upwards in prayer, begging us to open the gate, to come out, to come home, to save ourselves, only please, oh, please to save ourselves before it is too late. Nobody calls for me, and so I, at least, can stand firm – but beside me, I see many anguished glances, and some of those glances are directed at me, and I realise my friends need somebody to give them faith. Somebody needs to give them a reason to stay—

A harsh and glorious cry! From the city, a mighty raptor comes, sweeping the air with its broad wings. Low over Abramo's head it swoops, turns in a whirling gyre, soars up and up, tucks its wings – and dives. He tries to strike it with his flail, but the bird's talons seize the trailing cords, tearing it free from his astonished grasp. Up it swerves, up and out and over the river, tumbling the flail into the water below. From there – how we gasp and stare – a great white swan rises up, speeding to where Abramo stands shorn of word and deed, and now its thrashing wings are beating about his head, so he seems to wear a feathered crown. He raises his hands to protect himself, to throw it from him, and briefly he grips its neck – but the raptor returns, the raptor dives, and he must flatten himself to the ground. Writhing, hissing, screaming, the birds snap and peck and pound, before retreating to the air above. With one last lamenting call, the swan flies upriver, while the raptor crests our walls – and comes to rest atop our cedar tree.

Politic or no, we all erupt in raucous cheers.

I gaze upwards. The bird is hunched and motionless. I hear somebody saying they can make out trailing jesses, that it must have escaped, that it must once have been a rich man's bird. I shade my eyes, look up, and smile, resolving to enjoy this moment – for I know it cannot last.

And, sure enough, in the swiftly gathering dusk, Abramo returns with what must be the entirety of the city's supply of black-powder – funded doubtless by my father's purse – and lays it against our gate. The stupefying blast sends us reeling to the ground, hands clapped about our ringing ears, noses stopped against the sulphurous stench. A cloud of nails and splinters rises above the gate – a gate no more.

The smoke blows away, and we behold him, his robes, his curls, now grey with drifts of ash. His arms are wide, his aspect joyful. Our gate is down. We are some hundred women – but they are more, and they are men.

Tighter, we bunch beneath the cedar tree, so that I do not know whose hand I am holding, nor who holds mine. Black-clad guards and white-robed Lambs, both are massing in the empty gateway, while before us stand the few women who are bold enough to hold a makeshift weapon – Hildegard and her girls, Timofea and Tamara – but although Diana turns and gives me the bravest of her smiles, I know – finally – that this, our day's defiance, this is make-believe.

Onwards they come, coils of rope upon their shoulders, clubs and staffs swinging in their hands. With a wonderful roar, Hildegard launches herself forward – and the others follow. The men are so surprised I hope wildly that yet we could prevail. But they rally fast, joining together to strike each woman down. I have never seen violence – never – and after the first blow cracks Hildegard's head, I find I cannot watch. Around me, women are begging them to stop, stop, please stop – and our brave friends, as they stumble and crawl back towards us, they are begging too.

The men cluster around Abramo in final conference, and I watch him point, watch him single me out, and then fully a dozen men advance upon me. They close the distance fast. They reach, they grab, they snatch me up, but Diana – blood streaming from her nose – and Maria are clinging to each of my hands with both of theirs. The pain makes me scream and scream, but they are resolute and do not let me go.

One man strikes Maria, and she reels. He strikes again, and she buckles, and I feel Diana's grip break as they tear me away – lift me up – carry me off. I strain my neck backwards, trying to see Diana, Maria, to see are they standing, to see are they hurt or no. Hopelessly, I twist my head, turning it and turning it again and again. Agatha kneels beside Maria, who is moaning and spitting teeth. Diana is trying to come after me, wrestling in vain with two red-faced men. Women are screaming. A bird is screaming. I am screaming. Blood tears sky noise branches cruel faces stone pain. I cry out. I cry the woman's dying words. I cry:

'*Mater noster!*'

And the cry is taken up.

'*Mater noster – Mater noster – Mater noster!*'

I plummet to the ground. The men have dropped me. One stumbles over me, trips and runs – they are all running, yelling, making for the gate, all of them running, running, running, and I am lying on my belly. Whatever they run from – it is behind me. I roll over and stare. My sight is shot with blood and my lids are swollen and—

My sisters have gone.

Gone.

And behind me is a forest of trees, but such a forest as never yet grew upon this earth – unless, perhaps, at the very beginning, in the very first land of all. A desert palm, I see, and yew and box, olive, willows and silvered birch, sweet chestnuts and mountain oaks, some barely more than saplings, some in full blossom, some ripe with fruits, some cracked and galled with age. I stumble to my feet and walk between them. I walk from tree to tree and touch their bark. I press my cheek against their trunks and hold their lower boughs in my hands.

Through their branches, under the darkening sky, I see Abramo striding from man to man, raining curses on their heads, calling them traitors to the Father, urging them to seize me, to be undaunted. He tells them that this is their last test, their final trial; that vision and illusion are the Devil's snares; that the Devil twists their eyes; that before them are only feeble women – he can see that – why, why, why cannot they? When he realises he is shouting at the backs of fleeing men, he picks up a sword and advances himself, crying out in terrible anger:

'I cut her down. I cut her down, and I'll do the same to you. Every last one of you – I'll cut you down. I'll kill you – I'll kill you all.'

He thrashes at trunks, swipes at branches. He roars and curses from a mad and twisted mouth. He is panting, maniacal – and then he sees me. He opens his mouth to speak, thinking the next word should be his, and the next and the next and the next – but I have one word of my own to say, and I shall say it first. I point behind him.

'Look.'

He whips round and – finally – fear scums his face. The Mother, it seems, does deal in visions of hell, but a different hell to the one Abramo conjured for us. There are no flails – no chains, no brands; no many-headed monsters; no bat wings, no lizard eyes. Only three women sitting, quite comfortably, in the lower branches of the cedar tree.

A young girl, grey and sad and thin, holding her rounded belly. A woman with long, dark curls, her beautiful face and bare limbs suppurating with the pestilenza. And Chiara, bloody, broken and burned even as he returned her to us. A snake coils out of this Chiara's mouth and round her neck, and in and out of his mother's matted hair, and round and round and round the wrist of the girl whose life he stole.

He backs away a pace or two, bumping into the trunk of a great pine, which groans and shakes its branches. He starts to run, but finds himself fighting with the swooping branches of a willow tree. He turns and tries to squeeze between the close-knit trunks of a stand of silver birch. He falls and cringes and moans and crawls, and all the while, the snake writhes from branch to branch in languid pursuit.

Now, with a wordless howl, he stumbles to his feet, and tries to attack it, hacking and whirling with his sword. But he misses, again and again, he misses, until finally the sword lodges in the trunk of the cedar tree, so deep he cannot hope to pull it out. And so he leaps for the snake, trying to drag it to the ground, but it winds upwards, higher and higher above his head. He scrabbles for a branch, struggles to haul himself after it, but he is not strong enough, and he falls to the ground, where he shakes his fist and punches the earth in a spume of rage.

The snake comes to a rest – and speaks.

Its voice is a rushing, a roaring, a whispering – it is the voice of the book, the voice of the Mother's old places, the voice of nyads dryads sybils seers sphinxes priestesses prophetesses, it is the voice of Mother Chiara, of all our mothers, of the Mother. And its voice – although it does nothing more than tell him what happened, what truly happened – its voice drives him mad.

'I'll tell everyone,' he screams, 'I'll tell the world. I'll tell them what you women are.'

And as he runs, before hurt and weariness overwhelm me, I have time to think,

'Yes. Do.'

The Gate

A few weeks later

⌘

THE SUN IS HOT. The sky is cloudless. The doves are calling up the spring. The old moon is pale in the blue sky, but there are new leaves everywhere, pale green and tiny, shuddering in the warm breeze. Grasses are starting to sprout. The green days are coming, the growing days.

I am sitting beneath the cedar tree, watching excited preparations for the holy tableaux with which we will mark Son-Rise, when we invite the smallest children of the neighbourhood to feast in the quadrilango. Cateline and Timofea are hard at work directing matters, and from what I have glimpsed – although they are keeping the details a surprise – I suspect we are to witness the great scenes of Chiara's life.

Ortolana enters through the parlour, and I make room for her beside me. She pats my hand, looks up, says, 'Is it not the most perfect day?' I nod. In many ways it is.

The news is travelling up and down the Peninsula. Everywhere, Brother Abramo is reviled as the man who tortured Mother Chiara to death, who concealed his wrongdoing by barbaric means, who attacked a convent lest his evil be exposed, whose cruel and inhuman actions sent him rightly mad.

This is the tale Silvia bade us tell – and we must give thanks to the Mother for sending no less a woman than the pontifex's daughter to us when she did. Frankly, we'd have been lost without her. She arrived at dawn, the day after it all happened, when the air still reeked of black-powder, and we all lay huddled beneath the cedar tree. She did not exclaim or cry out or ask a thousand questions. She told us it was over. She told us we were safe.

That same morning, she summoned the Bench and the Board to bear witness to the devastation. Her father, she informed them, would be outraged to learn that Mother Chiara and her daughters had been so abominably used. They did try to question her more closely – rumour, as you can imagine, was running rampant – but there was only one story she would tell. That after Abramo breached our walls, we adopted the only recourse available to women of the faith. We took to our knees, we closed our eyes, we prayed to Mother-Mary – and she heard us.

'What would you rather I said?' she demanded – for it was plain many of us weren't happy with this account. 'The *truth*? They none of them are ready for that. Abramo – he *is* telling the truth, word for word in his cell, but they think he's insane.' She surveyed our despondent faces. 'The truth will out, I promise,' she says, more gently. 'Give it time.'

After that, she left. Already, I feel that what happened – to Chiara, to us – has drifted beyond our reach into the realm of statecraft and canon law, political and theological intricacies we none of us can follow. Pontifical emissaries are already on the road north, charged with apologising to Albion for the murder of its envoys upon the mountain road. We've heard Queen Ana is to present Pope Silvio with precious relics of the Son, which were her late husband's greatest treasures. Apparently, the foremost scholars of St Peter's and Northwich are to meet in some secret place – that last, I heard from Tomis, who has been a frequent and most welcome guest.

'καὶ ἄφες ἡμῖν τὰ ὀφειλήματα ἡμῶν,' he said the first time he came – the words of the Father's prayer that beg forgiveness. He held his hands up – and I had to look away. 'I am sorry I am not a braver man,' he said. 'When they tore out the first nail, I didn't tell. I promise, Beatrice, I did not tell. But by the third—'

'I wouldn't have made it past one,' I said.

'Chiara—' he began.

'I don't want to know,' I said, quickly. 'I don't want to know what he did to her.'

'No,' he said, 'that's not it. No – I wanted to tell you that when she – changed, when her branches cracked the walls and the sky poured into my cell, I wanted to tell you – that moment crowned my life.'

'Even better than watching Silvia lock Abramo away?'

A laugh: 'Even better than that.'

During his visits, he has been telling me how, in the years he has been travelling across our lands, always he has seen evidence that faith in the Mother endured, like a seed asleep underground, waiting only for the warmth of spring. 'These have been long, hard centuries for her, Beatrice,' he told me. 'But now—'

'The wheel turns?'

He nodded. 'At long, long last.'

Tamara sees it all very simply, enjoying any chance to relive our triumph. 'To think it happened to us! I'm glad I didn't turn into a scorpion or something. Could I of turned into a camel? I wonder how it works.' She's full of schemes and plans. 'This convent is going to be filthy rich, Beatrice,' she keeps telling me, rubbing her hands. 'Silvia says Chiara's beatification will be swift. Her Pa is going to see to it. We're going to be up to our necks in pilgrims.'

I can see her now, over by the chapterhouse, arguing some point with Giulia, who has indeed returned, and is making herself everywhere indispensable. Bianca, too, says she means to stay here, now that my brother has left the city – yes, I've seen him, too.

He came, very nervous, to the parlour. He is slight, like our mother. His hair has darkened. His eyes move quickly, like hers, but where she is watchful, he looks hunted. Certainly, he could not look directly at me.

'Is it true?' he asked. 'That she's—'

'Not quite herself? That's true.'

'Can I see her?'

I shook my head.

'I'll return,' he said. 'I am going – away – with a friend. Over the sea. Might you – give her this?' And he handed me my father's red ring. 'Say goodbye to her. And Bianca.'

'And your son?'

'And him.'

We all knew where she was. Sometimes, at dusk or dawn, we would hear her cry – see her swoop between cedar tree and chapel roof. I didn't know what to do, but Bianca did. Unabashed, she stood in the quadrilango, day after day, and shouted up, 'Come down, come down! Tiberio needs his grandmama. Come down, you silly, come down.' And at last, one night, she did. We found her on the bench on the way to breakfast. She recovered fast – and, with Silvia's help, she has secured a place on the Bench and the Board. She is already petitioning for Giulia's mother to accompany her husband to their meetings, now his dotage makes his understanding unreliable. She thinks they'll agree to it. We'll see.

Who else?

Arcangela has returned – although, not truly, not quite. Her eyes have darkened to black, and she does not speak, only drifts up and down the riverbank, occasionally circling the quadrilango or walking in and out of the chapel. She seems not to know us, but nor does she seem to want to leave.

And Hildegard, she is reassuringly the same as she ever was. In fact she's just yelled to me, demanding to know what am I doing sitting there idle-boned when there's work to be done.

It's a good question. What am I doing? I thought I'd go back to being me, more or less. I climbed the library stairs, thinking to lose myself in the business of my books, checking what was damaged, what was burned, what had survived. I had hoped for a sense of homecoming. Instead – a curious and unwelcome void.

I did think about the evangelists, how after the death of the Son, amidst their grief and joy, they sat down to write, to record everything that occurred. *The Book of Beatrice*, whispered my old friend, pride. I took up pen and ink and thought perhaps to make a start. But when I dipped my quill, I found myself tracing abstracted circles, meaningless lines.

A few days ago, I was standing in the chapel, puzzling up at the Mother's letters, but I couldn't read them as once I did. Their meaning had already trickled through my fingers, until only a few drops of memory remained. Behind me, I heard somebody enter and was pleased to see Diana. I smiled, pointed to the walls, and asked when she was going to start painting again.

She looked at me curiously. 'Are you mad? I'm leaving.'

'But—' That was a blow. 'But you said this was a good place.'

'I did. It is. But I'm not living here forever if I don't have to – and I don't. The Shepherds are licking their wounds. No – that doesn't sound right. They're lying low. Maybe for a while. Maybe forever. Anyway, I'm free to go.' That was when she said: 'Come.'

'Where?'

'Away!' she said, laughing. 'Away, away, away. Somewhere. Anywhere! Who knows where? Tomis is heading to Albion, with letters for Queen Ana. I thought I might go with him—' she talked on, while I listened – envious, enchanted.

A dozen times, I have placed my scant belongings in Sophia's old packbag. A dozen times, I have emptied it, telling myself not to be absurd. I packed it again this morning. It is with me now, tucked out of sight beneath the bench.

Behind me, I hear the sound of the gate opening. I hear children's voices, clamouring to be let in. And, coming closer, the rumble of Tomis's wagon. Ortolana turns to look. She has heard it too.

'They're leaving today?' she asks.

I nod.

'Have you decided?'

I shake my head and, not for the first time, say, 'Please tell me what you think I should do.'

'I've told you. Obviously, I want you to stay, but—'

'You think I should go?'

She smiles. 'I think you should choose.'

At that moment, Diana comes racing across the quadrilango. She greets Tomis, drops a packbag of her own onto the wagon, and now she's running towards us – towards me.

'Hello, Ortolana,' she says first. 'Nice ring. And thanks for the . . .' She pats the pocket beneath her skirts and I hear the clink of coins. Then, to me, 'You ready?'

My mother stands and moves a few paces away.

'I don't know,' I say.

She scowls at me, impatient. 'Listen, Beà, you know your own mind. Only – well—'

Her hand circles my wrist, gives it a little tug, and suddenly the impossible is easy. I find I am embracing my mother. I am promising to return soon – she says she knows I will. I am promising to write – she says I better had. I am scooping up my bag – and my mother is asking, is that really all I'm taking and Diana is telling her not to worry – and then we are turning, running, jumping onto the back of Tomis's cart.

Diana nudges me. 'Wave,' she says.

And I look. They are waving. All of them. My mother, my sisters, my friends.

And this is possible. To leave. To leave the walls behind and stand on a wagon, swaying, as Poggio shuts the gate behind us. There is sunlight rising, higher and higher. The wagon's rail is almost too hot to touch. I can feel the warmth of the wood through my skirts. The sun on my face. I turn to feel it. And Diana is there too, in the sun. And I think of her light: how I have been watching it, fascinated, for so long; how I have edged further and further out of the shadows, until I find the light is not so unbearable after all.

Acknowledgements

I would like to say thank you to:

Victoria Hobbs, my agent. Between my second novel and *The Book of Eve*, two unfinished manuscripts have been gathering dust on my hard-drive. Thank you for telling me – firmly; how else? – not to give up. Thank you for introducing me to Alex. Thank you for being sage, irrepressible and a very, very dear friend.

Alex Clarke, my publisher. Thank you for having the frankly brilliant idea – 'is there a feminist novel to be written about the Voynich manuscript?' – that set this book rolling in the first place. Thank you for being astute, incisive and heroically blather free. Thank you for telling me to 'turn the magic up to 11': best note ever.

Serena Arthur, my editor. You took on *The Book of Eve* when it was a tangly, knotted, lumpy mess, all dropped stitches and gaping holes. I owe a great deal to your perspicacity, tenacity and conviction. Thank you, too, for your commitment to the characters. It always felt like you were fighting their corner, for which they (and I) are eternally grateful.

Jack Butler, Ella Gordon, Areen Ali and **Kate Stephenson**, Wildfire editorial, past and present. I was extremely lucky to have your eagle eyes on *The Book of Eve* at the beginning and the end of the road. Thank you for teeing me up so thoughtfully – and for shepherding me through the finishing gate so adroitly.

Rosie Margesson, Elise Jackson, Lucy Hall, Joe Thomas and **Caitlin Raynor**, Wildfire's fantastic marketing and publicity people. Thank you for coaxing me on to Twitter. I realise I've been missing out all these years ...

Tara O'Sullivan, copyeditor. Thank you for your superlative work. You read with an enviable blend of sensitivity and scrupulousness, and the book is much, much better for it.

Rachel Malig, proofreader. Books need eagle eyes. Thank you so much!

Tim Peters (TimPetersDesign.co.uk), cartographer. I like maps almost as much as I like words. Thank you for turning my risible sketch into something useful *and* beautiful.

A hundred and one other writers. This book, like so many, leans heavily on the hard work of countless others. My thanks, therefore, to Somerset Libraries in general and Bishops Lydeard Community Library in particular. Without you, my advance would be long gone.

Here are but some of the people to whose writing I feel I owe a particular debt. Needless to say, any historical, philosophical or metaphysical infelicities are mine not theirs.

Raymond Clemens, Deborah E. Harkness, *The Voynich Manuscript*. Where it all began.

Sharon T. Strocchia, *Nuns and Nunneries in Renaissance Florence*. This book taught me never to underestimate the meaning and autonomy some women found behind a convent's walls.

Marina Warner, *Alone of All Her Sex: The Myth and the Cult of the Virgin Mary*. A landmark book from an inestimable scholar. Chiara's insight (201): 'Many a man has found his way into an honest girl's bedroom by calling himself a god,' is hers.

Erich Neumann, *The Great Mother: An Analysis of the Archetype*. Tomis's observation (139) that the Father desires permanence, not change, is one possible synopsis of this exhaustive and illuminating work. By the time I finished it, I was ready to tell a little of the Mother's story.

Arcangela Tarabotti, *Paternal Tyranny*, translated by Letizia Panizza. A seventeenth-century nun's denunciation of society's systemic misogyny. It appears (somewhat anachronistically) as *Letters from the Lagoon*, and is the source of the quote (122): 'A man says submit to the Father, but he means submit to him.'

Paul Strathern, *Death in Florence: The Medici, Savonarola, and the Battle for the Soul of a Renaissance City*. Thank you for introducing me to my world – and for giving me my baddie.

Ross King, *The Bookseller of Florence: Vespasiano da Bisticci and the Manuscripts that Illuminated the Renaissance*. All the bibliophilic detail I could dream of in one riveting book.

Stephen Greenblatt, *The Swerve: How the Renaissance Began*. I put Lucretius in Sophia's chest as a small thank you for what I learnt from this superb book.

The poem in Tomis's ledger (133) which begins, 'this was the day of her return,' is actually a few words of prose lifted from Peter Hoyle's book, *Delphi*. Until I double-checked, I had myself convinced I'd copied out a Homeric hymn. The following poem (134), is cobbled together from fragments of the Greek poet, Sappho.

Frederick Rolfe, also known as Baron Corvo, *Chronicles of the House of Borgia*. My mother plucked this from her shelves, gifting me the phrase (95) 'this lewd and lovely city'.

My copies of Robert Fagles's translations of Homer's *Iliad* and *Odyssey* are two of my oldest friends (until my dog ate the former when my back was turned last night). Tomis's rendition (139) of the beautiful lines from Book VI of the *Iliad* ('Like the generations of leaves . . .') is his.

Clive James's translation of Dante's *Divine Comedy* opened my eyes to this extraordinary poem: no prizes for guessing why Beatrice is called Beatrice. Her quote to Prudenzia (238) and Abramo's to her (245) are but two examples of his exceptional skill.

I also ransacked the *London Review of Books*'s digital archive, benefiting hugely from essays by, amongst others, Hilary Mantel, Barbara Newman and Marina Warner (again). More specifically, Tiberio Stelleri's opinion (150) that 'Apollo could not have been nothing' is borrowed from William Empson's review of *The Occult Philosophy in the Elizabethan Age*, by Frances Yates.

The National Gallery. The seventeeth-century painter Artemisia Gentileschi (again, anachronistically) is the inspiration for Diana. Sadly (thanks, Covid), I couldn't visit the gallery's exhibition of her paintings, but I spent happy hours on their website, admiring her work. A quick image-search will show you how Diana's picture of Judith might have turned out.

The trinity: wikipedia.com, thesaurus.com, etymonline.com. You guys don't get nearly enough credit.

The pestilenza safekeeps: Chris, Mary, Eira, Seren; Sophie, Dennis, Frankie. Thank you for keeping me sane (and fed!) during the beastly first draft.

And finally, the Littlecourt compound. Writing *The Book of Eve* has absorbed a vast proportion of my time and energy. If the people around me hadn't backed me to the hilt, practically and emotionally, I'd have been, to mix my metaphors, sunk. Rupert, Rowan and Bruno; Jane and Jonny; Ennea and Hugo; Kay and Jack; Natasha: this book would never in a million years have been written without you. I owe you all. Big time.